THE
ROMA
PLOT

MARIO BOLDUC

THE
ROMA
PLOT

A MAX O'BRIEN
MYSTERY

TRANSLATED BY JACOB HOMEL

DUNDURN
TORONTO

Published under arrangement with Groupe Librex, Inc., doing business under the name Éditions Libre Expression, Montréal. QC, Canada

Printer: Webcom

Library and Archives Canada Cataloguing in Publication

Bolduc, Mario, 1953-
[Tsiganes. English]
    The Roma plot / Mario Bolduc ; Jacob Homel, translator.

(A Max O'Brien mystery)
Translation of: Tsiganes.
Issued in print and electronic formats.
ISBN 978-1-4597-3606-1 (softcover).--ISBN 978-1-4597-3607-8 (PDF).--ISBN 978-1-4597-3608-5 (EPUB)

I. Homel, Jacob, 1987-, translator II. Title. III. Title: Tsiganes. English IV. Series: Bolduc, Mario, 1953- . Max O'Brien mystery.

PS8553.O475T7413 2017   C843'.54   C2017-901852-3   C2017-901853-1

1 2 3 4 5   21 20 19 18 17

We acknowledge the support of the **Canada Council for the Arts**, which last year invested $153 million to bring the arts to Canadians throughout the country, and the **Ontario Arts Council** for our publishing program. We also acknowledge the financial support of the **Government of Ontario**, through the **Ontario Book Publishing Tax Credit** and the **Ontario Media Development Corporation**, and the **Government of Canada**.

Nous remercions le **Conseil des arts du Canada** de son soutien. L'an dernier, le Conseil a investi 153 millions de dollars pour mettre de l'art dans la vie des Canadiennes et des Canadiens de tout le pays.

We acknowledge the financial support of the **Government of Canada** through the National Translation Program for Book Publishing, an initiative of the Roadmap for Canada's Official Languages 2013 -2018: Education, Immigration, Communities, for our translation activities.

Printed and bound in Canada.

VISIT US AT

Dundurn
3 Church Street, Suite 500
Toronto, Ontario, Canada
M5E 1M2

AUTHOR'S NOTE

While this novel's foundations are anchored in historical truth, the story itself is fictional. A troop of fictional characters was added by the author to the living and dead historical characters who make an appearance. What's more, the real-world chronology of certain events was modified for narrative purposes.

Romani culture is rich and varied. As much as possible, the Romani words and phrases used are those of the Kalderash of Eastern Europe. However, some expressions and customs of other Romani groups, notably the Manush and Romanichal, are also woven into the story.

So long as we travel the paths of justice, honour and duty, no one and nothing can turn us from our goal, because we have at our side a devoted and honourable ally — suffering.

— Gheorghe Nicolescu, 1936,
quoted by Donald Kenrick and Grattan Puxon
in *Destiny of Europe's Gypsies* (1972)

PART ONE

The Emperor's Son

1

Auschwitz-Birkenau, August 23, 1943

The Paolo Soprani was in rough shape — one of the mechanism's supports had come unglued, and part of its veneer had begun to peel. In other times, the accordion, the *gormónya*, would have been destined for the trash heap. But young Emil Rosca had disassembled the keyboard, refurbished the pallets, and glued both supports back on after reinforcing them with threaded shafts made of old barbed wire. All that did nothing to mend the hole — right in the middle of the bellows. A disaster. The accordion's owner had probably fallen headfirst off a freight car. He'd attempted to break his fall with the instrument and only managed to tear a hole two inches wide. Emil folded a piece of cardboard that had previously been luggage lining along the bellows' folds. He made a strap out of an old belt stolen from the camp's depot, the *effektenlager*, also called "Canada." The *effektenlager* was where the detainees' goods were held. Poor souls coming out of the showers at the far end of the ground were registered and given an identification number. At Auschwitz those numbers were etched directly on their left forearms. In the case of children whose arms were still too thin, the number was cut into the leg instead. They then dripped black ink directly in the open wound.

Emil wasn't stupid. Since he disinfected clothes, he knew that many of the new arrivals who were told they were being quarantined were never seen again after being marched toward the showers. "The final shower," the veterans said. "Hell," others whispered. Day or night made no difference at all; smoke rose behind the barracks, right over there, over the crematory ovens. It never ceased to surprise Emil how disinfecting the clothes of a convoy of prisoners took more time than erasing their existence from the surface of the earth did.

They were fifty or so assigned to the chore, all Roma prisoners of the BIIe sector, the Zigeunerlager. Most of them were older, more worn to the bone than Emil — but they were all as clever as him. They made piles of coats, pants, dresses, entire wardrobes, really, under the bored supervision of SS officers, all the while secretly going through every pocket. Results were scarce. Others had gone through the pockets before them, officers responsible for the reception of the convoys. Even they rarely found something worth stealing. Sometimes a watch, maybe a wallet, pictures. Junk.

Surprisingly, Emil had been the only one to notice it: the Paolo Soprani buried under a pile of suitcases the newcomers had abandoned, jostled ever forward by the guards and the barking dogs all around. Its trip to Birkenau's Judenrampe had been long and difficult. A sunbeam reflected against the instrument's keys, a sudden burst of light that caught his eye. Emil walked discreetly toward it, pretending to pick up discarded clothes. A meaningless precaution: the guards weren't paying attention. The accordion's owner? Gone, disappeared, evidently without having managed to keep his instrument with him. It was a small miracle he'd kept it so long, anyway.

Emil covered the *gormónya* with a long dress shirt, wrapped three or four others over it, and managed to bring it back to the Roma camp. Young Emil received a hero's welcome when he returned with his bounty. The children danced and jumped around him as if he'd won the lottery. Emil had always been a little vain. He wasn't going to refuse the attention. He played a few notes before even taking the time to repair the instrument and then began a longer piece. A Romani lament his father had learned somewhere along the travels of his *kumpaníya*. Emil and his family were Kalderash, a Romani people who specialized in the traditional making and repairing of cauldrons — in short, metalworkers. Since forever they had travelled Romania far and wide. At the beginning of the war Emil had been separated from his family in a police raid — he still had no idea what fate had befallen them.

The Paolo Soprani whistled out of every hole and crack in its bellows but still managed to hold a tune. Suddenly, a shadow fell over the young musician.

"Do you know how much we can get for that?"

Emil Rosca raised his head. Standing before him was Martin Hofbauer. He was a tall, brawny Sinto man, born somewhere in northern Germany, a horse trader who'd quickly made friends with the SS when he got to the camp. He'd become the long arm of the law, making sure the rules were respected — "his" rules, really. His size helped make him more persuasive. For his participation in the invasion of Poland with the Wehrmacht, he'd been decorated with the Iron Cross. But after the decree on German Roma was signed by Heinrich Himmler in December 1942, he was picked right out of his battalion and sent to Auschwitz. The idiot still proudly wore his medal on his shirt.

Emil didn't hesitate for a second. "The *gormónya* is mine. I'm keeping it."

It had taken all of Emil's courage to answer him. Once, he'd seen Hofbauer break a man's skull for stealing his tobacco — under the amused watch of the *kapos*, common criminals who supervised the work of Auschwitz detainees. Emil hadn't been a big guy even back when he'd had three meals a day. And here, in the camp, he was barely more than a hundred pounds. Little Emil, who'd never thrown a punch in his life.

But just as Hofbauer was about to punch him and steal the Paolo Soprani, a hand came down on the giant's shoulder. A delicate, frail, sickly man was behind it. Even smaller than Emil. Hofbauer could put him out of his misery with a single blow, Emil was sure. But the man, whom Emil had never seen before, spoke in Romani: "He is a descendant of Luca le Stevosko."

Hofbauer hesitated. The Sinto had lost some of his confidence. The sickly man's declaration seemed to have frozen him in his tracks. His enormous arms suddenly hung limply. He mumbled something, then turned and left, without another word. The stranger — Emil's guardian angel — also departed. Emil suddenly felt filled with prodigious strength despite his tiny frame. He stuck his chest out and held the accordion against him. More proof that all of the Hofbauers in the world couldn't do a thing against a direct descendant of Luca, son of Stevo.

Emil's ancestor had fought alongside Mihail Kogălniceanu, the Romanian statesman who'd contributed to the abolition of Romani slavery in 1856. Since that day, the Roma offered his family limitless respect. As *bulibasha*, or local leader, Anton Rosca, Emil's father, led the *Kris romani*, the tribal council of Wallachian Roma. He was known throughout Europe. Even in Auschwitz, the Kalderash, Lovari, and Tshurari respected the Rosca family. Once again, Emil had evidence of their respect.

The Zigeunerlager was a privileged place. Within the BIIe, the Romani camp, the prisoners were kept with their families, and no one wore a prisoner's uniform. Almost five thousand Roma in all. Oddly, the SS hadn't broken them up, for a reason Emil didn't know. Their skills were put to use. The Kalderash, metalworkers, maintained the barbed wire. Others, like Emil, worked in the *effektenlager*. There was even talk of a zoological garden at Buchenwald. A Rom there took care of a bear.

Here, in Auschwitz, the *Zigeuners* were never beaten. The rest of the camp, however, was pure hell. Emil knew the Jews and the politicals, the "red triangles," resented the Roma for the preferential treatment they enjoyed. Fights would break out among the prisoners. And so the Roma had to look out not only for the SS guards but for the other prisoners, as well.

Often, however, the *gadje* pressed their faces along the metal fencing, watching the Roma. Men without children, without wives, women without husbands — emaciated creatures, all of them. The shouts and laughter of Romani toddlers tore holes right through their hearts; it killed them, in addition to the forced labour. A small death preparing them for the larger one. Emil saw them wander about the camp, those they called the "Muslims," the famished, who no longer had the strength to breathe. Compared to those poor souls, the Roma gave the impression of being on vacation.

The Zigeunerlager, a sinecure.

Almost.

Last spring more than a thousand Roma had been gassed to prevent a typhoid epidemic.

"Give me your accordion."

An outline in the door frame, Otto Schwarzhuber, son of the SS-Obersturmführer. Otto was six. Every day the child left the Kommandantur buildings and wandered among the prisoners to get a bit of air. He wasn't given permission to come near the ovens and gas chamber — the guards made sure of that — but the rest of Birkenau was open to him. The detainees knew him, bowed low when he passed, the son of one of the most important camp officers after SS-Obersturmbannführer Rudolf Höss. His mother joined him sometimes. A stern-looking woman, always in a dark blazer. Her hair pulled back tightly, her lips tighter. Proper manners were essential to her. When Otto stepped in a puddle of mud, she'd chide him right in front of the astonished prisoners.

More often than not, however, Otto went on his peregrinations alone. To protect the boy from newly posted, overzealous SS guards who might take him for a young prisoner and send him to the showers, his mother had tied a small placard around his neck with a strap of dark leather: I AM THE SON OF SS-OBERSTURMFÜHRER SCHWARZHUBER!

For the past month or so, the child had been coming to listen to Emil play his Romani songs. That day, when Emil finished his piece, Otto reached out his hand and asked for the accordion again. Emil refused, shaking his head. Of course, if Otto made his request, just once, through the offices of a *kapo*, gone would be Emil's precious instrument.

But Otto added: "I'll trade you your accordion for this."

He pointed at the sign around his neck. Emil burst out laughing. Otto showed the hint of a smile. Emil had never seen him laugh. The little German boy didn't have an easy smile, probably because of his mother, who seemed so austere. Among the Roma, children were treated like royalty; they could do what they wanted when they wanted. Emil felt sorry for little Otto, who never laughed — for him and the other officers' children. Romani children ran and played and laughed and brightened the cesspit of their lives. The camp's authorities seemed to enjoy it. At Christmastime the SS brought the Romani children gifts, and the children would sing "Stille Nacht, heilige Nacht" in return … and there were New Year's gifts for the mothers and sisters. Many of the officers would have sex with them. And when Emil played the accordion, the SS listened. They stood stiff as boards behind the children, but they listened. Emil was no virtuoso, but who would complain? There wasn't much competition at Auschwitz-Birkenau.

"Happy children! What joy!"

Little Otto quickly turned around. Behind him Dr. Josef appeared. A large smile, warm eyes. The doctor passed his hand through his hair, while the Romani children hurried over, having recognized the doctor's kind voice. The same enthusiasm every time. Uncle Josef, the children called him. He pulled candy out of his pockets as the children ran toward him. They tugged at his sleeves, demanding sweets. The son of the SS-Obersturmführer was jealous in his own way. Meanwhile Emil, seventeen years of age, felt too old to be joining the fun. And, anyway, he was wary around Dr. Josef.

There were stories about the doctor. He loved Romani children so much because they were useful to him. In his Stammlager clinic in Block 10, strange things happened behind closed doors. Experiments, for the advancement of science. At least that was what the rumours were. He was particularly fascinated by twins. When the convoys arrived, Dr. Josef stood on the platform, a bit apart from the crowd, scanning it, selecting promising patients. He had an eye for them. He'd find prospects, inspect their teeth, feel their arms, their heads — was he checking for lice? And if the shipment was a quality one, it was straight to the lab for the chosen few. Other times he'd select his patients at the entrance of the gas chambers. Those he chose were marked with chalk so that members of the *Sonderkommando* wouldn't toss their bodies into the cremation ovens with the others.

The doctor had always ignored Emil. But that day he gestured him over. Emil obeyed nervously, holding his accordion tightly against him. Being noticed in Auschwitz usually meant trouble, sometimes even death. It was doubly true today, with Dr. Hans Leibrecht accompanying Dr. Josef. Leibrecht's stares had always made Emil uneasy. If Uncle Josef seemed reassuring, Dr. Leibrecht's angular face, his brusque movements, ensured that kids avoided him like the plague. Luckily for him, Dr. Josef's smiles were wide enough for the two of them. And he smelled so good.

"Tomorrow you're transferring to Block 10," he told Emil.

Still smiling, as if this transfer were the greatest of gifts, an exceptional privilege. Emil didn't want to go anywhere. It wasn't as if he could refuse, of course. Dr. Josef noticed his worry. He added, glancing at his colleague, "You can bring your accordion if you like."

Like the other prisoners, Emil Rosca had never seen a place that was so *white*. Inmates lay in beds placed one after the other. They were young, most of them. He recognized a few Roma. Jews, as well. Nurses came and went dressed in immaculate white uniforms. They looked like angels. A few moments earlier a truck had dropped them off in front of Block 10, now transformed into a medical laboratory. A dozen children, including two pairs of twins. It was Emil's first time in the main camp, also called the Stammlager. This was the oldest section of the camp and held the administration offices. The construction of Birkenau — where the Romani camp was — had been completed after Emil's internment. It was three kilometres southwest of Block 10.

A prisoner, Dina Gottlieb, was drawing a picture of a foot on a tablet placed on an easel. She didn't bat an eye when Emil — his accordion slung over his shoulder — and the others crossed the room. Emil felt a hand on his shoulder. It was Dr. Josef, bringing him along to another section of the block. Although he let himself be guided to the far end of the row of beds, Emil was uncomfortable at being so isolated. This move, the doctor's attitude — nothing good at all could come out of this.

"The operation is tomorrow," Dr. Josef said. "You'll sleep until then."

Emil wanted to tell him that he wasn't sick, that he felt a little weak, sure, but that was normal considering the circumstances. A few good meals, two or three days of rest, and he wouldn't need the operation, whatever it was. He was certain of it.

Dr. Josef had him lie on the last bed in the room. A nurse ordered him to take his clothes off and put on a gown. The cloth was coarse but clean. As white as everything else. There were a few drops of blood on it, he noticed, but they were pale, almost invisible. An old stain that hadn't come out in the wash.

Emil heard a wheeze behind him and turned around. In the next bed over, a small shape. A child. All he could see of him was a tuft of hair poking out from the sheets.

"That's Samuel," Dr. Josef said. "He was operated on this morning by Dr. Leibrecht. Look, the operation went smoothly. You've nothing to be afraid of."

Emil wanted to scream but didn't dare. Dr. Josef placed the accordion on the bedside table. He went through his pockets and pulled out a piece of candy, handing it to Emil. The doctor watched him for a long time, lost in thought, then left the dormitory. The lights were turned off soon after.

Then silence.

Broken by the whistle of a nearby train.

Emil couldn't sleep. He couldn't believe the operation would lead to anything good. He hated Dr. Josef's good manners. Emil turned on his side. A row of beds, lost in the half-light at the far end of the room. The same wheezing sounds startled him out of his thoughts. Emil turned again and looked at the boy, Samuel, in the bed next to his. The operation had gone smoothly, a satisfied Dr. Josef had said. But what operation, exactly? What had happened? After a moment's hesitation, Emil put his hand out and shook the young boy. The boy moved a little and muttered in his sleep but didn't wake up. He might still be under the effect of some painkiller, Emil thought. Tomorrow the lad would be better and Emil could talk to him, ask him questions. But Emil didn't have the patience, couldn't wait until tomorrow; he had to know now.

Emil put his hand out again. He grabbed the edge of the sheet and lifted it gently. Suddenly, Samuel woke up and turned his head toward Emil. His eyes were full of fear, his face bloodless. Emil yelped: on each side of the boy's face, two red stains.

The young patient had no ears.

2

Bucharest, November 26, 2006

Max O'Brien had headed straight to the Intercontinental Hotel to drop his bags off after coming in
from New York City. An hour later he was off to wander through — and lose himself in — the streets of the
Lipscani District, a maze of lanes filled with Bucharest's
citizens out for a bit of Christmas shopping. At some
point he burst out of the maze of small commercial
streets and onto Unirii Boulevard in front of the Palace
of the Parliament. The sheer monstrosity of the monument startled him. Like a wedding cake with its top
layer missing, crushing the capital around it, it was one
of the largest buildings in the world. The dream of a
megalomaniac tyrant, Nicolae Ceaușescu. The People's
House — though the people themselves had renamed

it the People's Madhouse. Around it, the Civic Centre, built over the ruins of a nineteenth-century neighbourhood. Twelve churches, two synagogues, and three monasteries, not to mention hundred of homes and shops, had been razed to build it. The destruction of a district twice as large as Le Marais in Paris. The Civic Centre was a city within the city, the place the dictator had ruled from to the end of his life. After the revolution in 1989, Romanians took over construction of the palace, which now housed the Parliament and various ministries. And yet it felt unfinished, as if it couldn't ever be completed.

Max kept on walking.

He had a meeting on the other side of the fountain, near the pond that ran along the boulevard.

The past forty-eight hours had been dizzying. Max had learned from a newspaper in New York that the Romanian police were looking for his friend Kevin Dandurand in relation to the murder of twenty-three Roma. Max had tried in vain to get in touch with Kevin's wife, Caroline, in Montreal. So he'd called Gabrielle, their daughter, who'd been living with her father since the couple had split. Kevin taught physical education at Collège Notre-Dame du Sacré-Cœur, but, according to the teenager, who'd been shocked by the news, Kevin had been on sabbatical since September. He'd been hiking the Appalachian Trail by himself. The trail ran from Maine to Georgia, the hike of a lifetime for an experienced outdoorsman. He could only be reached through email. And what about Caroline, what was happening with her? Gabrielle had explained that she'd locked herself in her house, refusing to answer the phone after being hounded by journalists following the accusations levied by the Romanian police.

Max had written a long email to Kevin, demanding an explanation, and left his cellphone number. Gabrielle had done the same thing — several times — earlier that very same day. As one might expect, Kevin hadn't answered a single one of her messages. Gabrielle told Max that Josée, Kevin's half-sister who worked as a lawyer in Paris, was already packing her bags for Bucharest. She was off to sort out the whole mess. She'd be there the next day.

In other words, total chaos. Kevin a killer? A murderer of twenty-three innocent Roma? Surely it had to be an error. Max would clear things up and get his friend out of whatever mess he was in.

On his way to Kennedy Airport, Max had left a message with Josée at her office on avenue des Champs-Élysées, setting up a meeting with her at the Intercontinental in Bucharest. He then reached out to one of his contacts in Prague, who put him in touch with a fixer. Max needed a guide and an interpreter. Someone for whom Romania and the internal dynamics of its judicial system held no secrets. Someone who might guide Max through the maze of Romanian society.

Toma Boerescu.

And so Max, feet frozen in his boots, now waited next to the fountain for the man. What about Romanian punctuality? Clearly, the fall of the Ceaușescu regime had wreaked havoc on good manners!

A crowd milled around Max: German tourists, their cameras strapped over their shoulders; older women negotiating with their tiny dogs at the end of taut leashes; teenagers on their skateboards, sporting esoteric tattoos, pants low on the hips, and enormous, untied running shoes. Those pimply teenagers were all amnesiacs, likely enough, completely unaware that the construction of the road they were risking their necks screwing around on had required the displacement of seventy thousand people.

Max circled the Christmas tree proudly displayed at the intersection. A gigantic tree that brought back memories of Kevin. Over the past two days, as he'd prepared for his trip to Bucharest, Max had relived the painful stages of their long friendship, all overshadowed by a horrible tragedy: the death of Kevin's father, Raymond, and of his infant son, Sacha. Max could remember every fresco painted on the walls of Chapelle Notre-Dame-de-Bon-Secours in Montreal, a few days after Easter. Raymond's family, his friends, and employees of Nordopak, the company Kevin's father had founded in the 1960s. It had been an emotional ceremony punctuated by sobbing from Kevin, Caroline, Gabrielle, and Josée, each more bereft than the last. Caroline was in a complete state of shock, blaming herself for having left her child with her father-in-law that day. How could she have known that he would stop on his way to have a drink with his friends? The autopsy had confirmed it: traces of alcohol in Raymond's blood. The businessman had been in no state to drive his Pathfinder.

Standing behind the crowd, Max had chosen to remain discreet. He'd surveyed the neighbourhood before coming, inspected the area surrounding the small church.

Once inside, he'd quickly made mental note of lateral exits and his most likely escape route, if need be. Max had come to Montreal under a cloud: he knew the Quebec provincial police, the Sûreté du Québec, was after him, and had been for years. His crime? Fraud. His victims? Hustlers, the nouveau riche, takers who exploited those without the means to defend themselves. Max was constantly changing his identity, and his appearance, too. A perpetual lie that was becoming progressively harder to bear.

That day he'd run a risk by being there. But he couldn't have stayed away; he just had to be present for his friend, to support him in this tragedy. In a way, Kevin and Max were responsible for these two deaths, the result of their mistakes.

After the funeral, once the rubberneckers had dispersed, Max made his way to Kevin's place, finding Gabrielle in a state of shock. Caroline was exhausted, having cried every tear in her body. Sacha had been the blood in her veins. Sacha-the-Red, Raymond had called him, because of the large birthmark on the back of his neck. Caroline felt as if she had killed her son with her own hands. She was entirely blameless, of course, but how could you convince a grieving mother that she was an innocent bystander? Josée, meanwhile, seemed incapable of getting hold of herself. She had cried throughout the ceremony, and she was still crying, huddled in a corner. She'd adored her father. She'd moved to Paris recently, and they'd spoken several times a week, Josée telling her father about her heartaches and her challenges and her joys.

Max couldn't stand it. He'd taken Gabrielle by the hand — she was seven years old back then — and they walked together to the Dairy Queen down the street for ice cream. Max would have given anything that day to be able to find the right words. But he had nothing to offer her. How was he supposed to explain to Gabrielle that she would never see her brother, her grandfather again? There was a crowd of children all bumping and pushing against one another at the counter for the first ice cream of the season, but neither he nor Gabrielle noticed; they were entirely absorbed by their pain.

"I'm not hungry," she finally said in a monotone.

Her ice cream had melted all over her hand. Max threw the cone into the garbage and took the girl's hand again. They walked to a park, its grass still covered in patches of grey snow despite the early spring. They were both incapable of saying a word, immured in their pain. The day was beautiful, the sunlight pouring through the branches of centenary maples. A magnificent day, intolerable, death wallowing in its power.

A few hours later Max found Kevin in a bar on rue Stanley. The two men drank into the early hours of the morning, along with the owner, a friend of Raymond's. By dawn their humanity had deserted them. Montreal's streets were empty, grieving. Kevin crossed the parking lot, toward a handful of idling cabs. All of a sudden the young man threw himself on his knees and howled. Max had never heard anything so violent. So unbearable.

Losing your father and your son in the same accident. What kind of cruel and vengeful God would permit such horror?

‡

Max first met Kevin in the fall of 1993 on the corner of Madison and Seventy-Second Street. Kevin was wearing a lumberjack's checkered windbreaker, but no hat on his head. He was shivering. Around him were a hundred or so Christmas trees, which that day didn't seem to attract the attention of a single New Yorker. Max hated Christmas. Like all single people, really. A holiday made doubly cruel by its seemingly interminable preparations. At forty-two, while most men his age were living lives within the bounds and lines of owning property, raising children, and getting ready to celebrate Christmas with them, Max wandered through the streets of New York looking for a bar to call home for the night.

Two years earlier Max had learned of Pascale's death. The woman he loved. He'd gone to India to witness her cremation on the banks of the Ganges. Since then, Max had had a few brief, meaningless relationships. Once trivialities had been exchanged, after the first few encounters, the same issue would arise. When it came time to show his true self, Max was trapped — all he could offer were lies. And so he would walk away, not unkindly, without making any waves, and return to the solitude he was forced into by his work. By his being a con man. The same solitude guided him toward an unknown bar that night as he scanned the storefronts on the corner of Seventy-Second Street.

Kevin was jumping up and down, shadowboxing against the wall. The dance of frozen feet. Seeing the guy jittering on the street corner, Max couldn't help but smile. Normally, he would have walked on, said nothing at all, but for some reason he engaged with the man.

"Merry Christmas!" shouted Kevin, waving his arms about. He added, "Want to go for a drink?"

So it would be coffee, first, in a nearby deli — a double espresso sweetened with a few drops of the cognac secreted in Kevin's inside pocket. Cab drivers jostled one another to reach the counter. The large outside window was all fogged up. New York in winter.... After coffee the two men found refuge at the Donohue, Max's local. They agreed on Irish whiskey, the universal remedy for the blues. Kevin told Max he was from Montreal and wasn't actually a lumberjack. The trees he was selling weren't even from Canada, but from a nursery in New Jersey, only a few kilometres away from Manhattan. The whole setup was just for show. Misleading representation? Kevin answered with a smile. Who cares about truth? Max wasn't about to contradict him.

The whole Christmas tree thing was only to make ends meet. It gave Kevin enough time to concentrate on his true passion: running. A former member of the Canadian Olympic team, he'd been to the Games in Seoul, as well as in Barcelona the previous year. He'd made a strong impression. No medals, but lots of hope for Atlanta — those were the next games. He trained with American athlete Richard Voight in New York.

At dawn Max stumbled home with a dishevelled Christmas tree in tow, which he couldn't remember why he'd accepted. He didn't think he'd ever hear from the fake lumberjack again. But after Christmas, Kevin called to invite Max to one of his training sessions at the Tribeca Sports Center. It was a dilapidated old gym next to a bus terminal — you could hear the buses changing gears as you ran around the track. Max sat in the stands and watched Kevin breathing hard, listening to the advice of a grey-haired man in a track suit — Richard Voight, a gold medallist at the 1972 Munich Olympics.

A few moments later Kevin threw himself down the track again. Despite his stature — he was tall, strong, something rather unusual for a marathon runner — there was something vulnerable in his movements, a semblance of fragility. He looked like a big kid who'd grown up too fast, running laps in a park.

"Ah! So you're the Robert Cheskin who's been carousing with my Kevin!" a young woman called out to Max from a few seats behind him. He'd been working with the Cheskin alias for a few months now. Max had noticed the woman when she'd first walked into the gym. Black tousled hair, a magnificent smile. Her name was Caroline. She and Kevin had just gotten married. Her belly was as round as a balloon. She was expecting a child soon: Gabrielle.

"Caroline is a journalist," Kevin explained later after he'd changed back into civilian clothes.

The young woman freelanced for small newspapers and magazines, usually those with a left-wing bent. The sort of papers whose mission was to fight against the cruelties and injustices of the world. The sort that sought to redress all wrongs, be they past, present, or future. Caroline dreamed of a job with the *New York Times* or the *Washington Post*; she was always looking for the next topic, the next story that would give her an opening, a foot in the door of those great papers. For now, however, she satisfied herself with what she had: contributing to sincere pamphlets with anemic print runs.

Back at the Donohue, Caroline asked Max what he did for a living. Where he worked, exactly.

"In a bank. Recovery and collections. I take care of outstanding loans and credit margins, that sort of thing …"

"So you pester people who can't pay?"

Max smiled. "Something like that."

Failure to pay, deadbeat creditors. They'd heard those words often enough, the both of them, Max would come to learn. Addicted to their credit cards, chronically in debt, they were acrobats of poverty. They lived in a pathetic little rental in Sunset Park in Brooklyn's Chinatown. And things weren't easy, that much was clear. Max didn't yet know that Kevin came from a family of entrepreneurs, that he'd had a golden childhood that had left its mark. Elegance, distinction, good manners. A beautiful garden to play in behind a manor on avenue Shorncliffe in Westmount. A summer home on rivière Saqawigan in Gaspésie — the biggest house in the entire region. Private tennis and horse-riding lessons. Extensive studies in management. Kevin was destined one day to take over the family business. What was he doing in New York pretending to be a marathon runner, selling Christmas trees to make ends meet? After having worked a few years for Nordopak, Kevin had cut all ties with his father. Caroline had told him this one night, not wanting to say any more than that. Max hadn't pressed. Secrets, like fruit, must be ripe to be picked without effort.

At one point that very night they had stood in front of a giant billboard in Times Square: an ad for the Boston Marathon with the year's previous winner, trophy in hand.

"Next year, Robert, it'll be my picture up there."

It was a dream that wouldn't come true, not the following year, nor any other. Disappointing performances, an injury that wouldn't heal. Voight fired, replaced with a guru from California. Yoga, relaxation, transcendental meditation. No results there, either. But Kevin wouldn't give up. After the Boston Marathon, after New York, he was offered a teaching position in British Columbia — he refused outright. He couldn't leave Caroline by herself; she'd just given birth. They were madly in love, the two of them, that much was clear. They couldn't bear the thought of living apart. Max had never seen such osmosis between two people, such compatibility. Even Max's relationship with Pascale those long years ago, the tormented, troubled, passionate moments spent together, seemed dull compared to the love between Kevin and Caroline. An intense love, destined for tragedy.

Max adopted their family, in a sense. They went out together all the time. Restaurants, museums, theatre, cinema: Caroline's world. Meanwhile, Kevin took Max out to baseball and hockey games. Max pushed Gabrielle's stroller through Central Park while the girl's father trained and trained. On Gabrielle's birthdays, Max would come over, his arms loaded with gifts. Gabrielle would throw herself at him, emitting shrill, joyful cries.

In other words, they saw one another as much as Kevin's schedule and Max's particular hours allowed. Max was often away, always on business. Sleazy business, which the couple knew nothing about, of course.

That always made Caroline laugh. "Your bosses are ready to send you to the ends of the earth for a few bucks out of some deadbeat's pocket! Now that would make a good story!"

The last thing Max needed was publicity. Caroline burst out laughing when he pulled a confused face. A loud, confident laugh that made you want to follow her anywhere. Kevin tried to make her happy, to do everything for her, and sometimes fell just short. As did she. But they always ended up back together after a fight or an argument, falling on their feet like champion gymnasts. Sometimes, right in the middle of a conversation, Max would notice a shared smile, a look between them. He'd glance away then, feeling as if he was intruding, not wanting to insert himself too deeply in their intimacy, especially because he wasn't revealing his true identity to his friends. Max made sure to keep them as far away as possible from his own scheming. To always play the role of protective older brother. It was a lie, another one, but it comforted him; it was the most beautiful lie in the world.

And so Max tried to help them out, giving secret gifts they knew nothing about. Like that training seminar in Colorado with a motivational speaker of some kind.

"He's just amazing! You should read his book, Robert." That was Kevin telling Max he couldn't go to the seminar because he was flat broke. So Max made a cheque out to the motivational speaker without telling Kevin.

Another time Caroline's computer suddenly died on her. Max knew they were tight on cash, so he came up with a prize she'd never heard of for her to win. One morning a representative from a technology company knocked on her door with a brand-new machine.

And then there were the jobs. Once the holiday season had come to a close, Kevin worked part-time as a personal trainer at the Manhattan Sheraton's gym. Max found him better employment with the New York City Department of Parks and Recreation. Kevin was none the wiser.

Max didn't get anything in return for his generosity. Kevin and Caroline weren't marks he was fattening for the kill. He had no intention of fleecing them at some point after winning their trust. No, that wasn't it at all. He was investing not in some grift, but in their happiness. He was always looking for ways to make them happy, to make their lives richer, fuller, to protect them from anything that might come their way. An impossible task, Max would come to realize. Fat and happy but in a cage is no happiness at all.

3

"Did you know Nicolae Ceaușescu loved Christmas trees? Each one of his forty villas was decorated with them. Isn't it ironic? There wasn't a single other Christmas tree in the country."

Max O'Brien whipped around, furious at being caught daydreaming. He hadn't known what to expect, but it certainly wasn't the man before him. Tiny, bent over, Toma Boerescu looked eighty years old on a good day. He was precariously balanced upright by a walker even older than he was. Could barely breathe, it seemed. And his breath stank of *palinca*, a moonshine expertly distilled in the slop buckets of Transylvanian farmers. On the lapel of what had to be at least a thirty-year-old pea jacket, he had a star — probably some sort of military decoration.

Before Max could answer, Boerescu added in approximate English, "Ceaușescu prohibited any Romanian from cutting down fir trees for Christmas. Environmental protection was the reason. Oh, how the Conducător was ahead of his time!" A twinkle in his eye, the man burst out laughing. "Robert Cheskin?"

Max shook his hand.

"Toma Boerescu. But you can call me Tom. I know you Americans love abbreviations. Tom Boerescu. Now that's not too bad a name, right? Sounds like a hockey player!"

The old man pointed down Brătianu Boulevard. "Let us walk, if you don't mind."

Boerescu continued to chatter idly about Nicolae Ceauşescu and his immoderate love of Christmas trees, which he had imported straight from Moldavia every November. "The army delivered the trees a few weeks before Christmas."

Ceauşescu didn't have many occasions to admire them, unfortunately. It was impossible for him to be simultaneously in every one of his forty villas. He could only visit them one after the other, according to a schedule kept entirely secret, established by his wife, Elena. For security reasons, of course. Despite his extensive powers, Ceauşescu wasn't gifted with ubiquity.

"One day he thought someone was trying to poison him. According to him, the branches of his trees were covered with some sort of substance that gave off a lethal gas of some kind."

Boerescu burst out laughing. "Because, you see, the trees came from the north! The Romanian gulags were there, where he'd sent many of his political enemies." He hesitated. "Not without reason, if you ask me."

He pointed to the small red star on his lapel, a decoration given to him by Ceauşescu, most likely. "Romanians realized too late they punished an exceptional man."

An old Communist! Just his luck.

A few tourists passed them on the sidewalk, hurrying toward their tour buses. Farther off, mothers with their strollers made their way between skateboard-riding teenagers and tiny dogs.

Boerescu hesitatingly gestured toward a bench a couple of lovers had just vacated. He dropped onto it heavily, inviting Max to join him. Pulling out a handkerchief from his pocket, the old man told Max in a muted voice how for more than thirty years he'd been a loyal servant of the Romanian police. Oh, those were the good old days! Thanks to their hard work, there was barely any crime. And when they did catch someone, you could be sure the culprit wouldn't commit the same crime twice. No, criminals were repentant: Romania's prisons had a way of knocking sense into even the hardest heads. These days, well, things had changed. In any case, Boerescu still knew a few people at the General Directorate for Criminal Investigations.

Max imagined the mocking smiles behind the back of this old shipwreck of a man as he struggled his way into the directorate straight from another time, coming for his annual inspection of his old stomping ground from all the way behind the Iron Curtain.

"You'd be surprised at what you can learn around a coffee machine," Boerescu offered, eyes twinkling.

"About Kevin Dandurand, for example?" Max suggested.

"Came in from Montreal by way of Zurich a week ago. He claimed to a customs agent he'd be staying at the Helvetia. Never checked in."

"His movements around town?"

"No idea. No one saw him, no one spoke to him. They couldn't even find the cab driver who brought him into the city."

"So someone might have picked him up."

"Maybe."

"Who's in charge of the case?"

"Inspector Adrian Pavlenco."

Boerescu explained that Pavlenco was conscientious and professional, an ambitious young guy impressed by American methods. He'd been confined to investigating criminal fires for the longest time, and hated it. He spent his days in rubber boots trudging through wrecked homes and smelling smoke. He did have a cordial relationship with the media, though, despite the lingering stench on him.

Boerescu made a face. Back in his day, the media had been nothing more than the mouthpiece of the Romanian police. Puppets, really, used to make the work of inspectors easier. Things had changed, unfortunately. The press gave itself licence to criticize. Asked questions. Demanded answers. Cloaked itself in irreproachable morals. Freedom of the press? Bullshit! The press had all the freedom, more like! Freedom to cause mayhem, which only helped the bad guys!

The old man blew his nose loudly. Then, with a tired gesture, he pulled a folded newspaper out of his jacket pocket, and showed it to Max. "Twenty-three Roma burned alive in a building on Zăbrăuți Street. For once a story about Gypsies makes the front page.... Usually they're somewhere in the middle, between soccer scores and lottery results."

"Maybe because the cops already have a suspect to throw to the press?"

"Maybe. But you know who the real criminals are? The city authorities, they're the ones who allowed the neighbourhood to go to hell."

Ferentari, the Bronx of Bucharest. Streets lined with boarded-up buildings filled far beyond capacity by Roma under the sway of local mafia types.

Kevin was a convenient patsy. Doubly so because Bucharest was currently hosting the Conference of European Cities, Boerescu explained. An organization dedicated to social and urban planning, dynamic management of human resources, alternative solutions to drinking-water supplies. Soporific subjects each and all, but this year the organizers were lucky. On the menu: the Romani "problem," which affected most European countries. And now this criminal fire everyone was talking about. Max now understood why, at the Intercontinental, he'd had to fight his way through a thick crowd. They'd been a harried bunch, computer bags over their shoulders, eyes tired after long flights. Handshakes and hugs, friendly pats on the back and laughter. Periodic reunions, probably. Paris one time, Rome or Venice the other. This year Bucharest and its damn Roma.

Pariahs who haunted the cityscape, an underclass to be wary of. Where were they from, exactly?

Northern India. Around the year 1000 they left their country for an unknown reason — perhaps chased off by an invader, Sultan Mahmud of Ghazni, it was sometimes claimed — and made their way west through Afghanistan, Turkey, then Greece, where they were first mentioned in the thirteenth century. The Greeks gave them the name *atzigani* — still used to refer to Hungarian Roma, or *tziganes* — a reference to a heretic sect that practised palmistry. Today they preferred Rom or Roma, meaning "man" in Romani, their most frequently spoken language.

After Greece, waves of migrants moved to Wallachia and Moldavia. They were enslaved, not to be freed until 1856. In the fifteenth century, other groups entered Europe, coming from the east through Bohemia. They'd been offered safe passage by the king. From then on they became known as *Bohemians*, or *Egyptians*, because they were believed to be from "Little Egypt," a part of Greece. The Egyptians mentioned in Molière's *The Imaginary Invalid*? That was them. In English, *Egyptians* became *Gypsies*. In Spanish, *Gitanos*. In Spain they were divided into two groups: those living in Catalonia in the north, and those in Andalusia in the south.

Over the centuries, Roma travelled across Europe, living from one end of the continent to the other. More often sedentary than not these days, they now lived all over the globe.

They'd always been choice victims for human cruelty. During the Second World War, they were exterminated in death camps alongside Jews. A tragic story that continued to this day. Second-class citizens in most countries. Foreigners in every land, characterized only with faults: chronic begging, knavery, black magic …

"Here, I want to offer you a gift." Boerescu held up a pin in the shape of a small candy cane. Max had noticed everyone in Bucharest was wearing similar pins, even tourists.

Max fixed the pin to his coat.

"Do you have time for a drink?" Boerescu asked.

"Another time."

The two men agreed to meet the next day after Max's meeting with Adrian Pavlenco. Max flagged down a cab and offered Boerescu a lift. A Dacia, the Romanian copy of the Renault 12. Max opened the door for his fixer, then folded up the walker and placed it in the trunk. "Intercontinental Hotel. But first …"

"Victoriei Avenue," Boerescu said.

Max hadn't been in Bucharest since 1989, in the last days of the Ceauşescu regime. He'd been on a job, promising to line the pockets of a bureaucrat responsible for IT procurement in the dictator's government if he chose Max's client instead of an Australian competitor. The city then had been dreary, whatever new construction there was in a state of almost immediate disrepair. He'd seen a tourist or two, at most. Eaten in awful restaurants. Stayed in cavernous hotels.

Today Bucharest was unrecognizable. Max had been expecting a sleepy city, still licking its wounds from the previous century. Instead, he discovered an animated capital, its sidewalks teeming with young people, teenagers who'd never known the Ceauşescu era, for whom the revolution of 1989 was already ancient history.

At a red light a group of Roma pestered tourists. Children were pulling on the clothes of passersby.

Boerescu turned toward Max. "They've got another trick. They saunter into a butcher's, right, and start feeling up the meat in the displays, waiting for the owner to notice them. When he does, he gives them the tainted meat just to get rid of the bastards."

He burst out laughing. "The Lovari, they used to be horse traders a long time ago. Well, now, they've become used car salesmen. Once upon a time, they applied wax on old nags to make them look younger. Today they tamper with odometers!"

Boerescu told him about other tricks of the Romani trade. Names, for example. They changed theirs depending on the country they were travelling through. Multiple identities to confuse the *gadje*.

"Gadje?"

"Non-Romani people, if you prefer. According to some historians, the word comes from Mahmud of Ghazni, the sultan responsible for their exile from India."

And other times, they all carried identical names, as in the Nazi concentration camps. Everyone was called the same thing to confuse the SS. Roma were absolute experts at fake papers: from forged passes given by King Sigismund of Bohemia in the fifteenth century to Guatemalan passports the Roma used to flee the Netherlands during the German Occupation …

"A wily bunch, let me tell you," Boerescu said.

Max felt kinship with the Roma. Fake papers, multiple identities …

Two world wars, forty years of totalitarianism. In Romania the Roma were only now beginning to recover from a century of atrocities. What would one more fire, one more tragedy change? And yet, since the fall of Ceauşescu, the situation of the Romani people had gotten worse, Boerescu explained. As if Romanians had been holding back from settling a few scores. Harassment, fights, even pogroms. Romanians were venting their historical misfortunes on the most unfortunate of them all, it seemed. Not a week went by without a new altercation between Roma and Romanians. Extreme right wingers, neo-Nazis, drunks, and lunatics. And this collective madness had migrated to other countries. The number of aggressions against the Roma in Eastern Europe was impossible to count. Since 1989 the Roma had taken advantage of the opening up of borders to migrate westward. In Germany outbreaks of violence had forced Berlin to react. An agreement with the Romanian government had been forged: Romania would take the migrants back as long as Germany paid for their return flights and gave a remittance to Bucharest. Same thing in France. The minister of the interior, Nicolas Sarkozy, chartered a few planes to repatriate these "undesirables" who squatted near Paris. A solution that truly wasn't one, according to Victor Marineci.

"And who's that?" Max asked.

A Romani MP. A star in Parliament, really, Boerescu explained. The Roma had been looking for a strong political leader for a long time now, after years of chaos among their ranks. They accepted no authority, according to Boerescu, though they would make you believe they did. Hence the proliferation of one-acre kings over the centuries.

Marineci, however, was cut from different cloth. A member of the International Romani Union representing all European Roma, he'd risen above the buffoonery. Elected to Parliament under the banner of the Vurma Party, he dedicated his life to the defence of the Romani people. He was the party's founder, actually. Călin Popescu-Tăriceanu's government took him seriously. Marineci was one of the most eloquent — and efficient — members of the opposition.

"Nomadic Roma are only a minority now," Boerescu continued. "Ten, maybe fifteen percent. The others are parked in shantytowns. Today the *kumpaníya* is in ruins. Awful, absolutely awful."

Marineci was positioning himself as a standard-bearer for these unfortunate souls, with some success, Boerescu explained. "He passed hate-crime legislation in Romania, making punishments for anti-Roma crimes more severe."

Anti-Roma crimes like the fire on Zăbrăuți Street where twenty-three Roma had perished ...

4

As the taxi trundled down the long boulevard, a memory overtook Max O'Brien. Another city, another time, but a long drive nonetheless, in New York instead of Bucharest. Kevin was being held in a police station in Astoria. Or so he'd told Max over the phone.

Max's ringing cellphone had woken him up. He was sitting on the side of his bed. Behind him, Susan, sleeping deeply. She was a young insurance broker who worked out of an office on Wall Street. He'd been seeing her for six months now in preparation for a grift.

"I need you to bail me out," Kevin repeated.

Caroline had no idea, of course. Kevin was calling his friend to pull him out of this rough spot before his wife was any the wiser. Max hung up and hurried to find some clothes, still holding the cellphone.

"Who was it?" Susan asked sleepily.

"My owner. Water damage in my kitchen. I've got to go down there."

Max leaned over the woman and slid his hand along her side. Her body was warm, heavy in the folds of sleep. He didn't want to leave the bed.

"You're insured, I hope ..." she murmured.

Max smiled. Even half-asleep, her job came first.

Max had raced through Manhattan in his new Saab, which he'd purchased to demonstrate his rapid ascension in the world of finance to Susan. He reached Astoria and made his way to the police station. A typical scene: officers warming their hands with paper coffee cups. A waiting room sparsely populated by friends and family come to rescue someone from themself. People, like Max, who'd been woken up in the middle of the night to be told that their cousin, their son, their brother had been up to no good.

Kevin Dandurand had appeared, haggard but relieved. He'd been implicated in a series of warehouse robberies, monthly rentals along the East River. Kevin had joined up with a gang of amateur thieves who hung out in a coffee shop near the gym where he trained. His accomplices all had criminal records, but not Kevin; he would be getting off with a fine and community service. Hours spent teaching young delinquents how to run the ten thousand metres, for example.

A heavy silence in the car. Max had felt as if he were driving home a teenage son caught destroying the flower beds in front of his high school. He didn't know what to say: he'd never been a good shoulder to cry on. No, encouraging words had never been his strong suit.

"They're going to take my green card away," Kevin finally said.

There was the crux of the problem. Sure, he could lie and keep his community service hidden from Caroline, but how could he possibly explain why he could never work in the United States again?

"They might even force me to leave the country."

It was a possibility, and a dark one at that, especially since things were finally beginning to line up for Caroline. Serious periodicals were knocking at her door, some even ordering pieces from her.

If she went back to Canada now, it would be all over.

Not to mention Kevin's athletic career. It was time for the young man to look at reality as it was and accept that his best performances were behind him. His private trainers were only exploiting his unrealistic dreams, his hopes. No one had the courage to tell him the truth: "Listen, Kevin, you've got to move on." In a way, he was paying these people to convince him to the contrary; if Richard Voight and others were interested in Kevin's career, surely it was because they believed in his abilities, in his future as an athlete. But he was slowly realizing it was just a pipe dream.

Kevin sighed.

"Your father could take you back," Max suggested. "You could work in the factory, maybe. You could ask him."

"Packaging?" he replied scornfully.

"I'm sure you could keep training in Montreal, right?"

Max didn't dare look at himself in the rearview mirror. He, the con man, giving a speech worthy of a priest.

"I'll never go back."

Kevin was never one to speak of his troubled relationship with his father. Max hadn't insisted. He was in no position to demand the truth. He respected his friend's discretion. He'd never really had a reason to get mixed up in Kevin's relationship with his father. It had nothing to do with him.

"So what are you going to do?" Max asked.

"No idea."

The two men fell silent, each lost in their own thoughts.

The night was full of light, the streets still wet from a too-brief rainfall. Taxis passing him, customers behind their windows. On the sidewalks, men and women desperately trying to find a cab in the small hours of the morning.

Max hesitated. There was something he could do for Kevin, but it might destroy their friendship. But Kevin was desperate. He needed help, and now; Max's small, secret gifts weren't enough anymore.

Or, Max thought, he could also do nothing. He could simply drive Kevin back home and return to Susan's arms. He could let the marathon runner deal with his own problems.

Not a chance, Max decided. "Listen, Kevin, I've got to come clean with you."

"What do you mean?"

"I don't work in a bank. What I told you and Caroline, it was all a lie."

Kevin turned toward Max, confusion on his face. Perhaps a hint of disappointment at being lied to by his friend all these years.

With a few words, Max told him everything. He was a con man, a thief, really, but a thief who made his life harder by making his victims consent to their own fleecing. He played on their worst instincts: vanity, greed, ambition. Max tried to reassure Kevin that he and Caroline had never been marks. Quite the opposite; he'd always seen them as friends.

"And, well, I'm not even called Robert Cheskin. My real name is Max O'Brien. But all over the world the authorities are after me. So I need to change identities early and often."

Kevin looked at him, speechless.

"These days, for example, I'm playing a broker for an investment company, luring a large insurance company."

"And how much is that going to bring you in?"

"A lot. But there are fees. Accomplices to pay, informants to compensate ..."

Silence again.

Kevin could have reacted by ordering Max to stop the car and let him out here, now, on the wet pavement. Clearly, his ventures with criminality had been a complete failure; he might not want to fall into the same trap twice.

But Kevin remained silent, as if he were trying to guess his friend's intentions.

Max told Kevin about his early days in the craft. The operations he'd been part of, then those he'd initiated. The bad experiences, as well. Painful memories. Time in prison, for example, time that had seemed to drag on even once he was out. The prison walls surrounding him now were made of fake names and counterfeit papers, of aliases and invented pasts.

"The work I can offer you is dishonest and illegal, of course," Max added. "And might just lead you straight to jail."

Kevin still seemed perplexed. He raised his head just as Max's Saab stopped in front of his building in Sunset Park. "And what would I do, exactly? I don't know the first thing about any of this."

Back in his room in the Intercontinental in Bucharest, Max tried to reach Josée Dandurand. No dice; she must've still been sleeping. He emptied two tiny bottles of whisky he found in the refrigerator. His appetite teased, he went down to the bar to have a bite. The place was full of conference-goers, and it was happy hour. The barman poured a Scotch for Max before moving on to the other end of the counter to settle the bill of a couple of Brits.

A commotion all of a sudden.

Max turned around. There was a group in the corner of the bar surrounding an individual Max couldn't yet see. Five or six people. The impromptu crowd was composed of ruddy, paunchy men, listening with interest to the speaker. The man got up suddenly to shake the hand of someone he knew, giving Max a view of him. Fifty-five years old, more or less, wearing a finely trimmed moustache over thick lips. Tanned skin giving him the look of a South American.

"Victor Marineci, the Gypsy MP." The barman was watching the man, as well. "This conference is quite the opportunity for him. With the elections coming up, Prime Minister Popescu-Tăriceanu is in trouble and Marineci might be part of the next government. Minister of the interior, maybe. Can you imagine? A Gypsy head of the police!"

Max turned around. "With you, no need to listen to the news. The lounge lizards in Romania must be the most informed in the world."

"I've got a Ph.D. in political science from the University of Bucharest. I got my diploma the day Ceaușescu was killed. And so — barman for life!"

Max smiled.

"Would you like another?"

"Sure, thanks."

"Me, too." A young woman had just slid onto the stool next to Max. Heavy makeup, friendly smile, provocative short skirt.

"Let me guess, you're an American," she said with a strong Russian accent. She offered her hand. "You can call me Tatiana."

Max saw Josée Dandurand walk into the bar. Tall, blond, elegant, her step confident. She scanned the room for Max among the sea of conference-goers. A man offered her a drink. She smiled politely, no thanks. Max turned toward her and she recognized him. She quickly closed the distance and they held each other in their arms hard, just as they'd done after the rivière Saqawigan tragedy a few years earlier. Max, comforter-of-all-trades. Josée hadn't slept since she'd heard the news, doubly so because the trip over to Romania had been difficult.

"I thought they'd gotten back on their feet, the Romanians," she said to Max. "This country is a disaster!" A crushing bureaucracy, lines in front of cash machines, the faces of the border guards drawn and heavy. "They took hours just to look through my papers!"

By the time she'd reached the hotel, she'd been so tired she collapsed on her bed. She was just waking up now.

Josée smiled. "You're not going to introduce me to your friend?" She pointed at Tatiana.

But the young Russian woman had turned her back on Max already and was now speaking to two Italians who'd approached her. Max led Josée to a table.

"I spoke to a few journalists," she began. "The authorities have no concrete proof. No witnesses. I'm sure we'll be able to get Kevin out of his bind."

"If we can find him.... Do you want to eat something?"

"I'm not hungry. All I can think about is Kevin."

"He's innocent."

"The fact he's vanished is rather incriminating."

Josée informed Max that a liaison for the Royal Canadian Mounted Police, Marilyn Burgess, would be present the next day for their meeting with Adrian Pavlenco. Max had been expecting it. Canadian authorities would surely want to follow the investigation closely, given the nationality of the suspect.

"Did you get in touch with a lawyer here in Bucharest?"

Josée shook her head. "I'm waiting to know what he's actually accused of. After that we'll see. I've got a few names." She smiled. "Strange to meet again in such circumstances. Are you still living in New York?"

"Yes."

"Still a banker?"

"Still a banker."

Josée looked him over carefully for a long moment. Behind her Max saw Tatiana leaving with the two Italians.

"We've got to get Kevin out of this mess," Josée finally said. "I'm convinced he's innocent."

Max nodded. It was imperative they help him, and quickly. But probably not using the methods the young lawyer was thinking of.

5

Three men, all dressed in white, were standing in front of a sort of workbench, their backs turned to him, working in silence. They weren't paying any attention at all to Emil Rosca, who was lying on the operating table. Among the men, Dr. Hans Leibrecht. Emil hadn't taken his hands off his precious ears since he'd been brought into the room, especially after a nurse had come to measure them that very morning. Sure, they weren't the prettiest ears around: they were a bit thick, slightly folded at the points, and stuck out from his head a little. But they were his ears, and the Nazi doctors were preparing to take them away from him for no reason at all.

His whole life Emil hadn't thought of his ears twice, like the rest of his body, really. It was his and he lived in it, and that was all. And yet today here he was envying the men and women sent directly to the gas chamber. At least their deaths were painless. Would he still be able to hear? The guards' orders? The music from his accordion? Last night Samuel seemed to have been able to hear his voice. Or perhaps Emil's movements had jolted him awake. In the dark, Emil hadn't dared to ask how the boy was feeling without his ears. By the time light returned to their dormitory, Samuel was dead. Two orderlies took his body away, leaving a brown stain on the boy's pillow in the shape of a butterfly.

Absorbed by their work, the men spoke among themselves in a German Emil could barely understand, despite his fair knowledge of the language. In 1940, when the Wehrmacht had come into Ploesti to secure its oil wells, the Roma had begun trading with the soldiers. Out of necessity, Emil had learned basic German, which he spoke as well — or as poorly, really — as he did Romanian. But he couldn't read or write either language. Nor his own language, Romani, the tongue of the Roma. And yet he enjoyed its musicality, its intonations. Every day in the camps he felt nostalgic for the *paramíchi*, the stories that had enthralled him as a child. And soon, maybe, he would never be able to hear anyone speaking his own language again. Or any other. A pang of anguish overtook him. He thought of his parents, who'd vanished. The SS had chosen not to split up Romani families in the camps, but his own family, for a reason Emil didn't know, was scattered to the four winds. The young Rom had discreetly asked around. He was the only Rosca in Auschwitz.

"As long as we don't have a solution for transporting specimens," Emil overheard Dr. Leibrecht say, "we'll face the same problems time and time again."

"The institute is supposed to take care of it."

"Dr. Josef refuses to ask anything of them."

"We've got the same issue with eyes."

Dr. Leibrecht turned around, adjusting his glasses on his face, then leaned over Emil without ever looking at him. Emil felt like an object, a piece of furniture, about to be repaired. Or broken. Leibrecht pulled a lever under the table, sending it upward suddenly. The movement surprised Emil, and he dropped his hands from his ears. The two others, orderlies of some kind, quickly grabbed his arms. Emil was far too scared to cry out. Within a few moments, he was tied to the table, his back uncomfortably pinned against the flat, hard surface. Leibrecht muttered something to one of the orderlies, who quickly went off to grab a metal tray on which were placed surgical instruments — all Emil could make out was the glint of the scalpel's blade.

The doctor put the tray on a small panel he'd pulled out of the table like a drawer. He examined his instruments, as if unsure which one he should use. Panicked, Emil struggled pathetically as one of the orderlies held his head firmly.

"Is the phenol ready?" Leibrecht asked.

A syringe appeared in the hand of the other assistant.

"Draw the sample as soon as the specimen's vital signs indicate death."

"As you say, Herr Doktor."

With a fidgety little gesture, Leibrecht daubed Emil's

ear with a liquid. It smelled horrible. But he'd put on too much, and swore as the young Rom felt the liquid slowly run down his neck and slip under the collar of his gown. A cold, sticky, viscous trail. Emil had never been so afraid in his life.

Leibrecht picked up a scalpel and placed a hand on Emil's forehead, preventing any movement at all. "Rainer, phenol."

The orderly was about to stick the needle in Emil's thorax, right above his heart, when Dr. Josef's voice sounded from across the room.

"Hans, can you come here a moment?"

"Just give me five minutes," Leibrecht answered.

"Now!"

The doctor sighed as he placed the scalpel back on the tray and left the laboratory, closing the door behind him. Abandoning the syringe filled with phenol on the tray, the orderly sat down at the edge of the table, the way you might sit on the hood of a car, and pulled out a pack of cigarettes, offering one to his colleague. Soon, acrid grey smoke filled the room, making Emil dizzy. Because of the liquid the doctor had daubed on his ear, he couldn't feel anything on the right side of his face. Emil kept glancing toward the phenol syringe, just out of reach. What would be the point, anyway? In a few moments, Dr. Leibrecht would return and finish his operation. It was the end. Death was coming. Death, which Emil had naively thought he could avoid in the camp, among his people. He saw in his mind's eye his father repairing a pot, face covered in soot. His father with a *gormónya* on his knees, teaching him how to play.

He could see the celebrations of the *kumpaníya* when the Kalderash, the Lovari, or the Tshurari met on the road. He remembered the feast of hedgehog served on long tables around which children ran, laughing, shouting. The *pavika*, the rejoicing, where wine ran more freely than water under the kind supervision of the *bulibasha*.

Suddenly, the doors to the operating room flew open. The two orderlies jumped to their feet, as if caught dawdling. A young woman walked in, her step straight and energetic, followed by Dr. Josef. She was a redhead with delicate skin in a tailored floral suit. She seemed lost, out of place in the midst of all this horror, though not surprised by what she saw. A German woman, without a doubt. Directly from the Kommandantur. The wife of an officer, perhaps. Emil saw Leibrecht gesture for his attendants to disappear. A guard stood near the doorway behind the doctor and the woman. He'd likely accompanied the redhead in.

"You've just arrived here in Auschwitz," Dr. Josef said, his voice stiff. "I understand that in Berlin, high society might have looked kindly on your initiatives …"

"High society has nothing to do with any of this."

"You have no idea who you're dealing with."

"With the best doctor of the Third Reich. But that doesn't mean you can disobey orders."

Emil was impressed this woman would stand up to Dr. Josef.

"And, might I add, it isn't my idea. It's Oskar's. I'm only the messenger."

Dr. Josef turned toward Leibrecht, who was looking at him with fire in his eyes.

"His requirement was clear, Dr. Mengele," she said.

Dr. Josef sighed. "The Kaiser Wilhelm Institute is urgently awaiting these specimens."

"Take them off someone else. You've got plenty to choose from."

"I don't like your attitude at all, Frau Müller."

The young woman seemed to deflate all of a sudden, as if she realized she'd gone too far. "I assure you, Dr. Mengele, no one is questioning the value and usefulness of your work."

"For which, if I must repeat myself, I received a clear mandate from the institute."

"Which no one is questioning."

Leibrecht burst out, incapable of containing himself further. "Leave, please. We have work to do. It's late. The day has been long enough already."

Frau Müller turned toward the doctor. "Hans Leibrecht. Sent away from Dachau for insubordination. Am I mistaken?"

Leibrecht was about to answer something, but Dr. Josef silenced him with a gesture. "Listen —" Mengele began.

"Anyway, this whole discussion is pointless," Müller cut in. "As my husband takes his orders directly from the SS-Obersturmbannführer.

The camp commander.

The sound of a paper being unfolded. A letter, perhaps, that the woman brandished. Emil couldn't see it.

"Signed by Rudolf Höss himself," she continued, with the consent of SS-Standortarzt Eduard Wirths, your direct superior. You can check with him if you still have your doubts."

Mengele quickly read through the letter, then raised his eyes level with Müller. He was furious, but there was nothing he could do. Leibrecht, meanwhile, had moved to the far end of the room. He was watching his superior be humiliated by this newcomer. Mengele returned the letter to her. Anger had transformed his face. Good Dr. Josef, always so generous with his sweets, now seemed like a lion trapped in the corner of a cage.

Mengele passed by the SS guard and left the laboratory without closing the door behind him. He spoke with someone at the Kommandantur over the phone — one of Rudolf Höss's subalterns, perhaps. A long tirade, which the others listened to in silence. Dr. Leibrecht observed the young woman as if trying to understand what in the devil's name motivated her. Ordinarily, officers' wives were happy enough to just parade about. The more ambitious among them worked in the Registratur, the prison archives, or at the Standesamt, the civil registration office. This one, however, seemed different, animated by some strange energy.

Dr. Mengele stalked back into the operating room, his anger barely contained. In a dry voice, he ordered Leibrecht to untie Emil from the operating table. The doctor hesitated, then, under Mengele's urging, undid the straps that held the boy. The whole time his eyes were fixed on the young woman, his stare cold enough to give you chills. Emil expected her to lower her eyes, but no. She held her own.

The SS guard moved Leibrecht out of his way and grabbed Emil by the arm, pulling him brusquely outside the operating room. As he was leaving, Emil heard Dr. Leibrecht say to the young woman, "You'll owe me one, Christina Müller."

She ignored him.

In the yard, the guard pushed Emil in front of him, shoving him without a care. In silence the young woman trailed them. They made their way toward the camp's entrance. Emil wondered what this stranger wanted from him, this Christina Müller, her hair fiery red. He would have liked to ask her, but speaking to her, even looking at her, would have been a grave error. He couldn't feel his right ear anymore; it was numb, frozen, really. He put his hand against it repeatedly; yes, it was still there. For now at least, and that was all that mattered.

Soon, Emil understood he was being brought to the Kommandantur, right beside the main guard post. The SS man pushed him through the door.

A corridor followed by a staircase and suddenly an office, with a desk and a German officer behind it reading through a pile of papers, a cigarette at his lips. Slicked-back hair, an aquiline nose — and the most beautiful ears in the world. In front of him, on a sheet of blotting paper, his officer's cap was laid upside down, his gloves inside it. Emil wondered why he'd been brought here, then noticed the accordion, his Paolo Soprani, abandoned on a chair in the corner. In an instant, he understood everything. He'd stolen the instrument during disinfection. Someone had sold him out. Otto Schwarzhuber, the SS-Obersturmführer's young son? Emil had broken a rule, the most important one. He'd taken something that belonged to the Reich. Every Rom was a damn thief, and here he'd given them more proof. He would be punished. Made an example of in front of the whole camp.

When the officer raised his eyes, Christina Müller said, "It's him, Oskar."

The officer furrowed his brow, sat back in his chair. "What happened to his ear?"

"Dr. Mengele. His research on racial characteristics. He mentioned it to us, once, do you remember?"

His face tightened. "I thought he was working on eye colour."

"Ears as well. Folds, curves, extrusions …"

The officer pointed at Emil. "Is he deaf?"

"I arrived right before the removal."

The man nodded. Emil understood that this high officer was Oskar Müller, husband to the young woman.

Müller got up, stepped around his desk, and stood in front of Emil, observing him for a long time. Finally, he pointed to the Paolo Soprani on the chair. "Play."

Emil couldn't understand what he was being asked. He understood the words, yes, but couldn't get his head around the meaning. Play? Müller became impatient. The guard shoved him toward the accordion. Without daring to turn around, Emil grabbed the instrument. His legs were weak, all of a sudden. He sat on the chair, got back up immediately, but Müller gestured for him to sit back down. Emil's fingers were fixed, rigid, as if he no longer had mastery over his hands. He raised his eyes. Everyone was looking at him, Müller, of course, the SS, and Müller's wife.

"Play!" the officer barked.

So Emil played. Timidly, at first, clumsily. His hands searching for the keys, his fingers slipping on the keyboard, his movements halting. But, soon enough, music filled him, occupying him entirely, the bellows working the fear out of him. He let himself be carried by the rhythm his fingers — now obeying him — imposed on the Paolo Soprani. Nothing existed anymore. These Germans, the Kommandantur, Birkenau, the entire Third Reich, the war, the endless war. Emil played what he felt in his heart; he played for his life, somehow knowing that the accordion was his only means of survival. He played and played, as if time no longer existed. And then, suddenly, weariness overcame him. When Emil finally stopped, on the verge of collapsing, he raised his eyes. No one had moved. They looked at him strangely; he was scared all over again. What did all of this mean?

Oskar Müller cleared his throat and told his wife, "The Jew, the other one, we won't need him anymore. This Gypsy is much better."

6

The official cause had been determined: the use of portable stoves and space heaters in a confined and insalubrious environment. During an early winter cold snap, all of this ad hoc heating equipment had been cranked to maximum power. A Romanian winter under a heavy grey sky. Bucharest's citizens stooped their shoulders as they quickly went about their affairs. Those on Zăbrăuţi Street in Ferentari, well, they wouldn't be going anywhere anymore. Twenty-three bodies last time they counted, including eight children who didn't even have the strength to leave their parents' squat. The fire caught them as they were sleeping; they didn't stand a chance. Bodies found in the trash-lined staircases, right in front of back exits on the ground floor. They'd been boarded up for years. Desperate men and women clawing at the doors, trying in vain to escape. Within five minutes it was all over, the smoke had taken them before any of the firemen had time to reach the building through the neighbourhood's mazelike streets. Six storeys in flames as gawkers and neighbours, most of them Roma living in similarly squalid conditions, stood by and watched until late in the night. Fellow Roma crying in the streets, guessing the fate of their brethren in the burning building.

"The preliminary investigation yielded traces of accelerants, which leads us to believe the fire was deliberately lit," Adrian Pavlenco declared from behind his desk at the Bucharest General Inspectorate.

Clearly, American TV detectives had guided Inspector Pavlenco's sartorial choices. The national Romanian television station broadcast police procedurals in the afternoon, with subtitles, of course. He was going for *Miami Vice*, *Hill Street Blues*, or maybe *Law & Order*. His clothes were a size too small, showing off his lean build. According to Toma Boerescu, Pavlenco had transformed his own basement into a gym. More gossip learned at the coffee machine.

"So what's the link to Kevin Dandurand?"

Pavlenco raised his eyes to Josée, who'd just asked the question. He then glanced at Max O'Brien and Marilyn Burgess, standing a little off to the side. Max thought this Burgess woman was small, delicate, and surprisingly wispy for an RCMP agent. He hoped she wasn't part of the Fraud Division. When they'd all introduced themselves to one another before the meeting started, she'd scanned Max's face for a beat too long, as if he reminded her of a person or a picture she'd seen before. However, he'd taken a few precautions. He'd played so many characters over the years for his scams that he'd become used to changing his appearance and wearing the clothes of other men. To Josée and the others, Burgess included, Max looked like a calm, collected New York banker used to conducting business on the golf course. The favourite pastime of his alter ego, Robert Cheskin.

Be that as it may, Max had a twinge of worry over Marilyn Burgess's insistent gaze. She might be an expert with a photographic memory, mentally riffling thought her department's open cases.

"The fire seems to have started in a fourth-floor apartment," Pavlenco explained. "An apartment left abandoned, in principle. A body — presumably the tenant — was found in a room that served as a kitchen."

"A Rom?"

"We haven't identified him yet. Always difficult with those people."

"Once again, I don't see the link to Kevin," Josée declared.

"Some of his personal belongings were discovered in the squat. Clothes and a suitcase, among other things."

That was Marilyn Burgess speaking. Her voice was confident, professional. She seemed to know her stuff, Max thought. Burgess appeared deeply connected to this whole mess, in a way Max couldn't quite understand. Was it ambition? Perhaps she couldn't stand the thought of letting an obscure Romanian police officer get all the credit for handling the investigation.

"That doesn't prove anything," Josée insisted. "He could have been robbed."

"Ms. Dandurand, please —"

"Neighbours witnessed a fight in front of the building, followed by both men going up to the apartment," Pavlenco said, cutting off Burgess.

"The tenant was stabbed to death," Burgess added. "Perhaps the suspect tried to hide his crime."

"Kevin is no killer," Max said.

The three others turned toward him.

"I wish I could be as confident as you," Pavlenco said. "The only way to know for sure is to find him. My men have gone through the whole city with a fine-toothed comb and we've gotten nowhere. Kevin Dandurand has vanished."

A silence fell.

"For now, all that we want to do is ask him a few questions. We need to know what he was doing in a building full of Roma. Know why he was in Bucharest, and in a neighbourhood like Ferentari." Pavlenco turned toward Marilyn Burgess.

She nodded. "Kevin Dandurand has had run-ins with the law. Thanks to Interpol I've obtained a copy of a police report out of New York."

Max closed his eyes. Here it came. The old stories he'd tried to hide coming to light. The East River warehouses.

"New York? What are you talking about?" Josée didn't have a clue. Max and Kevin had never revealed their secret to anyone.

"It is, in fact, Mr. Cheskin here who paid for his friend's bail," Burgess said, turning to Max.

Josée faced Max, too, waiting for an explanation.

"Ancient history," he said. "Kevin had nothing to do with the fire. You're wasting your time. Going down the wrong path."

Adrian Pavlenco ignored the remark.

"That's not all," Burgess said. "Victims of fraud in New York, Chicago, and Atlantic City have identified him as a con man by his picture. In the 1990s, Kevin Dandurand was part of a gang of thieves led by a so-called Max O'Brien, well known by the police. Dandurand was in Bucharest for a reason, likely related to the murder of this Gypsy. Fraud perhaps."

Max could see it now: Pavlenco and Burgess couldn't care less about the death of the twenty-three Roma. They were solely interested in catching this high-profile criminal who'd been avoiding Interpol for years.

Josée was speechless, stunned by what she'd just heard.

"Your brother may not be guilty of this tragedy," Burgess continued, "but he's got something to hide. That much is clear. If we don't get him for the murder and the fire, we'll get him on other charges, no doubt about it." She let silence fill the room, probably as an intimidation tactic. Then she added, "And if he gives us O'Brien, that'll be a start."

In the corridor, as Max headed toward the exit, Josée grabbed him by the arm. "What's all this about? Why did you never mention the robbery? Does Caroline know?"

"A youthful mistake."

"And what about this fraud business? You knew about that, too?"

"No, I swear I've never heard a word about it."

Josée peered at Max for a long moment, as if to make sure he wasn't lying. For Max, lying was second nature. He held her stare.

She added, "Anything else you've been hiding from me? Anything else I should know before I put my reputation as a lawyer at stake?"

Back at the hotel, Max finally got a hold of Caroline in Montreal. There had been dark days after Sacha's death, but she had gradually recovered and come back to herself. In the midst of her deepest pain, she'd often ended up at Refuge Sainte-Catherine to help others. There, the director had asked her to write a newsletter, which they distributed to donors and volunteers three times a year. Caroline had thrown herself into the project, hoping it would distract her from her grief. But no, this simple act of writing reminded her too much of her career as a journalist and her old life, when she'd been happy and carefree, when her son was alive. Volunteering, yes. She was ready and able to serve warm soup to runaways and give clean syringes to drug addicts, but there was no way she'd go back to journalism, even for a newsletter.

Max had been through Montreal a year ago and had taken the time to visit her. He hadn't seen her since the Saqawigan tragedy. Without attracting attention, he'd watched her sort through old clothes that other volunteers would give to the homeless once night fell, their hands frozen, standing shivering behind paper cups of black coffee. The beautiful, irresistible young woman he'd met in that gym in Tribeca was little more than a memory now. Caroline's hair, which had been so magnificent before, was cut short, a dense tuft of hair framing — highlighting, really — the bones prominent under almost translucent skin. Only her eyes were the same. Those penetrating eyes.

To the runaway teenagers and the homeless, she was simply Caro, the woman who handed them a bowl of soup or a used blanket in exchange for nothing at all. The young people had watched Max suspiciously, as if he were a cop. Or a journalist looking for a story on the urban jungle. They'd scanned the space behind him for a photographer, the obligatory appendix, but Max travelled light.

A volunteer had replaced Caroline, who left her post to join Max. The cafeteria was closed; it wouldn't open until the afternoon. Another volunteer mopped the floor, his thoughts elsewhere. The whole room smelled like industrial detergent, though it wasn't enough to convince anyone for a second that the place was clean.

"Why don't we go out for coffee?" Max had suggested, ill at ease.

As they trudged toward the Second Cup together, kids standing at street corners with squeegees and water bottles waved or spoke a few words to her. Even some cops, both in and out of uniform, stopped her in the street to ask her about a runaway whose parents were worried, or a john who'd turned violent on a prostitute.

Caroline, transformed into Mother Teresa. The former journalist with a promising, bright future, the elegant Caroline with the devastating smile, had become queen of Montreal's gutters.

Once outside the slums she'd come to know so well, her confidence disappeared. It was all a show.

"You're married, Robert? Finally hitched?"

In New York, Max had spoken of Pascale and their relationship, which had ended so abruptly. Caroline had scolded him: what was the point of staying tied to the past, to a memory, no matter how beautiful it was? You had to move forward, start fresh. Of course, that was before Sacha's death. Today Caroline lectured no one at all.

At a nearby table a man and woman sat facing each other in silence, chain-smoking in front of a full ashtray. They weren't exactly homeless, but they were close enough. Caroline watched them from the corner of her eye.

"I was like them," she said. "I spent two years wandering the streets, trying to convince myself I was the only one who'd ever suffered. That my pain was unique, one of a kind." She smiled. "Vanity. Even in my wretched state."

Over the phone from Bucharest, Caroline's voice seemed thin, used, as if she hadn't slept since the news broke about the accusations against Kevin.

"Everything they're saying about him, Caroline, it's all a lie."

At the other end of the world, radio silence.

Max asked, "Do you know what Kevin was doing in Romania? Did he talk to you before he left?"

"Yes." She hesitated. "He was acting strange, like restless, you know? We talked about all sorts of things, but I felt like he was hiding something from me."

Kevin might have been working an angle, as the cops were saying. Max could remember the mood he'd get in before an operation: like an actor about to walk onstage. A mix of nervousness and excitement.

Stage fright.

"Do you remember anything out of the ordinary?"

Caroline hesitated again, then said, "He just hugged me hard, that's all. Like he hadn't done in a long time. I felt all … strange." She muffled a sob. "I felt like he was saying goodbye."

7

J ack Straub, Bill Collington, Jiri Schiller, Larry Walberg, and the Kiwi Tom Farraday. Kevin became the newest member of the talented team Max had gathered around himself over the years. The group had since dissolved; gone were the heady days of operation after operation. Each was on his own path now, each following his own way. Back then, when Max called, they answered, even if they were running their own jobs on the side. They were the best: all specialists, all discreet, all terrifyingly efficient.

Max got Ted Duvall to train Kevin. Ted was a Franco-Ontarian with a loud voice and rolling gait. He usually worked on his own but always collaborated with Max when the latter required his services. Duvall knew every cop from Toronto to New York and could impersonate any one of them. He was the one to play the police officer when a job needed an authority figure or a representative of the law. Duvall clearly enjoyed this role, which he'd gotten down to a fine art over the years. He shared with Kevin all the tricks of the trade without hesitation, believing Kevin to be a promising young man — those were his own words. If you could be a convincing lumberjack in Midtown Manhattan, surely you were born to play any role.

Kevin fit in with the group easily. He was cautious, careful, and most important, he followed orders. He never put the safety of the rest of his team at risk. Fraud was a crime committed in the light of day and amid formidable banality. Kevin understood that right away.

Max and Ted built Kevin a new identity, one that would deceive Caroline. Kevin had just signed with a new sponsor, which meant he could now train without any financial worries, allowing him to quit his job with New York City's Parks and Recreation. A masquerade, a perpetual lie that Caroline believed hook, line, and sinker, despite being an investigative journalist. Thanks to the lawyer Max had hired for Kevin, he'd be able to stay in the country following the seizure of his work permit. Life could go on.

On weekends, Max, Kevin, Caroline, and Gabrielle ate together at the house. After the meal, once Gabrielle had been put to bed, Caroline locked herself in her office to write about the fate of illegal Cuban refugees, victims of the power struggle between Fidel Castro and the United States. Or to reveal to readers of *The New Yorker* the true motivations and intentions of Slobodan Milošević, the monster tearing through ex-Yugoslavia. Max and Kevin opened a bottle of cognac, put on a few jazz albums, and waited for the sun to rise. Family day, in a sense. A strange little family, but a family nonetheless.

As the first rays of morning light came through the window, Max would fall asleep, and Kevin would put on his track suit and go off running in the neighbourhood. He ran circles around Sunset Park, breathless, forgetting his failures, his disappointments, his wasted youth. Did Kevin have regrets about abandoning his running career? Probably. But Max came to believe that he'd gotten mixed up with the riff-raff in Tribeca precisely because he was looking for an excuse to justify an end to his dreams. As if he wanted some external force to make the decision for him.

Because of Kevin's new job, his relationship with Caroline changed, naturally, despite his swearing that nothing was different. His secret forced him to create a barrier between himself and his wife. She realized it but said nothing. Max, of course, understood exactly what was happening. It seemed clear that their relationship would slowly be poisoned. The lie, the secret, would only be followed by more lies, always essential ones, of course, all inevitable. Max saw in Kevin the repetition of his own life, of his own strained relationship with women, Pascale first among them.

Why had he done it? Why had he offered Kevin this poisoned apple?

The answer was simple: by making himself indispensable, he was forcing someone else, anyone else, to tie their fate to his. On the surface of things, Max was interested in people, yes, but they'd always been disposable. With Kevin he was trying to act differently, to be different. Max was proving to himself that he was capable of real relationships, ones worth more than a few drinks, quickly discarded and forgotten. Worth more than those he built for a scam, only useful to him for a short time. He'd adopted Kevin, in a sense, and along with him, Caroline and Gabrielle. And, together, Kevin and Max had vowed to protect mother and daughter through their silence and complicity.

Curiously, Max felt responsible for his friend's professional failures. Giving Kevin work on his team wasn't showing confidence in him. It was quite the opposite really: with his offer Max was signalling an end to Kevin's career as an athlete and an honest man. He was saying that Kevin didn't possess the necessary qualities to compete on the same level as world-class marathon runners. From then on it became necessary to lie, cheat, cover up the truth. What seemed like a hand offered to a man in need was really a way to cover his friend's failures.

Kevin had lost the will to fight. He'd given up his dreams, which had become unattainable. Max regretted having given Kevin the excuse he'd been waiting for to simply declare that he had forever forfeited his passions.

Something his father had never done.

Kevin rarely spoke of Raymond, and never in kind terms. And yet, in the business world, Raymond's star shone brightly. His company, Nordopak, founded in the basement of his house on a credit margin and a second mortgage, had become within a few years a packaging company with thousands of corporate clients. At the company's height in the early 1990s, Raymond had had some two hundred employees, a factory, a warehouse, and a fleet of fifty trucks. Nordopak distributed some ten thousand different packaging products in Canada and the United States. And in Europe, as well. Aspekt-Ziegler, the Dutch giant of prefab furniture, was responsible for forty percent of the Montreal-based company's revenue.

To his happy employees, Raymond Dandurand was God's gift to man. Their insurance against joblessness and poverty. Every February 19, Raymond's birthday, employees got the day off. There were great end-of-year bonuses, a well-funded retirement plan, generous summer employment programs for children of employees. In other words, it was a model company. Everyone at Nordopak called Raymond "the emperor" as a kind joke, but according to Kevin, this affection wasn't mutual. Raymond considered his employees to be foils for his own genius, his incredible success, his knack for business. He was a man of changing moods, taking all the credit for success and distributing blame to everyone but himself.

"A megalomaniac, seriously," Kevin said about his father. "And self-centred. A schmuck, plain and simple."

No love lost between the two of them. Kevin had always felt he was bothering his father just with his presence, by being in the way. Raymond had ignored the existence of his son. His eyes might come to rest on Kevin, but he didn't see him. While other fathers — normal fathers — played baseball or hockey with their sons, Kevin had had to find his own path. When he'd become more serious about running, when his ambitions had grown, not once had Raymond come to see his son run, never having been interested in his performances.

Kevin had found the affection his father denied him in his mother, Roxanne. A tender woman, but always willing to take a back seat. She was much younger than Raymond and took Kevin's side when things went from bad to worse between father and son. They spent a lot of time together, and Roxanne's kindness was the only thing that prevented Kevin from blowing up.

"He loves you, Kevin," Roxanne would say. "He doesn't know how to say it, how to show it, but he loves you."

"He's an idiot."

"Don't say that. Come on, tell me about your day."

And so Kevin would give her a full account, rocked in his mother's arms, forgetting for a moment his father, who treated him with complete indifference. Sometimes he caught himself wishing his father beat him or slapped him around from time to time. But no, Raymond never rebuked his son; he remained silent, unbearably silent, disinterested.

One afternoon, as Kevin had returned from school — he was eleven or so — he found an ambulance leaving the house. Inside, his father was standing by the china cabinet. His suit was rumpled, his tie undone; he'd rushed back home from work. Roxanne had collapsed in the kitchen. A neighbour had found her.

Kevin and Raymond sped to the hospital and made their way to her room in neurology.

It had been a stroke.

Kevin's world fell apart. Just the idea of life without Roxanne sent him into the depths of despair. Kevin simply couldn't believe it. Couldn't believe in this stroke. It had to be some sort of trick to pull them apart. He wanted to get the police involved, sic them on Raymond, force him to admit a crime.

Roxanne never returned to consciousness. After school Kevin would go straight to the hospital and hold his mother's hand, without knowing whether she was aware of his presence or not.

One Saturday Kevin had hidden out in a stall in the hospital bathroom to cry. He stayed there for hours. At some point Raymond walked in. Kevin didn't reveal his presence, but Raymond leaned against the metal door.

"Kevin, I know you're there. I can hear you snivelling."

Kevin closed his eyes. He'd never played hide-and-seek with his father before. Why now?

"Your mother died," Raymond said, concise as ever, announcing the death of his son's mother as if he were telling his employees about a recently fired colleague.

Kevin ripped the door open. "I want to see her."

"It's over, Kevin."

Pushing his father out of the away, Kevin bolted for the corridor. Nurses were busying themselves around Roxanne's room. A stretcher was waiting a bit farther off. Morgue employees were already on the scene. An orderly brought Kevin back to his father, who said, "It just happened a little while ago. I've been looking all over for you."

Kevin ran. He ran away from the hand offered to him in comfort. He rushed down the stairs at the end of the floor, ran into the street, and kept running for hours, hoping exhaustion would kill him so he could join his mother in heaven. Hours later he collapsed from fatigue in a part of the city he didn't know, hoping he was lost forever.

No dice.

After the funeral, Raymond had found solace in the arms of his mistress, Sharon Jankell, who'd been a lawyer for Nordopak for a time. It had been an open secret for years. Once a week, Raymond and Sharon would have breakfast at Chanterelle, a restaurant on rue Sherbrooke, accompanied by Josée, the child Raymond and Sharon had conceived early in their relationship. Even the day after his wife's death, Raymond hadn't strayed from his habit. More than once Kevin had gone to spy on his father's second family, observing his father the way you would a stranger, from afar, without daring to intervene.

And so the day after his mother's death, Kevin respected his own tradition, and in his Sunday best, spied on his father's second family through a window. A family together preparing for what was coming next — without Roxanne, of course. Kevin had tried to get his mother to act for months, tried to convince her to hold her own against her husband. When he'd told her about this second family, Roxanne had been happy enough to close her eyes and ignore the truth.

"Don't be mad at him," she'd told him softly. "Don't resent him for anything. Ever."

Such submission had disgusted Kevin. As he watched his father's second family, Kevin was filled with an aching desire. No, he didn't want to join his mother in death anymore — that was just childish. All he wanted to do now was kill his father, kill the perfect businessman. To get rid of him once and for all. To obtain revenge for his cruelty and indifference.

8

Glancing quickly about, Max O'Brien got the lay of the place. Beer mugs on every table, which the harried personnel hadn't had time to pick up. At the counter, prostitutes, attracted here by the presence of hundreds of foreign conference-goers, just like the young Russian woman at the Intercontinental's bar the previous evening. Two prostitutes were chatting over a glass of cognac: a blond one, tall and skinny with a nose that had had been worked on. The other smaller, rounder, with black hair and waxy skin.

At the far end of the room Max discovered Toma Boerescu hiding behind a slice of chocolate cake the size of his head. Max ordered an espresso and sat in front of the former cop after almost tripping on the man's walker carelessly left lying around.

"It's stuck," Boerescu spat out between two bites of cake. "I can't get it to fold."

Max pushed the walker away.

"And this glorious piece of cake is a gift from some of my old party friends to celebrate fifty years of membership."

With his fork, Boerescu looked like a mountain climber about to reach the top of Everest. Instead of eternal snow, however, he was facing down a mountain made of whipped cream and diabetes. Next to him, the rest of his meal: a Moldavian *tochitura*, pieces of pork, liver, and smoked sausages cooked in pork fat.

"Either your doctor's your uncle," Max said, "or you're not being entirely honest with him."

Boerescu pushed the dessert away. Took out a pill bottle. Max helped him open it. The old man swallowed blue, red, and yellow pills with a sip of mineral water. Finally, he asked, "Do you have the money?"

Max nodded. He'd taken out $200 from a cash machine near the hotel, using a credit card with one of his pseudonyms.

Boerescu raised his head and spoke in a conspiratorial tone. "The one on the right, with the brown hair. You can have her half off." He smiled as if he'd just told a funny joke.

"What are you talking about?"

"The two whores there at the bar. The one with the brown hair is cheaper."

"Why?"

"Didn't you notice? She's a Gypsy."

‡

The "Little Paris" of the Balkans had had its own Baron Haussmann, though one completely mad and afflicted by early senility: Nicolae Ceaușescu. A cobbler, son of a drunkard from Scorniceşti, he'd fought his way to the top of the Romanian Communist Party by using Joseph Stalin's method: backroom deals and treachery. Vestiges of his presence as head of state were visible throughout the country. As if, even years after his death, it was still impossible to get rid of his stink. Romania was changing, though; soon enough the country would be the newest member of the European Union, joining the other former people's dictatorships of Poland, Hungary, and the Czech Republic.

"Good old Vlad Ţepeş," Boerescu said as the taxi turned onto Brătianu Boulevard. "You see tourists looking for him all over the city, as if he should be remembered, as if he was the George Washington of Romania."

Max looked at him without understanding.

"In America every fountain, every tavern, every river or stream or puddle quenched the thirst of your national hero. But Vlad Ţepeş … a statue here and there. A few words in a brochure. So the tourists are disappointed, of course! On the other hand, this whole fascination for him … for the character. It's a bit exaggerated, don't you think?"

"Vlad Ţepeş?"

"Fifteenth century. He resisted the Turks, the fight of his life. He used to impale prisoners, traitors, all sorts of people. Impale them while they were still alive, of course. It was a common practice back then."

"A charming fellow, clearly," Max added.

"You might know him by his stage name — Count Dracula. Dracula meaning 'dragon.' Back in the good old days of Ceaușescu, the Bram Stoker novel was forbidden, banned! After all, it was an attack on the good standing of all Romanian people. Another fantastic policy destroyed by the revolution of '89."

A few minutes later Boerescu asked the driver to drop them off near a church. The two men walked up to the forecourt. Actually, it was more like Toma Boerescu struggled over the paving stones, leaning heavily on his walker. He'd managed to digest his meal, which was reassuring. A few passersby smiled at them. How wonderful to see a son being so attentive to his old man! Max sighed. His fixer was costing him $300 a day. He wasn't sure he was getting his money's worth.

A handful of young touts were milling in front of the church selling concert tickets. The eternal George Enescu's suites, sonatas, and rhapsodies for bored tourists.

"So not the best performance, these ones, but better than some of the others," Boerescu said, grabbing a flyer. He gestured at a second group of touts trying to lead music lovers toward another church.

The old man paid the woman at the booth for two tickets and led Max inside. The crowd in the nave was sparse, a few courageous souls, like them, braving the humidity of the place to listen to the concert. In the choir, musicians were blowing on their hands, warming them up. Max was beginning to wonder what this whole escapade was about.

Boerescu pulled out a handkerchief and blew his nose loudly under the scandalized stares of a few tourists. To them, Boerescu certainly looked like a homeless man come to warm up his feet for a few pennies while listening to Enescu's music.

The orchestra started, according to the program, with Sonata No. 3 for Violin and Piano. Despite a few blunders, they attacked the piece with an energy that surprised Max. For a long moment, he was rooted in place, completely transfixed by the music. In the middle of the piece, a half-frozen pigeon flew across the nave — which was covered in droppings — without breaking the attention of the spectators. At least, Max told himself, the day wouldn't be a complete loss. The violin, darting, throbbing, wailing sometimes, with almost a Romani air, made him deeply melancholic.

Max's thoughts returned to Kevin and his family. In 1998, for Gabrielle's birthday, Max had gone over to the Dandurand household, ready to celebrate the day with them. He'd had the impression his friend was avoiding his eyes, was hiding something. Caroline, meanwhile, was simply beaming. She was holding back, trying to keep whatever it was she wanted to say a secret for now, a surprise. Over a few drinks, while Gabrielle was tearing through the gifts, Caroline, incapable of holding back any longer, announced she was pregnant. Max was over the moon. More than Kevin, it seemed. Why did he have that air about him?

"We're going back to Montreal," Caroline had explained.

She'd been offered a job with the *Gazette* that included generous maternity leave. When Raymond had heard the news, he'd invited his son to work for Nordopak.

"I forced Kevin to agree," Caroline said.

Kevin smiled. A sad smile that hid plenty behind it. "Marketing. Folding flyers and stapling brochures … you get the idea."

"Kevin, please …"

It was only after the meal that Max found a moment to speak alone with his friend. "What does this mean?"

Kevin remained evasive. He'd been wanting to tell Max for a while but hadn't dared.

"And what about your father? You always told me you couldn't stand him."

"We've made peace."

He wasn't very convincing. But, once again, Max wasn't about to call his friend out on his lie.

That night, as he left, Max had wished good luck to the three of them. No, actually, the four of them. Caroline made him promise he'd come visit in Montreal. In only a few days, or so it seemed to Max, they packed everything they owned and got on the road. Max felt abandoned. All these years he'd been there, supporting the family from behind the scenes. And now, suddenly, they were gone from his life. He decided to not chase them to Montreal, to not show any neediness. What would it look like if he came to visit them? As if he were living the family life vicariously. Whatever the case might be, with their leaving, Max was bereft of the only genuine friendship he'd ever developed in New York.

Had it really been genuine? Once again, Max was being delusional. Caroline had known nothing of his true identity, what he did for a living. And she certainly hadn't known what he'd dragged her husband into.

No, when it was all said and done, it was probably best for the Dandurand family to get far away from New York.

Months later, Max was sleeping soundly when his cellphone rang. Still half asleep, he'd felt Isabel turn and stretch out for his phone. Isabel, a secretary for a real-estate developer in Spanish Harlem — a bit player in the operation he was currently running. He startled awake and grabbed the cellphone out of her hand before she could answer. Isabel shrugged, mumbled an insult in Spanish, and got up to go to the bathroom. A few moments later Max heard the shower running.

"Robert? You're with someone? Am I bothering you?"

"Caroline …"

She was calling from Montreal to give him the good news. It was a boy. Sacha.

Sacha-the-Red.

Max felt someone tugging on his sleeve. Toma Boerescu, his eyes insistent. Time for his medicine, probably. Instead, the former cop nodded at a small man seated alone a few rows away. Boerescu whispered in Max's ear, "Petru Tavala."

Confused, Max looked at Boerescu. The old man added, "He owns a café on Gabroveni Street. More of a restaurant, really."

Max gestured for him to go on.

"Early in the morning last Thursday he served breakfast to your friend, Kevin Dandurand."

Max glanced at the Tavala character, then back at Boerescu. The old dog had managed to pull a lead out of thin air, after all. He'd probably realized he was about to lose his cushy gig with Max.

The old man smiled. "Petru Tavala loves music. A shame these amateurs are just ruining poor George Enescu!"

Petru Tavala had no interest in confiding in two strangers he encountered in a church, but the café owner did love to talk. About this or anything else, why not? He didn't have much time, though, only a few minutes. It was high season, after all. With this conference, with the holidays in full swing, all he had time for was working himself to the bone. But better that than starving, right? It could be worse; it's always worse, or better! Who knows anymore! Anyway, sure, he'd seen a foreigner in his coffee shop early one morning.

"Kevin Dandurand?" Max asked.

"I only learned that was his name when the others came asking about him."

"The police?"

"No, no. They were these guys who reminded me of the Securitate … you know what I mean? Serious, austere, looking like there was a conspiracy afoot! They snooped around, asking the same question ten different ways, as if to trick me." They'd wanted to know whether he'd heard anything, overheard the conversation.

"What conversation?" Max asked.

"Dandurand was with another man. He had a moustache, the other one. I heard everything, but I didn't understand a thing. They were speaking English together ..."

Boerescu was translating for Tavala.

"Who was the other guy?" Max pressed.

"A Gypsy. That's why I remember. They sat at the table farthest from the door. They ordered coffee and breakfast. They seemed on good terms. They started laughing all of a sudden."

Old friends?

"Like I said, me and English ..."

In any case, whether or not they were close friends, it was clear they weren't strangers.

But a Rom who spoke English?

"They stayed, I don't know, maybe an hour, maybe a little more."

"And then?"

"Then they shook hands and the Gypsy left. The stranger seemed worried. He paid for the coffee and the breakfast. Then he left."

"And you didn't understand a word they said?"

"For years they forced us to learn Russian," Tavala said. "And now they say English is the language that matters! Do you think that's fair?"

The decline of Russian in Eastern Europe didn't matter much to Max, but he was intrigued by the idea of Kevin meeting a Romani man in Bucharest. The guy from the Zăbrăuţi Street dwellings maybe, where Kevin's personal effects had been found?

"I saw the picture of the man who died in the apartment," Tavala said. "It wasn't the same man at all."

Clearly, Max would need to find this strange Romani man to understand what had happened. His meeting with Kevin had preceded the fire by a few hours at most.

They left the café owner behind and made their way out of the church. Once outside, Max turned to Boerescu. "Do you think the authorities are trying to hide something?"

"Because of the two agents?"

Max nodded.

"They weren't police, according to Tavala."

"Okay, besides the police, there might be other groups, no? More secretive organizations?"

"The Securitate doesn't exist anymore, hasn't in a long time."

"Don't you find it strange that some unknown organization is after Kevin? They weren't cops, it seems. And what about the English-speaking Rom? Why hasn't he come forward?"

"He's a Rom. He's got everything to lose by revealing any ties to Dandurand." Boerescu sighed. "Does your friend, Kevin, have anything to hide? I mean, besides the murder of Gypsies?"

"Maybe."

The weather had warmed a little, and a fine fog had replaced the previous night's snow. Winter was a lost cause in Bucharest. Max raised his collar and began to walk toward Unirii Boulevard, followed by Boerescu.

"Did you know that, traditionally, Gypsies stayed away from multi-storey buildings?" his fixer asked.

"Nothing worse to them then all living stacked one on top of the other."

Which hadn't stopped the poor souls from piling up in that hellhole on Zăbrăuți Street.

"Are we far?" Max asked.

"What are you talking about?"

"Ferentari. Are we far?"

The first three cabs refused to take them to their destination. It was a rule taxi companies had put in place a few years earlier. Even the buses, the trains — barely anything made its way into the neighbourhood. There was less public transportation in Ferentari than in the rest of the city, but more police stations. Ferentari, the Bronx of Bucharest. The whole place had been left to rot, while the Roma, chased out of the countryside, scrabbled for a living in its ruined streets.

Much worse than the Bronx.

Only the walls of buildings remained, all lined up in Soviet fashion. Between them, trash heaps and dozens of wild, famished dogs. It was hard to even figure out which building it was that had burned. The Roma — the vast majority of the neighbourhood's population — had already settled back into their apartments, moving their worthless knick-knacks back into soot-darkened rooms never to be repainted.

Probably the most unusual part of this whole story was that fire trucks had actually come to the neighbourhood that night. And that an investigation had been opened. It was a rare thing indeed for anybody to do anything to help the Roma's lot. They were left to fend for themselves, to deal with their own problems and catastrophes. And yet, on Zăbrăuți Street, an exception had been made. More signs of a setup.

Max tried to put together the pieces he'd found so far. Kevin had reached Bucharest a week earlier and met a Rom in a coffee shop. He'd then gotten into an argument on Zăbrăuți Street with another Rom. There he'd allegedly killed the man and lit a fire to hide his tracks. But why, then, had he left personal belongings in the building, making himself easy to identify? Whomever had set him up hadn't known about Kevin's training. The first thing Duvall had taught Kevin was how to cover his tracks — unless he was leaving them purposely to confuse whoever was looking for him. Why was Kevin in Bucharest? A job gone bad? Which one?

"Do you want to see inside?" Boerescu asked.

The two men were leaning against a taxi, staring up at the building. The cab driver was nervously glancing this way and that. Max turned toward their driver, who, he noticed, had pulled out a handgun and was very visibly holding it aloft as a warning to whoever might be looking. It was clear now why he'd agreed to bring them to this neighbourhood: he was prepared.

"Let's get out of here," Max said. "I've seen enough."

After taking his leave from his fixer and paying for a cab back to wherever the man wanted to go, Max thought of returning to the hotel but couldn't resolve to end the day between the four walls of a poorly sound-proofed room — despite the five very optimistic stars on the establishment's brochure. Lost in thought, he wandered up Nicolae Bălcescu Boulevard and opened the door to a bar near Traian Vuia Street. Max ignored the conversation between the men at the counter dissecting the last World Cup results for — Max was certain — the hundredth time. Instead, he walked to the back of the room and sat down beneath a very old air-conditioning unit that probably hadn't worked since King Michael's abdication.

The television was playing on low volume. Max could see flashing images reflected in the large mirror placed behind another row of seats. On the news, tears, lamentation, and anger. Roma demonstrating in front of Parliament, begging for compassion for their brothers and sisters. And a speech by Victor Marineci. The Romani MP was demanding justice for his brethren. Pleading for a more just and fair Romania, even for the travelling people, as they were sometimes known. The patrons sitting at the bar clearly couldn't care less. Another small tragedy of life.

"Let them all burn!" the barman shouted in English before approaching his new customer. "What can I get you?"

"Peace and quiet. And a pint."

Max sank deeper into his seat. Those who were trying to hang Kevin Dandurand out to dry clearly lacked imagination. According to Pavlenco, in the past six months, there had been four other fires in derelict buildings inhabited by Roma.

After the first beer, another. And a third. The server's animosity had turned into indifference. Max had almost forgotten the man's existence when he approached the table again. "Someone on the phone for you."

Max raised his head. He wasn't sure he'd understood. But the bartender was pointing to a phone booth on the other side of the room. Max got up and squeezed himself into the cramped, dusty phone box, closing the door behind him. He picked up the phone.

"As cold as in New York, right? Nice weather to sell Christmas trees on a street corner."

Kevin.

"What's going on? Where are you?"

Close by, clearly, since he'd seen Max walk into the bar.

"I'm in a bind, Max. I need your help."

Kevin's specialty. Calling Max to the rescue. After Astoria, Bucharest.

"Tell me where you are. I'll be right there."

"It's more complicated than that, Max. Too complicated."

Silence on the other end of the line. Max was waiting for the rest.

"I didn't set the fire. Didn't kill the Roma."

"I know that. Just tell me what happened."

"All in good time. For now I've got more urgent matters. I need to ask you a favour."

"Nothing is more urgent than getting you out of here. I'm bringing you back to Montreal and —"

"Listen, Max, I don't have much time."

Max fell silent.

"Tonight you'll get a phone call from a friend of mine. Cosmin Micula."

"Kevin, this isn't the time to —"

"Let me finish." Kevin's voice was firm, bordering on hard. "Just do what he says, okay? Go with him. You can trust him."

"Kevin, please, this isn't the time to play games."

"Don't tell anyone anything, Max." He added, "And be careful. The people who are after me, well, suffice it to say they're powerful. Very powerful."

"Who?"

Kevin ignored the question. After a long silence, he continued. "I knew you'd come. I knew I could count on you." Then, "Be careful, Max."

"Kevin …"

But he'd hung up already.

9

Auschwitz-Birkenau, September 28, 1943

Emil Rosca glanced through the crack in the drapes. That was when he saw it for the first time: a gigantic birthday cake, transported by three camp aides assigned to the Stammlager's kitchens. A celestial vision for Emil, who still went hungry every day. The men had transported the cake through the camp right before the eyes of famished detainees.

The young Rom let the curtain fall back. Behind him the other musicians hadn't noticed a thing. Emaciated faces, half-dead men and women barely able to hold up their instruments, much less play them. An hour ago they'd been ordered to wait in this large room, a former office, perhaps. There was no furniture here now, and the floors were covered in dust.

Upon reaching the house of SS-Obersturmbann-führer Rudolf Höss, they'd been forced to remove their rags and put on fresh clothes. Real clothes. This did nothing at all to improve their looks — quite the contrary. One knew what to expect when everyone was wearing stripes. Prisoners looked like prisoners. Man and costume were one. But now, floating in a dark jacket and white shirt two sizes too big for him, Emil felt as if he were participating in a sinister masquerade.

The sight of the cake reminded him he hadn't eaten anything yet that day. Being in the orchestra was no picnic. Every morning at dawn the musicians played military airs to accompany the *kommandos* as they left for the work sites. At night, more music, this time for the return of the detainees. Between the two, the musicians also had to break their backs over piles of rocks. Except for Roma like Emil, who'd been exempted from forced labour for reasons he didn't quite understand. Perhaps it was so that Dr. Josef's guinea pigs could remain in decent shape to be harvested.

Usually, Oskar Müller could be counted on to be tolerant, even understanding. Other times, however, he'd lose his temper. On the ground floor of Block 24, where the rehearsals were held, he'd snap his conductor's baton in two and go on a rampage, breaking everything around him. The first few times Müller had gone mad Emil had folded himself protectively around his Paolo Soprani, making himself as small as possible, trying to become invisible.

Soon enough, however, Emil had seen that Müller's outbursts — as spectacular as they might look — were fundamentally harmless. The officer would eventually calm down, give a few taps of a replacement baton on his lectern, exactly like Herbert von Karajan had done at a concert Müller had seen in Paris in 1940, a little after the German invasion. Backstage, Oskar had had the exceptional privilege of shaking the hand of his idol, the famous conductor, the Third Reich's favourite child. No, in the end, Müller's anger was usually without consequence. But if the conductor came near a musician to tell him softly, "The way you play is a complete insult to Carl Robrecht," it meant he'd just received his death sentence. The man would disappear with his violin or his flute, soon to be replaced by a new musician. Emil sat in the still-warm chair of a Jewish accordion player, a Pole from nearby Kraków. Another musician was likely waiting in the antechamber, ready to take Emil's seat if his accordion squeaked.

In order to last, to survive, the only thing he could do was to play his best. Until the orchestra, the accordion had simply been a distraction for him, a pleasant one, surely, but a way to pass time. He couldn't even remember the first time he'd held a *gormónya*; it had simply always been a part of him. Emil's father loved the instrument, played it magnificently himself, and had shown his son how to hold it. The accordion was kept under a satin cloth in a corner of the *vôrdòn*, their means of transport. Emil was too small back then to hang it over his shoulder, but he'd managed to play it, anyway. He played casually without looking to improve. What would be the point of that? He played the accordion naturally, as others breathed, without effort. But in Auschwitz, improving was the only way to survive.

And so for the first time in his life Emil made an effort. He was getting better, learning what made Oskar Müller tick. Müller was completely unsophisticated when it came to the accordion, despite what he claimed. What he loved best were flights of lyricism, painful memories that induced tears, throbbing sounds. Emil gave him as much as he could. He'd conclude every one of his solos with pirouettes, acrobatics, flash, and thunder, keeping one eye on Müller's face. Sometimes, carried away by his false enthusiasm, Emil exaggerated and could sense a grimace taking shape on Müller's face, could sense his mood darkening. Immediately, Emil would change approach, adjust his interpretation. The others, bent over their instruments or looking elsewhere, didn't adopt the same strategy. They never saw the storm coming.

Emil had left the Romani camp, and for the past ten days, since he'd joined Müller's orchestra, he'd lived in one of the Stammlager's Cell Blocks in the main camp. He shared the place with the other musicians, Jews mostly. Also at Stammlager, the women played in the orchestra of Alma Rosé, Gustav Mahler's niece. Altogether there were six orchestras in Auschwitz, all of them led by prisoners, except for Oskar Müller's.

As well as accompanying morning and evening work crews, Emil Rosca and his colleagues played at special occasions. The day following his enrollment, Emil had been summoned to the camp commander's home. A reception that gave Oskar Müller an opportunity to impress Rudolf Höss and his wife, both lovers of Verdi.

And of Romani music. Attracting Höss's favour had been Müller's reason for integrating an accordion player into his orchestra. That night Emil had seen, among the guests, Dr. Josef and Hans Leibrecht, his dreaded subordinate. When Leibrecht noticed Emil, he walked over and posted himself right in front, observing him, a sadistic smile on his face. Immediately, Emil's fingers lost the rhythm. Müller noticed. He rebuked his accordionist as Leibrecht left for the buffet, caressing his own ear menacingly.

That night at the reception Hans Leibrecht wasn't the only one to show interest in the orchestra. A corporal, a young man named Matthias Kluge, kept humming along to the sounds coming from Emil's Paolo Soprani. At one point in the evening Emil overheard a rather heated argument between Kluge and Dr. Josef over the costs of Block 10. Emil understood that the former worked as an accountant for the SS-Standortverwaltung, which was responsible for the camp's administration.

To the others, the cream of the crop of Auschwitz-Birkenau, the musicians didn't exist; it was that simple. The music could have come from a phonograph; it would have made no difference. As he played, Emil had scanned the room, trying to find Christina Müller, the woman who'd saved his life. She didn't seem to be there. Emil overheard Oskar Müller telling another officer that his wife was tired and wouldn't be joining them that night. It didn't seem to bother him overmuch, quite the opposite. Over the course of the evening, Müller moved from one woman to the next, like an excitable butterfly. Perhaps Christina knew her husband's habits; she might have preferred not to witness his shenanigans.

‡

Back in the dusty room, the door burst open suddenly and Oskar Müller appeared, clapping his hands. The collar of his tuxedo was tight around his neck, making his face an impressive shade of red. Or perhaps it was his nerves at the thought of leading his little orchestra in front of all his superiors. The Paolo Soprani strapped around his shoulder, Emil followed the other musicians through the corridors of the house plunged in half-light. He could see the cake farther on, decorated with candles and carried by three aides. The other musicians were seeing it for the first time, unlike Emil. For those getting barely any food — and vile food at that — the birthday cake they would not be able to sample was, of course, additional torture. Müller, naturally, didn't have the slightest idea what was going on in the detainees' heads. He was as nervous as a young conductor getting ready for his first concert, even redder in the face now than only a few minutes earlier.

On Müller's signal, they began playing, with varying levels of success, a German birthday song. Two officers carried the cake to a table festooned with balloons and a banner, around which sat a few children but mostly adults, officers, all applauding loudly. It was all a surprise for Höss, who laughed and clapped like an imbecile. The same held true for Johann Schwarzhuber. Little Otto was seated in front of him, Johann holding him by the shoulders, the sign around his neck nowhere to be seen. A bit farther off, his mother, looking as austere as always. As he played, Emil scanned the room. It was the usual crowd: Mengele, Leibrecht, Kluge, and the others. Once again, no sign of Christina.

It was little Otto's turn, and he blew the candles with as much energy as he could muster. More applause, more encouragement.

Oskar Müller's performance over and done with, the members of the orchestra were directed toward the living room, where they were to wait for the end of the meal. Once the children were sent to bed, the adults would need to stretch their legs to the rhythm of dancing music.

Through a door left ajar, the prisoners could see and hear the action in the dining room: the sound of cutlery on plates, the shouts of children, the laughter of their parents. An evening of celebration like any other, it could have been anywhere. But it was in Auschwitz, where the victims of the Third Reich were disposed of. Auschwitz, little more than a landfill for undesirables.

Emil Rosca was hungry. Perhaps made hungrier by the officers he saw coming and going between the kitchen and the dining room, making sure Höss and his guests were eating their fill. Emil pushed the door open wider. The kitchen was right at the end of the corridor, nearby. With only a few steps, he could slip in, grab something, anything, and slip back into the living room. He knew there were only two officers taking care of the service — the third man had disappeared. Sometimes both men were in the dining room at the same time, leaving the kitchen unattended. That was when Emil had to act.

Emil looked around. The other musicians were all slumped against walls or napping on the ground, taking full advantage of the precious minutes of rest. His absence wouldn't be noticed.

He stood and watched the aides-de-camp coming and going for a long time. They were, unfortunately, almost perfectly synchronized. They passed each other in the corridor, where Emil could hear their perfectly polished shoes screeching on the wood floor. Each time Emil hoped one of them would turn around and go back to the dining room, giving him an opportunity to slip by unnoticed. But no such luck. Soon the noise from the nearby dining room, that of the children especially, lessened, a sign they'd be sent to bed soon. Emil was heartbroken; a small dream was slipping between his fingers.

Suddenly, the sound of broken glass, a slap to the face, crying. And the aides-de-camp were running toward the dining room. A child had spilled something; the two men were coming to the rescue.

It was now or never.

Emil opened the door as softly as possible. There was no one in the corridor. The child who'd dropped something was still crying; the aides-de-camp were nowhere to be seen. Emil moved in the opposite direction, all the while looking behind him. He was soon in the kitchen, a large, well-lit room. On every countertop, remains of the feast. Empty bottles of champagne, as well. A pile of plates, some of which still had pieces of ham on them. Emil didn't think, didn't look for something more substantial. No, those leftovers were a banquet for him. He rushed toward a plate with half-eaten ham on it, and just as he was about to put the food in his mouth, he felt a presence behind him.

Christina Müller.

Emil realized he was lost. He was standing there with a piece of ham in his hand. He would pay the piper for this — with his life, most likely. He could hear the aides-de-camp in the corridor, making their way back to the kitchen. Soon he'd be arrested, sent to the showers.

But Christina Müller kept her calm. Without any particular emotion, she grabbed Emil by the arm and pushed him into a pantry, just as the two aides-de-camp hurried back into the kitchen. They didn't seem surprised to see her. The guests were asking for more coffee, one of them said, a touch of nerves in his voice. Christina offered to prepare it herself, and they were only too happy to accept. The two men were overwhelmed, that much was clear. He heard them rushing back to attend to Höss's guests.

The pantry door opened. Completely puzzled by the young woman's decision, he didn't even take the time to thank her. He moved right past her and into the now empty corridor, and slipped back into the living room. Emil had been right: no one had noticed his absence.

Emil Rosca often saw Christina after that day. She began accompanying her husband to the Kommandantur receptions. As he played the accordion, Emil, of course, kept his attention on Oskar Müller. But sometimes he'd take a moment to glance at the young woman's face, and their eyes would meet. Emil would immediately look away, confused about why she'd let him go free from that kitchen. Twice the young German woman had saved his life. Why? What sort of interest did she have in him? She'd saved him from Dr. Josef to serve her husband's ambition and her own taste in music. But the second time? It could have been for the love of music again. If Emil had been arrested, he would have been sent back to the Zigeunerlager. Or to the gas chambers. No more music, no more accordion for him. But the look Christina gave him from time to time wasn't that of a music lover. No, it was that of a woman in love. Emil couldn't help but smile at the thought. The German wife of a German officer in a German concentration camp falling in love with a prisoner of the Stammlager! And a seventeen-year-old Rom at that! Emil was getting carried away, as usual. He dreamed, which was the most dangerous escape.

A few weeks after the kitchen incident, at another party, the men were chatting away, ignoring their wives, ignoring the orchestra. Müller was there, Kluge, as well, and others Emil didn't recognize. He overheard a discussion on German forces in Russia retreating following their defeat at Stalingrad in February, after six months of brutality and carnage. On the Western Front, France was still in the grip of the Third Reich. The officers spoke of how they expected the invasion of Great Britain would compensate for losses on the Eastern Front. But no one seemed entirely convinced of that. What was more, the Americans had just landed in southern Italy …

Emil had no idea where all these countries were. Stalingrad even less so.

"You are Emil Rosca?"

The young Rom was startled out of his thoughts. Christina, the wife of an SS officer, was speaking to him — simply inconceivable. She stood there, hands on hips, in front of the assembled orchestra, expecting an answer. Behind her the officers talked with one another in a cloud of smoke. Emil nodded imperceptibly, as if he were afraid to commit himself. Christina kept her eyes on him.

"Anton's son?"

Emil felt dizzy. His father? Why was this German woman speaking of his father? Why here, why now?

A voice broke the spell, a man's voice coming from the group of officers behind her. "And you, Christina, what do you think?"

Without losing her cool, the German woman turned toward the group of SS officers. "Do you really believe the Russians will be able to maintain their offensive?" she asked, her tone emotionless. "Don't forget that Stalingrad exhausted them, as well."

"Christina is right," Matthias Kluge said. "The Red Army is an empty shell. Sooner or later they'll be forced to slow down and fall back."

The others nodded without conviction.

"What if we danced?"

As Emil started to play, Christina grabbed Oskar Müller in her arms and dragged him into an energetic waltz, soon to be followed by the other women in the group. Emil observed her looking happy, joyous even, completely serene. She seemed like a different woman, he thought, and she didn't even glance at him for the rest of the evening. Once again, the young accordion player was sure he'd simply been dreaming.

Back in the barracks, Emil couldn't sleep a wink. He was so confused. This magnificent woman, this apparition, speaking of his father, Anton, of whom he hadn't heard a single solitary word of since the scattering of their *kumpaníya* a year ago now. Was Anton alive? Held in a camp just like this one perhaps. Worried for his son and the rest of his family. How did Christina Müller know of his existence?

The next morning little Otto Schwarzhuber was waiting for him outside the barracks. His eyes steady, looking straight at Emil. Expecting Emil to play his accordion for him. Emil had no desire to do so, had no desire to do anything, except maybe to dream a little, to escape. A hand fell on the boy's shoulder. Emil raised his eyes. It wasn't Otto's mother, but Christina Müller, looking after the child.

"Play, Emil. Play like yesterday."

Emil lifted his Paolo Soprani and played again, but for her this time. Little Otto couldn't guess what was happening, of course. Emil played and Christina looked intently at him, just as she had during the Kommandantur party. What did she want from him, exactly? His first song ended, and as he was about to start another, Christina sent Otto back to the officer looking after him a few metres away. The little boy grumbled but obeyed.

For the first time they were alone, Christina and him. Emil asked in his clumsy German, "You've seen my father? You've talked with him?"

She hesitated, then answered, "Your father is dead."

A break, his mind like a handful of pebbles thrown into a roiling sea. He'd believed, he'd hoped, he'd dared to dream, and now all of it was crushed once again. Would his misfortunes never end? Emil wanted to speak but didn't know how anymore. All he could muster was a questioning look.

"He was in Birkenau," she told him. "But not with the Gypsies. He was hiding. He was pretending to be someone else."

Emil didn't understand. Why would he be hiding, pretending to be someone else? What false identity? The Roma only used borrowed names, in any case, depending on the country they were passing through with the changing seasons.

"Come closer."

Emil hesitated. What did this woman want? He had to know more about how his father had died. And so he stepped forward, a single step. Carefully, Christina lifted her hand so very gently, as if wary of startling a savage, famished beast. She caressed his face, as if it were the most natural thing in the world. It was, of course, but not in this place, not in this hell on earth. In another world he would have expected it, in another world he was now sure he would never see again.

"Emil, I was sent by your father."

10

After Sacha's birth, Max O'Brien lost contact with Kevin Dandurand and his family. Max did visit them in Montreal a few times, but for Kevin and Caroline, Kevin especially, he represented the past. Gabrielle was the only one whose attitude toward him hadn't changed. The girl was growing so quickly. She'd started school and was learning, little by little, to go without her mother, who was often off to Toronto for work. The family now had the means to pay for a full-time nanny to take care of Sacha when Caroline was away.

Kevin seemed to enjoy his job at Nordopak. His truce with Raymond held despite Sharon's now-official role as his new wife, a role that still bothered Kevin, though his mother had been dead for years. Kevin had convinced himself that Raymond could do whatever he wanted with his love life. He wasn't cheating on anyone anymore. Perhaps Raymond had even been sensitive by keeping this woman — and their daughter, Josée — far from his first family. Kevin had learned that his father's relationship with his mother had soured long, long before. They'd only remained married for Kevin. Ironically, Roxanne's death had put an end to an impossible situation for both of them.

At the time, all of eleven years old, Kevin had interpreted Sharon and Josée coming to the house on avenue Shorncliffe as a betrayal. His father's betrayal, combined with his mother's defeat: a painful shaming Kevin sought to avenge. And yet, curiously, Sharon had ended up being a wonderful substitute mother, in some ways better for him than Roxanne had ever been. She had often come to Kevin's defence, though he wasn't her own son. The situation with Josée, his half-sister, was entirely different. While Kevin hated his father, the little girl adored him, and felt much closer to her father than to her mother, Sharon. This powerful affection negatively impacted her relationship with her half-brother, four years older than she. A sort of cold war had begun, unchanged by the passage of the two children into their teenage years. In fact, Raymond had been forced to intervene a number of times between the two of them, usually to Josée's advantage. Kevin had had the impression they were ganging up on him to make his life miserable.

Sharon had been the neutral arbiter. She was interested in Kevin's day-to-day life and treated him with respect. She was the one who remembered his birthday every year and drove him to the hockey rink on Saturday mornings. She was the one who made sure his grades were good in school, who waited for him when he came home late from a party in high school while Raymond slept soundly in their bedroom. Kevin was especially impressed by how Sharon could hold her own against his father's mind games, something Roxanne hadn't been able to do. Kevin had never understood his mother's seemingly shameless and total submission toward Raymond. He'd even talked about it with Roxanne — he was nine, maybe ten years old at the time. Even back then he had been able to intuit that the relationship between his mother and father was a strange one. But, as always, Roxanne had avoided the question. Kevin had insisted, and so she'd answered, "Your father can do whatever he wants. Do you understand?"

No, he hadn't. But Roxanne had refused to say more.

A few days after her death Raymond had told him to get in the passenger seat of the Cadillac. Without another word, father and son drove to the countryside. They eventually reached a small river, made famous after a local newspaper's exposé on young people drinking beers and smoking grass around campfires on its banks. To the great despair of the neighbours.

Raymond parked his car near the river and got out. Finally, he broke the silence. "Come on. Give me a hand."

In the car's trunk, Roxanne's personal effects. Boxes filled with her clothes, books, perfume. A scarf she had loved dearly. Raymond had lit a fire on the pile of ashes left by the previous night's revellers and thrown all of his wife's possessions on it. Soon, the objects were only smoke in a clear blue sky.

Raymond took his son by the shoulders. "Your mother's belongings are with her now. She'll need them up there."

Carried by the wind, a half-burned piece of paper floated above the trees. Raymond didn't notice it. Kevin ran after it, finally catching it at the foot of a tree. He recognized his mother's writing, the sharpness of it. A piece of paper saved from the flames. Half a sentence printed on it in a language he couldn't read. He thought for a moment of asking his father what it meant, but just then, a voice called him back to the car. It was time to go. His father's shouts wiped the thought from his mind, and Kevin simply put the piece of paper in his pocket and hurried back.

Years later, as Kevin and Max had been getting ready for a con, Kevin emptied his wallet out to get into character. Among the usual IDs and documents, that small piece of half-burnt paper, which Kevin had kept all those years.

"The only keepsake I have of my mother."

Kevin had told Max how Raymond had gotten rid of all her posessions.

"And what does it say?"

"'I miss you, I think of you all the time.'"

Max had looked at Kevin, waiting for him to continue.

"It's in Romanian. My mother was from Bucharest. A letter to her father."

‡

First an Olympic runner, then a thief, now a respectable man who'd settled down. Kevin had given up on marathons, given up on fraud, and had retreated into his own world. Through a long, complicated detour, he'd finally squared his circle, and Caroline was happy for it. Neither Kevin nor Caroline called Max asking him to visit more often, or rebuked him for coming too rarely. Max did what was asked — or more precisely, what wasn't asked — of him.

And so it had been a surprise when Kevin, travelling through New York, had contacted Max for a drink. The two men — who hadn't seen each other in more than a year — agreed to meet at the bar of the Plaza Hotel near Central Park. Max arrived a few minutes late and was surprised to discover Kevin seated with a young woman he didn't know: Claudia Ferrucci. Brown hair, blue eyes, small, a few pounds overweight, with a nervous disposition. Next to calm, collected Kevin, Claudia Ferrucci, with her nervousness, seemed even more out of place. She was from Toronto, Kevin explained, and had travelled with him. To talk business, he added, with exaggerated mystery. Max couldn't believe his friend had turned a friendly get-together into a business meeting. Especially when he learned that Kevin and his new business partner were working on a major con and wanted Max's help.

Kevin rambled on to Max, who was mostly concentrating on Claudia. He'd never heard of her, and he didn't like that. The whole thing could be a trap; she might just whip out a badge at any moment.

Finally, the young woman excused herself to go to the bathroom. Max waited until she'd disappeared to turn toward Kevin. "What the hell is wrong with you? And who is she?"

"I checked her out. She's fine. I can vouch for her."

Max was far from convinced. "I want nothing to do with any of this, Kevin."

"Wait, I haven't even told you about it yet …"

"I choose my teams, not the other way around."

It was one of Max's rules. There was nothing more dangerous than joining someone else's plan, working for someone else's interests. Naturally, early in his career, Max had joined teams he'd known little about. He'd been lucky to get off easy. But today it was different. No way he'd risk prison at his age.

Kevin had been expecting Max's reluctance. Kevin looked at him, an ironic smile on his face. "Always a wall with you. Open arms, sure, but only when you're offering. If anybody makes a move in your direction, you're gone."

Max furrowed his brow. "You want my help? Let me give you some advice. Run, now, and don't look back at whatever idiotic job you're planning."

"You haven't even heard me out!"

"Every con is the same. You know that as well as I do."

Max couldn't understand why Kevin would risk his family's happiness over a roll of the dice. Years before, Kevin had had run-ins with the law and Max had gotten him off the hook. Today the situation was different. He lived in Montreal, happily, had a new life. Why screw it all up for a minor score?

"So you're just going to say no to a friend asking for your help, is that it?"

"Don't you dare use our friendship for this."

"What should I use it for then?"

Max was already standing. This discussion was going nowhere. "Say goodbye to your friend for me."

Max left the bar without looking back, furious with Kevin. Early the next morning he called around to his contacts; he would find out who this Claudia Ferrucci was.

Two days later he was almost disappointed to learn that the young woman was indeed who she claimed to be. From Italy, no husband or boyfriend, a Ph.D. and a master's in geology from Queen's University in Kingston. Her last boyfriend was a computer scientist. He'd left her two years earlier after a six-month relationship. She sent money back to her family in Italy — who still lived in Sardinia — despite her meagre salary with Dominion Diamonds, an import-export owned by a mining exploration company. She, too, like Kevin, was the sort of person to fall into debt and not be able to drag herself out. She had several maxed-out credit cards, which likely explained her desire to get in on Kevin's job.

In other words, Claudia Ferrucci didn't have much to hide. She must have felt a lot of frustration, glancing up at her wall full of diplomas after receiving her paycheque. At Dominion Diamonds some of the employees who made the same salary as she did had left school at sixteen. She would correct this injustice, whatever the cost. She'd punish her employer. She was broke and ready to team up with a thief to make things right.

Max had forgotten all about Kevin's offer when, six months later, he called out of the blue. This time he wasn't looking for a partner, but advice. After Max had refused, Claudia and Kevin had gone at it alone. Max met up with Kevin in an out-of-the way restaurant in Brooklyn. Without Ferrucci. Between visits from the server, Max listened to Kevin describe the con. It was a classic job: you slowly seduce an avid businessman, gaining his trust. Then, out of nowhere, a situation arises, an emergency, an opportunity. Trust has been built by then and now comes the time to act. Listen, we'll never get another opportunity like it, if we don't act now, we'll miss out …

Max had run the same con several times over the years. Surprisingly, the job Kevin was describing seemed doable, plausible. Especially with Claudia Ferrucci as the inside woman, an essential element of any successful operation.

"And she has access to the boss? She can convince him to move? Quickly, I mean."

"Who?"

"Ferrucci."

"What are you talking about? I'm the inside man."

Max tried to hide his surprise.

Kevin added, "Raymond is the mark. My dear father. I want to hit Nordopak."

Max was almost out of the door before Kevin finished his sentence. Kevin was right behind him. Max was tired of this bullshit. Tired of Kevin's anger toward his father. Enough was enough; at some point you just had to move on. Raymond was overwhelming, controlling, but he couldn't possibly be as hateful, as odious, as Kevin claimed. What Kevin was about to do to his own father was disgusting.

Kevin listened to Max spit all this out before grabbing him by the arm. "Oh, so you're defending him now?"

"I'm trying to stop you from making a huge mistake."

"For years I've been trying to figure out a way to get back at the bastard."

"Keep looking."

"Listen, Max —"

"I thought you'd patched things up."

"I've wanted to get back at him since I returned to Montreal. I made peace with him, but only to soften him up. I wanted him to let his guard down."

"If you keep this up, I'll call him. I'll tell him everything."

Kevin closed his eyes, took a deep breath, then spoke almost inaudibly. "Look, I want to open a gym in Montreal. Modern facilities, a pool, an exercise room, a track to run on, the whole thing. I need some money to do it, and he won't lend me a goddamn penny …"

"I can help you."

"He's the one who should be helping me. He should be the one to pay."

Max stayed silent.

Kevin added, "A few million. That's all I'm asking. He owes me that much, the bastard!"

11

Bucharest, November 27, 2006

Max had fallen asleep on top of the duvet. A thick cover silkscreened with a hunting scene in the Carpathians dating from the reign of Carol I. Hares and a fox fleeing from mounted nobles in period costumes. A phone rang, once, twice, as Max wondered why the nineteenth-century hunters were after him. He hadn't done a damn thing to them, after all. A moment later he was pulling himself out of his dream. Shaking out the cobwebs, he picked up the phone.

"Mr. O'Brien?"

Was it room service? Max couldn't remember ordering anything.

"Cosmin Micula."

Max sat against the bedrest. "Is Kevin with you?"

A silence, then: "He spoke highly of your professionalism."

Micula had a very slight accent. The flow of his speech was faintly stilted, as if he were reading from a script.

"Mr. Micula ..."

"When Kevin learned you were coming to Bucharest, he immediately thought of you to help with our little problem."

"What are you talking about? What problem?"

"You'll see him soon enough. He'll tell you everything, I'm sure. For now, his situation is rather delicate."

"What's going on? What do you mean?"

Once again, a long silence on the other end of the line. The usual crackling of poor-quality cellphones, then, "I've something to give you. Have you heard of Herăstrău Park?"

Max answered yes, though he had no idea where the park actually was. The man on the other end of the line added, "Very popular with newlyweds. They sit under the trees. It makes for beautiful pictures."

More static on the other end of the line. Max thought he'd lost the connection.

"You can walk to the park gates from the Arcul de Triumf. I'll see you there in, say, thirty minutes? Please don't mention our appointment with anyone."

According to the map he'd picked up in the hotel lobby, Herăstrău Park was on the north side of the capital at the far end of Aviatorilor Boulevard. Max asked the doorman to hail him a cab, which appeared a few moments later.

In the car, speeding across the city, Max parsed the conversation he'd just had with this Cosmin Micula character. It sure seemed as if Kevin had gotten in over his head in some scam or another. Kevin, once again in a bind, counting on Max to save his skin. Once more waiting until it was too late to give Max a call and ask him to bail Kevin out. It frustrated Max, Kevin's attitude, far too similar to the one he'd had during his operation against Nordopak six years earlier. Conning his own father? It had been a ridiculous idea, and Max, like an idiot, had helped his friend, though it went against all of his rules. To this day, he still regretted having followed Kevin's obsession, a spoiled child's tantrum.

Well, hindsight is 20/20. Kevin had been going to con his father, anyway. Might as well support his friend, try to protect him. Within a few weeks, Max had learned everything he had to know about Raymond Dandurand's company. Kevin was his guide. By then his friend had been promoted. As an executive, Kevin knew Nordopak inside out.

Raymond had certainly earned his nickname, the emperor. He would occasionally listen to his board of directors, sure — especially since it was composed of old friends of his — but never when it came to what he considered to be an important decision. Anyway, no one could really complain. The company had always made money, or so it seemed, and had been steadily growing for a long time. The only real setback had come in 1998 when Aspekt-Ziegler decided to cut ties with its Montreal-based partner. Raymond had gone on the road then, refusing to let his company fail: he'd managed to charm a few contracts out of American companies enticed by the lower value of the Canadian dollar. Soon enough he'd found replacements for Aspekt-Ziegler.

An almost perfect record had made him overconfident.

The perfect mark.

Raymond had lacked supervision and believed that the mix of luck and skill that had brought him this far couldn't fail him. It had made him easy prey for an experienced crook like Max.

The con was made doubly simple by the fact that Nordopak was in the market for acquisitions, especially in Europe. Raymond had his eye on a number of modest-sized companies well established in their national markets. A Turin-based company, Cambiano, was particularly appealing. However, brothers Dino and Ricardo Negroni were jealous of their autonomy and had no interest in giving part of their company away. So Raymond had begun talks with other European companies, but negotiations were slow and arduous.

An impasse then. Until the day Carlo Negroni, passing through Montreal, had sent an emissary to ask Raymond for a few minutes of his time.

Carlo Negroni?

Cambiano's third owner. He was the youngest brother, and more discreet, leaving his two older siblings to lead the company as they saw fit. But here was Carlo, who'd been going through a rough patch. He'd lost money in a string of unlucky investments. And there was the matter of a minor gambling problem, barely worth mentioning. Anyway, he had a small liquidity problem and …

The emissary was Claudia Ferrucci, of course, who knew all about Raymond's interest in the Italian company.

Raymond had reacted just as Max had predicted. Instead of calling on his board for advice and guidance, he acted alone, without wasting any time. However, thinking himself prudent, he didn't trust the emissary's word alone, no matter how credible she was. He wanted to meet Carlo Negroni directly and hear the proposal straight from the horse's mouth.

Claudia had agreed. She'd arrange a meeting as quickly as possible.

A few days later Carlo Negroni would be passing through New York. He would take the time to meet Raymond Dandurand, accompanied by Claudia. The real Negroni was somewhere in the Bahamas. Max had made sure of that before making his move. Once the meeting concluded, Raymond, already convinced it was a good deal, would rush back to Montreal and urge the board to act quickly. Carlo's shares would be bought the following day.

For $38 million.

At the Plaza, where the whole scheme had first been discussed, all the pieces of the puzzle were in play. Max had recruited Flavio Morelli from Cincinnati, who'd been practising his best Carlo Negroni for weeks. Soon Morelli knew everything there was to know about the Italian businessman. His mannerisms, sure, but also his personal life, taken from Italian gossip sheets. According to the script Max had written, Negroni was travelling through New York — where his collaborator, Claudia Ferrucci, was waiting for him — unbeknownst to his two brothers. For this reason, Raymond couldn't verify the Negroni he was about to meet for the first time was truly the family's younger brother. A useless precaution. Raymond was seeing green and never doubted the story. Negroni was asking for his help, so Raymond believed himself to be in a position of power. He thought the Italian was desperate. Raymond was no fool; he knew how to take advantage of a golden opportunity.

Negroni's suite was on the hotel's top floor. Eight rooms with a view of Central Park. The neighbouring room — a suite, as well, but smaller than Carlo's — was also occupied by Max's people. Strategically placed bugs allowed them to hear everything said in the other room. A small transmitter in Morelli's ear allowed Max to guide his collaborator in case things soured.

Ted Duvall was waiting at the airport, able to warn the team if anything seemed off. Raymond was expected to arrive in New York alone and negotiate without the help of any financial consultants or lawyers, according to habit. But Max thought he might have gotten his board involved. They might have decided to come to New York in secret to ensure everything about Negroni's offer was kosher.

In the end, Max hadn't needed to worry. Raymond had gotten off Air Canada flight 746 from Montreal. A limousine ferried him to Trump Tower, his favourite hotel in Manhattan, only a few blocks from the Plaza. According to Ted Duvall, there wasn't a whiff of outside counsel. Raymond's ego knew no bounds. He was throwing himself headfirst into the trap Max had laid.

At the Plaza everyone took a breath. Kevin, who'd chewed his fingernails halfway to his knuckles, was most relieved. Carlo Negroni had flown in from the Bahamas where his yacht was docked. His flight plans had been a secret. He only had a few hours for the Canadian businessman. He wouldn't waste a second or drag things out: he was in New York to find out whether Dandurand was a serious businessman, ready to commit. If he wasn't, fine by Carlo; others would be glad to have his piece of the business.

Raymond left Trump Tower ten minutes before his meeting. He walked quickly toward the Plaza. He entered the lobby and made his way to one of the elevators. The fake Carlo Negroni and Claudia Ferrucci were already in their respective positions in their penthouse suite. She opened the door, welcoming the businessman. They exchanged pleasantries, which Max could listen in on in the other room, where he was accompanied by Ted Duvall and Kevin. Claudia was nervous, Max could tell. Raymond didn't notice a thing, or didn't remark on it. He was wearing his own mask: that of the confident businessman who signs multi-million-dollar deals before breakfast. A professional.

Flavio Morelli made his entrance. Bathrobe, slippers, very Old Europe — a character trait Max had read about in *Oggi*. Carlo Negroni saw himself as a member of the decadent Italian nobility. And yet the three brothers were the grandsons of manual labourers. Their father had founded a small packaging company in the early 1970s just as Italy was becoming more prosperous. He was the one who'd taken all the risks. The three brothers had simply reaped what was sown by their father — a father dead at fifty-eight from exhaustion and overwork.

A friendly handshake. A boring discussion on the nightlife in the Bahamas, and that one restaurant with all the freshest fish. An exceptional glass of port, which Raymond politely refused. In short, they broke the ice. But the Italian tycoon was in a hurry; he had to be out of New York by mid-afternoon. He wanted to close the deal as quickly as possible.

"I read through your offer," Raymond began. "I can't say I'm pleased. A lot of risk, a lot of uncertainty …"

Behind him, in the other room, Kevin jumped to his feet. Max remained calm; he knew Raymond was simply negotiating.

"I don't understand," Morelli replied. "We agreed on a price. I even mentioned it to my financial consultant. And now —"

"Now things have changed. The board of directors is reticent. They're interested, but not to the extent of putting our company's future at risk."

Behind him, Max heard Kevin call his father a bastard. The board of directors knew nothing at all, of course. Another negotiation tactic.

"You're getting a deal at thirty-eight million."

"A fire sale, more like."

"Are you trying to insult me?"

The conversation was moving in a direction Max didn't like. Discreetly, he ordered Morelli to back off a little. Yes, he absolutely needed to put up a fight, but he shouldn't be hitting to bruise, only to graze Raymond's chin.

"So what are you offering?" Morelli asked begrudgingly.

"Half. Nineteen million."

Kevin swore. Raymond was flexing his muscle. The battle was won, but Kevin wanted to crush his opponent.

"Thirty million," Morelli replied.

The two men negotiated for a few more minutes, but it was clear both of them had the intention of coming to a deal.

Raymond relented a little. "Okay, twenty-five million."

Max had hoped for more, but Raymond was a hard bargainer. The operation had been going on for long enough; time to put an end to it. He gave Morelli the order to accept the offer.

A handshake. Negroni wanted to get to the airport as quickly as possible. Raymond left. The meeting had lasted less than an hour.

Max was outwardly calm — if you discounted the sweat rings on his shirt. He whipped around. Kevin was staring at the floor, repeating like a mantra: twenty-five million, twenty-five million, twenty-five million.… All that was left was for Raymond to convince the board, but Kevin couldn't imagine there would be any resistance.

With reason. Raymond had negotiated behind the board's back, but to the company's advantage. At least that was how he presented the offer to his son, who answered with false admiration. The board agreed, their trust in Raymond complete. Asked a few questions, but didn't press overmuch. At a sharp discount Nordopak would finally get back into the European market. Raymond was over the moon.

Within forty-eight hours, $25 million was deposited into the fictional Carlo Negroni's bank account in Milan.

The very same day the real Carlo returned from the Bahamas, a communiqué was released announcing the transaction. Of course, the Negroni brothers, Carlo first in line, denied the affair. Confusion, retractions, and a sudden realization. Nordopak found itself on the wrong end of a $25 million bargain, without a single share in Cambiano. Raymond Dandurand and his team alerted the police, who tried to track the fake Carlo Negroni. A lost cause. And the money had already gone through two other bank accounts, both immediately closed once the transactions were completed.

Max had disappeared. His team, as well.

12

Ancient buildings, as elsewhere, but the streets were calmer here. A prosperous residential neighbourhood that seemed to be on a different planet entirely than the streets of Ferentari. The post-Communist nouveau riche who lived here probably paid top dollar for these affluent homes. Beyond the old, tall trees, Herăstrău Park began, the largest in Bucharest. It would be impossible to see Cosmin Micula from here. Max asked the driver to go around the block, but the man's English was a bit too rudimentary. And so Max simply paid for his fare and got out of the car near the Arcul de Triumf, the "Little Paris" of the Balkans. Max now understood the comparison. The taxi made a U-turn and disappeared into the night.

Suddenly, Max felt very much alone. Shipwrecked after a storm. Gusts of wind made him shiver. He continued toward the park entrance. The night was thick with silence. A feeling of isolation, of extreme solitude, as if he were all alone after the end of the world. Thankfully, the moon was there to cast a kind light over the scene, showing him the way forward.

Micula was late by at least twenty minutes, just like Boerescu was on Max's first day in Bucharest. Max looked around, trying to imagine couples in love holding hands, walking here in summer along paths flanked by rosebushes. Families, children, idle men and women taking in the greenery. But here and now there was no one. All were warm inside, away from the winter cold. Max was sorry he couldn't do the same.

"What did I tell you? It's a nice place, isn't it?"

Max turned around. A man stood behind him, a silhouette against the light of the moon.

The man walked forward and said, "It has been forever a favourite of lovers. Even back when it was called Stalin Park. I tell them, I say: 'Perhaps somewhere more original, somewhere as beautiful as here,' but they say this park and not any other. It's now a superstition of sorts, you understand? The rosebushes of Herăstrău. A guarantee of a happy family, prosperous and full of love." He offered his hand. "Cosmin Micula, the photographer."

He wore a beard, his hair wild, and probably looked much the same now as he had when he was a young man thirty-five years ago, albeit with some grey in the hair and a bit of a paunch betraying a fondness for beer. His shirt seemed more like a straitjacket around his generous belly.

"You weren't followed, I hope?"

"I've no idea."

Micula took him by the arm. "Come, we shouldn't just stand here in the open. My car is over there."

As they made their way to the parking lot, Micula spoke of himself. Of a career launched by a spectacular and shocking photo report. He'd accompanied a Romanian regiment to the north of the country, showing the solitude of young men sent to garrison the border with the Soviet Union. Micula, one of the regime's golden sons, had been invited to take pictures of the Ceaușescu couple. For months he'd followed both of them, immortalizing even their smallest gestures for posterity.

"Did you know they lived right near here? In a street barred to mere mortals and under permanent watch by the police and the dictator's personal guard."

Max certainly hadn't crossed half the city in the middle of the night to be told the life story of a jaded photographer. But Micula continued his tale, which now turned to vinegar. During the 1970s, Ceaușescu became acutely megalomaniacal, along with developing an irrational fear of germs. Nicolae and Elena constantly washed their hands with rubbing alcohol to avoid potential contamination. Paranoia became a constant in their lives. The young court photographer, celebrated for his courage and sensitivity, was thrown out of the palace along with drivers, cooks, bodyguards, and various other servants. The Securitate became interested in Micula, who could no longer practise his job as a photojournalist for the regime, since the regime no longer wanted him. And so, after 1980, he began to take pictures of weddings and christenings. He landed in prison, anyway, after a jealous colleague denounced him as a counter-revolutionary since — according to Micula at least — the man couldn't compete with his talent and vision.

Max cut him off. "Fine. Where's Kevin? What's going on?"

"Follow me. You'll see." When Max reached the passenger door of the man's old Dacia, Micula turned to him. "You really need to give the handle a good tug or it won't open."

The photographer systematically avoided all major boulevards, as if wary of a potential tail. Around them the capital was plunged in darkness.

They drove in silence for a long time. Finally, Micula turned right into a dark alley. Max was beginning to worry. He glanced at the driver, but the man didn't seem to be paying attention to him anymore. Another right turn and the Dacia stopped in a narrow driveway between two buildings. From the other side of the block of houses, Max could hear the sound of an occasional car or two in the night.

Another moment of tense silence. Max expected the photographer to get out of the car, but instead he leaned over and took an envelope out of the glovebox.

"Kevin is in Bucharest helping someone get out of the country. The other day he had a meeting with one of his contacts on Zăbrăuți Street. Things didn't go as planned."

"What happened exactly?"

"He fell into a trap. That's why he's hiding. And why he needs a messenger."

A messenger? Max was completely lost.

Micula turned the interior light on and emptied the envelope out onto his knees. A Canadian passport. A stolen passport, most likely. The photographer held it up proudly. "Oh, how our friendly tourist will remember her stay in Romania!"

Micula handed it over, and Max examined it. The photo was of a woman, approximately thirty-five years old. Laura Stelea. Born in Tecuci in eastern Romania, a naturalized Canadian citizen since 1998.

"The colours are the hardest part," Micula apologized.

Excellent work, nevertheless. That was clear despite the weak light. The photographer watched him, waiting for a compliment.

"Good job."

Micula smiled, then added, "She's actually called Laura Costinar. Wife of Ioan Costinar, the former leader of the Romanian Gypsy community. During the revolution, in 1989, he returned to the country in order to mobilize his people, after being asked to do so by the International Romani Union."

"With Victor Marineci, the Romani MP?"

"Yes. They were a team."

The International Romani Union, Micula explained, was an organization that had represented all Romani people across the globe since the early 1970s. The organization's mandate was the promotion of Romani culture, but also the creation of political entities for the Roma. Without land, divided by clan, living under different laws according to the countries they resided in, it was hard for the Roma to organize. But things were changing. In 2004 Marineci was elected an MP in the Romanian Parliament.

In subsequent elections, other Roma followed. In great part thanks to Costinar, the Roma now had a war chest to lean on to fund their political activities.

"Money collected from the Romani Diaspora all over the world," the photographer added.

Ioan Costinar was inspired by Golda Meir's fund-raising among American Jews to help finance the Israeli State, and he worked to mobilize the Romani Diaspora to fund the well-being of Eastern European Roma.

Micula shook his head. "But you can't compare them to Jews. That would be a mistake. Yes, they both suffered terribly under the Nazis. But there's a better comparison. African Americans. In the 1920s, in the United States, before they were organized, before they fought collectively for civil rights."

"Ioan Costinar is a sort of Martin Luther King then?"

"Both murdered in cold blood. Costinar was shot in the head in Canada."

Micula stretched toward the glovebox once again and took out a flask of *palinca*. He offered some to Max, who accepted. Boerescu's favourite drink. Max almost choked on it. He passed Micula the flask, and the photographer took a long swallow.

"Romani people have lived near Winnipeg since 1963. They're rich, too. In 2000 Costinar travelled there, after a stint in Chicago and New York, to raise funds for literacy programs, as well as other, more political work. And that bothered some people. In 2007, when Romania joins the European Union, the Roma will become the largest minority on the continent. And yet, do you see how they live?"

"Ferentari."

"It's the same all over Romania. To varying degrees, of course. Marineci, and Costinar before him, they told the Roma: 'Stop being victims, rise up and fight to change your lives.'"

"So what's the relationship with Laura?"

"Kevin said that she knows who her husband's killers are. But she's sure she won't get a fair trial in Romania. Killing Roma here is almost legal! That's why she's trying to get out of the country."

"With a fake passport? Why not use her own?"

"As I say to you, Costinar's political activities made him many enemies."

"In government?"

Micula fell silent. He seemed to regret having said too much already.

"So what's your role in all this?"

"Kevin needed someone to make fake papers for him. He recruited me." Micula hesitated for a moment, then turned and looked straight at Max. "And we're practically cousins, he and I. His mother was from Romania, did you know?"

13

Auschwitz-Birkenau, November 5, 1943

Emil Rosca and Christina Müller were wound together amid the half-empty luggage and countless children's shoes, abandoning themselves to their passions without an ounce of guilt. Without any qualms, they held and caressed each other among forgotten clothes smelling of sweat and pain. Emil had never loved before, and love seemed, all of a sudden, the most unjust thing in the world. When he was alone in the barracks, he sometimes thought that it simply wasn't possible to love in a place like this. And yet every time they had an opportunity, Christina and Emil threw themselves against each other without worry, without regret, a wave against a cliff. Love had erased any trace of compassion. The suffering of others no longer touched them. Egoists, they only thought of their unexpected fortune, their unexpected happiness that put both of them in deathly danger.

Thanks to her good relations with SS-Obersturm-bannführer Rudolf Höss, Christina had managed to get Emil assigned to laundry duty for the Stammlager's guards, whose back door gave on a warehouse in which stolen objects were stored. The place was a cavernous mess, devoid of life, where the lovers could steal a moment when the laundry room guards went off on a break. After making love, Emil closed his eyes and could hear nearby the Kraków-Berlin express. And every time, that same emotion: the strangeness that life went on as usual outside Auschwitz, beyond the crematoriums spitting human ash into the sky, beyond a stolen moment of love between a German and a Rom.

On the other side of the rails, another section of land had been confiscated by the camp authorities to lodge officers and their families. That was where Oskar Müller and his wife lived. Christina smuggled food out of her house for Emil to eat or trade, though he was rather skittish at the idea of joining the black market. His situation was delicate, and he didn't want to take undue risks and compromise it. But the black market went full steam ahead in the Stammlager, as well as in Birkenau. A market in which the Roma were particularly active, thanks to their privileged status. Martin Hofbauer, for example, the Sinto who'd had his eye on Emil's accordion, dominated the pharmaceutical market, selling drugs to fight the typhus epidemic that devastated the barracks.

One day Emil asked Christina, "Tell me what happened to my father."

‡

Two months earlier Christina and Oskar Müller had gone straight from their honeymoon in France to Auschwitz. Müller had been an officer at the camp since Rudolf Höss's nomination as camp commander. Höss and Müller had met at Konzentrationslager Sachsenhausen near Berlin, and the camp commander had brought him to Auschwitz.

Christina had hated the camp from the very first day. While still in Berlin, before the honeymoon, Oskar had described the place in detail, but no description could have prepared her for what she saw. The ovens, the gas chambers. Organized, planned, bureaucratized death. But what revolted her most of all was the attitude of the officers and their families — including Oskar, her husband — who behaved in Auschwitz as they would in any other garrison. Gossip, lies, power games. She was now part of this procession of monsters. Every day the smoke coming from the cremation ovens made her nauseous, sometimes to the point of vomiting.

And yet Christina still hated Jews. Parasites, blood-suckers. They specialized in plots and ruses with the ultimate goal of dominating the world. She kept *The Protocols of the Elders of Zion* at her bedside. She was the only and adored daughter of a long-time Nazi supporter, a personal friend of Adolf Hitler. Christina had always admired her father, and she had never doubted the truth of his ideas. The world was a filthy place that Jews and Communists, their offspring, dirtied more every day. Hitler and his disciples, including her father, had endowed themselves with the mission to clean up this imperfect planet. Who could oppose such a project? Auschwitz and its horrors opened her eyes. Helpless before so much cruelty, realizing the extent to which her life to this point had been marked by so many lies and such duplicity, Christina locked herself into guilty silence.

And then, one night, everything had changed. At the Kommandantur there was a spark in the air, an excited energy that preceded great events. Heinrich Himmler, the second-in-command of the regime, minister of the interior, and head of the Gestapo, was passing through Auschwitz for a series of meetings with the camp's directors. Himmler, the man who built or destroyed careers. The one in front of whom the whole garrison trembled — Oskar Müller first in line. In 1941 the Nazi leader had designated Auschwitz as the main location for the extermination of Jews. Since the opening of Birkenau and the utilization of Zyklon B, the pace of exterminations had increased at a phenomenal rate. The cremation ovens worked day and night. There was no doubt: Himmler was proud of Auschwitz, proud of his work.

The head of the Gestapo was on his third visit. The first one, in March 1941, was to announce the construction of nearby Birkenau, which would house one hundred thousand prisoners. And the construction of Monowitz a little later. In July 1942, Himmler came back in the middle of an epidemic of typhoid fever, during which the Nazi commander witnessed the gassing of Jews.

And now this visit in September 1943.

Christina knew the Nazi leader personally. When her father had been alive, Himmler was among the guests who'd stayed at the family residence in Charlottenburg. She remembered, as a girl, being seated on his knees, playing with his round glasses while the adults talked among themselves.

In the great room of the former Polish Tobacco Monopoly where the SS were lodged, mired in protocol, his attention demanded by everyone, Himmler didn't immediately recognize her. Dr. Hans Leibrecht, the accountant Matthias Kluge, and the others fluttered around the minister of the interior like *fraülein* at their first summer ball. SS-Standortarzt Eduard Wirths had shadowed Himmler since he'd first arrived in the camp, trying to convince him of the "enormous" problem that was Joseph Mengele. Fearing a new typhoid fever epidemic, the doctor wished to gas all Gypsy prisoners as a preventive measure, just as he'd done the previous spring with deportees from Bialystok and Austria. The minister of the interior was to give him an answer before leaving.

At the end of the reception Himmler approached Christina and apologized for giving her the cold shoulder earlier and began reminiscing about the magnificent evenings he'd spent at her family home. The head of the Gestapo, nostalgic. Christina's father had died of a heart attack in 1935 only two years after Hitler had come to power. Her father hadn't had the joy of witnessing the triumphant march of the Nazis throughout Europe. Since she'd reached Auschwitz, Christina had often wondered if her father would have been disgusted — as she was — by the extermination policies of the Nazi regime. She didn't think so. He, too, like her husband, would have become blind and deaf, an accomplice to the massacre.

As Christina exchanged banalities with Himmler — she couldn't bear to look him in the eye for more than a few seconds at a time — an SS officer rushed toward him and leaned over to say a few words. The latter nodded, then turned back to Christina and sighed. "Work, always work." After a moment of reflection, Himmler took her delicately by the arm. "No, you should come. Come and witness the power of the Third Reich."

In the small living room on the other side of the building, officers of the Kommandantur waited for them, looking rather satisfied with themselves. When they turned to welcome Himmler, Christina noticed at the end of the room a man sitting on a wooden chair, his back bent. Sallow, weak, he wore the garb of a prisoner employed outside the camp: stripes of grey and blue. The outfit was torn. His shoes were wooden soles strapped to his feet with strips of leather. The same shoes all detainees wore, in winter as in summer. Between his knotted fingers, a striped cap. The prisoner looked as if he'd been beaten; perhaps he'd tried to escape? An officer explained to the head of the Gestapo how the man had stuffed a piece of a paper bag under his uniform for extra insulation against the cold. The paper bag had been used to transport cement to the building site he was labouring on, one of the Buna-Werke factories. It was a serious crime.

With one hand, Himmler dismissed the other others from the room. Only one SS guard, Himmler, and Christina remained. She didn't know what was expected of her, and her glances at Himmler in no way at all helped her to understand. The Nazi leader was entirely focused on the prisoner, who turned toward him but without raising his head. The man was only skin on bones now, a dry grey skin that gave the impression of being about to crack. Himmler smiled. He walked to the man, and with a sudden gesture, tore off the red triangle sewn to his uniform identifying him as a political prisoner. Himmler let out a dry cackle. "The Gypsy king is suddenly ashamed of his origins, is he not?"

So the man was a Gypsy and should have been wearing a Z on his uniform for *Zigeuner*. For a reason Christina didn't fathom, the man had attempted to conceal his identity in the mass of prisoners. But why? She remembered listening to impassioned conversations at her father's house in Berlin about the fate of the Gypsies. For some theorists, they were the true pure race at the origin of all other European races, including Aryans. Others, more pragmatic, including Himmler, saw Gypsies as the bastardized, corrupted version of the original Aryan race. And so they would need to be exterminated just like the Jews. What's more, their fortune tellers sapped the morale of the German people by predicting the defeat of the Nazis.

For a few years both theories competed. In 1939 a few Gypsies were liberated on Hitler's birthday. A proposal went around that would allow some nomadic groups free circulation in Germany. Another option was the settling of *Zigeuners* in a model village, like a zoological garden, allowing Germans to visit the quite charming — though inferior — race.

In Auschwitz, since the beginning of the war, the ambiguity persisted. Exempted from forced labour, allowed to wear their own clothes and keep their hair, Gypsies received preferential treatment.

And now it seemed this prisoner had chosen to hide instead of staying among his kin. Christina was intrigued.

Himmler circled the Gypsy as if trying to gauge the man. He seemed to be evaluating his opponent, a man waiting to die, a man he could have finished with a single punch. A "Muslim," as the other prisoners called them. So much care and caution surprised Christina.

Finally, Himmler said, "They speak of you in Bucharest, Anton Rosca. Of you and your family. Well, you knew that already, didn't you? We intercepted your messages, your coded communications. You thought you'd be protected behind your little red triangle. But we've found you now. You can't hide from the Reich."

Christina realized that the prisoner's skin was particularly pale for a Gypsy. Certainly, it had helped him hide from the Gestapo among the camp's population for so long.

The man seemed neither upset nor fearful. His head was bent over his chest. He breathed heavily. Himmler stopped behind him. Christina expected Himmler to strike the man or order the SS to execute him, but instead he spoke again. "King Michael is sabotaging the prime minister's war efforts, allowing members of the government to secretly negotiate a separate peace with the English and the Americans. Even the Russians."

Christina knew little about Romania, though she did know that Michael, who'd replaced his father Carol II in 1940, had been playing behind Germany's back since the progress of German troops had halted in Stalingrad. The king had perhaps glimpsed the hordes of Red Army troops coming over the horizon from the east and sought to minimize the pain they'd inflict on his country. To maintain their influence, the Germans didn't have a choice: they had to invade the country.

The prisoner still looked down at the floor, twisting his cap in his hand.

Himmler smiled. "Anton Rosca. I've got an offer for you."

Christina couldn't believe her ears. The head of the Gestapo wasn't the sort of man to make an offer to anyone, especially not an enemy. Even less so a prisoner. The Nazi leader took his glasses off and wiped them with his handkerchief before moving away from the Gypsy.

"Adolf Hitler has a vision. Stalingrad is only a small setback. Soon the war will be over. Russia will be on its knees, the United Kingdom, as well. The Americans will no longer have the means for their ambitions. The Jews who advise Roosevelt will have to accept our conditions for armistice. Then we'll need to govern all the territories. A colossal task, only possible with the collaboration of locals. France is a wonderful example."

Himmler began pacing around the prisoner again. He didn't seem to be addressing him directly any longer, but simply thinking out loud. For a brief moment, he made eye contact with Christina. This was a show, a performance. He wanted to check the impact his words had on his privileged audience. She didn't wince.

"Romania presents a particular problem. Because of the Gypsies, of course. For centuries you've been shuttled back and forth from one place to the next — one garbage heap to the next, more like. King Michael despises you, all Romanians hate you. And yet you still ally with them against the forces of civilization. Skirmishes, attacks, sabotage. We're arresting Gypsies all over the country. Resistance, as you call it, Anton Rosca, is pointless."

Rosca flinched, and Himmler continued. "One name, Paul Vaneker. The Dutchman is working for the British. You know it as well as I. Because of what he's done, King Michael has turned against his prime minister. Today Vaneker leads a network of Gypsy saboteurs across Europe and in Romania in particular. Vaneker has been hiding for months, but you're in contact with him and his men. You know where he is."

Rosca remained silent, not denying Himmler's words.

"Paul Vaneker is taking advantage of the good faith of the *Zigeuners*, just like the British, just like King Michael. It's time to change that. To choose the right side this time, something Gypsies have never been able to do over the course of their long and painful history. Adolf Hitler is your only chance at salvation."

Himmler stopped for a moment, as if expecting the prisoner to say something. But the man stayed silent.

"Give me Paul Vaneker, Rosca. Lead the Gypsies down the path of reason. Abandon King Michael and the people who take advantage of you. Support Prime Minister Antonescu in his effort to conserve power in Romania. And, in exchange, the Third Reich will give you Romanestan."

For the first time, Anton Rosca raised his head. From her position at the other end of the room, Christina saw his eyes. Piercing eyes, black, with intelligence and strength shining through despite his physical state.

"A country, Rosca. A territory to call your own. A Gypsy enclave inside New Europe, Nazified, pacified, civilized."

Himmler continued, describing a territory west of Romania, from Hungary to Serbia, where the concentration of Gypsies was the greatest. In Timișoara. Or perhaps farther west, in Austria, in Burgenland. An autonomous government, independent institutions, an end to harassment and discrimination.

Himmler came closer to Anton Rosca. "A country you and your family would lead. Thanks to Adolf Hitler and the Third Reich, you have a date with history, Rosca."

A long moment of silence. The minister of the interior was waiting for his answer. Anton Rosca had kept his eyes on him since he'd first mentioned Romanestan. He seemed to be hesitating, to be evaluating the Nazi leader's offer.

"Just one word, Rosca. Just one. And you'll be the true King of the Gypsies."

Anton got to his feet slowly, painfully, as if every movement was excruciating. Standing, he was as tall as Himmler, though he seemed so frail, his body made weak from hunger and violence. As soon as he got to his feet, Himmler insisted, "So?"

Instead of answering, Rosca spat in his face. A stream of viscous saliva, disgusting, as if, during Himmler's entire monologue, the Gypsy had been drawing all the moisture in his emaciated body, everything he had left, just to spit in the face of the Gestapo chief.

Himmler seemed as surprised as Christina. The guard was already rushing toward Anton to beat him. Himmler took out his handkerchief and wiped his face as best he could as he stalked away from Rosca. Christina couldn't bear to watch. As the guard began repeatedly striking Rosca, she leaned against the wall and closed her eyes. Luckily for her, Himmler seemed to have forgotten her presence. She heard footsteps in the corridor, officers coming to help their comrade. Christina was still ignored. When she finally opened her eyes, the living room was empty. Anton had been dragged out, unconscious most likely, to be shot. The execution would take place in the yard between Blocks 10 and 11. A place called the sandpit; the SS threw fresh sand on red blood spilled when the deed was done.

Still shaking, Christina was about to leave the living room when she noticed something under a dresser. It was Anton's cap. He'd dropped it while being beaten by the SS. Christina bent to pick it up. The only sign left of the courageous man. He had stood stalwart against the full strength of the Third Reich without regard for his own life. Comparing herself to him, Christina couldn't help but feel like a coward. Her only acts of resistance against the horror that surrounded her were her fits of impatience with her husband. She ignored Oskar's need of her in social situations and played the snobbish, capricious Berliner. The courage of this diminished, weakened man only highlighted how pathetic her resistance was.

As she fiddled with the cap, Christina felt a rigid mass along its lining. She tore at the lining and discovered a piece of cardboard. On the back, a series of numbers.

An identification number.

Emil knew the rest.

Thanks to her husband, Christina had access to the list of prisoners. From that she learned the name of the prisoner who matched the number in the hat. Suddenly, it seemed imperative to save Rosca's son by any means necessary. The spirit of Anton Rosca guided her. She wanted to be as courageous as the man himself. In the Gypsy camp, an SS guard had informed her that the man in question had been requisitioned by Dr. Mengele and his team of doctors.

"A shame," the guard had added. "He played the accordion so well."

14

While Josée Dandurand had lost no time at all, she was convinced the Romanian police weren't working as fast as they should. Despite Inspector Pavlenco's efforts, Kevin was nowhere to be found. Josée had gotten in touch with a Romanian criminal lawyer who'd given her an overview of what Kevin could expect once arrested. According to the lawyer, the suspect would be held in custody for twenty-four hours, during which he'd be interrogated by Pavlenco and his men. And the Romanian police didn't have a reputation for patience when it came to stubborn witnesses. Which meant Kevin would likely be roughed up, as they say, until he admitted his crime. The most important thing, according to Josée, was to be able to intervene before Kevin cracked under pressure and admitted everything and anything just to get Pavlenco's goons off his back.

Marilyn Burgess was also working on extradition papers, but the minister of the interior wasn't quite open to letting his number one suspect just waltz out of the country. For once the authorities actually had a presumably guilty man, and they were going to take full advantage of it. Especially since the Romani MP Victor Marineci was demanding concrete actions against those responsible for the fire. With the arrest of the main suspect, it was becoming clear that Prime Minister Popescu-Tăriceanu would follow his recommendation.

In other words, the future was far from bright for Kevin.

In the Intercontinental's dining room, among the conference-goers, Max O'Brien and Kevin's half-sister looked like two co-conspirators. Josée had regained her appetite. She seemed to enjoy the *mămăligă cu brânză*, a sort of cheese-and-lard polenta, a peasant dish out of the Romanian repertoire.

"I called around trying to learn more about this Max O'Brien," Josée was saying between mouthfuls.

A rap sheet a mile long, according to her. He'd mostly worked in real estate, especially in New York and Chicago. More recently he'd been suspected of being involved in the fraud of a dog-racing promoter in Florida. O'Brien, according to Josée, worked several cons at once, appearing out of thin air to finish a deal.

"What was Kevin doing with a guy like that?" Max asked, all innocent-like, after taking a sip of Silva, the local beer.

"They can't prove a thing. For Kevin, I mean. They're fishing. Except for the whole East River business."

Max could feel the rebuke in Josée's words. Thankfully, the scam against Nordopak had been hidden from the public by the board of directors — as well as by Cambiano's own board. There was no point in showing the company's vulnerability. Until the very last minute Raymond had refused to accept the facts. There had to be an error. It couldn't be that he — the better, smarter man — had fallen for such a scam. For the first time in his life, Kevin had seen his father hurt, fragile, injured. A crack in his facade. Raymond didn't care about the money; at least it wasn't his main concern. His pride was more important. He knew he could no longer walk into the boardroom with his head held high; he wouldn't receive the respect he was used to when he was batting a thousand. He'd been duped like an amateur. From the heights of Mount Olympus, lost in the clouds, he'd been blinded by hubris. He'd never seen it coming.

To Max it seemed that Kevin had gone after his father with the sole purpose of humiliating him. Money wasn't the motivating factor at all. The whole gym project was nothing more than an excuse. He'd wanted to have the upper hand, the moral victory. He'd wanted to hand his father a devastating defeat. That seemed more important than anything else to Kevin, more than the millions of dollars he was making. The God Walking Among Us made into a mere mortal.

Max had come to understand that the logic guiding Kevin had been more twisted still. Incapable of rising to the same height as his father, the son had found a way of reducing him, of bringing his father down to his own level, forcing him to interact with Kevin on equal terms. And so it wasn't only about humiliation; it was also a way of forcing Raymond to see Kevin, to make him understand that the ingrate, hapless son existed — had always existed — by his father's own fault.

There could have been better ways, simpler ways to get the same result, but Kevin had chosen this winding path. Max, naively, had let himself be pulled along in turn.

Kevin, Claudia, Ted Duvall, and Max had divided amongst them the profits from the operation. Once all expenses were paid, Kevin had come out of it with a few million dollars. He had no intention of resigning straight away. He gave himself six months, so as not to raise suspicions. Discreetly, he began laying the foundation for his new gym.

Raymond had taken his humiliation in stride, trying to revaluate his management approach. The board didn't blame him openly — they were his friends, after all — but their blind admiration for him was gone. Controls were put into place, experts brought in, to avoid the same sort of mistakes in the future. Raymond agreed. He accepted his fate. Almost serenely.

He still spoke up during board meetings, but with less confidence. He listened more, nodding to signify agreement to others' proposals. He insisted less even when he was sure he was right. The whole adventure had shown him his limits as a businessman. He'd thought he had succeeded thanks to his talent and intelligence. He wasn't so sure anymore. In other words, Raymond

Dandurand had become a man again, a man like any other, with doubts, weaknesses, disappointments.

The following Easter the family got together for a week off at the house on rivière Saqawigan near Grande-Vallée in Gaspésie, a week that would change everything. Josée had flown in from Paris, between two cases, her cellphone always by her side. One day, Raymond offered to take little Sacha for the afternoon to give Kevin and Caroline some time off. Raymond had babysat Kevin's son before. Caroline trusted her father-in-law with her baby, and so did Kevin, despite their problems.

But tragedy lay behind the stillness of that day.

The bridge's railing had been under repair. The roadside signs were unclear. Raymond was distracted at the wheel of his Pathfinder, as always. Max could easily imagine the scene. Sacha seated in the back, Raymond speaking to him, turning around to look at the boy from time to time. Glancing in the rearview mirror. Suddenly, he'd lost control of the 4x4. A lethal drop into the roiling river below. Raymond trapped behind the wheel. Sacha dragged out of the car by the Saqawigan's rushing waters.

The news of the accident had struck Max hard. He'd found Caroline a few days later in Montreal, completely undone by grief. He was never able to find the right words. Tears welling in his eyes, his tongue silenced before the grief of a mother, his friend.

Sharon had been bent in two, almost unconscious. She was stuffed to the gills with sedatives, her eyes lost in the void, completely numb. Raymond's wife would never get over her husband's death. A year later she would die of a heart attack while she slept.

Josée had cancelled her flight back to Paris to take care of her mother, even though the young woman could barely take care of herself. Raymond, a man like no other, an exemplary and exceptional father, in her eyes. She just couldn't come to terms with the death of a father she loved so.

Kevin was made dumb by grief, wandering all day in the family house on avenue Shorncliffe. Or collapsing on a chair behind his father's desk, emptying his bottles of Scotch. Max had found him one morning, his eyes red, unable to believe what had happened, a succession of misery.

The young man pointed to a pile of documents on the desk. "Financial reports. The real ones. Raymond made us all into fools."

Max didn't understand.

"He made his entire board into fools. Fictional revenue, creative bookkeeping." Kevin sighed. "Aspekt-Ziegler was never replaced. Raymond came back from his American tour with nothing at all. All the contracts, all of them! They're not real."

Raymond hadn't been the golden child, after all. He'd hidden his failure by digging deep into the company's reserves.

Kevin took another draw of Scotch. "Isn't it ironic? While we were scamming him, Raymond was scamming his board. While we were passing him on the left, he was passing his board on the right."

Kevin got up, walked around the desk. "When they saw what was happening, it was already too late. And in addition to that, he'd just lost twenty-five million for a lie."

Max could now see the sheer extent of the disaster.

"Nordopak is bankrupt. Raymond had known it for a long, long time." Kevin raised his eyes toward his friend. "My father killed himself. I'm sure of it."

Max felt beaten, exhausted. Raymond's death — whether it was a suicide or not — they were both responsible for it. Well, all four of them, really, with Ted Duvall and Claudia Ferrucci. If he'd indeed killed himself, they may not have pulled the trigger, but they'd bought him the gun. The thing that bothered him the most was Sacha; why would Raymond want to bring his own grandson into the waters of rivière Saqawigan? Because he'd discovered Kevin's role in his downfall? To punish his son by taking away from him the thing he cared about the most? Max couldn't imagine that level of cruelty in Raymond. But Kevin's father could be twisted. He might have answered cruelty with cruelty.

Was Raymond Sacha's killer?

"I hate myself for dragging you into this mess," Kevin spat out.

Max should have known better than to go along. Oh, sure, he'd rebuffed Kevin's advances, but not for very long. He'd joined the scam, and now Kevin's guilt was rubbing off on him. Max couldn't bury his head in the sand this time. He'd participated; he'd helped Kevin push his old man into the void.

As soon as the server moved to another table, Max leaned toward Josée. "I had no idea you and Kevin had reconciled."

Josée shook her head. "It's ancient history."

After Raymond's death, Josée and her brother had stopped seeing each other, hadn't spoken a word to each other for years. Ancient history? She was referring to the rivière Saqawigan accident.

"The day he died I felt like Kevin blamed Raymond for the accident, blamed my father for taking Sacha away from him."

"There never was conclusive proof that Raymond killed himself," Max said.

"Kevin always believed it was suicide."

Josée was right.

"At first it just made me so angry that he could blame my father, our father, like that."

Max waited for her to continue.

"And then, well, I understand Kevin was completely distraught. He just hated Raymond so much …"

"Maybe he accused his father so he wouldn't feel responsible for the accident. Sort of putting a wall between himself and his darkest thoughts."

"I've been waiting to make peace with Kevin for months. I waited too long for the right moment. When I heard he was in trouble, I didn't hesitate." Josée smiled sadly. "I hope I'm not too late."

Max encouraged her with a smile. "It'll all work out, you'll see. Kevin isn't a killer."

"I asked to go on unpaid leave. I mean from my job in Paris. I want to be here when they bring him in. I'm worried about the skeletons in the closet, though. And you were right about this Marilyn Burgess character. She's ambitious. Very ambitious. And she wants to return to Canada with Max O'Brien in her trophy case."

After the meeting with Adrian Pavlenco, Josée had spoken with a man by the name of Luc Roberge, a detective with the Quebec provincial police. He'd been humiliated by O'Brien in India not long ago. The man had been obsessed with the thief for years, seeing O'Brien as the challenge of his career. But now Roberge had been put aside. He was tending to his wounds in Cozumel, Mexico.

"Marilyn Burgess has taken up the torch," Josée added. "She's got carte blanche from her superiors to get her hands on O'Brien."

"I'm sure they've made a mistake about Kevin. Why would he have been involved with some con man?"

Max felt defenceless. Faced with Josée's curiosity and intelligence, with Marilyn Burgess's determination, all he had was a fixer who couldn't go two steps without his walker, surviving on handfuls of pills, incapable of speaking a whole sentence without stopping for a breath.

And then there was this story Cosmin Micula had told him. Max hadn't known that Kevin kept connections with family overseas.

"Almost cousins," Micula had said. What did that mean, anyway?

Max couldn't wait to ask Kevin his questions and figure out what had really happened.

According to the photographer, Kevin would soon get in touch with him. Plane tickets had been purchased, and they would meet at the airport.

But it had been radio silence from Kevin since Max had met with the photographer.

After Josée left for her room to write a few emails, Max skimmed through Ioan Costinar's biography, which he'd gotten off the Internet. Thirty-six years old in his last picture. With glasses and a well-trimmed beard, he looked like a professor of Latin. Didn't have the appearance of a Rom, that caricature in *Paris Match* or *National Geographic*: poorly shaven faces, overcoats in tatters, caps screwed permanently on their heads, holding the reins of a dozen horses while walking toward a market. Or chasing chickens in a coop, with beaming, toothless smiles.

In another document, Victor Marineci praised the Romani leader. According to Marineci, by his actions, Costinar had helped the Romani community take giant strides forward. Before him, the Roma had been seen at best, as circus animals, and at worst, as vermin that needed to be exterminated. But where could they be sent back to? India, which they'd fled a thousand years before? Get serious. The Indians did care about the fate of their long-lost cousins. Indira Gandhi had helped fund the first World Romani Congress in London in 1971. But the Indian government could never go beyond symbolic measures. The fate of the Roma was in the hands of and depended on the goodwill of European authorities, who had to solve the claims of these people forgotten by history. His whole life, Costinar had striven to make the lives of the Roma better, and that was why he'd been killed, according to Marineci.

Another martyr.

Max left the hotel. The university was on his right, the National Theatre on his left. Bucharest had worked hard to forget its painful past. All of the street names were changed, parks and squares beautified and renamed. Since the revolution, the collective memory of postwar socialist heroes had been erased. Gheorghe Gheorghiu-Dej, a Stalinist, mentor of Nicolae Ceauşescu, was but a faraway memory now. Ceauşescu himself was harder to erase because of his House of the People, which had become the Palace of the Parliament.

Max could still remember the news items he'd seen on television showing the tyrant's decline. In Târgovişte, the small man gesturing toward the revolutionaries, accusing them of betrayal. A few hours earlier Ceauşescu had fled by helicopter off the roof of the Central Committee of the Romanian Communist Party's building in the middle of Bucharest. Elena had stood by his side, unable to help him this time. The dangerous Elena, whose fancies were legendary. A sort of Marie Antoinette who'd never quite gotten the dirt off her smock, despite the jewellery and other extravagances. The austere Joséphine to this stammering Napoleon who made himself emperor, he, too, with a sceptre and serious glare. The couple had met in 1939 during a strike. Ceauşescu had fallen in love with the textile worker seeking to better her lot in life. Older than Nicolae, she cheated about her age later in life, subtracting one year, then two, to make sure her husband was her elder. In 1965, after the death of Gheorghiu-Dej, when Nicolae succeeded him, Elena became his number two. She took advantage of this new power to invent a scientific career for herself. She was the recipient of several honours for a thesis on polymers — which she'd never actually read — that was written by Ioan Ursu, a professor at Timişoara University. He'd even left a few mistakes in to make it more credible.

The destruction of residential neighbourhoods, the construction of the House of the People, and even the destruction of Romanian villages were all projects she'd supported and perhaps even suggested. She was the one who'd whispered to Ceaușescu as he laid his head on his pillow: they are right to fear you, for you are fearsome.

They were a coarse, ridiculous, and bloodthirsty pair, welcoming the great men and women of this world in one of their twenty-one palaces, forty-one villas, and twenty-two hunting lodges. Charles de Gaulle, Queen Elizabeth II, Richard Nixon, and Pierre Elliott Trudeau. After swimming with Fidel in Cuba, Trudeau had visited Bucharest with Nicolae, all to promote CANDU, the Canadian nuclear reactor.

Max also remembered the summary trial of the dictator. And his execution. Shot at point-blank range, facing the soldier who killed him. Elena was shot in the back. Both with machine guns. Their bodies, sprawled in the dirt, seemed so small and insignificant. A death befitting the couple who'd made all of Romania tremble for twenty-five years.

Max's cellphone rang, startling him out of his thoughts.

"Max O'Brien?"

A man's voice. Max waited.

"Not so many people know your real name, Robert Cheskin."

"Who are you? What do you want?"

"I am calling to offer a simple trade. You have the passport, do you not?"

Max could guess what was coming.

"And I have Kevin Dandurand. It would not be a problem at all for me to give him to the police. But your friend is, for now, more useful to me if I can obtain something in return, would you not say?"

"I want proof of life."

A few moments of silence. Then Kevin's voice. "Max? Is that you?"

"What did they do to you?"

"I'll tell you on Wednesday."

Wednesday? What the hell was he talking about?

"Are you okay, are you —"

"Wednesday …" Kevin groaned on the other end of the line.

Max understood he'd just been punched.

The man's voice came back. "I am a serious man, O'Brien. I want the passport. You bring the passport to me and you leave with your friend."

Max sighed. He didn't have a choice. "Where are you?"

"Near the bus terminal — 208 Alexandriei Boulevard, third floor."

15

The vicar's rumbling tone had rung against the cavernous roof of the nave in Chapelle Notre-Dame-de-Bon-Secours. He'd been a friend of Raymond, the vicar, though that day he was delivering his eulogy. He spoke of a citizen, first among many, a job creator who'd remained, through his whole life, humble, serene, detached from the material world. The tearful audience clung to his words. Max O'Brien glanced toward the front row filled with higher-ups from Nordopak. Naive men and women who'd been swindled by their CEO, their friend. For months, they would all be involuntarily involved in a tragedy. They had chosen to hide their dear leader's activities. His honour would remain safe beyond the grave.

The following day a succinct though eloquent communiqué: Nordopak remained open, but the trustee was amenable to takeover bids. Cambiano was first in line. The Italian company, the real one this time, was glad to scoop up a competitor at a bargain price.

In short, bankruptcy ruined Nordopak. Kevin had helped create the whole mess. And what was more, amid the uncertainty, one thing was clear: the employees were straight out of luck. Their pension fund was an empty husk; Raymond had funded the company out of it for years. Even those who'd retired ages ago felt it: suddenly, the cheques stopped coming.

Within a few hours, the coverage of Raymond's death, which had so far been mostly about his accomplishments and his successful career, now took stock of these new developments. Stories came out about the fate of the unfortunate employees. People began wondering how such a respected man could have stooped so low, how Raymond Dandurand could have ripped off his employees. One article asked for stricter controls over companies' private retirement funds. An editorial blamed businesspeople's lack of ethics. And then a few days in, another scandal, a new tragedy, something else to distract the cynics.

A week later Claudia Ferrucci came in from Toronto and Ted Duvall flew in from Chicago. The four accomplices were parked on a calm street in Dorval in Max's rental car.

Kevin spoke through the silence. "I have no intention of keeping the money. It feels tainted to me. I don't want any part of it."

Tainted was the right word for it, Max thought. Blood money.

"The trustee in bankruptcy has agreed to do what he can to help out the employees before resolving the rest of the debt. He's going to try to fund the pension plan."

"So what are you going to do about it?" Ted Duvall asked. "Drop a duffle bag full of cash at his front door, ring the bell, and run away?"

"Why not? Look, maybe Raymond kept cash on him, in his office, you know? He kept other secrets. Why not that?"

That was Kevin's plan? Max didn't like it; it amounted to sullying Raymond's reputation even further. "That'll lead them to think your father was the one responsible for the scam."

Kevin shrugged. Raymond's reputation wasn't worth much anymore, anyway. What mattered most was to replenish the pension fund. Repair what Raymond had done using the profits of the fraud he'd fallen victim to. The fraud that had driven him off the bridge. The gold medal for convoluted redemption went to Kevin.

"The man killed your son," Claudia said.

In other words, why do you feel so guilty? Why are you forcing your guilt on us?

Kevin remained silent. His mind had wandered back to his father again. They were quits now. Kevin had led Raymond to his death, and Raymond had taken Sacha with him.

Game over.

Faced with his silence, Claudia got out of the car and slammed the door behind her. She raised her hand and waved down a passing taxi. Her answer was clear.

Duvall turned toward Max, as if to ask permission. "I need the money, Max."

Max nodded. Duvall got out of the car.

Max sighed. It was an unusual proposition, but the scam had been rather unusual itself. A son robbing his father. Raymond bankrupting his company. The son wanting to make amends for the father's mistakes. If it took a weight off Kevin's shoulders … why not?

"Okay," Max said.

The building had been erected in the mid-1940s, right at the apex of triumphalist Stalinist architecture. Max had gotten out of the cab one block earlier to walk the rest of the way. In his pocket, Laura Costinar's counterfeit passport. He turned into an alley, hoping his entrance wouldn't be noticed. This area was somewhere between a garbage dump and a vacant lot. A container had been knocked over a little farther away, garbage scattered across the yard. Someone had gone through it, it seemed, taking what could be recycled or sold.

Max looked up at the dwellings. Five storeys that included a mix of apartments and offices. There were chairs on the roof, placed along the parapet. A summertime terrace, probably. Max didn't want to go in through the front door, where he'd likely be expected. On the right, in the neighbouring building, the back door was ripped off at the hinges.

He crossed the lot and walked into the second building, stepping over discarded boxes and soiled clothes and climbing the stairs to the roof. From his new position, he could see below him now the chairs of the rooftop terrace. He could reach it by jumping. Two metres at most, but he wouldn't be able to come back the same way.

The sound of his drop was muted by the gravel spread on the surface of the roof. A low wall, maybe a bit less than a metre high, surrounded the rooftop. Rusted flagpoles stood at attention every metre or so, probably installed decades earlier for May Day celebrations.

A large door opened on a staircase. Max went down. On the third floor, he reached a deserted corridor, half-light revealing grease on the walls. At the far end of the corridor, a door left ajar. Max moved toward it, anxious. He'd expected a greeting party with the usual hardware. He'd expected to be dragged into a window-less room where Kevin would be tied to a chair. That was what kidnappers usually did, or at least that was what TV shows told him. But the place was empty.

Max pushed the door open. He could make out desks covered in dusty paperwork, filing cabinets, a coffee machine. On the wall, ancient frames showing model airplanes. On a work table covered in newspaper clippings, a coffee cup. Still warm.

"Kevin?"

No answer.

A worrying silence, broken by a passing car in the street.

Max called after Kevin again.

No dice.

He looked for the switch on the wall. His hand slid on something sticky. The light flicked on. The wall was covered in blood. Blood on the floor, as well. Fresh blood, which hadn't had time to dry. Drops, stains really, growing steadily toward the door at the end of the corridor. Max rushed over to it and ripped the door open. Blood everywhere. A battered arm stuck out from the bathtub in a sort of macabre salute. Max rushed toward the body.

A woman.

She hadn't been dead long. Her body still warm. Her eyes open.

Laura Costinar. Max recognized her from the picture on the counterfeit passport.

She'd been stabbed several times in the chest. Just like the tenant in the Romani building. Probably the same killers, then, whom Max had missed by only a few minutes.

Where was Kevin? Whoever was keeping him hostage had likely gone after the Romani leader's wife. What had they done to Kevin? What the hell was his friend doing with these sorts of people?

Max felt frustration, anger, growing inside him. What a mess. He was the one who'd led Kevin down this path of violence that night, when he'd first offered Kevin a job on his team. How would he ever forgive himself for introducing Kevin to the criminal life? How would he ever erase the image of a woman soaking in a pool of her own blood?

A siren broke the silence. Then another. Footsteps coming from street level. As if the whole city had suddenly been alerted to Laura Costinar's death. From the other side of the office door, from the corridor, Max heard voices.

A trap. He'd fallen for it like an amateur. No time to think about that now, though. Max climbed through the window and onto the fire escape. Down in the street, police cars, their lights revolving. To the roof then. The blaring of sirens continued. Max reached the railing. Down on street level, on the north side of the building, a heavy metal fence. However, it didn't go all the way around the building. On the south side, an alley, police cars filling it, with more incoming. Max was trapped. Soon enough the cops would climb to the roof.

His cellphone rang.

Max hesitated for a moment before answering.

"Robert Cheskin?"

"Boerescu?"

"What are you doing?" the fixer shouted.

Surprised, worried, Max looked around. He felt as if he was being watched. Had Boerescu been tailing him?

"Behind you, on your right, there's scaffolding."

Max glanced in that direction.

"Go. Now. You don't have much time."

Max ran across the length of the roof. He found a pile of supplies leaning against the wall. Basic tools and a harness used by construction workers.

"Take the one on the left. It's already tied to a cable. Use it to rappel down to the roof of the building next door. Do you see it?"

Two or three storeys lower, another squat office building. From there, Boerescu continued, he could reach street level without being noticed.

A moment's hesitation.

"You're not afraid of heights, are you?"

Max jumped off the roof.

PART TWO
Sacha-the-Red

16

Auschwitz-Birkenau, January 18, 1945

A rumour had been confirmed the night before. It threw the officers of the Kommandantur into a state of extreme panic. The 60th Army of the 1st Ukrainian Front was advancing all along the Vistula, heading to Silesia, aiming to encircle — in conjunction with other Soviet battalions — the German forces around Kraków and its vicinity. The plodding, disorganized Russians had moved far more rapidly than expected. Their tanks were tearing through Central Europe already. In their wake: theft, rape, pillage. The dream of a global Aryan civilization was over. In a few days, the barbarians would be at the gates of Auschwitz. The SS officers in the know had become feverish. There were no more parties, no more dancing. No more champagne from Occupied France.

The Americans had driven the Germans out of that country and pushed them eastward. The Nazi empire was shrinking like fresh leather under heavy sun. Soon Poland would fall into the Allies' hands.

And there would only be one Rom left in all of Auschwitz: Emil Rosca.

Following his humiliation in September 1943, Heinrich Himmler had left the camp, giving Josef Mengele free rein: to prevent typhoid fever, he could gas as many Roma as he wished. A little before August 1, 1944, from his office in Berlin, Himmler had called for the elimination of the family camp. A number of Roma had managed to flee but were caught early the next morning. Martin Hofbauer, the Sinto man who had managed the black market, was led to the sandpit with the other fugitives. They were all shot in the back of the head.

During those days, the gas chambers and crematory ovens of Birkenau were reserved for Roma. Late in the evening members of the *Sonderkommando* relentlessly pursued their exterminations. Over Auschwitz the stars in the sky paled in the light of constant braziers. A stench of burned corpses permeated the air, making the enclosed barracks smell of death. Thanks to Oskar Müller's intervention, Emil had once again avoided the ovens.

The only survivor of his kin.

In order to flee from the coming Russian invasion, the SS gathered every prisoner who could still walk from the three camps at Auschwitz — the Stammlager, Birkenau, and Monowitz — and sent them on the road, heading toward Germany. Emil never learned who had decided on this mass evacuation, or why. The war was lost, anyway. The prisoners could barely stand. Many were shot and killed where they fell. Oskar Müller refused to leave. The orchestra conductor on the *Titanic*.

"We'll play as civilization collapses," he said. "Our final contribution to music."

In the now-emptied Block 28, its former occupants on the road or in mass graves, Müller gathered the last members of his orchestra, wretches holding on to the instruments that had kept them alive, believing with all of the spirit left in their weakened selves that these violins, flutes, or horns would save them at the moment of the final debacle. Emil had believed it, as well. He never kept his patched-up Paolo Soprani far from him. It was a talisman more than a sword. A cloak more than a shield.

The musicians felt a twinge of hope when Oskar Müller arrived dressed in his finest. They all knew that Müller had interceded with his superiors to spare his protégés from the evacuation along a road the Soviets had already begun to bomb. The members of the other orchestras hadn't had the same luck, including the women's orchestra, who'd been without Alma Rosé for a few months after she'd died of natural causes. Emil knew, however, through Christina, that Müller and some others — Eduard Wirths, Dr. Josef, Hans Leibrecht, and Matthias Kluge, notably — would soon be high-stepping it to Berlin to prepare their escape to Switzerland. Naively, Emil thought Christina would bring him with her on this uncertain voyage. Another illusion.

It all happened so quickly.

Oskar Müller went mad. He pulled his Luger out of its holster and opened fire on the musicians, one after the other, damning the Russians, those barbarians — they would never put a hand on his masterwork, his magnificent orchestra. Emil was at the far end of the room when the shooting began and managed to avoid the first few shots by jumping behind a wooden bed. If he tried to get up and flee, he'd be spotted.

Then the firing stopped. An intolerable silence filled the barracks. Emil held his breath, listening. Perhaps Müller thought him dead? Perhaps he was gone already for Switzerland? He heard footsteps, a sound he'd waited for expectantly every day for weeks and weeks. Christina's footsteps. She would lead Müller out the door. She'd saved Emil twice already. She would do it again.

"Emil …"

Her voice was soft, unyielding, beguiling. Emil could still see Müller's boots among the corpses. Unmoving, waiting to finish the job before leaving the barracks.

"Emil," Christina went on. "Come out. You've nothing to fear."

For once, Emil doubted Christina's sincerity. The woman he'd held in his arms so many times in the past few months now seemed distant, even threatening.

Then her feet appeared next to her husband's.

Christina leaned over as if she'd known from the start where Emil was hiding. She smiled, ignoring the bodies around her. Emil hated her for that smile, which seemed like a threat. The young woman stretched her hand out to him. That hand he had kissed countless times, now taking him out of his safe place toward death. Emil knew he couldn't resist her charms now, in the same way he'd never been able to resist them in the past, though his life hung in the balance.

He slipped his hand into Christina's, and she pulled him up with all her strength. Oskar Müller was smiling. His gun in his hand, he watched Christina help Emil stand. Emil had left the accordion under the wooden bed. A separation, he thought, that could only lead to tragedy. He had lost everything: the woman he loved, the musical instrument that had kept him alive in the midst of this hell. Christina was smiling. The same frozen smile.

The conductor sighed. "A shame to lose such a talented musician."

Müller brought his weapon to Emil's head. A last glance at Christina, her face frozen.

"Let me do it," she interrupted.

Emil shut his eyes. She had chosen to end this life she'd saved twice already. The betrayal of the woman he loved seemed far more terrible than the prospect of his impending death.

Müller glanced at Christina. Intrigued? Perplexed? It was hard to say.

She smiled. "I'm the one who recruited him, no?"

Müller lowered the Luger and handed it to Christina, its barrel pointed at the floor. Emil discovered in his lover an expertise with weapons: she knew exactly what she was doing. There was no surprise at the heft of the weapon in her hand. She had likely killed before, other prisoners, other men she'd used to her satisfaction.

Christina stepped toward Emil and raised the gun. Emil closed his eyes.

Gunshot.

Emil wasn't dead. He opened his eyes and saw Christina already leaning over her husband's body. A red dot at his temple, a single shot. Emil was rooted in place, shocked, not knowing what to do.

Christina turned toward him. "Come on! Hurry up!" She pulled a uniform out of a canvas bag Emil hadn't noticed before and tossed it to him. "Your name is Reinicke. SS-Sturmmann Reinicke, private first class. Not that ranks matter anymore …"

"Christina …"

"Hurry!"

Emil slipped the uniform on. It was far too big, but there was no time to do anything about that.

Christina handed him documents. "His papers. It'll be enough to pass the guard post. No one will stop you, anyway. The war is practically over, Emil."

The young man wanted to take her in his arms, but she pushed him back, raised her hand, and pointed at the far end of the room. She barely shook at all. "In that direction, Russians. Maybe a day's walk away."

"Let's go together —"

Christina put her hand over his mouth. "Too dangerous."

Emil didn't care. He would go where she went; he'd follow her every footstep. His freedom was meaningless if he couldn't be with her.

Christina could read Emil's determination in his eyes but refused to relent. She took his face in her hands, kissed him, and stared deeply into his eyes. "I love you. I've always loved you. From the very first day. I'll never forget you."

Emil took his accordion from beneath the bed. By the time he'd gotten back to his feet, Christina was gone. He could hear footsteps, fading fast. Emil rushed out of the block, hoping to catch up, but once outside, he couldn't find her. Officers were rushing toward canvas-covered trucks. Other vehicles criss-crossed the camp, picking up stragglers. Soldiers rushed toward the crematory ovens with explosives, ignoring the "Muslims." They were too weak to flee, anyway, barely had the strength to stand. Already the sound of explosions could be heard. The SS had planned to destroy the evidence before the Russians arrived, but the Soviets had moved far too quickly. Now it was every man for himself.

He found himself alone among the corpses. He had to flee. To go where Christina had directed him. A handful of guards appeared out of nowhere and shouted at him, recognizing his uniform. They pulled him with them: "Hurry!"

The blast of a horn.

Emil turned around. Christina was running toward a moving truck, already halfway to the gates. Her arms were extended, trying to haul herself into its covered bed. Just as she was about to climb into the back, Emil saw Hans Leibrecht poke his head out, holding on to the canvas. He smiled and kicked the young woman in the chest. Christina tried a second time, and he kicked again. She stumbled for a few steps and fell. The truck kept moving, leaving Christina behind. Emil wanted to run to her, to save her, but he was trapped. The soldiers flanked him still, carrying the man they thought was a stunned comrade with them. More explosions. A cloud of heavy smoke, of ashes, floating in the grey sky over Auschwitz.

He undid his belt and tied each end of it to the Paolo Soprani, allowing him to use it as a strap to replace the one that had broken. He could carry the *gormónya* on his back now. However, his pants were falling down. It didn't seem to raise any questions. The SS he'd left the camp with had all rushed south. Meanwhile, Emil was following train tracks toward the Vistula. He passed soldiers, all in a panic, fleeing every which way. They weren't guards assigned to prisoners in Auschwitz, but troops in the regular army, abandoning their positions. Clearly, all that was left on the soldiers' minds was to save their own skins, to escape from the incoming disaster.

No one noticed Emil's dishevelled air; no one asked him questions about his destination. He was walking east while everyone else was rushing west. Anything but the Russians, the deserters seemed to be saying. The hell of bombardments, a long road to an impasse in Berlin, was preferable to what the Soviets had in store for the Germans. The rumour had reached the ears of the Auschwitz officers. The Red Army was paying in full the soldiers of the Third Reich for the horrors the SS had visited upon them. Emil didn't care. Christina had ordered him east, so he followed her command without question. Nothing could be worse than Auschwitz.

The young Rom walked for hours in this no man's land, characteristic of territory abandoned by a fleeing army. The population was boarding up their homes as best they could. The roads were deserted, destroyed, impracticable for anything more than a man on foot. The burning fires lit by bombs bursting in the distance made the horizon glow, an unceasing sunset. Emil found a dead soldier. He was slumped in tall grass, his leg ripped from his body. His abandoned mess kit still contained biscuits and margarine. Emil took the food and walked on. Christina had said a day's walk. Emil thought he'd been dragging his feet for at least thirty-six hours. He was tired, famished, but didn't dare stop to sleep. And where would he sleep, anyway? All of the homes, all of the farms, everything was burnt and in ruin. His German uniform made him a tempting target. He would need to get rid of it but couldn't guess where he'd find fresh clothes.

In the morning, he collapsed in a ditch, overcome with exhaustion. He fell asleep, his head on his accordion. Hours later the sun woke him. It was time to go on.

"Don't move!"

Emil whipped around. A rifle greeted him. A young soldier speaking a language he had never heard. Russian, certainly. The soldier was hardly older than Emil, threatening him with a heavy rifle he could barely keep steady.

"Don't move!" he repeated.

Emil was expecting a shot, but the soldier called for someone, without taking his eyes away from Emil. Another soldier appeared; this man was older, perhaps an officer. He told Emil in German to get up and put his hands behind his head.

The older soldier walked toward Emil and took the accordion. The sight of the instrument seemed to intrigue him. "It's yours? You're a musician?"

Emil nodded.

The man handed the Paolo Soprani back to the young Rom. "Come."

Emil was made a prisoner.

He wasn't the only one. Farther along the road, sitting beside a muddy field, others like him, hands tied or on their heads. Haggard soldiers waking from a nightmare six years in the making. Emil looked for guards who might know him from the camp. He recognized none of the Germans. He'd surely be shot now. Summary execution. Why would the Russians want to take prisoners? The Red Army had advanced so rapidly because they'd executed everyone who'd surrendered, Emil thought. They'd travelled light. And yet no gunfire for now — the soldiers left sitting on the side of the road. They were given meagre rations, which seemed like a feast to Emil, who was used to the food in the extermination camps.

He was told by a German soldier that Kraków had already fallen. The Russians had been in Auschwitz for days already. German officers had been captured in their flight back to Berlin. They were hanged or shot. Emil worried about Christina, she who'd saved his life once more. He would never be able to return the favour. Yes, he was free, and there was gladness in that, but his heart was rent at the thought of never seeing her again.

Next came the interrogation. The prisoners stood in a long line, giving their names and ranks. His Paolo Soprani strapped to his back, Emil stuck out his chest. He sought his courage, his strength. He had survived the worst carnage of the twentieth century. The future was his.

"My name is Emil Rosca. I am no soldier. I'm no German. I am Roma, son of Anton Rosca, King of the Roma."

The Russian soldiers looked at him, confused. Emil crouched and drew a *Z* in the dirt. He showed the number tattooed on his forearm.

"From this day forth, I am the King of the Roma in Romania."

The Russians burst out laughing. That was a good one! The King of the Roma! A dynasty fit for a travelling circus! King of half a rubbish heap!

17

Bucharest, November 29, 2006

The conflagration caused by Laura Costinar's death reached Max O'Brien all the way to his hideout on Sepcari Street. Toma Boerescu had sent him to a single room in a building. The apartment was on the fifth floor of an ancient structure without an elevator. Right over him, the attic, with the sound of pigeons cooing. In the distance, a steeple, Bărăția's church tower, if he wasn't mistaken. A stone-faced woman handed him the keys, soap, and towels without asking questions.

The next morning at a press conference Adrian Pavlenco stated that fingerprints had been found in the bathroom of the Alexandriei Boulevard building. They pointed in one direction: Robert Cheskin, also known as Max O'Brien, a Canadian-born con man operating out of New York. He was to be treated as a potential accomplice of Kevin Dandurand in the case of the Zăbrăuți Street fire. O'Brien had killed a Romani woman who could have denounced him. The woman in question had been a pillar of the community: Ioan Costinar's widow. O'Brien and Dandurand had both fled, which was rather incriminating.

However, Pavlenco wanted to reassure the Romani community and MP Marineci in particular that the police were doing everything in their power to get their hands on these Romani-killers. They would see that Romanian justice took its fight against perpetrators of hate crimes seriously.

Max turned off the television, disgusted.

That damn Pavlenco, using Laura Costinar's death to peacock.

More news came, this time from Canada. A man on Cambiano's board of directors claimed that Raymond Dandurand had been a victim of fraud, conned by a man calling himself Carlo Negroni. The man had never been found. Asked about this by investigative journalists, executives at Nordopak — now a branch of the Italian company — confirmed board members' allegations. Was the suspected killer of Laura Costinar also responsible for a fraud orchestrated by Kevin? Why not? The story was becoming far more scandalous and intriguing, and another dark mark was added to Raymond Dandurand's ingrate son.

The following day, Canadian media outfits began speculating on the deaths of Raymond and Sacha. There had to be dirt there, as well. Perhaps the deaths could be pinned on the murderous duo, talking heads on one news channel suggested. Max O'Brien and Kevin Dandurand: bloodthirsty killers, accomplices since forever, travelling the world and leaving death in their wake. Max could imagine Josée thinking that she, too, had been deceived by this inveterate liar, this thief. Adrian Pavlenco was asked how in the world he could have had the thief in his office and not catch him! Max guessed that Marilyn Burgess was cursing herself for not having been more careful. Thankfully, she had the decency to stay far away from the spotlight. Though Max knew a woman like that wasn't about to let such a humiliation lie. She was sharpening her claws, laying a trap this very instant, he was sure. Max O'Brien, the elusive con man, had been unmasked. He'd been lucky so far to have escaped the law, as had Kevin Dandurand. In a foreign country, unable to speak the language, the two suspects wouldn't last long. Their silver tongues would be useless. Sooner or later the two men would turn themselves in — unless the Roma themselves decided to hand down their own brand of justice.

A Romanian television reporter, the most syrupy of the bunch, described in detail in a falsetto the formidable *Kris romani*, the Romani court before which troublesome and quarrelsome delinquents were brought to justice. The *kumpaníya*'s degenerates, killers, thieves. Sometimes they were sent to face *gadjo* justice, but more often than not, punishment was handed down by the family, informally, without giving notice to outsiders. Of course, the *Kris* only handed out judgments to Roma, but the journalist insinuated otherwise, perhaps to cause a little shiver of fear and delight in his audience. These Gypsy killers would get what was coming to them … and from the Gypsies themselves! Their brand of justice was no stroll in the park, no! Max O'Brien and Kevin Dandurand would be found somewhere in a ditch, their heads chopped right off! Like the chickens Gypsy parasites were known for stealing.… Oh, yes, they would be tortured with hidden Gypsy magic …

In short, Max was screwed. And Kevin, as well. The Romanian police, humiliated, would try to get back in the good graces of the public, who'd begun demanding answers. And Marilyn Burgess was right behind the good Romanian people, pushing the cops as hard she could, desperate for that promotion. Not to mention the Roma themselves, out looking for justice. Max felt surrounded, encircled by three groups who all had the same objective: to neutralize him. The Romanian authorities would certainly demand harsh justice as an example. He'd never be extradited. The two criminals, Max and Kevin, would face a Romanian judge. They'd get a well-publicized trial with lights, camera, action. That was if they weren't caught by the Roma beforehand, of course.

Max was boxed in. Nowhere to turn.

On the third day, Toma Boerescu walked up to his bolthole, half carried by the owner. He laboriously reached Max's room under cover of church bells ringing nearby. Max's saviour collapsed in a wicker chair, and it took him a good ten minutes to catch his breath. The old man would have probably climbed all the way to the top of the Arcul de Triumf just to contemplate the sight of a bested Max O'Brien.

"So how did you know where I was?" Max eventually asked when Boerescu had caught his breath.

"I bugged you the other day, Cheskin. Or should I say O'Brien?"

"Please, Max is fine."

"Your pin."

Max examined it closely and noticed a micro-emitter.

"And your cellphone." Boerescu smiled. "Old habits die hard in Eastern Europe. Forty years of totalitarianism will do that to you."

Clearly, Max had underestimated his fixer.

The man added, "More bad news. This morning Pavlenco's men found the body of a photographer in the southern suburbs. The poor bastard was found stabbed in his Dacia."

Cosmin Micula.

"An anonymous call to make sure the body was found quickly."

It was a foregone conclusion who the suspect would be.

Max sighed. "Of course, they found my fingerprints in the car."

"Do you touch absolutely everything on purpose?"

Max had fallen straight into a trap as deep as it was wide. He was a lamb to the slaughter. Who were Laura Costinar and Cosmin Micula's killers — the same killers, presumably, who had lit the fire on Zăbrăuți Street? What did these people want? To make sure Max and Kevin took the fall, clearly. They would be thrown under the bus.

Why?

To Max it was clear that Kevin was still being held by his captors, if he wasn't already dead. One thing was certain: his friend was in grave danger. No way would Max abandon Kevin to his fate. Max had no intention of disappearing. The bastards behind this whole affair didn't know who they were messing with.

"You've got another passport?" Boerescu asked.

"For what? I'm not leaving. I'm going to find Kevin."

Boerescu sighed. "You'll get nowhere with the cops after you."

And Max still needed to figure out why Kevin was in Bucharest in the first place. The photographer, Micula, had been vague about that. How had he gotten mixed up in this whole affair? He probably didn't care a whit about Ioan Costinar's killer. So why this sudden flurry of activity?

Max realized he might just find a few answers in North America. He could start in Manitoba, where Costinar had been murdered. His killers were likely the people responsible for the fire in Bucharest. Back in Canada, Max would be able to move freely and investigate as he saw fit. He'd have room to breathe.

Boerescu sweetened the pot. "I'll put my friends on it. You can trust them. They'll leave no stone unturned, and those who don't want to talk, they'll get them to talk."

Boerescu was right.

"I promise to find your friend. So, the passport?"

Max always kept two or three backup passports in the lining of his coat.

His fixer scanned them critically. "This one should work."

"The airports are going to be under surveillance," Max replied. "We need to find another way out."

"You'll drive toward Serbia. You'll cross at Orşova and be in Belgrade a few hours after that. You could also cross through Bulgaria, but Giurgiu is too close to Bucharest, and the cops will likely be looking for you at that border crossing."

Boerescu smiled. "I'll go with you. Killers and thieves don't normally drive around with old men. Especially not former cops. It'll be good cover." He sniffed. "You've got money, of course? Cash?"

Max nodded.

They would leave the next day. Max slept fitfully, the slightest noise waking him. He woke often that night, and his mind turned to Kevin and what was in store for him. Kevin's presence in Romania intrigued him, especially since Laura Costinar's murder. What relationship did he have to the country? Surely, the link was his mother, Roxanne. That Max was sure of. Had she some connection to Costinar's cause, and through her, to Kevin?

As dawn broke over the city, the stone-faced owner climbed up the stairs and woke Max. A waft of coffee tickled his nose through the open door. Boerescu waited for him in a rusted truck. He was wearing his heavy coat, a spit-shined medal pinned to it. Boerescu ordered Max to sit in the middle seat, between him and the driver, without introducing the man. The vehicle rumbled off through the deserted capital. No police patrols to bother them this early. Soon the city turned into suburbs, and the suburbs into countryside.

According to *Nine O'Clock*, an English-language daily printed in Bucharest, the Conference of European Cities had ended on a statement reaffirming the desire of each and all to look into the concerning state of the Romani people in order to find a permanent solution to the deplorable situation that had lasted for centuries. The representative for Copenhagen — a tall blond man — spoke of a new era for stateless peoples. A statement supported by Hamburg's mayor and three other politicians from Western Europe. In short, the usual. Next year, in Venice or Lisbon, it would be on to another theme, other worries, and the same soothing speeches without action. In front of an assembled media, Victor Marineci called out the Romanian authorities, who were dragging their feet in the Zăbrăuți Street fire investigation. Where were Max O'Brien and Kevin Dandurand? Hadn't the authorities promised to apprehend them quickly? Surely, if fine, upstanding, pure-blooded Romanians had been slaughtered, there was no doubt the criminals would be behind bars already!

Max crumpled the newspaper and threw it under the seat. Next to him, head against the window, Boerescu was sleeping, despite the truck bouncing up and down on the rough road. He was sleeping a bit too deeply for Max's taste. Maybe he'd gotten his medication mixed up? But as soon as the vehicle neared Alexandria, the old lizard awoke from his torpor. He demanded the driver give him peanuts, almonds if they were straight out of luck, then complained about the weather, which had been so much warmer back when Ceaușescu was in power. To freshen his breath, he pulled out a flask of *palinca* and loudly cleared his throat. Good morning, Toma.

"So when are you going to introduce me to your driver?"

"He doesn't know you, he's never seen you, he's already forgotten you."

The man was called Juvan, in fact. Friendly, but not very loquacious — which Max appreciated — and rather impressively cross-eyed. And asthmatic to boot. A sight to see him drive with one hand, holding his inhaler in the other, looking in the wrong direction. And yet, according to Boerescu, Juvan knew the country like the back of his hand, especially the Danube region out west, where his family was from. All of his knowledge would be needed to cross the border.

Max watched the landscape go by, the first time he'd been out of city since he'd arrived in Romania. Carts pulled along froxen roads by horses or oxen, men wrapped up in heavy clothes. The country didn't seem to have really left the dark years. Back under Ceaușescu, food was rationed, citizens — comrades — condemned to malnutrition. Even famine. In winter, to prevent blackouts, it was prohibited to heat homes over fourteen degrees. Bucharest's downtown core was not the only place to have suffered from Ceaușescu's madness. In the 1980s, the dictator had had dozens of villages, churches, and historical monuments destroyed, trying to emulate what he saw as the success of the Chinese Cultural Revolution.

Peoples are like individuals: some are lucky, others aren't. Some slip off into the deep waters of history without causing waves, others crash into the reefs of dictatorship and totalitarianism.

This was the fate of Romanians.

Boerescu's fingers yanked at his pill bottle, which he couldn't seem to open. The vehicle's bouncing didn't help. Max wanted to give him a hand, but Boerescu refused. A moment of pride.

"You were a hard-liner?" Max asked after a time.

"I'm sorry?"

"As a party member, I mean. The picnics, the parades, the demonstrations. As a child, you wore the little red scarf?"

"Yes."

"And you were never tempted to cross the fence? To say goodbye to Joy?"

"Abandon socialism?"

Max nodded.

Boerescu said nothing at first. He swallowed a handful of pills, then said, "The retirement plan I worked for all my life with the Bucharest police department was annihilated by the devaluation of the Romanian leu. I live in a tiny apartment bought directly from the city by a corrupt promoter living the good life in Turkey. The pills I take that used to be free now cost me a fortune."

Boerescu hiccuped. He had spoken too quickly. After catching his breath, he added, "Socialism abandoned us, don't you see? In '89 it was socialism that jumped the fence."

He gestured toward a family on the side of the road, children running about covered in ash. Their parents searching through roadside trash for something that might be recycled to make a meal. Roma, no doubt, shunted from one landfill to the next.

"And that's what we got for it. Ceauşescu would never have let the situation get so bad." A long silence, then, "The greatest statesman this poor country of ours has ever known. The greatest defender of the Romani people. On his death, they lost a true father."

Max had his doubts. "A bogeyman, more like. Why would he ever have cared for the Roma?"

"Because he was a Gypsy himself."

18

They reached Craiova toward the end of the day and made their way to a hotel Juvan knew and recommended — his stepbrother's. The next day they would cross the Serbian border one hundred kilometres to the west. The hotel was freezing, of course. After a lukewarm shower, Max walked down to the practically deserted dining room. On the wall, a Caribbean tapestry: sunset over a beach. Enough to make your teeth chatter even more. Toma Boerescu, who'd kept his coat on, was seated with the driver. The two of them were attacking their vodka with gusto. Max thought they looked like two party members back in the good old days. Travelling on Romanian roads, announcing the good news, terrorizing whomever crossed their paths, just because they were bored.

The menu was recited in a monotone voice by Dracula's little brother. The Ceauşescu special: not much, and none of it tempting. Max had noticed, as he'd walked by the kitchen to the dining room, a crate of vegetables that might conceivably have been fresh at some point. No way he'd risk it with anything too fancy. Boiled vegetables, it was.

In Europe, history had gotten a bit too enthusiastic, not only to the detriment of Jews, but to the detriment of the Roma, as well, who paid their pound of flesh for Adolf Hitler's madness. After the war, the situation didn't get much better for the Roma. Some of them had stayed in the camps because they had nowhere else to go. In Germany, repression continued. The racist laws of 1938, adopted by the Nazis, remained in practice against the Roma until 1965. Things were even worse in Eastern Europe. There were countless initiatives to pull the Roma out of their misery, of course, but they were always promoted for the benefit of the totalitarian regimes that funded them. Be it forced sterilization to avoid the "proliferation" of families — which the Czech government called an act of socialist humanism — or the removal of children from their families to be educated by the state. In East Germany, for instance, Roma children were placed in classrooms for mentally handicapped children. Punishing measures taken without consulting the Roma, of course, who only sought to survive.

"Except in Romania," Boerescu said. "Here their situation was better than anywhere else."

"Thanks to the Genius of the Carpathians, as Ceaușescu called himself, right?" Max added.

"Don't you dare make fun of him! Even worse coming from a thief!" He glared at Max, disgusted.

"So why are you helping me, then?" Max asked.

"If you're arrested, I lose my three hundred dollars a day."

"Clearly, Toma Boerescu, capitalism has corrupted you!"

The revolution of December 1989 had begun in Timişoara. Students and workers demonstrating, encouraged by what was happening across Eastern Europe in the dictatorships of the people. The Berlin Wall had fallen in November; a wind was feeding the fires of freedom in Poland, Hungary, and Czechoslovakia. Everywhere, rusty, corrupted regimes — empty shells, really — imploded, incapable of resisting the popular pressure of the discontent. In Romania, however, the powers that be held strong, even if the troubles in Timişoara began to spread to the rest of the country.

Ceauşescu's answer to the agitators was the old tactic of totalitarian regimes: organize in Bucharest a counter-demonstration in support of the dictator, in front of the Central Committee headquarters. On the balcony, surrounded by a few apparatchiks, Nicolae and Elena, the "father" and "mother" of the Romanian people, or so the propaganda claimed. But the initiative went south. Some in the crowd began booing the Conducător. Others supported him. Furious, Ceauşescu ordered the security services to open fire on the crowd, which they did. But the Romanian army didn't comply.

From that moment on the game was up. Ceauşescu ordered his minister of defence executed, but it was too late. Ceauşescu had to flee. The deposed couple rushed toward the helicopter parked on the roof of the building while street battles raged. The army against the security services. The erstwhile leaders were trying to reach Switzerland, most likely, where Ceauşescu had several secret bank accounts. Four hundred million dollars' worth of possessions outside Romania, according to certain estimates. But the pilot chose to land his plane in Târgovişte, where the revolution's leaders were already waiting for them. In Bucharest the army had triumphed. Hundreds had died. A mock trial, a summary execution, mowed down by a machine gun, all of it filmed by the insurrectionists who claimed to be part of the newly founded National Salvation Front.

"We recognized them," Boerescu grumbled. "Ion Iliescu, the front's founder, was the former head of the Union of Communist Youth."

Iliescu became the first elected president in 1990. He'd always hated Elena, who'd preferred her son, Nicu, to him — a corrupted alcoholic who died of cirrhosis of the liver at forty-five.

The Romanian revolution, a perfect opportunity for this apparatchik and his accomplices.

In short, Boerescu concluded, Ceauşescu's guard dogs rebelled against their master. They settled the score — that was what this whole affair had been. The triumph of the heir apparent and the profiteers who'd fed off the regime for years before turning their backs on it in response to popular pressure. It had been pure mathematics: joining the people, associating themselves with their rebellion to stay in power. The Ceauşescu couple, symbol of the people's suffering, could be sacrificed. Without regrets, without remorse.

"Except for the Roma," Boerescu added.

"Hard to believe."

"They had supported the regime way back in 1949. It was natural for Ceauşescu to reward their loyalty." The old man sighed. "Ask any Gypsy today. They all miss the Conducător." Boerescu kept eating, nose deep in his plate.

"Tell me about Ioan Costinar," Max said.

For years, an inspiration to Roma living in Romania. Closely followed by Victor Marineci, of course. In a sense, they were the Gandhi and Nehru of the Roma. Marineci was a political organizer and represented the Roma to the *gadje*. He was the face of Romani demands for equality and respect. Meanwhile, Costinar worked on a more philosophical level. He was sought out to describe and teach the world about the place of the Roma in world history, and European history in particular. He travelled around the globe, raising funds for his initiatives.

"What about his wife, Laura?"

"Discreet. She always stayed far from political turmoil."

"Did she accompany him on his travels?"

"Sometimes."

Juvan woke Max at dawn, informing him that Boerescu, who'd come down with a cold, would remain at the hotel. The rest of the trip would proceed without the old man. They had breakfast in the dining room before leaving.

Max joined him as Boerescu was swallowing his medication with a glass of water. His heavy coat was draped over his back to warm him up. He seemed worn to the bones and admitted to having slept poorly.

"When you get old, the weight of your memories becomes harder to bear."

Max realized he hadn't taken the time to learn anything about this man he'd judged so quickly. "Are you married? Do you have a family?"

"My wife died in 1986. My daughter works in a cannery on the Black Sea. I haven't spoken to her in twelve years. She hates policemen." His face was a picture of sadness.

"The money I owe you will be transferred to your account as promised," Max announced. "As soon as I get back to America, I'll take care of it."

Boerescu nodded. "Be careful."

"You, too," Max replied.

Curiously, Max realized, he would miss the old man. He had gotten used to his fixer's habits and mood swings. They'd become companionable enough. Boerescu invited him to sit and have a cup of coffee before hitting the road. Juvan was packing the truck. After getting Max across the border, the driver would come back and pick up Boerescu, and the two would return to Bucharest together. Max and his fixer chatted amicably, knowing they'd already said everything that needed to be said. As soon as Boerescu located Kevin, he'd get him out of the country in the same way as Max. Until then he'd keep Max informed of his search, and Max would do the same from North America.

Soon enough it was time to say goodbye. Leaning against his walker, Boerescu followed him to the vehicle where Juvan was already waiting, door open, as if driving royalty to a ball. Max threw his bag onto the seat and turned to Boerescu to embrace him. The old man smelled like cheap aftershave.

"*Mulțumesc*, Boerescu. Thank you."

"Please. Toma."

"Thank you, Toma."

Without Boerescu, the truck was silent. Juvan was becoming increasingly nervous, taking deep breaths from his inhaler. Thankfully, the road was deserted. Busy with tourists in the summer, in winter it was used only by the rare rusted tractor or old Dacia. On each side of the road, forest and mountains.

The Danube appeared suddenly. In antiquity the Romans had built a bridge here, right over the water. The road followed a one-hundred-and-fifty-kilometre-long gorge. A police car passed them without slowing down, giving Juvan another asthma attack.

Just before Orşova, right where the road to Deva and Timişoara began, Juvan parked his vehicle behind a motel frequented by truckers. Many of them were sleeping poorly in frost-covered cabins. Max thought Juvan wanted him to cross the border with a truck driver, though that seemed too risky. A patrol might come by and catch them. Or a curious border guard might ask a few questions and that would be it for Max.

The motel's owner led Max and Juvan to the edge of the Danube behind the property. A hangar in ruins at a twist of the river where a cliff had collapsed millions of years earlier. On the rocky beach, a fishing boat.

"We can go now, but it's safer to wait until night," the small man gasped. "Because of the guards on the shore."

They had to be careful not only of Romanian border guards, but Serbian ones, as well, in the village of Tekija, just across from Orşova. You could see the houses on the other side of the Danube. In the darkest days of the Cold War, Yugoslavia was often the destination of choice for citizens fleeing Ceauşescu's reign of terror. Border patrols would pick up desperate refugees along the Danube. Today the situation was far less tense, but they would still need to be careful.

The owner gave Max a room to wait out the night. While Boerescu had told him Juvan was used to ferrying illegals, Max was devoured by anxiety. He twisted and turned, trying to find sleep, but again all he could think of was Kevin. After a time, he managed to fall fitfully to sleep. The sound of a car door slamming shut woke him. Max looked through the window and saw a police car parked in front of the motel. Before he could react, the door to his room was flung open and Juvan burst in, more agitated than ever. It was time to leave. Now. Not a minute to lose.

A patrol was ending its day at the bar. The policemen had dropped their hats on the counter. Max and Juvan slipped out the back door while the cops laughed loudly at a joke from the owner. The two took the path to the shore where the fishing boat was beached. A young man with sideburns was waiting for them, and as soon as he saw the pair appear, he began pushing the boat into the Danube. Just as Max was about to climb into the boat, Juvan grabbed his arm and handed him an envelope. A plane ticket from Belgrade to Brussels, bought with Max's money. His fixer had left nothing to chance.

Juvan disappeared into the night, and Max found himself on the Danube, whipped by the wind blowing through the high cliffs along the river's course. On the other shore, the winking lights of Tekija's homes. Boerescu had assured him that the place was frequented by Serbian truck drivers, and that with their help, he would have no trouble finding his way to the capital.

The young man rowed swiftly and silently, scanning the other shore from time to time. He seemed to know the waters well, not hesitating as he skirted rocks and trapped logs.

Soon enough Max heard the boat drag against the bottom. The young man jumped into the water and pulled the boat ashore. With a gesture of the hand, he showed Max the way to the road, higher up. Then he pushed his boat back into the water and disappeared.

The night's darkness was complete, and Max struggled his way up the small path climbing the cliff. A few minutes at a slow, plodding walk and he'd reached the top. He heard a truck coming, its headlights bursting through the night. For a brief moment, Max saw a few houses lined along the road, all plunged into darkness. The village was behind him. He chose to walk westward until he could find a gas station or a truck stop where he might pay a few dollars for a ride to Belgrade.

Max had been walking for a while already when he heard voices coming from his left, accompanied by the crackling of a fire. He made out the silhouette of a few caravans, old cars hitched in front of them, mostly massive, rusted American cars. A Romani camp, of course. The chattering around the fire fell silent when the dogs began barking at a stranger in the night. Children ran out, surrounding him. The women quiet behind them. Men got up from around the fire, watching him intently. They seemed worried at first, but when they realized he was alone, relief was clear on their faces. Here was a lone stranger, a man as rootless as they, at least in appearance. Max O'Brien, the killer of Roma, according to the Romanian police, the fox in the henhouse. Luckily, no one recognized him. He didn't move.

The oldest of the Roma, the *káko*, spoke a few words in a language Max couldn't understand — Serbo-Croatian, most likely. The man didn't seem particularly offended that the stranger was unable to comprehend him. A child pulled Max by the sleeves to offer him a guided tour of the caravans. He was given food, then a tune on a violin broke the deep night. The child who'd pulled him by the sleeve was playing to impress his new audience. If he'd pulled Max to the fire, it was to make a show of it. The child played skillfully, effortlessly. Max was reminded of a joke by a music teacher he'd read somewhere once: there were two ways to play a violin: well, or like a Rom. After the meal, after the music, Max was offered a bed in one of the cars, a bit away from the camp. He let himself sink into the back seat and fell deeply asleep almost immediately, a wool blanket over him.

At dawn, when Max finally opened his eyes, he realized the Roma were preparing to break camp. He was offered a cup of very strong coffee. Farther off, in a river that fed into the Danube, women washed clothes according to old traditions. The men's clothes higher up the stream, the women's lower, and even lower still, women's underwear and the clothes of pregnant women. Max knew the Roma had inherited from their Indian ancestors various taboos related to impurity.

The *káko* approached Max, and with difficulty, Max finally understood that the *kumpaníya* was going toward Belgrade. Max was welcome to join them on the road if he had nothing better to do. He accepted without hesitation. Romani hospitality definitely beat out that of a Serbian trucker.

19

Chimneys spitting ash like pillars holding up a dreary Russian sky, leaving Emil Rosca's clothes drying on a rope tied between his barracks and the next, with long dark streaks. Striped like his uniform in Auschwitz. In the dank streets, the only vehicles were owned by the mine and factory owners. They splashed infrequent passersby with thick mud sprays. A veiled sun hid, never piercing through heavy grey clouds, spending its day concealed as if ashamed this corner of the earth existed. At night, military dogs barked ceaselessly, tied by long cables along the path of foot patrols near the *vychki*. All of this didn't mean Emil couldn't sleep; quite the opposite.

Poorly fed, exhausted by his work in the mine, he collapsed every evening, surrounded by the two hundred other men in his barracks, as soon as his eleven hours of forced labour were over. All he got was the dry ration, as it was called: smoked herring and bread. And it was never enough. Four hundred and fifty grams a day, half of what the guard dogs got! And he was always thirsty. Rations were meted out according to the output of workers. Those who fell ill or became physically exhausted received less and less to eat, until they died of starvation or dysentery. The first summer, when Emil was put to work building railway tracks, he'd been able to pick small fruits and eat them out of sight of the guards. But once winter came he was sent to the mine with other *zeks*, all trying to survive, as well.

Emil had gone from one prison to another. One hell had been replaced by another. Every morning, in fifty-below-zero weather, the men marched toward the mine, heads down, dressed only in cotton short coats. On their swollen, frozen feet, they wore shoes made from old tractor tires. At least in Poland there had been hope that the war would end. Even atheists in the camps had prayed for the Germans to be defeated. Here there was no war, no hope, no prayer. There would be no defeat. There would be tuberculosis phlegm in the shared sink. There would be *zeks* with rotten teeth. Grey snow stuck to the boots of deportees — many of whom had survived Nazi concentration camps. Revolt? Five thousand men had been gassed in a nearby camp after going on strike. The whole world ignored their existence. The Soviet Union had won the war and none could resist its strength.

Emil had the impression that he was slowly going mad. Thankfully, he'd managed to keep his Paolo

Soprani on the train ride that had brought him here. In the evenings, exhausted, he could barely find the strength to play the accordion. The music reminded him of Christina. It was for her that he made an effort. He thought of her constantly. Maybe she'd reached Switzerland. Or she might be in prison, just like him. Or dead, which was more likely still. Emil would have given anything to save her life, including giving his own.

One day, exhausted, Emil collapsed in the bottom of the mine on a pile of coal. He wanted to die — enough, enough — but two guards picked him up, brought him to the surface, and left him in the infirmary.

When he came to, three men stood at the foot of his bed: two short, large men with close-cut hair, and a thinner, younger man, who held a handkerchief over his nose. The whole place surely smelled like unwashed latrines and sweat and death. Emil couldn't tell anymore; he was part of the smell. The three men wore clean clothes. Canvas coats lined with fur, likely not as warm as the mine guards' heavy pea jackets. The youngest of the three, the smaller one, was dressed far too lightly, as if he'd misjudged the weather. He shook visibly, ready to get on with it.

When the older man realized Emil had regained consciousness, he leaned over and put a hand on Emil's shoulder. "Emil Rosca?"

It was the first time someone had called him by his *gadjo* name since he'd gotten out of Auschwitz. What did these men want from him? He'd been in this prison for three years and not a soul had come to see him, except for a handful of KGB officers in charge of his "re-education."

Trick questions and exhausting interrogations. If a single one of the KGB emissaries wasn't satisfied with his answers, he knew he'd be sent to another camp where the conditions were even worse.

"You are Emil Rosca?"

The young Rom knew Russian well enough by now to notice the man didn't speak with a Muscovite accent. The two other men observed Emil attentively, as if he were a strange creature. What was all this about?

"Do you understand what I'm asking?"

Emil nodded.

The man smiled. No one had smiled at Emil in months. The stranger took a coat from one of the beds behind him and handed it to Emil. "Put it on. We're going to go for a stroll, the four of us."

That invitation would mean only tragedy — that much Emil was sure of. He remained motionless, staring at the three men in turn. But the heavy coat seemed so warm, so comfortable, so much more so than the thin cotton sheets that covered him. So Emil dragged himself into a sitting position on the side of the bed. They draped the coat around his shoulders, slipped boots onto his feet.

Outside the infirmary was an enormous ZIS-110, its motor running. Frightened, Emil took a step back. "What do you want?"

"We need to talk," the older man said. "You've got nothing to fear."

"Will I be able to keep the coat afterward?"

The three men looked at one another.

"Yes," the older man said.

"And the boots?"

"Come, Emil."

The young Rom didn't have much choice. If he tried to run, he'd be shot in the back. It was better to risk the car ride, especially since it seemed so warm and comfortable inside. He sat in the back seat beside the youngest of the three men, the one with the handkerchief. The eldest of the trio sat at the wheel. Inside, the car was as comfortable as it had seemed. Emil had been right to go with them. Behind him, over his shoulder, was a small lamp, the height of luxury.

The ZIS-110 rumbled off toward the camp exit. They were stopped once beneath a gate over which hung a sign on a steel wire: *ZAPRETNAYA ZONA* — "restricted area." A junior officer peered through the window and almost tripped over himself as he backed up quickly and waved them through, saluting twice for good measure. Soon enough they'd crossed a few more coils of barbed wire and were out of the camp altogether. Free. The car drove right past the kennels. Soon the entire city of Vorkuta was behind him, growing smaller. They drove across the Pechora coal basin.

A few kilometres into the tundra, the driver glanced at Emil in the rearview mirror. "My name is Gheorghe Pintilie, but they call me Pantiuşa. Let me introduce you to Oleg Charvadze, who works for the Soviet minister of foreign affairs, Andrey Vyshinski."

The man seated in the passenger seat turned slightly. He was the most austere of the three, but the most physically imposing, with an immense neck stuffed into a too-small coat. He looked like a former wrestler.

"And this is Nicolae Ceauşescu."

The young man on Emil's left offered a small smile. He seemed shy, uncomfortable in his poorly tailored clothes. Emil later understood that Ceauşescu didn't speak Russian. Everything had to be translated for him.

Pintilie added, "Nicolae is Romanian, just like you. He, too, was in a concentration camp. In Târgu Jiu, where he became the head of the Communist youth."

Ceauşescu smiled again, clearly uneasy at being a topic of conversation.

"Three years ago Nicolae was elected to the National Assembly. Today he's in charge of agriculture. Romania's biggest challenge, right, Nicolae?"

The young man nodded. "If our agrarian reforms are successful, everything will be different," he added in Romanian.

Ceauşescu couldn't help his stammer. Painfully, he explained that Petru Groza's government had begun the collectivization of farmland throughout Romanian territory.

"A colossal task, made doubly hard by landowners united around the National Peasants' Party, who oppose it."

Since their defeat in the 1946 elections, Charvadze explained, the bourgeois parties were attempting to block reform. Today they could no longer count on King Michael's support. He'd abdicated and left the country. Yet Stalin still feared Romania might veer back into fascism.

Charvadze's voice was curiously melodious. The giant spoke softly, like a man trying to sell a pillow.

"The battle hasn't yet been won in the country-side," Ceauşescu continued. "There are peasant revolts throughout the country, unfortunately."

"Partisans hiding in the mountains, resisting socialist progress," Charvadze corrected.

"Partisans?" Pintilie interjected. "No, more like terrorists who don't hesitate to murder civilians. For this reason, we must all be vigilant. Even if the victory of the people is close at hand."

Emil listened to them converse with one another as the car drove past other labour camps, some of which seemed to still be under construction. He felt as if he were at a party he hadn't been invited to. They spoke to him, but through each other. What did these people want? All Emil cared about was the coat. And the boots.

The ZIS-110 was driving through forest now. The three men spoke of Romania, ignoring the landscape around them. They were talking strategy, time frames, balance of power. Emil listened to them distractedly. He watched the forest instead, a forest he'd never had an opportunity to visit. Snow was a rare sight this winter. Large off-white patches hid the grey of the undergrowth. To the east, he saw a mountain range. The Ural Mountains most likely.

Pintilie brought the car to a halt at the end of a small road beside a rotting wooden grain elevator. A bit farther off, an abandoned cabin, its roof collapsed under the weight of snow, probably last winter. What remained of a camp that might have been active in the 1930s.

The three men climbed out of the car. Charvadze stretched, cracked his knuckles. Ceauşescu lit a cigarette and offered it to Emil, who thanked him with a movement of his head. Stepping around the snowdrifts, Pintilie came near the two men, as if to continue the conversation. More of a monologue, really. Emil was still wondering why he'd been invited on this little trip. Wondered what the answers were to the questions they weren't asking him.

Finally, Pintilie addressed the young Rom. "Do you know what the biggest obstacle to collectivization is, Emil?"

He shook his head.

"Gypsies."

"Pantiușa is right," Ceaușescu continued. "The Gypsies are afraid of losing their privileges as seasonal workers."

"When they've got nothing to fear."

"Of course, some comrades haven't always been entirely honest with them."

"Mistakes were made."

"Mistakes were made toward all Romanian people," Ceaușescu admitted.

What were they trying to say, exactly? Were they speaking of their attitude during the war? If so, the Communists had a lot to answer for. They had completely disregarded reality when Hitler and Stalin signed the non-aggression pact in 1939. And then the silence of Romanian Communists when the Soviet Union annexed large portions of the country. Emil would later learn that Petru Groza's victory in the 1946 elections had been the result of widespread fraud. Clearly, Romanians could pin some blame on the Soviets.

Ceaușescu threw his cigarette into the woods, saying, "One thing is certain. We can't build socialism in Romania without the Gypsies. Romanians owe a debt to you for your opposition to Ion Antonescu, and later, the Nazis."

"Paul Vaneker, a Dutchman, led sabotage and infiltration operations for London," Pintilie continued. "In Moscow, Stalin knew all about the operations. Right, Oleg?"

The giant nodded.

"Gypsies are essential for the new Romania," Ceauşescu said. "The second most important minority in the country after Hungarians. And the one most often ignored."

"They certainly need a bit of rest after all their centuries of wandering," Pintilie added.

Charvadze spoke, even more softly, almost a lover's tender whisper. "Romanestan, Emil. An autonomous territory where you'll be masters over your own fate."

The three men stood in front of the young Rom, who looked back at the trio in turn.

Romanestan. His father's old dream.

"Look at the Jews," Charvadze said. "The United Nations gave them a state. And what about the Gypsies? Nothing, not even crumbs.... In Nuremberg they even refused to speak of what was done to you as genocide. Your people were exterminated in the camps and yet you won't get a penny of compensation."

"Did you not suffer?" Pintilie asked.

"The Jews don't want Gypsies to be associated with the Holocaust," Ceauşescu said. "They want everything for themselves."

Charvadze laughed. "Rabbis with their shekels, am I right?"

Finally, Ceauşescu laid his hand on Emil's shoulder as if they were the oldest friends in the world. "Without us, you're all alone," he stammered. "The entire world gave up on your people."

Emil turned his head away. Heinrich Himmler had made a similar offer to his father in Auschwitz. A pact with the devil. Anton had refused by spitting in the face of the Nazi's second-in-command. These Communists were offering him the same thing. Should he refuse, as well? Spit in the face of these three emissaries? Pintilie was right, wasn't he? The world had changed. Still hangmen, each and every one of them, but of a different flavour now. Emil's experience in Vorkuta, what thousands of other prisoners were going through in similar camps, was only a variation on the Nazi theme. The urgency of murder wasn't as strong as in the Nazi camps. But the result came down to the same thing. A hundred and sixty kilometres above the Arctic Circle, death was the true master, just as in Auschwitz. The Soviet Empire would last forever: why hurry?

Himmler, Pintilie? Two sides of the same coin? Satan on one hand, Lucifer on the other. But these three men were right. Moscow led the world today. At least the world in which the Roma lived. The hangmen couldn't be ignored; you couldn't take your *vôrdòn* and cross the border. There were no more borders, only one country now. A single horizon scattered with watchtowers like those of Vorkuta.

"Our offer is a serious one, Emil," Ceauşescu said. "Pantiuşa has just been named the director of the Romanian political police."

"The Securitate," Pintilie added.

Ceauşescu continued. "But no matter how good a security service is, there are always limits. I need the help of Gypsies to convince the peasants to support collectivization. In exchange we're ready to guarantee a territory to your people. Near Timişoara, for example, on the Hungarian border."

Pintilie smiled. "And Stalin has already agreed. Right, Oleg?"

Charvadze nodded. He seemed overjoyed. He was the one who'd convinced Stalin, most likely. Later, Emil learned that Ceauşescu had travelled to Moscow to convince Stalin to accept his offer, only two days before coming to Vorkuta.

Pintilie took Emil by the shoulders and walked with him a few steps away from the others. "The Rosca family must be part of the greatest revolution in history. The world needs new leaders like you, like Nicolae. You're of the same generation. You were both victims of Nazi horror. Emil, you can't rob your people of this opportunity."

The young Rom hesitated. He wished his father were beside him now so he could ask for the man's advice. Should he trust these *gadje*? He disengaged from Pintilie. A small voice was telling him that the Soviet envoy was right. The Roma had stayed too long outside humanity, missing out on its evolution. He understood why his father had spat on the Gestapo chief. He would have done the same thing. But these three weren't offering him war; quite the opposite. They were offering peace. And to be a part of the future of the world.

Emil turned around. "All right, I'll follow you."

Smiles lit up the faces of the three men.

"But I do have one condition. I want to find a German woman. I want to know what happened to her."

They looked at one another, confused.

"The wife of a German officer who died in Auschwitz. Christina Müller."

There was a long silence, which Ceauşescu finally broke. He took a step toward Emil. "I'll find her. I promise."

"A plane is waiting for us in Vorkuta," Pintilie said. "We'll be in Moscow tonight. And in Bucharest tomorrow."

"My accordion."

Charvadze opened the trunk of the ZIS-110. The Paolo Soprani was already there. His only possession.

Pintilie smiled again. "We've got no time to lose, Emil. Each moment wasted slows the triumphant forward march of socialism."

Emil hadn't seen Bucharest in seven years. Back then the Kalderash lived far from the centre, beside awful-smelling landfills, abandoned industrial sites, fallow fields. The Roma criss-crossed the country, following the seasons, the harvests. And the rest of the time they juggled, wove baskets, told fortunes. And, of course, repaired pots and did minor metalwork, the Kalderash's traditional activities. Emil still remembered the story his mother had told him about Roman soldiers searching for nails to crucify Christ. All of Jerusalem's smiths refused the thankless task, and so the soldiers turned to a Kalderash, who made three nails for them.

As he was forging the fourth, he learned what the nails were for: crucifying the Son of God. The Kalderash refused to continue his work, but it was too late. Christ was nailed to the cross due to a Rom's handiwork. A nail in each hand and the third nailing both feet together — the fourth nail missing. A divine punishment followed, and the smith and his kin were condemned to wander through the world until the end of time.

There would be no more wandering, Emil told himself, as the small Tupolev landed at Otopeni Airport, still filled with military planes. After the end of the war, Stalin had refused to pull back his occupation army. There were Russians everywhere in Eastern Europe. Trade had begun again, but only the regime's highest cadres could afford to take a plane.

Ceaușescu told Emil they had a room reserved for him at the Capitol Hotel. He himself was looking forward to seeing his wife, Elena, again. They'd been married for three years. Like many other members of the Communist Party, the couple had adopted a war orphan, Valentin.

Emil thanked Ceaușescu for the offer of a room but turned it down. Instead, he climbed into a GAZ-4, a Russian jeep, which took him into the suburbs. A young, smooth-faced Soviet soldier was at the wheel. Along the road Emil saw Bucharest's citizens hunting through still-ruined buildings for supplies. The war had been over for four years! The Russians had promised law and order. It was likely the same across Europe, Emil thought. Reconstruction would take years, if not decades. And yet, later, Emil would realize that the seeds of doubt were planted on that car ride. What if the promises made by the three emissaries were all smoke and mirrors? But Emil didn't have the means to think critically. He was being offered a throne, a crown — why would he be difficult about it?

In the plane, Ceaușescu had revealed that the Roma, the few who'd survived the camps in Hungary and Czechoslovakia, were returning to the country and were now occupying land west of Bucharest. Land the municipality had given them as a stopgap until it figured out what to do with these people. Doctors and nurses had visited them to make sure they weren't an epidemic risk, and then they'd been abandoned. In 1946 the Communist Party had insisted that these refugees be given a right to vote, but they hadn't voted, not for the Communists, nor for anyone else. Thousands of people no one had any idea how to deal with, politically or otherwise. That was where Emil came in.

He got out of the vehicle at the entrance of a shantytown built from whatever had been pulled from the rubble of bombed-out homes. A rivulet overflowing with garbage ran through the site. Children in rags played in the fetid waters. No *vôrdôná*, at least not yet. Those from before the war had been destroyed, of course. Those to come were only promises. For now travel was a faraway project. A fantasy. These Roma were trapped in this landfill near Bucharest through no fault of their own.

Emil grabbed his Paolo Soprani, which he'd kept close by for his entire trip, and slowly, painfully, walked into the shantytown. His body hadn't had time to recover from the years of deprivation in Auschwitz and

Vorkuta, but it was his time to lead. Men repairing pots lifted their heads. Women and children poked their heads out of their miserable lodgings. They all watched this newcomer as if he were a strange beast. Other Roma appeared, dressed in filthy clothes. Right around the middle of the camp, Emil stopped. A curious silence fell around him as his brethren watched this strange, thin, beaten man. Then Emil raised his chin, puffed out his chest, and spoke with all the confidence he thought his father might have had in a moment like this. "I am Emil Rosca, son of Anton Rosca, *bulibasha* of Wallachia, descendant of Luca le Stevosko."

A woman walked out of the group. An old woman, or one worn to the bone by a hard life. She bowed deeply in front of him, forehead practically in the mud. "The King of the Roma," she murmured in Romani.

One of the men gestured at the Paolo Soprani. "Play."

Emil didn't need to be asked twice. His *gormónya* seemed imbued with a life of its own. Even the sad songs, which were his specialty, suddenly became light, full of joy. Emil played for all Roma everywhere, for all his brothers and sisters. Now he had a mission. An extraordinary project. After centuries of wandering, he would offer his people, who'd been abandoned by history, a country.

Romanestan.

20

Minneapolis, December 7, 2006

The airport teemed with Boy Scouts back from a winter jamboree in the countryside around Bruges, Belgium. Flags, whistles, calls to order. A general in shorts, despite the weather, leading his troop. Max weaved through the crowd of parents come to pick up their offspring. He took the Hilton shuttle downtown but didn't get out at the hotel where he'd booked a room. Instead, he got off at the bus stop on Hawthorne Avenue. He hadn't been followed, hadn't been noticed.

Grand Forks, North Dakota. Six hours of fitful sleep in an overheated room at a Holiday Inn. European newspapers, picked up at a magazine stand, devoted a few lines to Adrian Pavlenco's hunt in Romania and to the disappearance of Max O'Brien and Kevin Dandurand. Not a word, however, about Marilyn Burgess. Out of desperation, the police had come down hard on other suspects to calm rumblings from the Romani community.

Max learned that Victor Marineci was getting ready to organize a major demonstration in front of the Palace of the Parliament to denounce the nonchalance, the lack of effort, the ineffectiveness of the Romanian police when it came to tackling crimes against the Roma. Marineci, answering a question from a journalist on why the authorities were so slow to act, had quoted an old myth, still alive fifteen years after the fall of Ceauşescu's regime. Supposedly, the Securitate had recruited informants, rats, spies, and torturers from within the Romani population. Ceauşescu, rumoured to be a Rom himself, chose among his own people those who'd practise the dark arts for his regime. For some, the Roma followed satanic rituals, drank the blood of *gadjo* children, and provoked earthquakes. Thankfully, the Roma had reached Europe after the great pestilences of the Middle Ages, or they would have been declared responsible for those, as well — instead of the Jews.

At breakfast Max sat at a rear table in a greasy spoon, his back against a window but still able to see the front door in the reflection of a mirror. He got the house special: toast, bacon, hash browns, and a couple of fried eggs. Max had located the washroom as soon as he'd entered, as well as the emergency exit, which led to the parking lot. This was no time to be careless.

He couldn't stop thinking about Kevin and his family. The blessed period in New York when he'd used to pop by the Dandurand house, arms laden with gifts. He feared Gabrielle's reaction when she learned his true identity. The venerated uncle now a notorious criminal. Max felt naked all of a sudden. His past revealed to everyone, his secrets bared to all. For a thief, a con man whose fuel was illusions and lies, this was the worst possible sentence. Max, who'd wanted to help this family, had only managed to slowly tear it apart.

And to destroy Caroline.

Back in New York, he couldn't remember ever seeing her without a pen in her hand, scribbling down notes or concentrating in front of a computer screen. After the rivière Saqawigan tragedy, Caroline had lost all interest in what used to be her driving passion. Journalism became meaningless to her; what used to be a pleasure became a chore. She worked on fewer and fewer contracts. And soon enough, the phone stopped ringing. *What would be the point, anyway?* Caroline seemed to be thinking. She no longer turned her computer on, no longer took notes about everything and nothing. She had stopped looking at the world through the eyes of a journalist. She had become completely disinterested in other human beings and circled the wagons around her grief. She had then begun to drink immoderately.

While Caroline drew back into herself, Kevin had begun training again. Through running he tried to exorcise his demons, free himself from guilt. The feeling that he'd ruined everything, his athletic career, his perfect family, his wife, his daughter, his son, whom he had so adored.

His father.

From far away, a broken-hearted Max had seen his two friends felled by grief and felt completely powerless to help.

The loss of Raymond and Sacha caused much collateral damage. To the silences were added absences. Two strangers who now rarely shared a meal and almost never a bed. Separation, divorce? It seemed like the simplest solution. But Kevin and Caroline had held on to their marriage as if it were the last life preserver in an endless shipwreck. Of Sacha, all that was left were pictures on every wall of that sky-blue room neither of them had the courage to repaint. It became an altar, a mausoleum, where Kevin and Caroline went to gather themselves.

Another victim of the tragedy was Gabrielle. Over one day to the next, the girl had simply ceased to exist. Sacha's memory was all that mattered to her parents, and they had no more room for Gabrielle. When she'd become a teenager, things could have gone from bad to worse, but surprisingly, she kept control over her life. She was the one to convince Kevin to leave Caroline, since the couple couldn't seem to come to a decision. Gabrielle and her father settled in a condominium in Old Montreal. After Nordopak was bought out, Kevin had started searching for a job. His Olympic past gave him a shred of notoriety, enough to get a job as a physical education teacher at a local high school. The life he'd lived with Caroline he continued with his daughter; they sought each other for comfort and reassurance.

After breakfast, Max wandered through the city. He saw nothing at all of Grand Forks; his sight was turned inward, centred on his solitude. Being a fugitive was making him realize, once again but perhaps more cruelly than at other times, the futility of his life. For years he'd had the impression of leaving in his wake only sadness and desolation, though all the while he'd tried to convince himself of the opposite. He'd fallen back on a very peculiar type of morality that allowed him to justify all the pain he had caused, not to mention all the people he'd exploited to suit his own ends, all the Susans, the Isabels he'd lied to over the years.

Max dropped heavily onto a bench outside a pharmacy. He was pathetic, insignificant. He always had been, would always be.

Under another counterfeit identity, Max rented a Pontiac from Hertz before heading for Manitoba. A few kilometres from the Canadian border, he abandoned the car in a mall parking lot, where another vehicle was waiting for him, this one left by his friend, Ted Duvall, with whom he'd gotten in touch from Brussels. Under the front seat were a new passport and a driver's licence. In the trunk, hockey jerseys. Max, a businessman returning from a fruitless sales trip to an American wholesaler.

At the Emerson crossing, named for a small village near the Canadian border, the officer examined Max's unsold stock more intently than his fake passport. He looked through the shirts and seemed sincerely sorry for the salesman's poor results.

"The NHL strike's been over for a while, so I thought people would be back into hockey," Max explained.

The officer held a shirt in his hands and smiled. "The Blackhawks. My favourite team."

Max tried to give him the shirt, but the officer refused, saying he'd be accused of taking a bribe.

A few questions, and Max was waved through.

Perhaps the Roma's greatest problem was literacy. Most Roma couldn't read or write, a contributing factor to marginalization. Romani families hesitated to send their children to *gadjo* schools, which they saw as tools of assimilation, often rightly so. And thus children weren't educated, or only occasionally, when laws in place forced them to. Little Romani children sat at the back of the class, ignored by teachers who preferred to concentrate on other students. Flexibility was the solution. And so, across Europe, several initiatives saw the light of day, funded by patrons or organizations intent on the development of Romani autonomy. In some cases, the classroom — teacher, blackboard, and all — would go to the Roma instead of the Roma going to the classroom. Ioan Costinar had crossed the Atlantic to fund these initiatives. The trip that had cost him his life wasn't his first journey, far from it, but perhaps it was his most important. Romania was mounting its dossier for admission into the European Union. The select club would soon open its doors, a golden opportunity for the Roma. Education would give them a chance to pull themselves out of their endemic misery and take advantage of the opportunities offered by a politically unified Europe.

Before Max had left Romania, Toma Boerescu had told him how Costinar first met Romanichals just outside

Chicago. Beginning in the nineteenth century, Roma from Great Britain had settled in villages in Illinois. Some of them even still lived a nomadic lifestyle, travelling across the border to Canada and back, enormous aluminum caravans hitched to their 4x4s. They were a prosperous community — one of the largest casinos in Atlantic City was owned by Romanichals — who hadn't lost their language or their culture, unlike many other European migrant communities. Spared from Hitler's atrocities — called the *porajmos* in Romani, the "devouring" — and from the subsequent Eastern European dictatorships, American Roma did not suffer from an acculturation similar to that of their overseas compatriots. Ironically, the country known for being a melting pot had given North American Roma an opportunity for wealth while still protecting their culture. It remained relatively intact, so much so that a nineteenth-century Rom wouldn't have considered his future compatriots alien in their behaviour.

After fundraising and giving a few speeches, Ioan Costinar had flown to Winnipeg, where a representative of the Vlach-Roma, a clan distinct from the American Romanichals, was waiting for him. They were originally from Romania and had been in Canada since the early twentieth century. Former slaves emancipated by the Romanian government, they'd travelled through Europe and across the Atlantic before settling all over North America. Contrary to the Romanichals, the Vlach-Roma had lived sedentary lives since the Second World War, which didn't stop them from hitting the road from time to time.

Costinar had also met with representatives of the Romungere community, Roma who'd found refuge in Canada after 1956, following the Soviet invasion of Hungary.

Three prosperous clans, all well integrated into North American society, all receptive to Costinar's plea to help Romanian Roma.

And yet in Manitoba, death was waiting for him.

Why kill him? What was the purpose of the assassins? Max had no idea. But he understood why the killers had acted in Canada instead of Romania. Laura, Micula, and the Roma dead in the Zăbrăuți Street fire had all been easy hits to orchestrate. However, in Europe, a man like Costinar, a high-profile political player, would be under a constant protective detail. In Canada, though, the security measures would be relaxed, since Costinar was touring in relative anonymity. He wasn't an internationally renowned political figure, not yet, and he was travelling mostly to meet private philanthropists. The Roma Committee was looking to extended its support base outside Europe, most particularly in countries where helping Roma wasn't as controversial a subject as it was in Eastern Europe, France, and Germany.

One thing was certain, however. This wasn't some random act of violence. The killers hadn't tried to hide their crime by pinning it on the back of a deranged loner. No, Costinar's murder had been the result of a coordinated operation, carefully planned, implicating many people. The crime felt more like an organized terrorist act than an isolated gesture by a man made mad by his demons or manipulated by obscure forces.

Max still needed to figure out Kevin's role in this whole story. His relationship with Costinar's killers, or with those who were trying to reveal the truth.

"And we're practically cousins, he and I," Cosmin Micula had told Max. "His mother was Romanian, did you know?"

21

Max arranged to meet with Sergeant Phil Garrison of the RCMP in front of a Saint Boniface liquor store. Garrison had volunteered for the force's Christmas decoration party and was on refreshments duty. Arms filled with bottles, he placed his bags on the hood of his car and turned to shake Max's hand.

"Mark Callaghan? Nice to meet you."

Garrison was open to lunch on Main Street. The sergeant had an hour to chat but not a minute more. He laughed. "My colleagues are anxiously waiting for me."

A ruddy-faced man whose belly had grown along with the stripes on his shoulders, though he was still physically strong. An archetypal RCMP officer. Max could imagine him on a brochure. Did he know

Marilyn Burgess? Probably not. While Max was sure pictures of him had circulated in every local RCMP office in Canada, the rank and file rarely paid attention to wanted posters. In Winnipeg, Garrison had other fish to fry — that much was clear. He wasn't focused on catching international criminals still believed to be in Romania.

Max claimed he was a journalist on sabbatical, researching a book on the Canadian Romani community. He was currently working on a chapter about Ioan Costinar. Garrison had been part of the team who'd investigated the murder.

"It was a spectacular crime. To me it looked like someone wanted to settle a score. Two men stopped their car alongside Costinar's at a red light. A single shot from a man in the back seat. Costinar was struck in the head. They used a Walther P99, a professional's weapon. There was blood everywhere ..."

Costinar's driver hadn't panicked; he'd peeled off straight for the hospital. But by the time he got there, Costinar was already dead.

"We found his ears next to his body on the back seat. Covered in blood."

"His ears?"

Prosthetics, Garrison explained. Synthetic material made to imitate skin. He'd lost his ears as a young man in a torture room at Rahova Prison. Costinar, another one of Ceauşescu's victims.

"The poor man took them off before going to bed at night, like dentures or a pair of glasses. Awful, right?"

"And the killers?"

"Not a trace."

Garrison knew Costinar had been in Winnipeg to raise funds. He had interrogated everyone the Romani leader had spoken with before meeting his untimely end. He'd even gone to Chicago to talk with Romani community leaders there, but no dice. They were all shocked, saddened, revolted. And they all had iron-clad alibis. It had been a real professional job.

"A hit, then? Sponsored by someone?"

"That was our conclusion. A perfectly executed hit."

Of course, they'd gone over every inch of the crime scene and interrogated the few witnesses. The bullet found in Costinar's body was sent to the United States for analysis: no previous crime had been committed with the same weapon. Another dead end.

"And you spoke to his widow?"

"Laura. Yes, I called her. She was terribly distraught." His face darkened. "And they got her, too, in the end."

Garrison knew about the killing in Bucharest, of course. Thankfully, he wasn't drawing a line between Max O'Brien, the number one suspect, and this journalist come to ask him questions ...

"Do you think the crimes are connected?"

Garrison shrugged. He didn't want to talk about it. He looked at his watch. He was anxious to get back to the office.

Max hesitated, then asked, "Do you think all the Roma you spoke to told you the truth?"

"The truth?"

"I've been told they like taking care of their own problems internally."

232

"The Roma collaborated with our investigation in an absolutely impeccable manner. The murder revolted them. They wanted to find those responsible as much as we did."

"I was referring to their reputation of hiding things from the *gadje*. A way of protecting themselves. Do you see what I mean?"

Garrison smiled. "No, they didn't lie to me, let me assure you."

"Lying is an art."

"I know how to recognize a liar when I see one."

"Still …"

"I come from a Vlach-Roma family. I speak Romani fluently. That's why I was put on the case." Garrison smiled at Max's surprised air. He glanced at his watch and sighed. "Fine, fine. I'll let them decorate the tree without me. Come."

Max left his Subaru behind and climbed into Garrison's patrol car. Soon Winnipeg and its large avenues gave way to seemingly endless fields covered in snow. Garrison told how his grandfather and his family had used to live in a mobile home and how they had followed carnivals and amusement parks across Canada and the United States. Garrison still travelled a little. Every summer he and his family drove all the way to Sainte-Anne-de-Beaupré near Quebec City. It was a Romani pilgrimage as important for North American Roma as the one in Saintes-Maries-de-la-Mer was for Europeans.

"Which doesn't mean we don't practise our own religion," he added.

Romaníya, inspired by Hinduism.

"Or respect *Kris romani*, the traditional Romani tribunals. Of course, participating in a *kris* doesn't mean you believe it has precedence over an actual *gadjo* tribunal."

From the Greek *krisis*, meaning "judgment," it was more of a mediation instrument than a tribunal. The *Kris romani* also played the role of a proto-parliament, a place for the Roma to hash out issues of concern.

The two men drove for a time, then Max asked, "Who do you think had it in for him? Ioan Costinar, I mean."

"Skinheads, neo-Nazis, anti-Roma radicals — in other words, Romanian extreme right-wing groups. They're probably behind Laura's murder, as well."

"Do you really think they're sufficiently organized to carry out such a complicated operation?"

Max had his doubts. Garrison shared them. So who could it have been?

Garrison finally answered. "Perhaps the Romanian government itself."

Max had had the same thought. To many, including Toma Boerescu, the fall of the Ceauşescu regime was little more than a palace coup. The pretenders to the throne had harnessed popular anger to get rid of the old dictator. Romania was the only country in Eastern Europe whose transition out of communism had been so violent. Since Ceauşescu's execution, the situation of the Roma had worsened. And probably that of mainstream Romanians, as well. Max remembered reading somewhere that in

1999 two-thirds of Romanians were at least a little wistful about life under Ceauşescu, despite the Securitate and the absence of freedom. After all, their democracy was no more than an exercise in the redistribution of power to former apparatchiks. Boerescu had spoken the truth plainly. The country had replaced the benefits of communism with the drawbacks of capitalism.

Phil Garrison's coming in with a stranger raised a few eyebrows in the village. They were sedentary Romani here, the policeman explained. Six generations since the Vlach-Roma first came. Three individuals walked out of a bungalow to greet Garrison and Max. Their hard eyes half hidden behind their hats, all three of them with thick moustaches. To their right, another man washed an enormous Chrysler by hand. He stopped, looked at them, hose in hand. Everyone watched the newcomers without saying a word.

In Romani, Garrison asked to see Jennifer. One of the men gestured toward the field behind them, and a troop of children ran in that direction. A brick home became visible behind a bouquet of trees. A young woman came out of it, chalk in hand.

"Jennifer works for the Woodlands School Board," Garrison explained. "She's responsible for the integration of recently immigrated Roma. She teaches them how to read and write."

The newcomers were refugees from persecution in the Czech Republic. They had come to Canada in 1997, under intense scrutiny after a number of Canadian media types had repeated tired old Romani clichés. While other waves of immigration had taken place in relative anonymity, the arrival of the Roma occurred in the public eye. Their integration thus became a priority for politicians, who sought to make sure they quickly joined the ranks of the eighty thousand or so Roma already well integrated into Canadian society. Jennifer was one of the people called upon to help this process along.

"Roma tend to blend in with the culture that welcomes them," Garrison explained. "In Muslim countries, they're Muslims. With Catholics, they become Catholics. In the past few years, many of us here have converted to Pentecostalism."

They also picked names based on common *gadjo* ones in their community of choice. Jean-Baptiste "Django" Reinhardt, for example, the inventor of Romani jazz. Or the guitarist Ricardo Baliardo, nicknamed Manitas de Plata. The Roma often changed names according to the country they travelled through. Today Dumont or Villard in a suburb of Paris. Tomorrow, in Great Britain or Canada, they became Walker or … Garrison.

A tradition of adapting. The Roma were history's chameleons.

The young woman had accompanied Ioan Costinar during his visit. The murder had happened on his way to the Winnipeg airport after three days spent with the Vlach-Roma of Woodlands and surrounding municipalities.

"What was his attitude like at the time?" Max asked. "Did he seem nervous? Did he feel threatened?"

"No, quite the opposite. He really enjoyed his stay. And everyone loved him."

So the hit had come from elsewhere and likely had nothing at all to do with the communities Costinar was visiting. The killers had chosen Manitoba for tactical reasons. Max was coming to the same conclusion as Garrison: a well-planned crime executed by professionals. Like the murder of Laura. And Kevin's cousin, Cosmin Micula, the photographer.

"We went over a list of all travellers who came into Winnipeg by plane over the few days before the murder with a fine-toothed comb. We looked at everyone who'd rented a car either downtown or from the airport."

Jennifer pulled a large binder from behind her desk filled with pictures taken during Costinar's visit. Max recognized the Romani leader. The man seemed happy, radiant even. Pictures of him holding an oversized cheque, surrounded by community leaders. Others were of him seated at a table, chatting away with his hosts. Max also recognized Jennifer, her hair cut short back then. She pointed to the picture of a man near Costinar with a shaved head. His driver and bodyguard, she said, the man at the wheel of his car who'd rushed him to the hospital, only to get there too late to save his boss's life.

Max looked most attentively at the un-staged photographs. Costinar embracing a friend or smiling at a joke. And in one, Max recognized a silhouette, someone who seemed familiar. He asked Jennifer, who'd flipped right by it, to go back.

No, it couldn't be possible.

Max found other pictures of the same event, and there he was, the same man, but this time there couldn't be any question. A man in a well-tailored suit shaking Ioan Costinar's hand.

Raymond Dandurand.

22

Bucharest, October 20, 1956

Bear handlers, musicians, and singers had travelled all the way from the Carpathian Mountains. Entire families in their colourful clothes making their way toward Bucharest. The *vôrdônă* trailed, one behind the other, on the long roads that stretched between the capital and the north of the country. On the shores of Lake Tei, tents had been raised, some absolutely gigantic. Marquee tents around which dozens of children played. Romanians avoided the site. For this weekend, they'd abandoned the lake to the Roma. The police watched from a distance.

Traffic had been diverted on Barbu Văcărescu Boulevard. Identity checkpoints farther up the road, around an enormous house surrounded by trees. In that house, since the previous spring, a certain Emil Rosca lived. Turrets, dormers, and colonnades in an Arabian decor. A castle of sorts, pushing kitsch to its absolute limit. Inside, a ballroom, a great staircase, all of it lit by chandeliers that would have been at home in Buckingham Palace.

The whole place felt like living in a layer cake. Emil had inherited it from Mircea Remescu, King of the Soroca Roma, who'd used the place as a pied-à-terre when visiting Bucharest.

A number of Roma had already settled nearby, families of his own *kumpaníya* and of others, as well. They lived in more modest homes so as not to cast shade on Emil.

The accordionist from Auschwitz was now thirty years old. At the recent *Kris romani*, the *bulibasha* of the Wallachia Kalderash had become the leader of all Romanian Roma, despite his young age. He had thus taken up his father's mantle. The others respected him as they had respected his father. Unfortunately, his power was limited to his own community and meant nothing to the *gadjo* authorities. Of course, thanks to the support Emil had lent to the Romanian government since his return from Vorkuta, he had friends in the halls of power. But the Romani leader was disappointed by the current leaders. He'd been promised Romanestan, and his people were still waiting for it. And yet Emil had fulfilled his end of the bargain. He'd supported collectivization of agricultural land. When those opposing the regime had found refuge in the Carpathian Mountains, using the inhospitable landscape as a base of operation for sabotage and violence, the Roma had lent no help. They hadn't hid those people or supplied them with food or weapons — something they'd done for partisans throughout the war.

There was no doubt the situation of the Roma had improved. Despite collectivization, the Roma could still work seasonally, just as Ceauşescu had promised in Vorkuta. And the regime guaranteed them work in the country's new economy. Low-paying jobs, unfortunately, but jobs that made the Roma full-fledged citizens, integrating them into Romanian society.

What was more, Emil could count on the discreet but efficient support of the government, which dissuaded his opponents during the assemblies of the *Kris romani*. The Securitate hadn't intervened, but the Roma knew it was there, close by, in the shadows, threatening. In his moments of doubt, Emil wondered whether he'd re-created among his people the same sort of dictatorship the Communist Party was imposing on Romanians.

More unpleasant still, Emil sometimes had the feeling he was becoming a *gadjo*. He almost never travelled anymore — even if he had the permission of the authorities — preferring the comfort of his Bucharest home to the inconveniences of the road. Emil was becoming less interested in the numerous social occasions he was invited to. It was a smokescreen, another one.

And now another betrayal. He'd learned how to read in order to be able to decode without outside help the letters and notes his friend, Nicolae Ceauşescu, sent him. Emil had applied himself. All these scribbles had only confused him at first, giving him headaches. But slowly, meaning emerged. Words, sentences — he could now understand documents sent from the various ministries. Any day now, he was expecting to be told the good news of the creation of Romanestan. But day after day the authorities pushed the date back.

"In good time" seemed to be Ceaușescu's motto.

And so, of all of Emil's dreams and ambitions, there wasn't much left. He had his little world, his luxury, which induced amnesia — the broken promises forgotten.

But on this day Emil had no intention of bemoaning his fate. It was a great moment for him. An important celebration: his marriage. Emil had fallen for a young Kalderash; she was just seventeen, from Târgu Mureș, at the foot of the Carpathians.

Of course, in his heart of hearts Christina was still his soulmate, his one true love. What was more, he'd learned the German woman had survived the war. Three months after his release from Vorkuta he'd discovered through Ceaușescu that Müller's widow had travelled west and been caught by American troops in April 1945. She'd managed to escape and had fled to Paraguay with some others from Auschwitz, including Josef Mengele. According to Nicolae, she'd married a notary from Asunción.

It was hard for Emil to believe, knowing how Christina felt about Mengele and the others, but he hadn't the means or the time to conduct his own search. Christina had survived, and that was all that mattered. He would never forget her, no matter the intensity of his attachment to Eugenia.

When they'd decided to live together, Emil had strictly followed Romani tradition. One night he sneaked into Eugenia's *kumpaniya* and "kidnapped" the young girl. He'd brought her back to Bucharest in the Mercedes he now drove, which inspired jealousy even among his party member friends. Eugenia's entire family were accomplices in the abduction, the *romni nashli*. An old Romani custom. Her parents had looked away so as not to see the suitor. Gunshots were fired in the air to add to the illusion.

The next day, in his shiny pre-war Citroën, Eugenia's father, a Kalderash who recycled scrap iron, King of the Roma of Târgu Mureș, had come to negotiate the union of his daughter with Emil, as per tradition. The two men determined the amount Emil should pay him to compensate for the loss of his daughter.

A great celebration was organized, with Eugenia's parents crying and wailing, according to custom, to demonstrate their grief at having been robbed of their child. A *plotska* followed a few days later. The bride received a necklace made of coins, given to her around a bottle of wine covered in a silk handkerchief.

Tonight, the *abiav*, the marriage itself. It, too, would conform to tradition. Among the community, before the *káko*, the clan elder, Emil and Eugenia would join hands and swear to be true and faithful to each other. After the ceremony, while the guests danced and drank to the tune of Romani music, the young couple would lock themselves into the nuptial suite in Emil's home …

"Might I have a private audience with the King of the Roma? Or must I content myself with the benediction you'll bestow on your subjects in just a few hours?"

Emil looked up.

Nicolae Ceaușescu stood before him, a bottle of champagne in hand. A smile on his emaciated face. Since Gheorghe Gheorghiu-Dej had replaced Petru Groza as head of state in 1952, Emil's friend had quickly risen in rank. He now sat on the Politburo of the Romanian Communist Party. Groza and Ceaușescu had met in a camp during the war. Former cellmates now leading the country, following the example Stalin had set. The young, timid activist who couldn't speak without a stutter, who'd been little more than a boy when they first met in the forests of Vorkuta, had transformed himself into a cunning politician.

While Emil was on poor terms with many apparatchiks, he liked Ceaușescu. And the man returned the favour. The Roma, meanwhile, appreciated the influence Emil exerted over this important political player, which explained, in addition to his family's origin, the decisive role Emil played among the Romanian Roma.

When a policy was proposed to house the Roma in depressing apartment buildings, for example, Emil had intervened. He'd patiently explained to Nicolae, with utmost seriousness, that the Roma couldn't tolerate a woman walking over their heads. Ceaușescu had burst out laughing. According to Emil, because of this ancient custom, the Roma could only live in one-storey homes. This complicated their integration into urban environments. Ceaușescu applied pressure, successfully, on the minister who'd come up with the plan.

Later, when the government had proposed to take Romani children away from their families so that they might receive a socialist education from the state,

Emil once again got involved. Family was sacred to the Roma. Yes, Emil had learned to read and saw the immense benefits of learning how to read and write. But he certainly couldn't consent to placing the future of the Kalderash in peril by allowing the state to take their children and turn them into second-class *gadje*. Once again, Nicolae made sure his friend's proposal won the day.

Now, Ceaușescu came forward and the two men embraced. Despite his good mood, the Romanian seemed tired. Exhausted, in fact. Emil, who now read the newspaper, knew that the government was fighting tooth and nail to maintain its independence from Moscow. Soviet politicians had learned a lesson from their conflict with Yugoslavia. The Soviets were only just beginning to rebuild their relationship with Marshal Tito. And so the struggle for autonomy was a daily battle, which Gheorghui-Dej's regime wasn't certain it could win. What preoccupied Romanian leaders most of all, Emil knew, was de-Stalinization, which the Romanian regime opposed.

"Nikita Khrushchev is making you thin, Nicolae! The Russians are ruining your appetite."

Ceaușescu smiled. He was seated near the low table. On it, an immense Bohemian crystal vase. He struggled to pop open the champagne. "You're like my wife, Elena. I can't hide anything from you."

As Ceaușescu gained in power, the little seamstress had increased her influence over her husband. Emil had never met her; according to what he'd heard, she despised the Roma.

The bottle popped open like a gunshot. Champagne poured out onto the table. Emil brought his glass over, which Nicolae filled to the brim.

"Long life to the *bulibasha* of Romania …"

"And the government's second-in-command!" Emil emptied his glass in a single gulp and dashed it against the wall, where it shattered. "That's what the Russians will do with Gheorghiu-Dej!"

Ceaușescu shook his head. "No, no …"

"You're playing with fire."

"I agree with you, Emil. It's a risk. But one that might just be very profitable in the end. At least that's Gheorghe's opinion. And the old fox hasn't been wrong yet!"

Since the end of the war, Romania's economy had grown more than any other country in Eastern Europe's. While Poland, Hungary, and Czechoslovakia, for example, couldn't pull themselves out of postwar misery, Romania's agriculture and economy were growing year after year. The country had more autonomy than its neighbours and could refuse Moscow's generosity.

"We must at all cost avoid annoying the Russians," Ceaușescu continued. "They can be so resentful …"

Gheorghe Pintilie and Oleg Charvadze, the two emissaries from Moscow who'd visited Vorkuta in 1949, had lost their influence since Khrushchev had come to power. A new generation now occupied the offices and dachas. Meanwhile, in Romania, Gheorghiu-Dej wasn't a fan of the new Russian leader, nor was Ceaușescu. When Khrushchev had come on an official visit, he'd mocked Romanian farmers for the methods they used in milking their cows. Ceaușescu had taken great offence to this. Instead of accompanying Khrushchev all the way to Braşov, Ceauşescu had gotten off at the next railway station and taken another train straight back to Bucharest. Certainly, that had done nothing to improve the relationship between the two nations.

Hungary was also rattling its sabre but was going about it the wrong way, in Ceauşescu's view. It was attracting world attention to the failures of Soviet policies. Hungary was thinking of turning its back on socialism as a solution to its problems, which Moscow would, of course, never tolerate. Hungarians hadn't forgiven Stalin for refusing Marshall Plan funds, which had so helped Western Europe get back on its feet from the devastation left by the war. Romanians had also had enough of the Soviets' tantrums, but the country was adopting a different approach. It would be even more socialist than its big brother. And, above all, it would avoid confronting the Soviet Union on the world stage.

It was a strategy that seemed to be working, as of now. In Romania, individual freedoms, be they movement or association, were severely repressed. More severely still than in the Soviet Union, especially since de-Stalinization. Collectivization had been more thorough in Romania than in the Soviet Union. However, on the international stage, Gheorghiu-Dej was looking for new friends.

"The United States?" Emil asked.

"As well as France and Great Britain. Countries that seek by any means to stand in Moscow's way."

And countries that couldn't care less about the living conditions of Romanians, Emil thought. Doubly true for the Roma. Who took care of the Roma, in the end?

No one.

Except for his friend, Nicolae.

Emil grabbed another glass. Ceauşescu poured him a drink. The two men toasted to their friendship and Romania's future.

"And the future of Romanestan!" Emil added.

Ceauşescu's face darkened. Always and still that same question. Emil needled his friend whenever he could on his unkept promise. Ceauşescu's excuses were becoming increasingly pathetic: geopolitics, border issues with Hungary …

Emil wondered whether Gheorghiu-Dej had any intention at all of respecting the promise his protégé had made. The Roma were more organized now than they had used to be. If Emil chose to gather his troops, to cause a little trouble here and there, he could easily create a serious problem for the Romanian government. Enough to destabilize the internal balance of power and justify Soviet intervention.

"A promise is a promise, Emil. The situation is more complicated than we had expected, but the project remains on the table."

Emil sighed. He was used to Ceauşescu's excuses by now.

"As long as I'm in government, you can be sure I'll have your interests at heart." The minister smiled. "Do you know what they're saying? That I have Gypsy blood in me."

Emil burst out laughing. "We might be cousins!"

23

In what way was Kevin's father involved in this whole affair? And what sort of relationship had he had with the Roma? A close connection, obviously, close enough to cross half the country to shake the hand of a public figure from Romania, practically unknown in North America despite his notoriety in certain circles in Europe. Surely, either the two men had met before, or Raymond Dandurand had had an in within the Vlach-Roma community. Had Kevin's mother kept tabs on old friends and political figures in her native Romania, leading to a meeting between Raymond and Ioan Costinar? But to what end? Max still remembered the story Kevin had told him about Raymond bringing Kevin to watch his mother's possessions burn on the riverbank. Roxanne's

Romanian past, gone forever. It was as if Raymond had wanted to erase his wife's origins.

Seeing his surprise, Jennifer showed Max a list of Roma living in Winnipeg and the surrounding area. Not a single name rang a bell. Neither Jennifer nor Sergeant Garrison knew Raymond, and neither of them had spoken to him when Costinar had visited. Jennifer, however, recalled the elegant man who'd shadowed the Romani leader at one event, although she hadn't spoken to him. Perhaps other members of the community knew him; they might give Max a clue concerning Raymond's reasons for being in Woodlands. Jennifer would ask around, as well, and keep Max in the loop.

Back in his room at the Fairmont Hotel, Max tallied the dates: only two weeks between Costinar's visit to Winnipeg and Raymond's death. Bankrupt, humiliated by the con he'd just fallen victim to, Raymond had reached Woodlands toward the end of March. Four days later Costinar was gunned down on his way to Winnipeg's airport — while Raymond was probably already back in Montreal. In April, Raymond pulled Sacha with him into the depths of rivière Saqawigan.

Were these events related? If so, how? Had Kevin played a role in these two tragedies? Was it now necessary to add the deaths of Sacha and Raymond to the murders of Laura, Micula, and the Zăbrăuți Street Roma? The edges of a plot were becoming visible, or so it seemed.

Max tried to consider every angle of this whole affair, and yet could find no meaning, nothing tying it all together. He was missing a piece of data, the keystone that would hold the edifice of truth together. And he was headed to Montreal to get Caroline to spit it out.

He drove all the way to North Bay and abandoned his Subaru in a Canadian Tire parking lot before continuing his trip by Greyhound. Soon enough rivière des Outaouais appeared under a sky heavy with clouds. A few kilometres north of Deep River, snow began to fall, first lightly, then abundantly. The driver slowed down, the cars behind following suit, as if all were suddenly participating in some ritual, some religious procession.

After a short night in a Best Western in the Ottawa suburbs, Max took yet another bus that dropped him off on boulevard Maisonneuve in Montreal, his back bent by three days of travel. The cold, humid weather reminded him of his childhood winters on rue Lajeunesse. It was no longer snowing. It was almost day. There were no taxis idling in front of the bus station. Max walked down rue Berri toward Old Montreal. He passed Chapelle Notre-Dame-de-Bon-Secours and stopped for a moment before it, seized by the memory of Raymond Dandurand's funeral four years earlier. The chapel's doors were locked. He would have liked to sit for a moment inside, to try to understand what sort of trouble Raymond, and now his son, Kevin, as well, had gotten themselves into. No point standing before a locked door. The chapel wasn't open for business.

Max suspected the accusations levied against Kevin had stirred up a wasp nest in Montreal. The media were hunting for the truth about Nordopak's bankruptcy, Kevin's potential role in the whole affair, and his friendship with a known criminal. The sort of high drama that would sell copies for weeks — a heady mixture of fraud, international crime, family tragedy, and the sickly scent of blood. Max couldn't just go knocking on Caroline's door; likely her apartment was under surveillance. And what was more, he'd have to find a way to explain everything. Max had little to offer her in terms of peace and comfort. All he could give Caroline were his regrets, and that wouldn't solve anything, wouldn't make anything better, just the opposite. And how could Caroline ever trust Max again? Or Kevin? Even if the murder accusation were untrue, they'd both lied, both betrayed her. She would never forgive them.

After serving breakfast, Refuge Sainte-Catherine put everyone back on the street in order to clean and prep the place for the evening meal. During the day, the volunteers could rest, take a moment to breathe, get ready for the rush hour.

Max walked around the block once, looking for surveillance, not noticing anything out of the ordinary. Outside the refuge, young men and women, lost at sea, packed together on the sidewalk, not knowing where to go to while away the day. Inside, other homeless men and women on washing-up duties were supervised by volunteers. They all ignored him. One of them, a man with grey hair in a musty ponytail, moved docilely away as Max made a beeline for the kitchen.

Caroline saw him first. She didn't seem surprised, as if she had been expecting his visit. Max grabbed two chairs and set them down on each side of a table in the dining room. They sat facing each other: time for confession.

He had expected she might be angry at him, at the whole world, or otherwise broken-hearted to the point of confusion. In fact, she seemed little more than discouraged.

Perhaps even desperate.

"Where is he?"

Truth, for once.

"Romania, probably. In the hands of very dangerous people. I don't know why they want him, why they've got it in for him, but I intend to find out."

He gave her a rundown of his time in Bucharest. His meeting with Cosmin Micula, Kevin's phone call, Laura Costinar's body. How he'd managed to flee thanks to Toma Boerescu.

He knew he was doing everything to avoid speaking about the elephant in the room: Kevin's criminal activities with his friend and mentor, Max O'Brien.

Caroline forced the issue. "Do you mind if I keep calling you Robert?"

Max closed his eyes. He'd anticipated this exact moment for months, years. It was just too hard to explain his past, to justify his actions. There were few good answers down that road.

"I'm responsible for what's happened to Kevin, what he's become. I led him down that path." Max sighed. "I wanted to help you, the three of you, really. But I went about it all wrong, and by the time I realized it, I'd painted myself into a corner."

He felt so discouraged, so miserable, engulfed by despair. "I wish I could do it all over again. From the very beginning, fix what I've broken."

"The scam against Raymond. That was Kevin's idea, wasn't it?"

Max raised his head. For the first time, he had his doubts. Caroline seemed to know more than she'd let on. Was it possible that …?

She confirmed his suspicious. "I knew. And I let it happen. I'm as guilty as you are."

Max didn't understand.

"The scam. He just wanted to get back at his father."

"Because Raymond didn't want to lend him money for the gym, right?"

Caroline sighed. She closed her eyes. "That was his excuse. But he would never have found the courage to go after his father if it hadn't been for …"

Max remained silent. This was all new to him.

"When we came back from New York —"

"What happened, exactly?"

"Raymond started flirting with me. At first I thought it was funny, that he was just messing around, wanting to make me feel at home. But then one night when he'd been drinking, he made advances, serious ones. He told me I deserved better than his son."

She fell silent. "I was pregnant with Kevin's child, and he was hitting on me as if I were some floozy he'd met in a bar. I told him to back off, to leave me alone, but he wouldn't."

"And you didn't tell Kevin?"

"At the time, no, I didn't. I was scared of how he'd react. And I felt guilty about dragging him back to Montreal, forcing him to make peace with his father." Caroline lowered her eyes. "But one day I couldn't help myself. I admitted everything. Kevin flew into a rage. I thought he was going to kill Raymond."

And that was when he'd decided to rob him.

Kevin had told her the truth then. About the lie he shared with Max, their desire to protect Caroline and Gabrielle. Max understood where things had gone from there. Kevin's motivation to rob his father, the gym simply a pretext. Raymond had gone too far; he'd committed an unforgivable offence. Kevin would make him pay dearly. In the end, though, his anger had turned against him. Kevin's father had had the last word.

"Raymond knew that Kevin was involved in the scam. I don't know how, but I'm sure of it."

Raymond's revenge had been complete: he'd driven off the bridge, Sacha in tow. An ultimate punishment, both to his son, and to Caroline, who'd refused him. Raymond died, yes, but he'd left desolation behind him.

Suddenly, Max caught movement out of the corner of his eye. On the other side of the cafeteria, something was going on. Max had been careless; he hadn't located his emergency exit before sitting down. Through the kitchen maybe. Not a minute to lose. Ignoring Caroline, he jumped to his feet and ran to the far end of the room, just as two men reached him. He was about to kick through the door when he felt a hand on his shoulder. He whipped around. It was the volunteer with the pony-tail. He didn't seem as old now. Or as docile.

Max threw a punch. The man parried and swung him around in a shoulder lock. Max tried to push him off, but the volunteer threw him to the ground with disconcerting ease. He felt a jolt through his back as his arm was twisted behind him. The two other men leaned over him, watching him like a wounded beast. Max at their mercy. His face against the floor, he heard footsteps, and from the corner of his eye, a woman's high-heeled shoe.

Marilyn Burgess.

She watched him writhing on the ground and smiled with satisfaction. "Welcome back to Canada, Max O'Brien."

24

They dragged him into an unmarked car, handcuffs around his wrists. Max couldn't help but think of his nemesis, Luc Roberge, who would never get the satisfaction of putting his hands on the collar of the thief he'd been after his whole career. Max couldn't help but smile ruefully. Poor guy.

Another car was parked a bit farther off in the parking lot behind the refuge. The ponytailed volunteer's car. Max looked for Caroline. She was beside the service entrance, speaking with Marilyn Burgess, who was handing Caroline her business card. He tried to catch her eye. She didn't even glance at him. He couldn't believe he'd been so naive.

Despite his delicate situation, Max thought about what Caroline had just told him. Raymond, playing behind Kevin's back, belittling him to his wife, trying to rob him of what he loved most. Kevin had been right: Raymond tried to destroy everything that stood in his way. Max couldn't imagine what could drive a man to act so disgracefully toward his own child, especially since he'd been such a good father to Josée: protective, but not excessively so, attentive, respectful. The ideal father. Meanwhile, for a reason Max couldn't understand, Raymond's relationship with Kevin had been the polar opposite. The son had suffered mightily from his father's rejection, and in a sense, had always remained under the man's sway. Returning repeatedly to kiss the emperor's ring, to ask once more: "Have I done enough this time?" He couldn't stand his father, yet couldn't live without Raymond's approval.

Their conflict had created one more victim. Raymond had dragged his grandson with him into death. A scorched-earth tactic. Yes, he'd given up ground, yes, he'd lost a battle, but whatever victory Kevin had claimed tasted only of ash. Raymond had destroyed Kevin's relationship with Caroline, taken Sacha away from him, and annihilated their futures, their dreams.

Raymond's punishment, cruel and irreversible, existed in a context Max couldn't quite grasp. Roxanne, of Romanian origin, her life cut short one October afternoon. Ioan Costinar, a murdered Romani politician friend of Raymond Dandurand, a successful businessman who'd fallen victim to a scam. Kevin, a hostage in Romania, accused of murdering Laura Costinar, Cosmin Micula, and twenty-three Roma in Ferentari. The Roma, Romania, death — whatever angle you looked at it from, those three elements were never far.

A room without an exit. A closed circuit. Max couldn't find the door, the opening, the ray of light. He peered at the enigma from every angle, and it seemed just as obscure. From the stranger Kevin had met in the Bucharest coffee shop to Raymond's presence at a fundraising cocktail affair for Ioan Costinar, it was all a series of unsolvable mysteries, of coincidences, of backroom intrigue whose rules he couldn't divine. There had to be a thread, of course, but he didn't know where to pull to unravel it. And if he ended up locked behind bars, there would be no way to figure any of it out.

Marilyn Burgess sat in the front, one of her goons driving and the other seated next to Max in the back seat. They turned onto rue Sherbrooke, heading east. The police light had been placed on the roof over the driver's head. Max evaluated his options. He could try to force his way out of the car, especially since the ponytailed man wasn't part of the escort. Although Max figured the other men would also likely be able to beat him to a pulp.

And what could he do, really? He might, for example, jump out of the car at a red light. But even if he managed to flee, he was handcuffed and the men were certainly armed. Still, even a small chance at avoiding extradition to Romania might be worth it.

Burgess glanced at him in the rearview mirror, guessing his intentions.

"There are two tail cars. You make a wrong move and you're a dead man."

The goon to his left laughed. The driver snickered. Clearly, they were a bunch of comedians.

Suddenly, to Max's surprise, the car veered left into an alley. Burgess didn't bat an eye. They kept going to an even narrower alley between two buildings, then came out on rue Jean-Talon and drove across it to a third alleyway. As if the driver were trying to lose a tail, he constantly checked the rearview mirror. Then, with no one in sight, the car turned into a car wash, its gate bearing a sign stating that it was closed for repairs. Once inside, a man in overalls lowered the garage door behind the car.

What was this all about?

As soon as the car came to a stop, Burgess stepped out and opened Max's door. "Let's go."

Intrigued, Max got out of the car. After taking his handcuffs off, Burgess guided him toward the manager's office, giving orders to her colleagues in a language Max didn't recognize.

Burgess noticed his surprise. "A week in the Balkans and you still haven't developed an ear for Romani!" She burst out laughing at her captive's confused air.

What were Roma doing here?

Burgess opened the door to the office. "I'm Keja of the Lovari clan." She offered her hand.

After a moment's hesitation, Max shook it.

Keja was her Romani name, the young woman added, which she only used in the presence of her compatriots. For the investigation, she preferred her pseudonym, Burgess.

"The investigation?"

"In 1971 in London, the Roma created an international parliament inspired by the traditional *Kris romani*. We chose a hymn, a flag, and created an organization that was to supervise the growth and development of Romani clans around the world — the World Romani Congress."

She paused for a moment before continuing. "The Roma are a people, recognized by the United Nations, but the only people who've never gone to war with anybody. Simply because we have no territory to defend." Burgess went around the table. "A nation without a home doesn't need an army, but it can't survive without information, without *intelligence*. In the 1980s, the Roma created a secret service. Of course, we didn't shout it over the rooftops."

"So you're not with the RCMP …"

"We've got our people with them. As well as in the FBI and elsewhere. Some police services have people who are either Roma or sympathetic to the Romani cause working on their staff."

"Including the Romanian police?"

"Of course."

The intelligence unit Marilyn Burgess was talking about was a tributary of the old Indian secret services — the original home of the Romani Diaspora — following an agreement with Indira Gandhi's government. Over the past few years, the organization had worked autonomously without reporting to anyone. It saw its mission as the protection of all Roma from potential sources of danger. Currently, that danger seemed to be the resurgence of anti-Romani racism in Eastern Europe and elsewhere.

"The world has always walked over us, our bodies fed to the dogs. Our organization is here to make sure that never happens again."

Two days earlier Phil Garrison, an informant of theirs, had gotten in touch with Burgess, detailing the curious visit of a journalist on sabbatical. A man named Mark Callaghan. Bullshit, according to him. It became clear to Burgess that the man could only have been Max O'Brien, who, after successfully getting out of Romania, was continuing his investigation into the deaths of Ioan and Laura Costinar. Sooner or later, she knew he'd be coming to Montreal.

"And so we've been keeping tabs on Caroline."

"Does she know?"

"No. She still thinks we're with the RCMP. So does Josée Dandurand."

Disappointed by the glacial pace of the Romanian police's investigation of Kevin and his accomplice, Josée had returned to Paris. She'd kept in touch with Adrian Pavlenco and Marilyn Burgess.

"So what is it that you want from me, exactly?"

Burgess took a deep breath. "Ioan Costinar's murder was never resolved by the *gadjo* police. It'll be the same result with Laura's murder and the killing of twenty-three of our compatriots in Ferentari. We're certain that something ties these three crimes together, but the local police won't get anywhere. That's why we've gotten involved." She stared Max down. "We're convinced you and Kevin were set up by the real killers to take the fall."

An anti-Romani organization was behind it all, according to Burgess. They had to be stopped. Since the end of the Cold War, violence directed toward Eastern European Roma had been mostly spontaneous acts, sparked by racism and frustration. The Roma made good scapegoats. And since existing laws and political structures cared little for them …

However, forms of more organized violence were increasingly beginning to appear — in Romania in particular. No one knew who was behind it all.

Examples?

A mob of a thousand villagers had attempted to lynch the two hundred or so members of a Romani community after the death of a Romanian man. Just as they'd done in Hădăreni in 1993. A few hundred farmers burned the homes of several Roma near Făgăraș. Romani leaders regularly received death threats. Victor Marineci, for example, always travelled accompanied by bodyguards. An extremist group, the Gypsy Skinners, led a campaign of violence and terror against the Roma. After a soccer game, Romanian hooligans had started a riot against Roma and Arabs.

"And governments have been giving ideological cover to the violence, sometimes even perpetrating it, like what happened in Belgium in October 1999."

Attempting to discreetly rid themselves of newly arrived Slovakian Roma, police had trapped a few families, inviting them to register at the police station on the pretext of regularizing their situation in the territory — they'd even sent the invitation in Romani to hide their true intentions. At the same time, other police went through the local schools and took every Romani child out of the classrooms before sending everyone to the airport for deportation.

"It was the first ethnically motivated mass arrest in Europe since the Second World War."

The police officers even wrote the seat assignments of the deportees on their forearms with a felt marker.

"Remind you of anything?"

Not a single person responsible for this abject act faced any consequences, of course.

According to Burgess, there were similar cases all over Europe: from the Czech mayor building a wall to isolate "his" community from a Romani district to a Romanian senator demanding the creation of special colonies to better supervise the Roma.

"So how is Kevin involved in all of this?"

"By allying himself with Laura Costinar, he found himself in the centre of machinations that were out of his depth."

"Cosmin Micula mentioned that Laura knew who had murdered her husband. That she was trying to leave Romania for a safe haven where she might be able to denounce them."

Burgess sighed. "Kevin Dandurand recently developed an interest in the Roma. We don't know why. We also have no idea how he first got in touch with Cosmin Micula or why he recruited him. He wanted to get Laura out of the country, but he had something else in mind." She came near Max. "We're counting on you to help us find his true motivations. Let's join forces, Max O'Brien. Naturally, our work together must remain a secret."

"And you would trust a crook?"

"Why not? The new Indian government holds you in high esteem after your involvement in Kashmir." She smiled. "For us that's enough of a recommendation."

‡

A change of clothes awaited Max in another room. He became a businessman in casual business attire. The sort of man who'd been looking forward to his game of squash all week. When Max had changed and come out of the bathroom, he realized the car that had brought him to the car wash was gone. A brand-new Jeep Grand Cherokee had taken its place.

Sitting in the passenger seat, the ponytailed volunteer gestured Max over to get behind the wheel. A suitcase on his lap, the man offered his hand. "I'm Laetshi. Sorry for earlier."

"Lovari, like your friend?"

"Sinto. A German Rom." He smiled. "Over there they know me as Kurt Dönitz."

"Exchanging pseudonyms is always a nice sign of trust, right?"

Laetshi chuckled as he riffled through his briefcase. He pulled out several documents and handed them to Max. "Driver's licence, passport, credit card, cellphone. And you've got a full tank of gas."

"A gift from your organization? Where did you get the money for all these goodies? Surely not from reading palms and weaving baskets?"

"Any other questions?"

"Where do I sign?"

Laetshi chuckled again. Cheery fellows, these Roma.

"We'll be in touch. If you need help, you know where to reach us." The Sinto handed him a key. "The Sheraton on boulevard René-Lévesque. You have a suite."

"A bit too ostentatious maybe?"

"The surest way to be found is to try to hide."

Max wasn't about to disagree; if he moved around in broad daylight, he'd be less noticeable to those hanging out in dark corners hoping to find him.

"Be careful."

"Careful? Where did you learn my middle name?"

"*Latcho drom*, safe travels."

25

Bucharest, June 14, 1968

Like most Roma, Emil Rosca held farmers in con-
tempt. The support he'd offered to Ceauşescu's plan
for collectivization hadn't been a sacrifice or compromise for him — quite the opposite. The damn yokels
hated the Roma, in any case. And, anyway, Emil lived
off hunting and trapping. Or off whatever dead animals he could find. Birds that crashed into his house's
huge bay windows. He would prepare those, or the
deer the regime's cadres hit on their way to or from
their weekend retreats from Bucharest in their luxury
automobiles. From time to time, a Rom knocked on his
door with some dead animal to honour his protector,
his *bulibasha*. Others stole chickens that they brought
to him, as well.

These gifts were all cause for celebration, an opportunity to pull out the old *gormónya*, his Paolo Soprani, and play late into the night while Eugenia and their eldest daughter, Alina, prepared food inside — all the while keeping an eye on the family's newest baby. Around the fire the men tore at the burning meat, knives in their hands. Eugenia was responsible for the purity of the food. There would be no eating of pork, or even chicken, unless it had been stolen. Boar, however, was another story. And hedgehogs especially, *niglo*, a favourite of the Roma, hunted at night, killed with large metal rods and cooked in boiling water.

That night Emil was entertaining two guests.

The first was a Tshurari from Bulgaria who'd been living in France since the end of the war: Rossen Markov. The other, tall, blond, smiling, his skin so white it was almost pink, spoke with a Romani accent Emil couldn't quite locate. Maybe a Lovari accent, or Linguari, a clan of woodcarvers. The two men were stuffing their faces as if they hadn't eaten in months. As a Rom, Markov's having an appetite for hedgehog wasn't surprising. The other man, however ... *gadje* never acted like this tall blond man. Usually, they were disgusted by the Roma — and doubly so by what they ate.

Rossen Markov smiled at him; he seemed to guess what Emil was thinking and nodded in his friend's direction. "Paul has known the Roma forever. Before the war, when he was a child, he travelled across Europe with Dutch Kalderash. He was born in Holland and learned Romani with them. Learned how they lived."

Emil had been introduced to the man earlier but had forgotten his name. "Paul?"

"Paul Vaneker," Markov said, mouth full, smiling.

That name tickled something in Emil's mind. A vague memory. Yes, he remembered now. Auschwitz. What Christina Müller had told him about Himmler's interrogation of his father.

"The spy Himmler was trying to catch, right? That was you?"

"I worked with the British a little bit, trying to mobilize Romani resistance. When it comes to transporting a message, to gathering intelligence, no one's better than the Roma."

Many Sinti who'd settled in Alsace had been useful to the Allies because they spoke German, Vaneker told him. And in Italy the Americans were able to count on Romani resistance. On the Eastern Front, while the Wehrmacht worked to stem the Soviet offensive, the Roma sabotaged supply lines from behind enemy lines.

"Thanks to Paul and his team, the Russians were able to push back the Wehrmacht more rapidly," Markov said.

That explained why the Nazi leader had so wanted to put his hands around the throat of the Romani-sympathizing secret agent.

"My father saved your life," Emil declared.

Vaneker nodded without understanding.

"He knew where you were hiding, you and your men. He resisted, with his life, and kept the secret from Himmler.

The Dutchman hadn't known that.

"And you're still a spy, right? Against Ceaușescu this time?"

Markov pushed his plate away. "Paul and I haven't come to Bucharest to spy on anyone. Quite the opposite."

"Is the Securitate aware of your presence in Romania?"

"We mean you no harm, Emil. You've got nothing to fear."

The Romani leader studied the faces of the two visitors. The fire's dancing light made their features uneven. He couldn't tell whether they were being sincere or not.

"Nicolae Ceaușescu is my friend," Emil said finally. "More than a friend. A brother."

"We know that," Markov said. "We also know Romanian Roma respect you and your family's name."

"What do you want then?"

In a few words, Markov told him that things were changing in Eastern Europe. There had been Budapest, then the wall in Berlin, an unfortunate event. Other things had been moving quickly in the past few months, history in action. Alexander Dubček in Czechoslovakia dragging socialism in an entirely original direction under Moscow's supervision. Since 1948, Marshal Tito had been leading Yugoslavia without the consent of the Soviet big brother. And in Bucharest, Emil's friend, Ceaușescu, had replaced the Stalinist Gheorghiu-Dej. He'd softened the regime, abolished work camps, eased travel restrictions, stood up to the Russians. On the other side of the Iron Curtain, Dubček's and Ceaușescu's initiatives were attracting attention, doubly true because both countries' economies were growing much faster than in the other dictatorships of the proletariat.

"Socialism is reaching a watershed moment," Vaneker added. "Thanks to Romania and Czechoslovakia."

"The Iron Curtain will soon open," Markov added. "A few months from now, a few years at most."

"Europeans in Western Europe talk of expanding their economic relations to make it a political union one day," Vaneker explained. "Europe will become a single country. A confederation of states like the Soviet Union or the United States."

"And what does that change for the Roma?"

Markov got up and walked toward Emil. He wiped his mouth as if preparing to make a speech, then described his project to bring all Roma together in an international association. There were Roma all over the world, and in Europe especially, from east to west. And all Roma were beginning to realize their political power. In Prague, the Union of Czechoslovak Gypsies had forced Dubček to tackle issues that concerned the Roma. In France, since 1912, all Roma had had to carry an anthropometric passport with them, which recorded, among other things, their names, birthdates, and morphological details. That passport had just been abolished and would soon be eliminated in Belgium, as well.

"And that's not to mention television," Vaneker added. "It's been introduced in *gadjo* homes, but in *vôrdôná*, as well now."

An incredible means of communication that cared nothing for borders, he claimed. Thanks to television, Roma could now establish relationships with one another across Europe, no matter the diametrically opposed interests of the governments of the various countries they lived in.

Markov leaned toward the Roma leader. "Romanestan, Emil. The dream of all Roma, which the *gadje* have been promising us forever. You were a victim of their false promises, too, weren't you? Where is the country promised by your friend, Ceauşescu? Under the pillow of the beautiful Elena?"

Emil sighed. The Bulgarian was right. Ceauşescu had been in power for three years, and the project hadn't been mentioned once. Emil reminded him regularly, but he refused to honour his promise. And yet Ceauşescu didn't owe anyone anything now; he could make whatever decisions he wanted.

"We can't wait for the *gadje* anymore," Markov said. "We must organize. Roma, Sinti, Manush, Kalderash, Tshuraria … all Roma, no matter what country they've ended up in. With the support of the United Nations, we'll be able to change things."

"United Nations?"

"A process has begun to recognize the Romani nation, with the help of the Indian government."

"A nation without a territory!" Emil mocked.

Markov fell silent for a moment before finally saying, "The first objective of the International Gypsy Committee will be to force the German government to recognize the genocide of Roma during the last war."

"Hundreds of thousands of Roma assassinated in concentration camps," Vaneker added.

Emil sighed. The enthusiasm of the Bulgarian annoyed him. Of the Dutchman, as well. Of course, he felt cheated by Ceaușescu. Almost twenty years after Vorkuta, Romanian Kalderash were still waiting for their promised land. Sometimes he would glance at himself in a mirror and see the memory of the Nazi concentration camps in his eyes, the memory of what they'd done to his people; the anger and sadness he felt overwhelmed him. But the Roma were finding their own way to deal with their past, different than what Jews had chosen to do. The Jews kept reminding the world of the Holocaust that had victimized them. The Roma didn't want to remember, to be reminded of their *porajmos*. What the Jews were trying to exorcise through remembrance, the Roma were exorcising through forgetting. Not remembering the dark years, not looking back on that terrible period, not cheering for the heroes and martyrs of the unnameable butchery. And here was Rossen Markov wanting exactly the opposite — to remind the world of what the Roma had been trying hard to forget.

Later, in a car driven by Paul Vaneker, they rode down Republicii Boulevard, the only other traffic being a few Dacias, Skodas, and Ladas. In their ZIL limousines with tinted windows and small flags on their hoods, drivers ferried friends of the regime to meetings. Interested by the two men's ideas, Emil had agreed to accompany Markov and Vaneker to a meeting of Romanian Romani leaders. Emil was expecting the worst. They were barefoot kings, all of them, a Romani specialty. Screwballs who took advantage of *gadjo* naïveté to proclaim themselves lifelong leaders of a handful of Roma.

A bit like Ceaușescu had done with the *gadje*. Like Emil Rosca himself.

A left turn, heading south, then a right turn. The car was in Ferentari now, where military barracks had been built. Already they were showing signs of disrepair.

Seated in the back by himself, Emil recalled his car ride with the Soviet emissaries in Vorkuta. He had the uncomfortable impression of déjà vu. His Indian ancestors were perhaps right: every life is repeated, treading the same ruts.

The two men hadn't stopped talking since they'd left Emil's house. Liberty, democracy, representation, compensation ... they were both dreaming in Technicolor.

Emil looked behind them. He expected there might be a Securitate car, since his movements were sometimes under surveillance. His detail was likely on a break tonight.

"Your family's blood has fertilized Romanian soil," Markov said. "They're part of its history. The kings who lead the several clans will only follow a Rosca."

Markov was right. In Poland the Kwieks had wielded the same power. But by collaborating with the Nazis — Rudolf Kwiek was tried and convicted in 1947 — they'd discredited themselves, an error that Anton, Emil's father, hadn't committed. Anyway, the results were the same. Janusz Kwiek, Rudolf's rival, was crowned king by the archbishop of Kraków in 1937 before dying in Auschwitz. Anton's end was the same. Joseph XIII, the Czechoslovak Romani leader, was killed in Bergen-Belsen.

Emil felt immense pride at being part of a great family but wouldn't let himself be fooled so easily a second time by the promise of Romanestan, whatever Markov and Vaneker said. Back in Vorkuta, he should have done as his father had and spat in the Soviets' faces.

Vaneker stopped the car in front of a building. Several windows were lit up. "We want you to lead the Romanian committee. You could give it the national profile it deserves."

"You've got the wrong man. I've no taste for politics."

"Think of the future, Emil," Markov said.

A big word that, a big lie. Ceauşescu had promised him a future in 1949 and what had it got Emil? His clan and the Kalderash in general were excluded from power. Victims of racism. Forced to rot in unsanitary districts.

"I'm not your man. I want nothing to do with your promises."

Markov and Vaneker stopped talking, out of arguments, mercifully. If they wanted to dream, good for them. Emil didn't want to risk his life and the lives of his family for an illusion. He had no intention of raising the ire of Romanians toward the Roma further still.

They climbed the staircase to the third floor and walked through a dirty, poorly maintained corridor. Emil was becoming increasingly uncomfortable with this clandestine meeting. Sure, he hadn't seen a Securitate car. But sooner or later his friend, Nicolae, would be informed of his conversations with the two strangers. He'd been foolish, imprudent, to welcome them into his home.

Emil turned around. Markov and Vaneker stood back in the corridor, as if they didn't dare walk any farther.

"What's happening?"

"Apartment 328, Emil," Markov said. "They're waiting for you."

"You're not coming?"

"Go, Emil."

Emil hesitated for a moment before his curiosity got the better of him. He pushed open the door to a large room plunged in darkness. Emil had expected to see the usual collection of fools, but the place was deserted. Slowly, his eyes became used to the darkness. A desk. A sofa. And soon a silhouette near the window. A woman. She turned around.

Emil couldn't believe his eyes.

Christina Müller.

"Good evening, Emil," she said in German.

He closed the door behind him as she walked toward him. His hands shook, and Christina's whole body seemed to do the same. For a moment out of time, they inspected each other, ghosts of the camp between them. Christina wore her red hair short. Her scent filled the room, paralyzing Emil. Speechless, he closed his eyes. Eugenia would shake him awake soon, wouldn't she? It had to be a dream, or some new form of torture, a terrible joke.

Finally, Christina raised her hand and brushed his face, as she'd done so many times before, long ago in Auschwitz. The spell broke and Emil took her in his arms, holding her tight against him, before they fell together on the sofa, undressing each other without a word. Christina gave herself up to Emil's touch, just as she'd done in Birkenau among the belongings of the prisoners and the disappeared. In the half-light, they made love passionately. The years, the lives they'd lived, none of it changed what had first brought them colliding against each other in a place of death.

Finally, Emil rolled onto his back, taking Christina in his arms.

She looked at him steadily, savouring the moment. "When they told me they'd found you, I didn't believe it. I thought you were dead, another body in the camps."

"And you in Paraguay."

"What are you talking about?"

"With Josef Mengele and the others."

Christina smiled. Emil understood that Ceaușescu had lied to him. The Securitate, as well.

"We managed to get out of Berlin in the last hours of the war. Among the ruins …"

"We?"

"Matthias and me. You remember Matthias Kluge?"

The accountant.

In the last hours of Auschwitz, when Dr. Hans Leibrecht pushed Christina off the truck, Kluge was the one who saved her and took her with him as they fled.

After the war, there were long months of privation in a devastated Berlin. A hunt was on for former Nazis. Matthias had been able to hide. And, slowly, little by little, a form of normalcy returned. The trial of those responsible for the horrors of the war in Nuremberg came and went. Reconstruction could begin. To many it was time to simply rebuild the present and put the past behind.

As with the Roma, so, too, with the Germans, Emil thought. To forget. To fall silent. To hide the painful events in the depths of memory.

"Matthias is a businessman now. He's been quite successful."

Emil couldn't believe the bastard was still alive, and rich to boot. You had to wonder who'd actually won the war. While Emil had spent four years in a gulag, Kluge was lining his pockets.

God was a *gadjo* — there was no doubt about it.

"You married?" Emil asked.

Not immediately. After the war ended, Matthias and Christina had lost sight of each other for a time. Then, in 1950, they met again at a conference. Christina was employed as an interpreter for an American envoy for the Marshall Plan.

Christina stretched and grabbed her handbag. She pulled out a picture and showed it to Emil. "My daughter. She turned twelve last week."

"She's very pretty."

Emil told her he'd married, as well. Eugenia had given him a daughter and a son. Nicolae Ceaușescu was the godfather.

Silence fell between them as it had in Auschwitz. Unease. Their lives had moved so far apart. Their love founded on a memory. On an intense, impossible, very precise moment in time, one they would never be able to recapture.

"Do you still play the accordion?"

Emil nodded.

Whenever he hosted a party, he didn't need to be asked twice. Other times, when dark clouds hung over him, he locked himself in a room and played for himself. Emil now regretted not having brought the *gormónya* with him.

"What are you doing with those two?" Emil asked, referring to Markov and Vaneker.

"The Roma need you, Emil."

"You're playing at politics now?

"They're convinced that soon the Soviets will be out of Eastern Europe. Germany will be reunited. That democracy will return to Romania, to Hungary, to Eastern Europe."

No need to believe them, according to Christina. The Soviet Union would last a thousand years. Adolf Hitler's dream was now the reality of Stalin's successors and their pawns in Eastern Europe. And socialism would only become more violent the longer it dominated the political culture of these countries. It was necessary to organize, to resist. Romanians couldn't look inward, not when so many foreign winds buffeted them.

Had Markov and Vaneker brought Christina here to convince him of their projects?

She seemed to guess his hesitation. "I've got access to a lot of money. I want to support the Romani cause. I want to do something for you in particular."

Emil got to his feet, confused. She'd helped him so much already. Saved his life three times. And now she wanted to do even more for him.

"I need forgiveness. But I won't get it. So repentance will do."

Why should he carry somebody else's guilt?

"Nothing has changed, Emil. My husband is only digging himself deeper into mediocrity, becoming as odious as my father was. He's a bastard."

Soon after they married, Christina had begun to notice strange behaviour. Matthias kept secrets, made excuses, lied. At first she thought her husband was seeing another woman. In the end, she discovered he was getting together with other former Nazi officers, those nostalgic for the swastika. Christina thought about confronting him, or leaving him after notifying the police. But, in the end, she didn't do a thing. Matthias offered financial stability, so she decided to use his money at the service of the emerging Romani movement.

That was how she'd met Markov, who introduced her to Vaneker. She was in Romania to convince Emil to assume the full responsibilities of his name and his family, his duty toward his people.

"It's my way to love you as much as I can now. To help all Roma. Indirectly, secretly, behind Matthias's back."

"With his money?"

"Yes."

Emil closed his eyes. He didn't care about the Roma. Or money. All he wanted was to take this woman by the hand and leave with her, go to some place unknown to everyone. To forget everything.

"I love you, Christina. I've always loved you."

"I love you, too, Emil. I'll always love you."

26

Max O'Brien sat in his Jeep, watching the scene unfold before him. A merry-go-round of low-level thugs selling weed or crack or whatever the house specialty was, waiting for their clientele in the park in front of the school. They were kids really, some of them with wispy moustaches, trying to look like hard men out of a movie. Several parents had parked their cars near the school entrance, a Hadrian's Wall of overbearing concern standing between their kids and those in the park.

A few students began to trickle out of the school, and all at once, the bell rang, the dam broke, and the streets were full. The dealers had disappeared from the park and were now mingling among the students, attempting to find their usual customers. Max scanned the crowd for Gabrielle. There were teenagers all over the place now, their faces half hidden by long scarves or wool hats.

Max grumbled. He heard someone cursing behind his car. Turning around, he saw one of the dealers beating a hasty retreat from a girl Max recognized as Gabrielle. She seemed to be shouting something at him about getting out of her damn way, using words Max doubted Caroline would approve of. Max smiled. The girl certainly didn't need Mom and Dad to get herself home safe and sound.

Max opened the door and shouted, "Way to go, Gaby!"

Gabrielle didn't bother to turn around to see who'd called out. "Go fuck yourself, you old pervert!"

"Gabrielle …"

She turned around, recognizing his voice. "Robert?"

"Come on, climb in."

Gabrielle hesitated.

"I've never killed anyone and neither has your father. He's got nothing to do with the murders you've been hearing about."

Gabrielle glanced inside the car, suspicious, before finally getting into the Jeep. She looked at Max questioningly, unsure of the reaction she should be having. With a pang of sadness, Max noticed how much her attitude toward him had changed. He watched her for a long moment. She'd become a beautiful girl, with her long black hair, her blue eyes full of life, intelligence shining through. Just like her mother a lifetime ago.

"The police came to talk to me. Is it true what they're saying?"

"Partially. My name is Max O'Brien. And I'm a crook. But I'm not a killer."

Gabrielle paused for a moment, clearly trying to determine what her next move should be. "I'm supposed to call them if you try to get in touch with me."

Max handed her his cellphone. "That's your choice."

Gabrielle didn't move.

"Again, I haven't killed anyone, nor has your father." She remained silent.

"Were the cops nice to you at least?" Max asked. "Were they polite?"

"Yeah, they were two young guys."

"They told you their names?"

"Giovanni something, an Italian. I have his card at home. I can't remember the other guy's name."

The flow of students had already dwindled; the dealers were gone, the streets almost empty again.

"Why don't we go find something warm to drink?"

A coffee on rue Saint-Hubert under the eaves of the plaza. The coffee shop had served smoked meat and cherry colas for several decades. The neighbourhood was changing and was now all almond-flavoured coffee drinks and triple-chocolate cakes. Max needed to put events in order from the very beginning, from Kevin's decision to go to Romania. And why had he chosen to take a sabbatical?

It had been a last-minute decision, according to Gabrielle. The high school he worked at wasn't happy. The school had had to find someone to replace him on short notice, though it had figured things out in the end. Kevin had said he was leaving for Maine in early September, wanting to hike the Appalachian Trail to take in the fall colours. He'd make his way to the southern tip of the trail in Georgia by foot before resting for a few weeks and flying back in January. At least that was the plan.

It turned out that was all a lie. Kevin had flown to Romania.

Why?

Gabrielle had been staying with a friend while her father travelled. He'd promised to send her news regularly as he walked south.

"Do you have his letters with you?"

In her bag, Gabrielle had a pile of printed-out emails. Entire pages full of anecdotes.

"Hiking with a computer? Maybe a BlackBerry ..."

Gabrielle shrugged. "So he never went to the Appalachians. Why did he lie about that, too?"

"He wanted to protect you."

"From what?"

"That's what I'm trying to find out."

Max studied the missives, mostly interested in when the emails were sent. Kevin had written to his daughter once a week, sometimes twice. Max understood what Kevin had managed to do: he'd disappeared without disappearing. Given signs of life to his family while being reachable only by email. No phone number, no address. Kevin all alone, hiking the trail. Meanwhile he was able to travel to Romania and get on with his true plan.

His last message was dated the same day he'd called Max.

"The road is long and often hard, but I'm moving forward," Kevin had written. "I'm sure of it. One day, you and me, we'll walk this same path together. With your mother, too, why not? Soon, Gabrielle, all will be as it was."

Max swallowed back emotion. Kevin's last message to his daughter just before being kidnapped.

Soon … all will be as it was.

What did that mean? As it was before the accident on the Saqawigan?

When Max looked back up, Gabrielle was watching him closely. "Do you remember taking me for ice cream?"

Max nodded. Today ice cream had a sour taste for him. As it did for Gabrielle.

"I'm sorry," Max replied. "I should have brought you elsewhere."

"I was happy to see you."

Gabrielle welled up. She glanced away, avoiding Max's eyes. She didn't want to cry in front of him. Max still felt terrible at having forever tainted the taste of what had been her favourite treat.

"I'd like to take a look around the apartment," he said finally.

From the living room, they could see a docked cruise ship in port, Île Sainte-Hélène behind it. A few pedestrians plodded through the cold cobblestone streets. Just below the window, a deserted bicycle path. In summer you felt as if you were participating in the lives of all these anonymous tourists who invaded the area.

Max could feel how the truth about her father had rattled Gabrielle. She'd always seen him as an honest man, and here he was accused of having caused a fire that had killed almost two dozen people on the other side of the world. Accused of being a crook, a con artist who'd ruined his own father. Too heavy a burden to bear for anyone.

He slipped into Kevin's room. On the wall, posters from races his friend had run years before. A few pictures of him as a young man, standing on a podium or in the company of other athletes. The mail he'd received during his absence was piled on a dresser.

Clearly, the police had already gone through his letters.

Max unfolded Kevin's credit card statement. The card hadn't been used since September. The right-hand drawer to his desk was half open. Scattered, disorganized documents, probably the result of the police going through the drawer. Max scanned the documents quickly, finding nothing of interest. Notes Kevin had taken for his classes. Photocopies of a teaching manual. Various training techniques for teenagers. A letter to the director of Collège Notre-Dame du Sacré-Cœur, the local high school, agreeing to the terms of his contract for the next semester. And another letter, this one from the school's principal, rebuking him for putting his colleagues in a bind just as they were preparing the new school year — a letter dated in July. Receipts from a parking spot near the high school, a late notice from bibliothèque de Côte-des-Neiges.

Curiously, among all the papers, a bill for renting some landscaping equipment signed by a Julien

Desmeules. Max compared the date of the rental to the principal's letter. Only a few days separated the two documents.

In the left-hand drawer, a pile of newspaper clippings. Articles about Kevin's performances in various marathons.

A bookcase lined one side of the wall. Mostly sports books. He recognized the one from bibliothèque de Côte-des-Neiges by the sticker on its spine. A piece of paper stuck in the last third of the book. Max pulled it out. It was a phone number. Long distance.

Max went through Kevin's phone bills, which were organized in a folder. He found the call. To Victoriaville in early June.

He opened a closet.

All of the Dandurands' pain was thrown in his face all at once. Pictures of Sacha everywhere. And objects, as well, toys, clothes. It broke his heart to see.

A sanctuary.

"One day I found him kneeling before the closet, crying."

Max turned around. Gabrielle was standing in the doorway, on the verge of tears. The girl threw herself into Max's arms, and he held her against him as he'd done that day in the park after the Dairy Queen.

Back in the living room, while Gabrielle made coffee, Max called the number in Victoriaville.

"Boisjoli, Michaud & Ranger," a feminine voice answered after several rings. Behind her, laughter, music. "We're having our Christmas party. Perhaps we can call you back tomorrow if you wish to speak with a notary?"

Max insisted. He'd found this bill in Kevin Dandurand's papers and all it had on it was this phone number. He was looking for information as to why this Dandurand character would have the phone number of a notary.

"And you are?"

"Sergeant Donald Gravel of the Quebec Provincial Police."

"I'll get you Mr. Michaud right away."

A hoarse voice, that of an older man. In his sixties at least, Max thought. An old small-town notary who'd seen it all before. Max wouldn't be able to deceive him easily. Thankfully, the Christmas party was in full swing, which might mean the man had his guard down ...

"How can I help?" he asked, chuckling, perhaps at a joke a colleague had just finished telling.

Max gave his spiel a second time. Michaud didn't seem suspicious, only surprised. He didn't know what the bill was for. Kevin Dandurand had never had any business with him or any other notary in his office. Likely an error.

"And yet you spoke in June, didn't you? A few times, actually."

Michaud hesitated, then said, "It was about something else entirely ..."

He wouldn't say any more, as if he realized, suddenly, how strange this call actually was. Max heard someone at the party laugh loudly. Then a voice calling for Michaud. The notary shouted back to wait a minute.

Max needed answers. He tried another line of questioning.

"A bill for a thousand dollars. That's not nothing."

Michaud laughed.

"I think Dandurand was trying to save on his taxes! I'm the one who should have billed him. Cost me $12.28 in postage to send an envelope to him in Montreal!"

"I don't doubt you're telling me the truth, Mr. Michaud, but it would certainly help our investigation if I could speak with your other client, whoever wanted to send a letter to Kevin Dandurand in the first place."

More laughter. Clearly, Michaud was enjoying himself.

"Six feet under, that's where old Lefebvre is! I doubt he'll call you back!"

"And why did Kevin contact you?"

"My client's affairs are confidential. If you wish to continue this conversation, please arrange a meeting. After the holidays."

"It won't be necessary."

"Merry Christmas, Sergeant."

Max hung up.

Lefebvre.

The name rang a bell, but why? And why had the notary sent an envelope to Kevin from Lefebvre after the man's death? Perhaps something to do with a will he had with Michaud?

Max returned to Kevin's room. No envelope to be found.

27

A rather curious chronology. In early June, Kevin had received a letter from a notary with a client named Lefebvre. A few weeks later he had asked to take a sabbatical, which his principal wasn't keen on. Then, in September, Kevin had left for the Appalachian Trail; at least that was the excuse he'd given Caroline and Gabrielle so they wouldn't worry. To maintain his subterfuge, he'd written to his daughter regularly. Of course, by then, Kevin was already in Romania for an unknown reason.

Everything had gone downhill from there.

First, the Bucharest police had tried to get Kevin for the Zăbrăuți Street fire.

Laura Costinar's fake passport, she the widow of a Romani leader murdered in Manitoba.

A Romani leader known by Raymond Dandurand.

And, finally, Kevin in the hands of his captors, and the horrible deaths of Laura Costinar and Cosmin Micula.

The next day Max met up with Gabrielle for breakfast at a nearby diner. The young girl usually wolfed down her toast with caramel as if she hadn't eaten in days. But, this morning, she seemed to have no appetite at all.

Max ordered a cup of coffee. He described his conversation with Michaud, the notary. Gabrielle had never seen such an envelope, and her father had never mentioned it to her.

"How was your father last summer? Was he acting strangely?"

"No, I mean, he was running in the morning, training …"

"For the Appalachian Trail?"

"No, just to stay in shape."

"He didn't seem different at all?"

Gabrielle thought back. "I went rafting with a friend, and when I came back, yes…. More nervous, I guess you could say."

"Rafting?"

Camping, actually, with her friend, Chloé, and Chloé's older brother in vallée de la Jacques-Cartier near Quebec City. Kevin had suggested it, which had surprised her. Since forever, Gabrielle had been nagging her father about the trip, but Kevin had always said no. He'd lost his son in the Saqawigan's currents. He wouldn't risk his daughter in the rapids of rivière Jacques-Cartier. For some reason, from one day to the next, he'd changed his mind. He'd even chosen the dates for her and made all the reservations.

He'd been a week without Gabrielle in July.

What had he been up to?

Back in his hotel, Max called Julien Desmeules, a John Deere dealer near Boucherville. His name was on the invoice for Kevin's rental. Desmeules rifled through his papers and found Kevin's reservation. However, he'd gone to the Grande-Vallée service point to pick up the equipment.

"I guess he called us to avoid the long-distance fees."

"What did he rent, exactly?"

"A bulldozer."

Max couldn't imagine Kevin operating a bulldozer.

"Comes with an operator, of course."

Desmeules didn't know the guy; Max had to get in touch with the Grande-Vallée office.

At first glance nothing seemed off. There's always work to do on a country house. But Max knew from Gabrielle that Kevin hadn't gone to Grande-Vallée since the accident. And neither Max nor Josée had actually been able to part with the house. On the one hand, the place was still filled with too much pain, and the idea of visiting might have seemed intolerable to both of them; on the other hand, selling what had become hallowed ground felt like a betrayal to both Kevin and his half-sister. Another relationship of love and hate, of affection and repulsion, just as Kevin had had with his father while he was still alive. Raymond, whose presence in Woodlands with Ioan Costinar still raised questions Max was unable to answer.

The affair Max was embroiled in seemed to be an echo of another sequence of events that had occurred four years earlier in another country. In both cases, people had died: Ioan Costinar and Raymond Dandurand in the first case, and now Laura and the photographer Cosmin Micula. Max felt as if these two series of tragedies were intertwined, though he still struggled with exactly how. The link might just be the letter from Michaud, the notary, received by Kevin this past June.

Lefebvre.

He'd been thinking about the name all day, and suddenly it came back to him.

Gérard Lefebvre, Nordopak's co-founder. One of Raymond's early collaborators, he'd left the company just as it was beginning to find real success. Max remembered now; he'd come across the man's name several times while studying Nordopak for the scam. Gérard Lefebvre had sold his stock in the early 1980s. Max had believed the man — much older than Raymond — to have died. And yet, clearly, Lefebvre had kept something of a relationship with Kevin's father after leaving the company. If it was indeed the same Lefebvre.

Max went on the Internet to find a list of retirement homes in and around Victoriaville. He called each of them in turn. Based solely on his age, Lefebvre had probably ended his days in one or the other of these establishments. After a few unsuccessful calls, Max reached an orderly with Cedar Residences. The woman told him Gérard Lefebvre had indeed been one of their residents. At the time of his death he'd been suffering from Alzheimer's for several years.

"Did he have any family? Friends?"

"No, no, he was all alone in the world. By the time you're ninety-three, you're often the only one left, you see."

Which meant there were more than twenty years between Raymond Dandurand and Lefebvre. An odd couple, indeed. The young businessman and his older partner. The mentor and his protégé.

Max asked whether Lefebvre had received any visits from a Kevin Dandurand over the few months preceding his death, but she was categorical: Lefebvre had died alone, without family, without any visitors, forgotten by everyone. There was a solitary soul at his funeral: Michaud.

"Maybe you should speak with him," the woman offered. "He was the executor for his will."

Max rang the notary again but was told Michaud was off for a few weeks over the holidays. Anyway, Max hadn't expected much from that call: Michaud would be sober now and much more conscientious about attorney-client privilege. As Lefebvre's guardian and later executor, he would be the one who'd paid for the care and lodging of the old man. Max could well play the policeman over the phone. But to get more from the notary, as the man himself had suggested, Max would have to go to his office in person. A risk he wasn't willing to take.

One thing was certain: at Lefebvre's death Michaud had disposed of his client's assets in compliance with his wishes and responsibilities. Kevin might have inherited a part of those assets. An envelope at least. A few weeks after receiving it Kevin had rented a bulldozer in Grande-Vallée.

The next day Max hit the road and headed for Gaspésie to visit the family house on rivière Saqawigan. Raymond had acquired it early on when Nordopak was halfway between a small family-run business and an important player in the Canadian packaging industry. Why Gaspésie? It seemed a strange choice: after all, Grande-Vallée was several hundred kilometres from Montreal. Raymond could have found as nice a place closer to home in the Eastern Townships or the Laurentian Mountains that could have satisfied any desire for clean country air. Maybe those places were too close to the city for his tastes.

Raymond had only visited his hideout on rivière Saqawigan a few times a year — over Christmas or summer vacation, sometimes at Easter. But every time he went to the place, he'd stay for a few weeks at least and usually with his family. First with Roxanne and Kevin, later with Sharon, Josée, and Kevin.

Kevin had told him once that when Roxanne was alive, Sharon and Josée would also spend their vacation time in Grande-Vallée in a rented house nearby. Raymond wasn't the sort of man to go without his second family, not even for a few weeks.

Kevin remembered his time in Grande-Vallée fondly. His father's constant pressure would lessen. Raymond, far from his court, was able to unwind a little, able to relax his expectations.

It was over the course of one of these summers that Kevin had come to appreciate Sharon, whom he had once so loathed. His stepmother was a good woman, after all, and the two had gotten along famously. And because of it, life with Raymond had become less tense, as if Roxanne's death had in a way made his father's life better. Sometimes, in a moment of laughter or joy with his stepmother, he'd be overcome with guilt, feel like a traitor.

In those moments, Kevin would run off and find refuge near the boating shed at the far end of the grounds. He'd go and sit in that dark, humid shack and let himself mope for hours. Once night fell, it was Raymond's voice calling him back that would signal the end of his episode. Kevin would come out, head bent over his chest. At the top of the steps Raymond would sometimes toss out: "You were off to see your mother again, is that it?"

Kevin would hate him then as intensely as ever before.

A few years later, after Caroline had come into Kevin's life, the atmosphere had changed once again. Josée would bring a boyfriend from university, a law student destined for a stellar career, according to the young woman. Raymond would transform himself into the patriarch then, bestowing counsel and advice without being asked, playing to perfection the role of the exemplary father. In law, as in journalism, he could give lessons even to the experts. His newfound court oohed and ahhed and asked for more while Raymond beamed. Meanwhile, Kevin made himself discreet, trying to offer a small target for his father's sarcasm.

With Kevin back in the fold after his return from New York, Raymond's attitude had evolved once again.

Kevin was now an example of a man who'd returned to the righteous path of a serious career. Raymond could be proud of how he'd expertly manoeuvred Kevin's entry into the business world. A former athlete with good to fine results — though his career had dragged on too long by half — was now finally becoming a man to be proud of. The reconciliation seemed sincere enough, though always tainted by an undercurrent of dishonesty. And then there was Gabrielle, and later Sacha, allowing Raymond to display his talents as a grandfather. Kevin was grateful for his children, since they took his father's attentions away from him, giving him room to breathe.

Sacha.

Such a beautiful child, a doll brought to life, as Gabrielle used to say.

Always the centre of attention, of love, of affection.

And then the tragedy.

Before entering the village of Grande-Vallée itself, Max turned right and drove along rivière Saqawigan for about twenty kilometres until he reached the site of the accident. He stopped the Jeep on the other side of the bridge and strolled toward the river. Then he walked back to the bridge and across it. It was a recent construction, all made of concrete, replacing the old metallic structure still seen higher up the river, though now unused. The accident had taken place just as construction on the bridge was ending, after it had been opened to traffic. Perhaps it had been opened too early.

Raymond had lost control of the Pathfinder and fallen into the water ten metres below.

Max leaned over the guardrail. The water frothed and jumped and sprayed where the river suddenly became much narrower between two cliffs. The accident had happened in spring, when the current was stronger still, fed by melting snow.

Standing there, watching the water go by, Max felt as if he were reliving the terrible tragedy. That single day had destroyed a happy family and ruined the lives of people he loved.

Max returned to the Jeep, inconsolably distraught. He turned it around and drove back to the Grande-Vallée garage, the John Deere service point. Max was given the name of Sylvain Drolet, the only qualified bulldozer operator this side of the Saqawigan.

He drove around for a while, completely lost. Finally, he accepted the humiliation and asked a passerby. Max got the direction wrong again and was forced to ask someone else. He had to take a right after the gas station and follow a dirt road for about ten kilometres.

"Watch out for your muffler!"

As he drove down the road — more of a gravel path between the trees, really — Max realized that farmers, with little success, had attempted to tame this land better known for its coastal fisheries. The farmhouses were in disrepair, many of them standing behind washed-out FOR SALE signs.

Max reached the place he was looking for. A dog ran, barking, sticking its maw between the slats of a wooden gate. The owner's voice was heard behind the dog, cursing the animal to take it easy, for Pete's sake. A man in overalls walked over, wiping his hands on an oily rag. Behind him, a pickup, its hood open.

"Sergeant Gravel? I'm Sylvain Drolet. I thought you'd be in uniform."

Max smiled casually. "We get to take it off when we become inspectors."

That answer was enough for Drolet. And a good thing, too, since Max hadn't had time to prepare fake papers. A gangly boy appeared behind Drolet — his son, Sébastien, the man informed him. A perfect copy of his father, twenty years younger.

Sylvain Drolet knew Kevin Dandurand well. The whole family, in fact. Raymond had been a gold mine for local jobbers. He was always off on some renovation project or other, adding sheds, storeys, or extensions every season, following his whims. From the patio to the pool, not to mention the garage and the aviary, Grande-Vallée's underemployed contractors had loved him. Raymond's death, with his house left in disrepair, had put an end to the good times until Kevin called him in early August to hire him. The two men agreed on a price, and Drolet waited for Kevin on the property early the next morning.

"What sort of work, exactly?" Max asked.

"He wanted to solidify the dock. And also build a small embankment. Sometimes, when the snow melted, the basement got rather humid, and in bad years could even flood."

Drolet ambled back to the pickup and lowered its hood. "He was also looking for someone to do some basic work on the house — repair the deck, clean the chimney, that sort of thing."

Drolet had started the work that very afternoon, despite the rain. Kevin, umbrella in hand, supervised him, sometimes offering suggestions but mostly listening to Drolet's advice. Three days later Kevin returned to Montreal, never to come back. Drolet finished the work the following week after checking on a few details with Kevin over the phone.

"He essentially gave me free rein on the renovations," Drolet added.

The following Friday he had prepared his invoice and dropped it off at the general store. A few days later he received a cheque with a thank-you letter from Kevin, promising to get in touch that autumn for more renovations.

"So he was thinking of coming back to spend time here?"

"That's what I told myself. I guess he'd mourned, you know, moved on. Or maybe he wanted to sell." Drolet rubbed his forehead with his hand. "But there wouldn't be much of a market for the house. Bit too rich for the area."

"Had he come back to Grande-Vallée since the accident?"

"That was the only time I know of. But someone in the village might know more than I do."

"How did he seem when you saw him?"

"Happy to see his house again. Happy, but worried."

"Worried?"

"I don't know. He was fidgety. I told myself it was the emotion of being back. I didn't ask any questions. It was none of my business. His father was like him, you know. Always a bit of mystery with Raymond. An incredible man, but you never really knew what he was thinking."

Drolet looked at Max, a frown on his face. "It's horrible what happened, isn't it? Is it true what they say? That he was behind his father's downfall?"

"You can't believe everything you read."

28

To protect drivers from the spring floods, the municipality had closed off the old, sinewy road and replaced it with a new one, straight as an arrow, and relocated it higher on the hill, cutting right through a field, far from rivière Saqawigan. Max had no trouble finding the place this time. He encountered a huge metal gate, the sort they'd have had in front of Versailles to make sure the peasants didn't come to lop off a few heads. It, too, was in disrepair.

Max left the Jeep in front of the entrance and slipped between two rusted bars. He walked for a while through tall grass before reaching the dirt path again, two overgrown tire tracks beneath an arch of maples. The residence appeared behind a row of birch trees. The place had a lot of character, Max thought. Two storeys, chimneys on both ends. A long gallery on three sides. A prosperous home despite the lack of upkeep.

Raymond had bought the home from a ruined gentleman farmer, who himself had acquired it from an American industrialist seeking solitude. Dandurand had had it renovated while still in Montreal, faxing plans and estimates back and forth from his offices at Nordopak. The result? A luxurious and comfortable refuge amid the undergrowth, undergrowth Raymond had always refused to trim and prune and control. The grass had only grown taller, the grounds wilder, since the house had been abandoned.

After being conned, Raymond had travelled here to lick his wounds and find his bearings. Sharon had come with him. Kevin, Caroline, and the kids joined them for Easter. Rumours of bankruptcy were in the air, and perhaps Raymond had been informed of the financial details of the trustees' agreement while at the rivière Saqawigan home. Perhaps, by then, he'd already decided to take his own life if his company went under. A double exit, a final show. He would impress them all one last time.

By taking Sacha with him.

Max walked around the house and headed toward the river, where the brand-new dock valiantly stood over the water despite the strength of the current. A great expanse of uncut grass led to it, covered with patches of snow. A supplier had piled a delivery of cut maple and cherry, but no one had come to store it in the basement. Clearly, Drolet hadn't been wrong: Kevin had expected to spend the winter in Grande-Vallée. A project he hadn't mentioned to anyone. Perhaps a Christmas present to himself?

A shovel, a broken ladder, old planks of wood with rusted nails poking out were scattered on the deck. The front door was solidly locked, of course. In Montreal, Gabrielle had gone through her father's effects but hadn't found the key. On the other side of the house, where the deck ended, Max put his hands on each side of his face and pressed them against the window of a double room, a living room, probably. Antique furniture in harmony with the exterior design of the house. Raymond and Sharon had purchased most of it at local antiques stores.

Max glanced around: there was no one. The Dandurand residence was far from the road, and not a single vehicle had driven by since he'd arrived. With a single punch, he broke a windowpane, unlocked it from the inside, and stepped over the frame and into the kitchen.

The sound of his boots resonated on the floorboards. The heat was set to a minimum so the pipes wouldn't freeze, and the rooms stank of humidity, making them feel colder still. Max crossed the kitchen and into the corridor leading to the front door. In the middle of the living room, on his left, an oval carpet, half hidden under a bright red sofa. Max looked around. In a corner, the space where a television normally sat. Perhaps Kevin had taken it, but Max hadn't seen one in his apartment. On the wall, lines left by an old bookcase — it, too, brought to Montreal, probably. This hideaway, this refuge, left abandoned to the ghosts of the rivière Saqawigan tragedy.

Max crossed the corridor. Another room that gave onto the deck, this time filled with cardboard boxes, the ruins of a hurried move after the accident. Kevin and Caroline had wanted to leave as quickly as possible. They'd never come back — until Kevin's recent visit. Frames leaned against a wall. An abandoned pillow. Their return to Montreal executed in complete disorder, made only more chaotic still by Nordopak's impending bankruptcy.

A few mismatched chairs. Max moved them around for no particular reason, just to fill the place with a bit of sound. There were mouse droppings in every corner; the mice, too, had found a way in without a key. In a closet, more boxes, all empty.

If Kevin had planned to make the place livable in time for Christmas, he still had his work cut out for him.

Max noticed a pair of paint-speckled shoes placed on sheets of newspaper on the other side of the room. Kevin's, clearly. He recognized the old pair from when he'd picked Kevin up, years earlier, at the Astoria police station. Kevin had tied his laces with a foot up on a wooden bench. Max grabbed the newspaper under the shoes. It was a copy of *Le Soleil* from early August. Those dates made sense with the story he'd heard so far.

Making his way toward the staircase, Max climbed it two steps at a time. Only bedrooms on this floor, bathed in sunlight. The repainting had been left unfinished. Light bulbs removed but not replaced. Furniture covered in plastic tarp. More newspaper on the ground. And a container of dried paint, a now unusable paintbrush abandoned. Farther off, a roller entombed in the dried paint of a plastic tray.

Kevin had grieved enough, as Sylvain Drolet had suggested. Perhaps he'd thought to take a vacation in Grande-Vallée, the three of them, Kevin, Caroline, and Gabrielle.

"Soon ... everything will be as it was," Kevin had written in his last message to his daughter.

In a room at the far end of the floor, a bed. The sheets were undone, a blanket on the floor. Obviously, Kevin had slept here during the renovations. Max sat down on it, trying to understand what had been happening in his friend's head. He'd received a letter from the notary, Michaud, which had had such an effect on him that he'd decided to renovate a house he hadn't set foot in for years and to make both his employer and his family believe he was off hiking the Appalachian Trail. So many mysteries, but to what end?

Then Max noticed the answering machine at the foot of the bed, half hidden by fallen sheets. He picked it up. The small red light was blinking. He pressed the play button. A single message: "Hi, Kevin, it's Marie-France. I've thought about it and ... listen, I agree. Okay? Okay. Call me when you get back."

Max searched for the cordless phone, which he found near a pile of old rags. In the phone's memory, a number of unidentified incoming calls, but also Drolet's name three times. Finally, an "M-F Couturier" appeared. Three calls, all in August. In the closet, Max found a phone book and located the entry for M-F Couturier. The numbers were the same. An address on a rural road outside Grande-Vallée.

Max drove north from the river, through a forest of conifers. Lakes dotted the landscape, glimpsed through the trees, and prefab houses, small fragile boxes, in front of which huge pickups were parked. Then the road narrowed, the prefabs disappeared, and even the most dedicated farmers hadn't tried to make a go of it. Hardscrabble land here, abandoned to wild nature, no human intercession at all. A hunter's paradise, Max thought. He glanced at a roadside sign alerting drivers to crossing moose — the sign itself was dotted with bullet holes. Clearly enough, in the fall, during hunting season, this was the sort of place you avoided.

Within that greenery a small school bus suddenly appeared, stopped in the middle of the road. A strange vision, a boreal mirage. A woman in overalls led three children, toques screwed on their heads, to the vehicle, attempting without much success to prevent them from jumping into mud pies made of melted snow and dirt. A last few minutes of play before climbing into the bus. Without losing her temper, the young woman walked back a few steps, grabbed a child by his waist, another by his huge school bag, and pushed them into the driver's arms, he standing on the footboard. Max halted the Jeep a distance from the bus so as not to interrupt the manoeuvre.

When the vehicle continued on its way, the young woman sent air kisses to the children, whose noses were glued to the glass. Once alone, she examined the disorder around her without noticing Max's vehicle. In their rush toward the school bus, the children had pushed over a sled and some ski poles, which had been leaning near the door frame. Time to tidy up. The woman could only be Marie-France Couturier.

Shovel in hand, she raised her head when the Jeep's door slammed closed. She straightened, watching Max approach, seemingly suspicious, on her guard.

The place was isolated, and Max realized he was likely a threatening sight. He stayed a little back on the road so as not to scare her. "I'm a friend of Kevin Dandurand. You're Marie-France, right?"

Kevin's name seemed to reassure her. And intrigue her. She took her toque off, releasing a flow of long hair that she brushed away from her face. "What can I do for you?"

"I just got in from Montreal. I heard your message on his answering machine."

She waited for what was coming next.

"Do you know the police are after him?"

Marie-France Couturier nodded. Clearly, she hadn't recognized Max despite the fact that his picture had been circulating. Perhaps the young woman never watched television.

"It's horrible," she said.

"I know."

"You're with the cops, too?"

"A friend of his, like I said."

"Do you believe what they're saying about him? I just can't."

"I'd like to speak to you for a few minutes."

A long silence.

"You've got nothing to fear. I promise." He added, "Kevin needs help."

She hesitated for another moment, then gestured toward her door. "Come."

‡

A cozy little house, low ceilings, its large beams visible. A snug nest filled with plants and old furniture. Max noticed a piano in the corner, an old Steinway, a couple of its keys missing. Marie-France had transformed part of the living room into a classroom. Tiny chairs, coloured pillows, a movable blackboard, and of course, children's drawings hung up all over the place.

"I tutor children," the young woman explained when she noticed Max looking around.

She'd taken a year off work and hadn't had the heart to go back to a bricks-and-mortar school. So, instead of going to them, she thought of bringing the children to her for remedial work. The school board gave her its desperate cases, and she tried to help the kids with a lot of perseverance and patience. Most of the time she succeeded. A small miracle each time, she said with a smile.

"Do you want something to drink?"

"Coffee. As strong as you can make it, if possible."

Marie-France smiled. Max followed her to the kitchen. He leaned against the door frame as she filled the drip machine.

On the refrigerator, more children's drawings. Her protégés.

"About your message. What exactly were you referring to?"

She and Kevin had known each other for years. In fact, they'd been in love once. Each other's first love. Marie-France's family came from Rimouski and took their summer holidays in the area. They, too, had had a country home, though farther up the river. A tiny house, uninhabitable in winter, that had more holes than walls. Nothing like the Dandurand castle, but she'd loved the place. Sooner or later, the two teenagers had been bound to meet.

Kevin was from Montreal, the big city, swaggering his way to rivière Saqawigan. He listened to strange music, wore trendy clothes, knew all about things she'd never heard of. In September, after a summer of total joy, the separation had been heart-rending. Life had slowly pushed them apart, as it does. Later, as adults, they'd seen each other a few times. They became friends again. Marie-France never married, but she didn't regret losing her chance with Kevin.

She returned to the living room, two cups of coffee in hand, and offered one to Max.

When Kevin started coming back to the house after having been gone for years in New York, they saw each other from time to time in the village at the post office or grocery store. She was happy to see he was a father.

"I thought it was a shame he wasn't competing anymore. I would still see him running, though, sometimes early in the morning. He would run right alongside the road."

And then the tragedy. Everyone still talked about it in Grande-Vallée.

"And he came back last summer?" Max asked.

"Right. I hadn't seen him since the accident. I thought they'd sold the house."

He seemed radiant. Happy, which had surprised her. His car was filled with brand-new tools. He explained he was renovating, that he planned to come back to Grande-Vallée.

The same story he'd told Drolet and the others.

Marie-France had been intrigued but hadn't pushed him for an explanation. She understood why he'd left in the first place. She would have probably done the same. The fact that he was returning seemed like a good sign. He had mourned and now was living again.

Then Kevin called her one evening and asked if they could meet. He wanted to talk about something important. She invited him over. Supper, just the two of them, old friends who knew each other well.

"We drank a little, not much. I've never really liked alcohol, anyway. We traded memories. We laughed. I'd pretty much forgotten why he'd come over in the first place …"

She fell silent for a moment, then said, "Over dessert he offered me money."

Max raised an eyebrow.

"I had the exact same reaction as you at first. Then he explained everything." Marie-France got up, opened a dresser drawer, and threw an envelope onto the table. "Look inside. You'll understand."

Pictures of a party. An open-air reception. A beautiful afternoon. Men in dark suits, women in long dresses, servers in their livery.

Some of the pictures seemed hastily taken, as if the photographer wasn't supposed to be there in the first place. Fifteen pictures in all. One in particular caught Max's eye: a woman dressed all in black, looking pensive, the only picture in which someone was staring straight at the photographer's lens.

He recognized the woman immediately. Laura Costinar, murdered in Bucharest. Widow to the Romani

311

leader, Ioan Costinar — he, too, murdered, but in Woodlands, Manitoba.

A low-angle shot showed part of the sky, azurine, the rest of it obscured by a palm frond.

"They were taken in Spain," Marie-France explained. "In Granada, actually. Taken by Kevin himself."

Max didn't understand why the pictures were so important to his friend. Except for the one with Laura Costinar.

"Look at this one."

At first glance it seemed as if Kevin had taken the picture by mistake. The people in the background were all blurred. But on the right side of the frame, very clearly, a child's head seen from behind.

Max jumped to his feet.

There, between the collar and the child's hair, on the nape of the neck, a red mark.

Just like Sacha's.

"That's impossible."

Another picture, this one better, taken earlier or later, there was no way to know. Among a group of children, there was Sacha-the-Red, seven years old, more or less, and seemingly perfectly healthy. In another picture, a man in his forties held the child by the shoulders, either in congratulation or in protection. Just as a father would hold his child. A man fulfilled, satisfied, happy with his life. A man who'd stolen someone else's son.

Sacha was alive.

PART THREE

The *Mulo*

29

London, April 7, 1971

The BOAC Boeing 707 bounced once on the tarmac
at Heathrow, startling Emil. He'd only ever been on
a plane one other time, years before, and they'd flown
across Europe so quickly he could hardly believe it.
When he was a boy, his father's *kumpaniya* could drive
down the same road for weeks and they'd still be in the
same country, the same province even! Was it really
Great Britain there, out the window, or some illusion
only Ceauşescu had the secret to?

Like an obedient schoolboy, Emil followed the
other passengers out of the plane and took his luggage
off the long piece of moving rubber his fellow travellers
grouped around. Now that he could read as well as any
gadjo, Emil recognized his name written on a piece of

cardboard in the hall. A young woman in a very short skirt and huge glasses held the sign.

She led him to a large van that already held several other Roma. He didn't know a man among them, but his guide introduced them all.

"Slobodan Berberski, Antonin Daniel, Jan Cibula, and from Canada, Ronald Lee," she said.

"Emil Rosca from Romania."

Emil had heard of Berberski, a famous Romani poet from Serbia. He'd fought against the Nazis in the Yugoslav resistance. Antonin Daniel worked tirelessly to increase literacy among the Roma, as well as being a member of the Romani Union of Czechoslovakia. Jan Cibula, a doctor living in Switzerland, promoted Romani culture around the globe. Ronald Lee, a Vlach-Roma originally from the Balkans, was a writer and journalist and had been fighting for years for the recognition of Canadian Roma.

Emil felt privileged being part of such a select group of Romani leaders and organizers. Doubly so since the trip had been so difficult to organize despite Rossen Markov's repeated intercessions. After Emil had asked permission from Ceaușescu, two Securitate agents had shown up at his door. Asking Eugenia and the children to make themselves scarce, the two men had politely, with smiles as wide and kind as a shark's, begun asking Emil question after question. They, of course, were only looking for a reason to deny him an exit visa.

And so, three days before his supposed departure date, Emil still hadn't received the necessary paperwork.

That evening he'd put on his best sports coat — the only one he owned — screwed his hat on his head, and gone knocking at Ceaușescu's private residence. A rather bold move, one very few Romanians would ever be brave — or foolish — enough to do. If the dictator gave himself permission to sometimes visit the King of the Roma unannounced, Emil told himself, the king had permission to do the same in turn. Over the years, Emil had deepened his friendship with the Conducător, though the two men hadn't seen each other in months.

As Emil approached Herăstrău Park, around which the party's most privileged comrades lived, he was intercepted by agents of Ceaușescu's personal guard, who forced him to stand under a street light on Primăverii Boulevard for more than two hours. At least a dozen people, from uniformed policemen to stone-faced men in civilian clothes, checked and double-checked and triple-checked his identity, one after the other, explaining each time that the president of the State Council was absent and it was best to return tomorrow, go to his office, meet with one of his subordinates, and schedule a meeting.

Emil answered the same thing every time. "I'm the leader of the Roma of Romania. Nicolae Ceaușescu is a personal friend and godfather to my children. If he learns that you're stopping me from seeing him, he'll send you all to gather bulrushes in the Danube delta!"

All evening Emil felt as if he were switching a tractor to make it pull a plough faster. But, finally, a handful of agents escorted him to Ceaușescu's home. They guided him through a great garden — where other agents stood guard — then led him to an office isolated from the rest of the residence, a vast room bright with fluorescent lighting.

Ceaușescu was waiting for him, seemingly worried, hands behind his back, head held high. Around the Conducător, pictures of himself among his collaborators, all retouched to make sure he appeared taller than the apparatchiks with him — they were members of his family, for the most part. Pictures of Elena, as well, who'd been exercising an increasingly important role in government. She was the new director of the Institute of Chemical Researches, even if she had no competencies whatsoever in the subject. It was said ambition burned in her. One day she would possess the same power as her husband and lead the country beside him. Just as his was, her birthday was a day off for the entire nation.

Emil walked toward his friend to shake his hand, but before he got there Ceaușescu ordered him to stop. He shouldn't come any closer.

"Because of the germs," Ceaușescu explained, pulling a bottle of rubbing alcohol out of his desk. He sprayed his hands generously while smiling to a rather confused Emil. "You Gypsies have built a strong immune system after having lived all those generations in the dirt."

Emil didn't like the tone of his voice.

"How are your wife and children?"

"Eugenia thanks you for the gifts you sent for the birth of the new baby."

Ceaușescu smiled. "I always liked your people, you know? Your family in particular. If I'm where I am, it's thanks to you people."

He was referring to collectivization.

"Or because of you, really. And I rewarded you well, didn't I? What would you have become in Vorkuta?

Another corpse?" The Conducător walked to the window. "Mao Zedong and Kim Il-sung succeeded where Stalin failed. Moral hygiene will lead to physical hygiene, and that should be one of the goals of the revolution."

Ceaușescu admired China and North Korea. He was particularly impressed by how order reigned — in North Korea espcially. He admitted to Emil that the leaders of both countries had invited Elena and him for an official visit. The trip would take place in June.

"She'll meet scientists there. Chemists just like her." Ceaușescu turned back to Emil. "Universities around the world are interested in her work — what an incredible woman!"

He gestured at the pictures behind him. "Now that you know how to read, I'll give you her thesis on polymers."

Emil made a step toward Ceaușescu. With an impatient gesture, the Romanian leader ordered him once again to move back. As if Emil was afflicted with some contagious disease.

"In Pyongyang no one touches anyone else is what I heard. Everyone greets each other from afar. Even the highest cadres respect this directive."

"Nicolae —"

"Here, however, we're still promiscuous. Our pre-revolutionary habits die hard. Our socialism is tired."

Ceaușescu had changed, Emil noted. He seemed harder, which was to be expected, but sharper, as well. Ceaușescu's stammering had used to make him timid, unassuming, and, at least in appearance, harmless. That was how he'd managed to become head of the party in

1965. You always wanted to console Ceauşescu. Even in Vorkuta, Emil recalled, the young man had seemed to him like a child lost in a world of adults.

Today that impression had vanished. Ceauşescu seemed to him both ridiculous and dangerous. This obsession with cleanliness of his was pure paranoia. According to what Emil had heard, Ceauşescu had armed guards posted in front of his closet to protect him against potential poisoners. He brought his own bedding during foreign visits.

"Why do you want to go to Great Britain?" Ceauşescu asked.

"It's the first World Romani Congress. There will be delegates from around the world. I was chosen to represent Romania."

Ceauşescu straightened, anger in his eyes. "Chosen! What are you talking about? I'm the one who chooses in this country! No one else!"

Emil sighed.

"And this congress is funded by the CIA, isn't it?" Ceauşescu continued. "Or by the KGB maybe? It's all the same in the end."

"By India, actually. Indira Gandhi in particular."

Ceauşescu relaxed. The Indians, like the Romanians, were part of the non-aligned countries, despite the fact that both countries' governments had warm relations with the Soviet Union. Ceauşescu believed himself smarter than the Indians, however. By keeping an ongoing relationship with the Americans, he thought he'd gain an advantage over time. Richard Nixon, who preferred the Chinese to the Indians, whom he found contemptible, called him regularly, and even referred to Nicolae as Nick, as if they'd grown up together in Yorba Linda.

Nick and Dick, friends for life.

Still, the dictator wasn't particularly enthusiastic about the Romani congress. "They'll fill your head with wild ideas."

"Like Romanestan?"

Ceaușescu gestured impatiently. "Whatever you might say, I'm still your best ally, Emil. Without me Romanians would burn your caravans and spit on their ashes."

"Most Roma are sedentary now — you know it well."

"It would be easier to find your people, then, to exterminate you."

Emil nodded.

"Romanians hate you, will always hate you," Ceaușescu went on. "All I'd need to do would be to loosen the grip, just a bit, and they would jump at your throats like wild beasts …"

"Not all Roma are so lucky as to live in a country governed by such a benevolent leader as you. Each day I thank the heavens for having put me in your path, Nicolae."

Ceaușescu was certainly not immune to flattery.

"You're a ray of sunlight on the long stormy path of all Roma," Emil continued, seeing the dictator's satisfaction. "And to me, you are the closest of friends. The only *gadjo* that I see as I do a brother."

Muttering words Emil couldn't' understand, the dictator sprayed alcohol on his hands once again, rubbing them together quickly. Then he turned to Emil. "You'll tell them it's a paradise here."

"Thanks to you. Thanks to Elena."

Paradise …

London wasn't too bad in its own right. Through the window of the small bus, Emil was surprised at how well stocked storefronts seemed to be, at how so many people from so many countries in the world walked right by one another in streets without suspicion or aggression. He was filled with wonder at the clothes people wore — colourful and varied and beautiful. Back in Romania, it felt as if the war had ended yesterday. In London it seemed as if there had never been a war in the first place! And the music on every street corner: rock and roll, jazz, and Romani airs, too! Seen from London, Romania seemed dull, lifeless. Romania was in a coma, held in half-life by artificial means. In the West, light from every crack, life filling the streets.

Emil had never met any of the British Roma, but he certainly was impressed by how organized they were. They'd created the National Gypsy Education Council and had participated actively in making sure this conference went from dream to reality.

"Your talk is scheduled for Saturday at three o'clock," a young man told him in the entrance hall. "Just after Miroslav Holomek."

The president of the Roma Union of Czechoslovakia, a colleague of Antonin Daniel.

"I haven't introduced myself — Victor Marineci. I'm of Romanian origin, too."

Emil watched him closely. A young Rom, educated, comfortable among the *gadje*. Dressed like them, his hair cut like them. He did seem kind, though.

"One day I hope I'll return to Romania. But for now I'm more useful here in London."

Emil nodded.

"Do you want to visit the city?" Marineci asked.

"I'm tired. I'd like to rest."

Standing in front of his bedroom mirror, Emil hated what he saw. For the first time, he thought of his clothes, of what he looked like in his ratty old uniform, his ancient, outdated clothes, almost rags. And he smelled terrible, he was sure. Should he put some of those lotions on, those he'd found in the bathroom? Emil decided against it. Instead, he'd bring the vials back to Bucharest and give them to Eugenia. She'd adulterate them with a bit of water or alcohol and give some to all her sisters-in-law. Emil smiled. His *kumpaníya* had never felt so far away as today.

He tightened the knot on his tie to emulate the London style, went down to the entrance hall, and greeted the Roma who were arriving, notably the Hungarian Vanka Rouda, a Lovari member of the International Gypsy Committee and a colleague of Rossen Markov. Emil asked a doorman to hail him a cab. He'd written the address he wanted to go to on the back of a book of matches, which he gave to the Pakistani driver. The man nodded. Luckily, he knew the place. Emil spoke three words of English on a good day and had no idea where he was actually going.

For a long moment, curiosity replaced the anxiety that had inhabited him since he'd landed. The wonder he'd felt in the minibus had returned. At a red light, on his right, Emil noticed Roma, his brothers. His sisters, actually. Two women, an older one and a younger one, panhandling. The younger woman was no older than fifteen and held a baby in her arms. Or it might have actually been a doll carried like a child. Emil smiled. The oldest trick in the book to gain *gadjo* pity.

It had begun to rain, which Emil hadn't been ready for. After paying the cab driver, he ran to the hotel's entrance. It was more modest than his. More discreet, as well. By the time he reached the hall, he was completely wet. The man at the reception handed him a key, as if he'd guessed what this stranger had come to do in his establishment.

Emil climbed to the third floor via a wallpapered stairwell. An enormous bouquet of flowers at every floor, befitting a mortuary more than a celebration. In the corridor, he heard a television blaring behind one door, a radio from another. Emil's heart beat even faster. Why was he acting like such a teenager!

He pushed open the door, and there was Christina staring out the window. He recognized her by her silhouette, which hadn't changed since the last time they'd seen each other three years earlier. Christina extinguished her cigarette in an ashtray on the radiator and walked toward Emil. He'd prepared so many things to say, and she, too, probably, but they were both conquered by the emotion of their reunion. Seeing tears beginning to well in her eyes, fearing she might cry and feel the need to apologize for it after, Emil took Christina in his arms and held her as tightly against him as he could, as if he might lose her all over again, just as he'd lost her too often in his life. It was raining hard outside, the drops a constant patter against the window, but the lovers ignored the world going by around them. When he opened his arms, he realized Christina had cried: his tactic hadn't worked.

"I'm sorry, I'm so sorry," she said, smiling. "I swore to myself I'd be strong."

The bed was covered with a duvet, it, too, flowered. Emil threw it to the other side of the room. Christina let herself fall onto the sheet, and Emil took her in his arms again to smell the scent of her once more. They made love without taking time to undress, as they'd done so often in Auschwitz. Were they scared of being discovered? No, not this time. It was instead the fear that this perfect moment might be taken away from them at the last moment. That something, somehow, would prevent this reunion they'd been pining for since their last.

When Emil flipped onto his back, his breath short, Christina followed him, leaning her head against his chest as if to make sure he was there physically, that this wasn't all a dream.

The rain had stopped, night had fallen. They hadn't left the bed in two hours, maybe more. Neither one of them dared get up first, fearing the significance of that gesture, sounding the beginning of the end, or more that the wait was starting again.

Christina brushed her fingers on Emil's face as she'd done that day at the Zigeunerlager. "I'm returning tomorrow."

Emil closed his eyes. He didn't want the dream to end. Not again.

"The Belgians are still refusing to give citizenship to the Roma living in their territory," Christina continued. "Czechoslovakia wants to put into place a program of forced sterilization."

Emil winced. It would never end, the violence, the horror, the discrimination.

Christina turned to him. "But this time we've got resources to tap, especially money. A lot of money."

"Thanks to you."

"Ceauşescu hasn't noticed? What about the Securitate?"

"They only care for the Roma when they're looking for someone to hurt."

For months now, Christina had been sending funds to Romania through intermediaries, money used to improve the living conditions of the Roma. Health care, education — Emil discreetly coordinating the initiatives.

Christina sat on the edge of the bed. "Tell me what else I can do, Emil."

"Leave with me … forever."

"Impossible."

Emil shut his eyes.

"Somewhere else, in another life, in another time, everything would have been different."

Emil wasn't convinced. Without their shared experience in Auschwitz, nothing would have brought them together. The horror had been necessary for them to meet, to fall in love.

"I think of you every day," Christina added. "I try to imagine you working, living, over there —"

"Don't speak."

She turned around. He took her in his arms again. They kissed passionately, time passed, a moment of happiness that couldn't end, a space in time stolen from their fates.

Somewhere else, in another life, in another time, everything would have been different.

Christina was wrong. Everything was different because of her.

30

Granada, December 18, 2006

In Málaga, as the tourists trudged back to their buses, soon to leave for Marbella or somewhere else along the coast, Max O'Brien jumped into his rental Peugeot and drove northeast. It felt like a holiday: warm sun, blue sky, perfect weather. In the hills, the wind held winter's intent, just a small chill, enough to remind tourists of the cold climes they'd left before reaching this place. It would get warmer in February or March.

Gone were the architectural monstrosities of the Costa del Sol: the Andalusian landscape on the other side of Salobreña gave Max the impression of going back in time. While real-estate developers had corrupted all but the hardiest points of the coastline, they had left the backcountry virtually pristine, to the immense pleasure of visitors and tourists and, it could be imagined, of its inhabitants, as well. Behind a hill, on the other side of a turn, Max saw his first Osborne bull. A German couple had parked their car — was it the same Germans he'd seen in Bucharest? — and were taking pictures of the iconic animal.

But Max wasn't in the area to slum about on vacation. He got lost, as per his wont, in Granada's suburbs before finding his way to the old city, in which the Alhambra reigned supreme. The red citadel was a marvel of Nasrid architects and indissoluble proof of the Arabic presence in Spain.

Most of the rather discreetly sized hotels were located in streets inaccessible by car. Max circled the Albayzín circuit three times before finding a parking spot near Iglesia de San Juan de los Reyes. He walked along the road he'd just been driving on toward Santa Ana Plaza, jumping to avoid cars speeding through tiny alleys full of life.

Granada, a sad, melancholy city, despite the bright blue of the sky.

The Alhambra like a tombstone obscuring the sun, a magnificent mausoleum, as if death had finally given itself a monument to the measure of its cruel beauty.

Throughout his trip from Montreal, Max hadn't stopped thinking of what Kevin had confided in Marie-France Couturier. His son was alive, he'd told her that night, not revealing how he'd come upon this surprising piece of information. Kevin was going to find Sacha and bring him back to the country, he'd added, without giving any inkling as to how he'd go about that, either. Kevin asked Marie-France whether she'd be willing to teach the boy French upon their return so that he might eventually rekindle a relationship with his mother tongue and culture.

A few weeks later Kevin told his family he was off to hike the Appalachian Trail while, in reality, he was landing in Bucharest to put his plan in motion. Marie-France hadn't seen Kevin between that supper they had together and the day he went away. The message she'd left at the rivière Saqawigan home was to agree to his proposal: she'd help his son. He had made her promise not to tell a soul.

"So he was in Bucharest to find his son," Marilyn Burgess had concluded when Max told her about his trip to Gaspésie.

According to the photographer Cosmin Micula, Kevin had been in Romania to take Laura Costinar out of the country so she might implicate her husband's killers from a safe place.

Perhaps.

"But Laura was important to Kevin for a different purpose entirely," Max explained.

She was the key to finding his son. Laura was in some of the Granada pictures; she might be able to help Kevin get Sacha out of Granada.

Burgess was quiet.

The extraordinary violence that followed Laura's murder, Kevin's kidnapping, and the attempted implication of Max indicated something else. The child was important for another reason beyond his father's love for him, but for now neither Max nor Burgess had any inkling of what it might be. Kevin hadn't only found his son; he'd also opened a Pandora's box — but hope hadn't yet shown its nose.

An anti-Roma plot, as Burgess suspected? Again, perhaps.

What was more, what could the relationship be between Sacha's faked death and the very real one of Ioan Costinar, except their proximity in time?

Raymond, of course.

Again, the hoof marks of Kevin's father on the ground. Gérard Lefebvre's death had sent Kevin after his son. In the envelope he'd received from the notary that day, he'd gotten proof that paid to the official version of events. A confession by a dead man, a forgotten document manifested out of thin air, now in Kevin's possession.

In it was information that had revealed enough of the truth for Kevin to demand an impromptu sabbatical and go down a path that had led so far to the deaths of Laura Costinar and Cosmin Micula.

While still in Grande-Vallée, Max had tried his luck a third time. He called the notary on his vacation, trying to wheedle more information out of him. This time Michaud was more loquacious. The envelope sent to Kevin had come from Gérard Lefebvre's safe-deposit box located at a National Bank branch in Victoriaville. It had been opened decades earlier. Max pushed a little, trying to determine what other objects had been in the box, but Michaud cut the conversation short. He had nothing more to say on the subject, and anyway, it was protected by attorney-client privilege, and even if he was forced to talk about it, he would say that the remaining contents of the box held nothing of any interest at all.

In short, Michaud had gotten around the law and confirmed that Kevin's envelope had been the only item that was out of the ordinary.

And so the first stop had to be Granada.

In July, as Gabrielle was rafting on rivière Jacques-Cartier with her friend, Chloé, and Chloé's brother, Kevin had gone to Andalusia and gotten in touch with Laura Costinar. It was still a mystery as to how the two of them could have possibly gotten to know each other. In any case, Kevin had likely obtained proof in Granada of the information the documents contained, whatever Gérard Lefebvre's posthumous confession actually was. Sacha was alive, and in the hands of a stranger pretending to be his real father.

And so Kevin had made an irrevocable decision: Sacha would come back home.

What, again, had he written to Gabrielle in one of his emails? "Soon …everything will be as it was."

When his family was together.

When Sacha was alive.

After Granada, Kevin returned to Montreal.

In August he hired Sylvain Drolet to work on the house and grounds. He'd travelled to Grande-Vallée to paint the house and to speak with Marie-France Couturier in preparation for Sacha's return. Meanwhile, Caroline and Gabrielle had been left in the dark. Sacha would be Kevin's surprise, a Christmas present.

Then the kidnapping in Bucharest.

"What about the man with his hand on Sacha's shoulder at the reception in Granada," Burgess asked Max. "Have you identified him?"

The adoptive father.

From Grande-Vallée, Max had sent Toma Boerescu the picture taken by Kevin in the Andalusian garden. The old man had paid a visit to Petru Tavala, the music-loving café owner. The man confirmed what Max had begun to suspect: yes, that was indeed the fellow Kevin Dandurand had met with that morning.

Without the child.

"Maybe Laura was grabbing the child at the same time," Burgess suggested.

"So the breakfast was a diversion?"

"Perhaps."

That still left the question of who the usurper father was.

No one had any idea.

One thing was clear enough: whoever this man was, he had ties to dangerous individuals, people who'd so far kidnapped Kevin and murdered twenty-five people: all to make sure the truth wouldn't come out.

The following day Max called Marilyn Burgess right after hanging up from a very informative discussion with Boerescu. The man from Granada was Peter Kalanyos, a Hungarian Rom who'd fled that country after accusations of drug trafficking and attempted corruption of civil servants.

Burgess completed the tableau a few hours later after consulting with her own sources. "Violent, dangerous, he's believed to be linked to Eastern European drug cartels. In Romania in particular."

In Ferentari, the Bronx of Bucharest, where the mafia was located.

Burgess called Phil Garrison in Woodlands. Both Jennifer and he were clear: Kalanyos hadn't been in Manitoba with Ioan Costinar. At least neither of them recalled the man's presence.

In short, Kevin had angered a very dangerous person. Someone who'd stop at nothing to get the child back.

But again and always: why Sacha?

And how had his death been faked so effectively six years earlier?

"Do you intend to tell Caroline?" Burgess asked.

Max hadn't said anything to Gabrielle, but he couldn't very well keep the truth from Caroline. Part of why he'd gotten involved in this whole mess was to help patch things up between Kevin and Caroline. The media had depicted Kevin as the patron saint of hypocrites, the worst kind of ingrate son. Max knew Caroline had been troubled by these attacks on her ex-husband. By telling her the truth about the reasons behind Kevin's presence in Romania, Max hoped to help begin to rebuild Kevin's reputation.

"I'll speak to her in Montreal," he'd told Burgess. "But I still need to meet with someone before then."

Louis Maranda, one of the policemen who'd taken part in the investigation at the time, was part of a model train club based in Delson, near Montreal. Next to the old mayor's office, a warehouse had been converted into a tiny triage yard where a hundred or so miniature trains were stored, some of them remarkably realistic. Max saw Maranda, dressed up as a railway worker, standing behind railway signals. The policeman gestured for Max to approach. The latter stepped over an interchange, around a tunnel, then shook Maranda's hand as he leaned against a small mountain. Max felt ridiculous among these scale models, an oversized doll in a dollhouse, a giant among the Lilliputians.

"A journalist interested in our little wonders! Let me tell you, that's a rare sight indeed! You're with *La Presse*, right?"

Max didn't want to disappoint. "Television, actually." He explained he wanted to meet Maranda not as a model train aficionado but as a former police officer with the Quebec Provincial Police who'd worked in Grande-Vallée for years.

Maranda's face fell. After being transferred from Montreal, he'd settled in Saint-Constant, birthplace of his wife. He agreed to answer questions, anyway. "As long as I can remember the answers!"

"I'm curious about the death of Raymond Dandurand and his grandson, Sacha."

"Ah, the Saqawigan accident. Careful …"

A Union Pacific Railroad 600 series locomotive was steaming right for them. Max shuffled a few inches to the right, avoiding a terrible railway tragedy by little more than a hair.

"Come." Maranda guided the visitor toward a small office where another man in railway overalls was reading a book on scale models. Maranda asked him to give them the office for ten minutes. Max and Maranda sat at the table. "What do you want to know exactly?"

Following procedure, Maranda had collaborated in the coroner's inquest. The boy had disappeared, swallowed up by the river. Maranda was surprised to hear people were still interested in the story.

"In a world without violence, condemned to eternal joy, sometimes we media types have to look back in time to find anything at all to write about," Max joked.

Maranda smiled. Quickly enough, he described the investigation's conclusions: it had been a tragic accident. Raymond Dandurand had been drunk, a victim of a seat belt he hadn't been able to undo once the 4x4 had tumbled into the river. Of course, the authorities hadn't made that detail public. Raymond had drowned. The responsibility for the accident had fallen on Grande-Vallée's roadwork planning board. The coroner's report had pointed the finger at a lack or confusion of signage, that sort of thing.

"Even sober you couldn't tell where you were going," Maranda added.

"Is it possible the child might have survived?"

Maranda raised his head, surprised by the question. "Why do you ask?"

"Well, they never found his body, right?"

It was unthinkable that he might have survived. His body had never been found, sure, but the Saqawigan — most rivers, really — are full of drowning victims whose bodies are never recovered.

"Don't forget. Here we're not far from the Atlantic, and the tides are strong."

What had the investigation found out about Raymond himself?

He'd been drinking with his fishing friends. Caroline had left her son with his grandfather around eleven. Together they'd gone to the local brewery where the old boys got together to solve all of the world's problems. Raymond was very popular, of course. He talked loudly and had two opinions for every topic. The men remembered the car seat perched on the bar. From time to time, between beers, Raymond checked on the child.

Max raised an eyebrow.

According to his friends, Raymond always did whatever he wanted.

Still, Max found it hard to believe that Caroline would trust her child to Raymond, considering their relationship. And doubly so because of the context of that weekend, right after the big score, just when Nordopak's bankruptcy was about to be made public.

The accident took place around three in the afternoon, according to the report. Raymond had left the bar only a few minutes before, but had been gone to the village for more than four hours. Raymond had been drunk, and his friends had let him drive, with a child in the back seat to boot.

"The guys told us that Raymond didn't seem drunk. And it wasn't as if he would ever accept anyone giving him advice. He was stubborn, is what they said. Always ready to get into an argument."

Max had no trouble believing that. "Any witnesses?"

A couple had been hiking near the river. They rushed down to the water to try to help, but it was too late. By the time they got there, the vehicle had already been lying at the bottom of the river for several minutes, with Raymond trapped behind the wheel.

"What about Sacha?"

As they were pulling Raymond's body out of the car, the paramedics noticed the car seat in the back. It was empty. After speaking with Kevin and Caroline, and Raymond's friends, the conclusion was that Sacha had been washed out of the car by the current.

Which meant, Max thought, that no one could confirm the child had actually been in the back seat at the moment of the crash. The last time anyone had seen Sacha had been at the bar.

What if Raymond had left the child somewhere between the bar and his tragic crossing of the river? By the time the six o'clock news flashed images of a terrible car crash on every TV screen, Sacha could have been in the hands of a kidnapper, who'd disappeared with no one being the wiser. The accident only a providential act, allowing him to escape public notice.

And yet something didn't quite fit. Max tried to put himself in Kevin's shoes, to understand how his friend had reacted when he learned his son hadn't actually died that day.

How had he gotten the news? The notary's documents sent after Lefebvre's death? Had those led him to Granada and propelled him down the rabbit hole?

Max had no idea.

The day the accident actually took place Max hadn't doubted the truth of it. Raymond and Sacha dead, an unbelievably cruel world, but no more. How could a child, some eighteen months old, have survived if an adult had died?

How could he have disappeared?

Raymond's accident had been no accident. His car had been tampered with, his brake lines cut, or whatever they did in the movies to make quick work of a man. And yet the investigation concluded that the car had been in good working order.

So what had happened? Max had no idea, but Kevin knew.

Perhaps thanks to Laura Costinar.

31

The Albergue San Miguel was an old barracks for the Spanish cavalry, transformed some three years earlier by a Norwegian couple into a luxury hotel. This refuge from the modern world set you back four hundred euros a night. Max didn't have a reservation, and didn't think he'd find a room, but a last-minute cancellation meant that the *mirador* was available. A room that had been added to the original structure, over the top floor of the hotel. It had a spectacular view of the Alhambra, whose fortifications dominated the city.

One of the receipts he'd found at the rivière Saqawigan house had pointed him here. Kevin had stayed at the Albergue for three nights in July before returning to Canada. He'd come to take pictures, Max guessed, either as proof that Sacha was still alive or to identify his kidnappers. He'd probably begun preparing the counter-kidnapping in his room, with Laura Costinar as his accomplice. Since he didn't have any forged documents to take his son back to Canada, he'd gotten in touch with Cosmin Micula, a talented forger.

At least that was how Max thought events had unfolded.

The Norwegian woman at the front desk couldn't remember seeing Kevin, even after Max showed her a picture of him. With all the guests coming and going …

Max dropped off his bags and left the room immediately to explore a city whose sights he could barely glimpse through the fog of his worry. He was insensitive to the beauty surrounding him, lost in thought, trying to put himself in his friend's shoes, to understand his motivations. He saw Kevin meeting Laura, telling her all about his family's odyssey, their hardship. Perhaps Laura, seeing his limited means, had agreed to help. He only needed to bring his child back to Canada, to start a new life — or more accurately, to return to his old one. But first Kevin needed to see his son for himself, to prove Sacha's existence to himself.

Or perhaps it was the other way around. Laura had contacted him, intrigued by this man taking pictures at a private party. She'd spoken to him again, or they'd met, and he'd told her everything. Touched by his story, maybe she'd suggested the kidnapping and agreed to help since she knew the family well.

Perhaps. Maybe. Too many unknown answers, questions he didn't know yet to ask.

Max recalled that sin, that dark trait often attributed to the Roma to rouse hate and anger toward them: they stole children.

Had a Romani man, this Peter Kalanyos, stolen Sacha?

Max found a chair on a street-side table at a small café and ordered an espresso. He contemplated the view of Iglesia de San Nicolás. The cold streets were deserted, but Max had no trouble imagining how busy this plaza would be come high season. As he drank his coffee, he forced himself to make sense of the Spanish-language newspapers scattered on the tables. Listened to the barking voice of a lottery ticket vendor. Distractedly watched a broadcast of a Christmas parade on Telemadrid through the café window.

Max paid and returned to his walk. Melancholy overcame him, despite the new knowledge that Sacha was alive. All that still connected him to his dear friend, Kevin, was the thinnest of threads, one that could be severed at any moment. Had Kevin wandered through these streets, as well? Had he met someone? Had he struck up a conversation with a stranger? Max almost wanted to wander the streets and show Kevin's photo to every stranger he passed. But instinct told him that attracting attention here wouldn't be a good idea, despite what the Roma in Montreal had told him about hiding in plain sight.

The information he'd gleaned from Maranda, the retired policeman-cum-train conductor, made him think back on that tragic spring. It seemed to him that the circumstances surrounding Raymond's death had been left purposely nebulous. When the accident had occurred, Max had tried to shut out the truth as much as possible. As if not facing facts would make the pain less difficult to bear, the guilt less crushing. Now, this picture of Sacha alive and well, his discussion with Maranda, it had all revealed to Max how little he'd actually taken the time to analyze what had happened.

"You're calling me from jail?" Caroline sounded more intrigued than scandalized.

They spoke over the phone as Max was driving back from Delson. "I'll explain. But we need to see each other, you and me."

"Have you heard from Kevin?"

"Not yet. But …"

"Yes?"

Max turned his hazard lights on and brought his car to a halt on the shoulder. "I don't want you to get your hopes up."

His words came out fretfully, slowly, almost a stutter. Why was he telling her what he'd learned over the phone? Caroline remained silent the whole time on the other end of the line. Waiting for the other shoe to drop.

"I'm not yet a hundred percent sure, okay? It's a hypothesis and …"

Silence from Caroline.

"Sacha might still be alive."

What reaction was he expecting? Tears? Shouts? Laughter and thanks? Anything.

Anything except that deafening silence.

"Why are you trying to hurt me?" she finally asked.

"Caroline, please, listen to me —"

"Sacha is dead," she said, her voice like broken glass. "How many months — years! — did it take me to … and now …"

Max thought she might hang up on him. "Kevin went to Romania to try to find him. That's why he left."

"Spoken like a true liar, like a thief!"

"I've got proof, Caroline."

More silence.

"A picture taken by Kevin in Spain."

"You're insane!"

"Do you remember the Second Cup, Caroline, the one we went to together last year?"

Caroline held the picture in her hand. Sacha-the-Red in an Andalusian garden. She took a deep breath, closed her eyes, the veins in her eyelids like stains on skin so white it was almost green. She seemed to be trying to get hold of herself. She pushed the picture back across the table. Around them, strangers came and went.

"What happened on the Saqawigan might not have been an accident," Max finally said.

Caroline looked up at him, confused.

"A setup. To fool anyone investigating the car crash."

Max talked of Laura Costinar, seen in Kevin's pictures. Of her husband's role in the Romanian Romani community. How he'd died in Manitoba, and his wife's murder in Bucharest. How Max was playing the role of messenger for Kevin. Raymond's presence in Woodlands.

"Sacha is alive, and he's at the centre of the storm, Caroline."

She didn't say a word. Lost in thought. Max's revelation forced her to think back on a period of her life she'd tried in vain to forget. Her past bubbled to the present, constantly, like heartburn.

"What happened, exactly?" Max asked.

Caroline described that tragic weekend when the family had gotten together for the last time at the rivière Saqawigan house. Kevin was morose, Raymond, too. The two men were incapable of thinking of anything except what had happened in Montreal.

"Nordopak's bankruptcy?"

"It wasn't official yet. Raymond was in constant contact with his board members, though unable to convince them to give him another chance. He'd lost all credibility."

Max nodded.

"Kevin and Raymond, tormented, avoiding each other." Caroline straightened. "Thankfully, Sharon was spending the week with us. And so was Josée. They both tried to drag Raymond out of his shell a little, without much success. I tried, too. Josée thought her mission was to support, reassure her father constantly, try to make him laugh a little. Sometimes there'd be this little moment of sunlight and he'd chuckle or smile, but the clouds would come back right away. Even darker than before."

Raymond only seemed like himself when he played with Sacha. The child helped brighten his mood. When Sacha was just a newborn, Raymond had been annoyed by his babbling; it exasperated him. But the boy had grown on him, and Raymond had become a doting grandfather. He could spend hours with the child, never getting bored or losing patience, playing with him on the living room floor. He kept all of his smiles for Sacha, as if punishing his family for being there, witnesses to his misfortune.

And then there were all his old pals, Grande-Vallée's fishermen. Every morning Raymond told Sharon, Kevin, and Caroline that he was off to pick up the mail in the village. While, in fact, he'd make his way to the bar to have a drink with his friends. He'd come back stinking of alcohol, but he never seemed drunk. Raymond had always been the sort of man to drink like a fish and not show the effects.

By early April, discussions with Nordopak's board were becoming increasingly fraught. Raymond was looking to gain a little time, which the board refused to give him. The vultures were beginning to circle, Cambiano the first among them, ready to fall upon what was left of the carcass.

Raymond couldn't sleep; he stalked the corridors of the large home all night.

One day Raymond simply disappeared. Kevin and Caroline thought he'd gone back to Montreal to confront the mob trying to sell his company out from under him.

Max now knew that Raymond had been in Woodlands, Manitoba, for an unknown reason. In any case, his trip had been fruitless; he returned from Manitoba more desperate than ever.

The end was unavoidable. Nordopak's corpse fed to the vultures, and gone was Raymond's life's work.

His last day, now intolerable by its banality.

Sharon and Josée had driven to Matane to shop for groceries. Kevin, Caroline, and Gabrielle wanted to go for a bit of a hike, to get some fresh air. Raymond had been in a strangely good mood, offering to take Sacha for the day. An offer Caroline had accepted. A decision she thought of every day since, a decision that had ruined her life.

Raymond, preparing to leave a void behind him.

Caroline wasn't telling Max anything new. He felt as if she was staying on the surface of things, giving him the official version of events. He had hoped for more. He didn't blame Caroline, though. Raymond's death had taken over their lives. A tragedy that, according to the official version of events, was no more than a common accident; no different in nature than the dozens or hundreds of other tragedies that happened every day. A death — two — caused by a moment of distraction.

Caroline's story seemed to have exhausted her. Max realized she looked even paler than before, as if the retelling of events had made them worse. The only remedy she'd found had been silence, forgetting, and here was Max forcing the past back on her.

After a moment, Caroline said, "And the man in the picture …"

"Peter Kalanyos."

Caroline closed her eyes. "I saw him in Grande-Vallée. With Raymond. The day before he died."

32

As he returned to his room at the Albergue San Miguel, Max was stopped by the desk clerk, who gestured him over while still on the phone. As he waited for her to finish her call, he looked over the postcards in the display stand. Typical Andalusian landscapes. *Pueblos blancos*, an Iberian bull, sunny scenes. Decidedly, he'd have to return on vacation to visit this beautiful part of the world.

The clerk hung up and glanced at Max. "Was your friend wearing a tuxedo?"

Max had no idea. But if Kevin had been invited to a party, or wanted to infiltrate one, he might have. In some of the other pictures Marie-France Couturier had shown him, several men wore tuxedos.

The Norwegian woman remembered Kevin now. "He had a stain on his shirt. I remember it now because

I helped him clean it. He was nervous. Like a teenager going to his first dance."

Max showed her Kevin's picture again.

"Yes, exactly, that's him. I recognize him now."

"A party during the day? Like a garden party? Do you know where?"

"He didn't tell me." Her eyes lit up. "Oh, wait a second! I called the taxi for him because he didn't speak Spanish."

She rummaged in a desk and came out with a card for the cab company the Albergue did business with.

A thread. A thin, thin thread, but a thread nonetheless. And Max had nothing better to go on. He went to his Peugeot and left immediately for the suburbs of Granada, to Radio Taxi Andalucía's headquarters. In a cul-de-sac, off a main street, a Repsol garage surrounded by a dozen cars, all taxis. Max had seen quite a few with the same branding in the streets of Granada near Iglesia de San Nicolás.

José López — or so the name tag on his overalls read — pulled himself from under a car he was working on and walked toward Max, chewing on a toothpick. Slightly round, bald, a sort of Sancho Panza disguised as the boss of a taxi company. He asked Max to go to the other pumps, not these ones, if he wanted to gas up his car. Max handed him a fifty-euro bill through his open window.

"I'm looking for a driver."

López hesitated. As in many countries in the world, taxi driving was the domain of insomniacs and loners, but also ex-cons. It was a common occurrence for some-one to want to know more about a driver, but it usually spelled trouble nonetheless. Only cops were interested in cab drivers.

"I run an honest business," López said gently. "I've got nothing to hide."

An honest man always cost more.

Max pulled out another fifty-euro bill; the second was enough to buy him a strong espresso behind closed doors in López's office.

"Every call is recorded, of course."

López turned to an old computer dirty with grease and tapped on even filthier keys one finger at a time. Information on the night of July 19 appeared on the screen.

"The Albergue San Miguel, right? A dozen calls during the day and … only one in the early evening. Ramiro Bugalla …" López snorted. "You're in luck. I'm about to fire him."

There were hundreds of drivers who'd be happy to have his job. López explained that drivers worked in pairs, and Bugalla's current partner wanted his step-brother to work with him. And so Bugalla would have to go.

"So where can I find him before you fire him, this model employee?"

López looked at the Cinzano clock on the wall. "Here, in an hour, like everybody else. I mean, if he's not throwing up his tapas in the bathroom of some bar somewhere …"

‡

Ramiro Bugalla seemed sober when he parked his Fiat in the garage. José López knocked on his office window and pointed out the car to Max, who was sitting on a pile of old tires. Max let Bugalla turn the engine off at the far end of the parking lot, between two cabs, before making his way toward him. The man was vacuuming the back seat and didn't hear Max approach. He startled when he saw two shoes right behind him, pulled his head out, and looked up.

"How's your memory, Ramiro?" Max was smiling, enjoying the driver's confusion.

Tall, lanky, grey hair falling to his shoulders, a hippie slowly approaching well-deserved retirement.

"I've done nothing wrong," Bugalla answered in halting English.

"I'm not accusing anyone. Just asking you how your memory is."

"You work with the FBI?"

Now it was Max's turn to be surprised.

"You look like a cop."

Max sighed. Clearly, he'd need to buy some new suits next time he was in New York.

"On July 19 you picked up a man in a tuxedo from the Albergue San Miguel. Sometime in the afternoon. He was off to a party."

Max showed him Kevin's picture. Bugalla examined it for a long moment, his brow furrowed, attempting to convince Max of how hard he was trying to remember. Max slipped him a fifty-euro bill to jog his memory.

"Yeah, something is coming back to me. Near the Alhambra."

"Do you remember the address?"

"Hard to say."

Max peeled out another bill.

"Yes, yes, it is all coming back to me now."

Max reached the top of a narrow street that led to the Red One, as the Arabs used to call it. The same street used by tourists, on foot or by bus, as well as by Granada's citizens. On hot summer days during the holidays, it was total chaos. In December, however, the street was almost empty. A few people out for a run, others walking dogs, a few students. Max followed a handful of tourists visiting the city during the low season. They'd probably driven from the Costa del Sol, disgusted by all the concrete there, looking for a bit of culture and beauty.

At the end of the street he moved away from the crowd. On the left, if you climbed higher still, the ticket booth and access to the citadel. On the right, a few hotels and restaurants. In the Antequeruela Baja, on the other side of those few businesses, the house Ramiro Bugalla had driven Kevin to that day. Four storeys, the last one high enough to glimpse the fortress through the windows. Max saw a covered rooftop terrace and what might be a dining room. From the street, you couldn't see the garden, but likely the view of the citadel was breathtaking from there, as well. An ideal site for a party.

The house was shuttered, though, and graffiti covered its walls.

Max was caught off guard.

Tall metal fencing, already beginning to rust at its highest points, encircled the house. Max was stuck; there was no way he'd be able to climb that fence. That was when he noticed a small sign on a gate. The phone number and name of a real-estate agency, which Max committed to memory.

Max's cellphone battery had died, and he made his way to a nearby café, right at the top of Peña Partida. The owner let him call from a phone booth at the far end of the bar whose door wouldn't close, unfortunately.

"Señora Zarzuela isn't available just now, but she'll call you back as soon as she can," the receptionist said. "Would you like to leave her a message?"

Max told the receptionist there was no need, that he'd call again a little later.

He walked back to the front door of the café. The barman behind the counter, the one who'd shown him where to make the phone call, was now staring at him, alarmed.

"You're looking at Werner Landermann's old house?"

He'd overheard Max's conversation. A professional busybody, clearly, with the thick moustache to match the startled eyebrows.

The barman leaned over the counter. "It's been in disrepair for three years. You saw the fence? It's even worse inside. Rats in the basement, the roof needs to be redone."

No doubt Señora Zarzuela must love this guy … Max could imagine the man discouraging every potential buyer who, just like him, came to make a phone call to the real-estate agent.

Max sat at the bar and ordered a beer. He described himself as an American tourist looking for investment opportunities in Andalusia. While his wife visited the citadel, he'd decided to wander around. The barman introduced himself as Javier.

"Can I meet the owner, this Landermann …?"

"He's been dead for a dozen years. Cirrhosis of the liver. An amazing man. Stayed strong to the end."

"Though he left his house rotting to pieces."

"That's the agent's fault. She's supposed to take care of it and then sell it. But she barely does anything, and the price is too high, anyway."

"Because it's near the Alhambra?"

"Right. But you couldn't turn it into a hotel or a restaurant. It's just not built that way. I'm not complaining, though, believe me. There aren't enough tourists during winter already, so if people start opening restaurants here and there and on every other corner, soon enough …"

A fine sort, Landermann was, Javier added. He'd come and have a drink regularly. And then he'd meet a German tourist and the whole thing would turn into drinks for everyone, every time. Must have cost him a fortune. The barman had even stocked German beers that he had specially imported just for Landermann.

"He hated the Spanish brands" Javier whispered. "He wasn't in the wrong there, either."

Sometimes the drinking sessions lasted into the wee hours of the morning. And so Javier courageously dragged Landermann back to his house, where his wife waited for him. The worst sort of stuck-up princess you ever saw, Javier claimed, and she'd order Javier to drag her husband to a couch upstairs in a small den.

Landermann's wife would hand him a bill or two, as if he'd returned her lost cat.

"He must've slept on that couch often, the poor man," the barman added.

"Quite the love story, right? What happened to her?"

"She died. Just like him. I can't remember when, but not too long ago."

"Cirrhosis, as well?"

"I doubt it."

And so the house was for sale. And the way Javier was advertising it, it wouldn't be sold for a long time.

At the foot of the Alhambra near Gran Vía de Colón, Granada looked like a typical European city again, with the requisite Mediterranean zest: angry drivers, their hands resting on their horns and their middle fingers on quick draw. Max called the Albergue San Miguel from a restaurant on Plaza de las Pasiegas where he'd stopped to have a bite to eat. The receptionist told him a Raquel Zarzuela had tried to reach him and left her cellphone number. Max called the real-estate agent from the restaurant, and they agreed to meet thirty minutes later in front of Werner Landermann's house.

Raquel arrived, glittering, energetic, with a smile full of straight white teeth that could be spotted a mile away. She reached the house a few minutes early, practically leaping out of her Volvo with the elegance of a predator. Though night had fallen, she had life enough for both of them. Ready to sell this godforsaken house she'd been stuck with for months. For once, a potential buyer wanted to visit the place! Max walked toward her to shake her hand. A cloud of perfume overcame him. He gave a small cough.

The woman stood straight as a rod, ready to spin her tale. "This house is just perfect for you." She looked Max over, seemingly satisfied by what she saw.

"Listen —"

"You didn't choose it, did you? It's more like it chose you among the hundreds of people who walk down this street every day. Do you believe in fate?"

"Señora —"

"What's your sign?"

Raquel took Max by the arm as if he were her son, though she was younger than him, leading him toward the Landermann residence. Max didn't know what to say but finally asked, "So how's business in Granada?"

"So-so. But my properties never stay on the market for long. Because I choose them carefully, take care of them personally … because I love them. As much as I love men," she added, a sly smile on her face.

"You knew Landermann?"

She burst out laughing. "Do I look that old?"

With her long, bright red nails, Raquel tapped a password out on an electronic keypad before inserting a card in a slot. The gate opened, and with it the lights that surrounded the entire property came on. Max felt as if a well-rehearsed play were beginning.

The *señora* indicated the window. "We had to board up the windows because of thieves."

"The neighbourhood's dangerous?"

Raquel had made a mistake. She found a way out elegantly. "The whole world, *señor*. Here as elsewhere. If you leave a house abandoned, it'll quickly become prey to looters! In every neighbourhood, the good neighbourhoods like the bad ones."

"Thieves! They lack all decency."

From up close the deterioration Javier had spoken of didn't seem quite so bad. But it was nighttime. Anyone who knew anything about real estate would tell you never to visit a house after dark.

Another card and another code for the front door. It stood tall, grand, really, double doors swinging open. Raquel turned the light on. An entrance hall two storeys high, a monumental chandelier hanging from the ceiling. A staircase, on the right, led to a mezzanine that continued to the back of the home. It felt like first class on a luxury liner.

"Sumptuous, isn't it?"

And of rather startling kitsch. Chandeliers, mirrors, friezes, and lace. As if the architect had been held back, contained when he designed the exterior, and had gotten his revenge inside, letting loose his mad imagination. From one moment to the next, Max expected to see a major-domo or a maid pop out from behind a carpeted door. The Landermann couple, clearly enough, hadn't had much of a sense of humour. Or they were the funniest people in Spain. Had to be one or the other.

Señora Zarzuela was already leading the way up the grand staircase, her earrings and bracelets echoing in the cavernous room like a handful of nails dropped on a marble floor. Her face red, breathing heavily, she showed Max to the mezzanine level. It was a living room, in fact. To the right, he could see a kitchen, the first one. There was a second one in the back of the house, and a third somewhere over there, she told him. The agent offered to show the bedrooms immediately.

Back on the first floor, they walked through another large area, which the Landermanns had used as a parlour, then various rooms that could be used as offices or children's bedrooms.

"If you have children, of course."

Her eyes twinkled. Perhaps she could get, as well as the commission, a friend for a cold winter night … an American perhaps?

Raquel pulled the drapes open to reveal two ceiling-to-floor windows giving onto the backyard. The reception had surely taken place in that garden. Outdoor lighting snaked around trees and paths. Finally, a stone wall behind which you could see Iglesia de San Cecilio and Hospital Militar. Max imagined Kevin slipping in among the guests, a glass of champagne in hand, trying to hide the stain on his shirt. A camera in the pocket of his dinner jacket. Circling small boys like a pervert. Looking for a red mark on the back of a child's neck. How had he managed to get in? Perhaps thanks to Laura Costinar. And why were they having a party here in the first place? What was the occasion?

With Laura Costinar and Peter Kalanyos there, it seemed to point to some sort of reception for Roma. A *Kris romani*? There was a time when the Roma came to find refuge near Granada in Sacromonte and its caverns.

The garden was definitely the highlight of the visit. Raquel had kept it for the end. Standing next to Max like a concert pianist after a stellar performance, she waited for the applause and the bouquets of roses.

He smiled, then threw out a line. "What a wonderful place for a party, isn't it?"

She took the bait. "You're right. Last summer we had, oh, two hundred people here for an event. The owners had the property cleaned and opened especially for the occasion."

"I thought the owners had died."

"The Landermann couple, yes, they both passed away. But the house was purchased by a company. Aspekt-Ziegler. Do you know them? They make furniture."

Max hid his surprise. Aspekt-Ziegler, who'd been behind both Nordopak's fortune and its ruin. Aspekt-Ziegler, Raymond Dandurand's goose that laid golden eggs. The lives of father and son intertwined again. What role had Raymond played in this whole affair?

Max felt like the answer was there right under his nose. Soon he would be able to see the whole picture. The notary's mysterious envelope, as per Lefebvre's posthumous demands. A document that had pushed Kevin, in utmost secrecy, to jump on a plane for Spain to attend a garden party in a home linked to his father, Raymond. At the garden party, a gangster usurping Kevin's fatherhood, pretending Sacha was his own. A gangster named Peter Kalanyos who had breakfast with Kevin a few months later in Bucharest. The same Peter Kalanyos Caroline had seen in Grande-Vallée the day before Raymond died. Everything tied together with a thread that remained invisible to Max. There had to be a relationship connecting Nordopak's bankruptcy, Kevin's con against his father's company, and the latter's links to Ioan Costinar, the Romani leader.

Roma, Romania, death. And Sacha-the-Red, of course, at the heart of the mystery.

"How do you like it?" Señora Zarzuela asked, her voice breathy.

"Very interesting. But first I need to speak with my wife."

33

When preparing for the scam, Max had done his research on Nordopak, discovering fascinating information about how the company had been founded. Gérard Lefebvre and Raymond Dandurand had spent years building their reputation, trying to convince potential customers to trust them.

Younger than his partner, and in better physical shape, Raymond became the travelling salesman. He journeyed across America and Europe, meeting important players, looking for contracts, softening up potential customers. There was some interest, surely, but most prospects were worried about Canada's production costs. In the early 1970s, the Canadian dollar was worth as much as the American dollar. Why pay for transportation if you weren't going to save on labour?

According to Kevin, his father spent interminable weeks criss-crossing the Old World and the New, with only middling results to show for it. Nordopak was barely treading water. It hadn't hired anyone in recent memory. Meanwhile, the whole continent was experiencing a period of spectacular economic growth Something was off, a hidden knot, a problem the mentor and his protégé weren't able to solve.

And then, all of a sudden, everything changed. A huge contract from the Netherlands.

Aspekt-Ziegler, an important producer of flat-packed furniture, one of the few companies able to actually compete with IKEA. Both businesses wanted to achieve a presence in North America. A race for market shares between two giants, and Nordopak set to profit from it. In order to avoid exorbitant transport costs, the Dutch company decided to deliver its furniture in bulk to a North American subcontractor — Nordopak — with its Canadian partner assuring packing and distribution throughout Canada and the eastern United States.

Raymond Dandurand's company was suddenly a money-making operation. Soon eighty percent of its profits came from this providential customer, finally assuring a certain stability for Nordopak, a stability that had been sorely lacking.

Aspekt-Ziegler gave carte blanche to its Montreal-based partner. The Dutch company was betting on a discreet infiltration, the complete opposite of IKEA's strategy of opening big-box stores in North American suburbs. Instead, throughout North America, you'd walk into any furniture store and find examples of

Aspekt-Ziegler products — this meant lower risk for the Dutch enterprise as it saved on infrastructure costs. It would have been foolish, anyway, to try to compete with IKEA at that company's own game; the Swedish firm's retail model was already well established in North America. Aspekt-Ziegler's infiltration strategy was entirely consistent with Nordopak's interests; in short, it meant more packing and more shipping.

After the contract was signed, gone were the days of constant travel for Raymond. Now customers came knocking at his door, wanting Aspekt-Ziegler's partner for themselves. Nordopak grew at an astonishing pace. The fleet of trucks doubled, tripled, and quadrupled. Dandurand's small operation — he'd become the only captain after Lefebvre's retirement — had become a prosperous, dynamic business, its potential for continued growth seemingly unlimited.

But in 1998, after years of profits, an unforeseen turn of events: Aspekt-Ziegler abandoned retailing and decided to reorient toward industrial furniture, prioritizing the Asian market. And so it dropped Nordopak. Kevin could remember his father's repeated trips to Amsterdam, trying to convince the Dutch firm to modify its decision.

In vain.

Aspekt-Ziegler's new management — there had been a generational change within the enterprise — wanted to geographically realign the company's activities, all the while renewing its clientele. Few buyers, but a lot of volume centred on emerging markets. Aspekt-Ziegler, in short, was admitting defeat at the hands of IKEA in America. They'd turn to China and India.

It was the beginning of the end for Nordopak, despite Raymond's creative accounting: fake orders, fake American customers.

Aspekt-Ziegler and Raymond Dandurand.

Max wondered what lay behind that relationship.

In the last few weeks of winter, the businessman had been desperately seeking a solution. Perhaps he'd gone to Manitoba not to meet with Ioan Costinar, but with Peter Kalanyos, whom he'd bring back with him to Grande-Vallée, and whom Kevin would later find in Granada.

But there was no evidence of the Hungarian's presence in Woodlands. Both Garrison and Jennifer had been unable to identify him.

Was Aspekt-Ziegler the link between Raymond, Laura Costinar, and Peter Kalanyos?

Was Aspekt-Ziegler linked to the Roma?

Was the Woodlands trip a failure? Perhaps not, since Raymond had come back and put his plan into execution.

Sacha's kidnapping.

In exchange for the child, money. A lot of money. Enough to fill Nordopak's coffers.

Money paid by Aspekt-Ziegler?

A deal with the devil then. Where the men on both sides of the handshake turned out to be Satan.

The drunken emperor, his deal done. He'd climbed into his car, his grandson already in the hands of Peter Kalanyos or accomplices. The accident on the bridge was supposed to take only one life, and a fraudulent one at that. Perhaps according to the initial plan, Raymond was supposed to survive, call the police, ask for help, guide the dredging teams. Raymond, the only witness, saving his company by … selling his grandson.

Kevin was right: his father was a monster.

Unfortunately for Raymond, events hadn't turned out as he'd expected. The deal hadn't been respected. Raymond was dead, the funds hadn't been paid out, and Sacha had disappeared.

One thing Max still didn't understand: what could the child actually be worth? Raymond had gone to Manitoba convinced he could get millions in exchange for Sacha, knowing how important he was to certain people. Anti-Romani activists, according to Marilyn Burgess. Who knew for sure? In any case, people who were ready to pay a tremendous sum for a toddler. The sheer level of violence exercised to recover him demonstrated that he was crucial to someone's plans.

Max was following his friend's footsteps, and he was now facing the same dangers. From now on the road would be even more fraught. The Romani man at the car wash had been right to wish him *latcho drom* …

Raquel Zarzuela hadn't wanted to reveal the name of her contact, the person with whom the real-estate agent communicated for questions related to the Granada property. She feared Max might make a deal directly with Amsterdam, making her lose her commission. But Max was persuasive — over the course of a passionate night in an apartment on Calle Pedro Mártir.

Dawn came, and Raquel poked her head from under the covers, her body still tangled in her satin sheets, a sleepy Madonna. "Do you still want that phone number?"

Max played the game. He kissed her passionately, and they made love again.

After, she coiled herself around him, simpering. "Frank Woensdag. You can reach him at his office every day except Wednesday. Funny, isn't it?"

Max didn't understand.

"Woensdag means Wednesday in Dutch."

Max thought back to his last conversation with Kevin in Bucharest: *I'll tell you on Wednesday.*

Frank Woensdag.

Max returned to the Albergue San Miguel in the early hours, his body beat, lost in thought. He noticed a shadow rushing to his right, emerging out of the half-light on Avenida de los Alixares. Footsteps. Before he could turn around, his arms were grabbed from behind and lifted over his head. Max struggled to free himself, attempting to elbow his assailants, trying to stomp their feet. He bent over at the waist suddenly, trying to free his arms, but all he got for his troubles were a few kicks to the back of the head. Struggling to remain conscious, he felt himself being dragged toward a car parked at the far end of the street. He was thrown onto the floor of the back seat like an old rug. Within seconds he heard the rumble of the car driving off into the night, then unconsciousness.

Max opened his eyes. He wasn't sure whether he was dreaming or the blow to his head had been harder than he'd thought. Around him, to his left and right, a hundred or so beds. He was lying on his back, long legs poking out between the metal bars at the foot of the bed, a thin cotton sheet thrown over him. Max scanned the room. Tall windows, some of them covered, took up an entire wall. Over his head, very high, ancient metal lampshades green from patina covering burnt-out light bulbs. Before him, between the two rows of beds, a long line of tiny sinks over which mirrors had been installed. Most of them were shattered or simply missing. The size of the bed, the size of the sinks. Max understood immediately. He was in a dormitory, likely in a boarding school, one that hadn't been used for years, if not decades, considering the state of the place.

Max sat up on the bed. His head still hurt, but little by little he was beginning to see a bit clearer. Whoever had intercepted him and taken him weren't cops — that much was clear — or he'd be in prison somewhere. This place was no prison.

He looked at himself in a scarred mirror. Bruises over his right eye, dried blood on his left cheek. The bastards hadn't gone easy on him. To the right of the mirror, a child's scribbling, drawn in chalk, which had somehow survived the years this place was left abandoned: a moon over a leafless tree.

"Granada isn't a safe city even for a professional crook like you, Max O'Brien."

Max had no trouble recognizing that voice. The same one that had asked him to meet on Alexandriei Boulevard in Bucharest … with Laura Costinar's passport.

Max turned around.

The speaker stood on the other side of the door frame, a heavy leather vest on his back and two henchmen flanking him, as if protecting a piece of millennial porcelain.

Peter Kalanyos.

Max recognized the two men as his attackers: they didn't seem any friendlier in the light of day.

Kalanyos walked toward him. He bore a long scar on his face, an old injury, probably won in his days as a petty criminal in the streets of Budapest.

"Where's Kevin?" Max demanded. "Where's Sacha?"

Kalanyos smiled.

Max noticed that the Hungarian's two bodyguards were armed, guns slipped in holsters visible whenever they raised their arms or moved rapidly. Fleeing wasn't an option. The two men would shoot him dead before he could get to the door.

"Where's Kevin?" Max repeated. "What have you done to him?"

"According to Romani traditions, children are raised like little princes in a climate of total freedom. We never reprimand them. Discipline isn't a popular value among the Roma."

What was he trying to get at?

"Which is a mistake," Kalanyos continued. "And so I chose a nanny who was fair but knew how to properly discipline a child. She was always with him, making sure he grew up right. Unfortunately, while I was off meeting someone who claimed to have access to European drug markets ..."

The character Kevin had invented.

"… Laura Costinar disappeared with the child." Kalanyos shrugged before continuing. "You're right to look at me like that. I got taken like an amateur." His face darkened. "The nanny paid with her life. I don't tolerate traitorous behaviour, as you well know."

Before dying, the nanny had incriminated Laura. Her information, and Sacha's, were sent to every *kumpaníya* in the country, which had led Kalanyos to Kevin.

"We caught both of them. They were interrogated without success. Laura wasn't able to survive our questions, unfortunately."

Anger rose in Max, masked by worry. He could well imagine what Kalanyos had done to his two victims.

"Leave Kevin alone. He's got nothing to do with your damn agreement."

"An agreement?"

"In Grande-Vallée with Raymond Dandurand. You had a deal with him but double-crossed him."

Kalanyos burst out laughing. "You've got quite the imagination!"

"What, you didn't kill him?"

"You ask too many questions, O'Brien."

"Why Sacha?"

Kalanyos sighed. He was getting bored — that much was clear. "My secrets are my own. I'm only here to tell you to go now and find the child."

"Sacha isn't your son."

"His name is Féro."

"You have no right!"

"I don't give a damn about your *gadjo* laws." Kalanyos walked closer to Max, sneering. "I'm still holding Kevin

Dandurand somewhere in Romania. He's in good health, don't you worry. But I'm not sure how long that'll last." He sniffed at Max and stared him down. "I care about Féro as if he were my own son. I'll do anything to get him back."

Including killing Kevin.

Max took a step back. "Just like you killed twenty-three Roma on Zăbrăuţi Street!"

"Collateral damage, as the *gadje* are so fond of saying." Kalanyos walked back to his bodyguards. "As soon as you give me Sacha, I'll give you Kevin. Alive and well."

The Hungarian was about to leave the room when he turned around for a last thought. "Oh, and by the way, don't count on your friend, Toma Boerescu, to play behind my back. He's slippery, the old man. It wasn't easy to get my hands on him. But it's done now. He won't be much help to you, believe me."

Boerescu . . .

Max's eyes were filled with hate.

There was no way to know whether Kevin was still alive. The son of a bitch could be lying to him. But Max had no choice. He was at the mercy of this madman.

"Do we have a deal?" Kalanyos asked.

He knew the answer already.

34

Emil Rosca had only seen his wife, Eugenia, a few times since he'd learned she was pregnant again. Though they already had three children, Emil was overjoyed when he found out that a fourth was on the way. He was hoping for another boy, though he'd be just as happy with a girl. According to Romani tradition, a pregnant woman became *marime*, or "unclean," which meant Eugenia had to leave the *kumpaníya*. In any case, due to uncleanliness again, it wasn't as if the birth could take place in the family home. Elias Hospital, Mărăști Boulevard, was used to admit pregnant Roma, who in exchange accepted to be touched by *gadjo* doctors, thus preserving tradition. Just before the expectant mother gave birth, Eugenia's friends would come and untie every knot in her clothes and hair to make sure the umbilical cord would also be free of knots. Nurses knew about these practices and worked around the rituals.

And so, until the day she gave birth, Eugenia would stay with a cousin in Chitila, a suburb of Bucharest, where the *kumpaníya*'s women regularly visited her, along with their only daughter, Alina. Besides them, Eugenia lived as a recluse. Anything she touched in her cousin's house was also considered unclean and would be destroyed after the child's birth. And even after her delivery, Eugenia wouldn't be able to come near her husband for several weeks and would be forced to wear gloves inside the house to avoid contamination.

Of course, such customs had loosened over the years. The world Emil had been born in had possessed far more unyielding traditions. But Emil was attached to his people's traditions, just as Eugenia was. For him, as for his father, the Roma weren't aimless wanderers on the road of life, but possessed traditions, history, culture.

In the kitchen, where the family spent most of its time together despite the size of the house, Emil had pinned a green-and-blue flag to the wall, a red wheel at its centre. The official emblem of the Roma, adopted at the London congress a few months earlier. The flag had similarities with the Indian flag, to remind all Gypsies of their roots. What was more, that word — Emil had to correct himself often — would no longer be used by the Roma. The word *Gypsy* was banned in favour of *Roma*, the Romani people, a decision made to change *gadjo* perceptions as well as to elevate the distinct identity of the Roma.

At the congress a national anthem was also adopted, composed by the Serbian Rom, Žarko Jovanović: "Opre Roma! Roma Arise!" And April 8, the date of the congress opening, would be forever known as International Romani Day.

Emil had never felt better than he had since his return from London. Romanestan wasn't spoken of much there except by a few doe-eyed romantics and nostalgics. The youth were elsewhere. As one participant had stated: "All of Europe is our nation. Why should we create another?" And since the greatest concentration of Roma in all of Europe was found inside Romania's borders, Emil's speech had been well attended.

Speaking in front of the delegates, Emil had recalled his family's exceptional trajectory. The Rosca had played a determining role in the emancipation of Romani slaves in the nineteenth century. His father, Anton, had spat in the face of Heinrich Himmler. Emil spoke of unity, of solidarity, words he'd never used — the words of Ceaușescu and his pals — but which that day, before the assembled Roma, finally came to mean something he endorsed.

Emil also spoke of the future, of the changing role of Romania, his country forgotten behind the Iron Curtain in the deep end of Europe. It would evolve, yes, like all nations eventually did. The Roma had a responsibility to help it along, to contribute to this evolution, by learning how to read and write, by becoming interested in *gadjo* affairs, by refusing to circle the *vôrdônă* and think only of themselves, as they had done too often over the centuries.

He received a standing ovation. Emil had never felt so important, so useful. The admiration he received had nothing to do with the blind, hypocritical adulation of the one-hectare Romani kings of his homeland. As the crowd applauded, he took a moment to think of his father and dedicate the moment to him.

When he returned to his room later, a woman was pacing in the corridor, waiting for him.

Christina, joy plain on her face.

She took him in her arms, hugged him close. "You were magnificent."

Back from London, Emil found that Nicolae Ceauşescu wasn't in a hurry to see him or hear his report. Emil attempted to talk to Ceauşescu but was simply passed from one secretary to another without ever managing to actually speak to the Conducător himself. Finally, Nicolae invited him to his own house.

Emil was forced to wash his hands with alcohol twice and put on rubber gloves and paper shoes before being admitted to see Ceauşescu. The dictator led him through the door to an immense room shrouded in darkness. Ceauşescu flipped a switch, and fluorescent light exploded in the room, blinding Emil. As he blinked back sight to his eyes, Emil realized that most of the area was taken up by a large table covered in a thick velvet sheet. Ceauşescu seemed as nervous as a child showing off a science experiment. With a single movement, he finally whipped the sheet off the table, and an enormous model appeared under Emil's surprised gaze.

"So?"

Emil looked at his friend, standing far from him as usual, afraid of his germs.

"My future House of the People …"

The Romani leader knew Ceaușescu dreamed of leaving something behind, a monument to posterity worthy of his achievements. But Emil had never thought it would be so … grandiose.

"It will be the largest building in the world, Emil. After the Pentagon in Washington. My beautiful Elena came up with the idea."

"And where will you build it?"

"In the capital, of course. We'll tear down the slums to build it."

Emil didn't know what to say. Anyway, Ceaușescu didn't care to hear his thoughts. Hypnotized by his fantasy, it was if Emil were no longer in the room. His eyes filled with a strange light, contemplating the mad model of a madder idea.

A long moment. Emil shifted from foot to foot. Finally, Ceaușescu spoke. "You wanted to speak to me, Emil?"

"About my trip to London …"

"London? Why the hell did you go to London?"

After that, Emil didn't go back to see Nicolae. When Eugenia had become pregnant, he hadn't told Ceaușescu the news. In any case, the King of the Roma was far too busy thinking of his new child. At night he would try to come up with two names to give the child. A Romani name that would be used in the *kumpaníya*, and a *gadjo* name that would change according to country, religion, and culture. On her end, Eugenia would give her son or daughter a third name, a secret one, known only to the mother, which she would whisper in his ear to protect him from life's trials. None of these names would be spoken aloud before the child was baptized in a ceremony in which he'd be washed in running water to clean him of all impurities.

Emil hoped only one thing for this new son or daughter, the same thing he'd wished before the birth of his other children: that they would never know the horrors, the pain, that had so filled his life and his father's life. Emil had hope. For the first time in years, he was optimistic. The London congress had made him realize the political strength of the Roma, and their future as a people.

Tires squealed, tearing through the night. Car doors slammed shut. The sound of feet running toward the house. Emil rushed to the window but didn't have time to open it. Police burst through his front door, filling the kitchen. Emil's eldest son — sleeping in the next room — woke and ran to his father's arms. Emil cowered against the wall. Other men in civilian garb strode in. Emil recognized among them the Securitate agents who'd interrogated him before he'd left for London. That was why they were here — his trip to London.

"Wait a minute! What are you doing?"

Emil sought to calm the men down, to get them to listen to him, but there was no point. He noticed through his window that several houses on his street, all of them Romani homes, had been raided in the same manner. All of a sudden Emil was filled with the memory of his family's arrest by the Nazis in 1942. He held his son against him even more tightly.

An agent came near him. He walked with the air of one in charge. A tall man, physically strong, face covered in acne scars, he wore a heavy leather coat despite the season. As the men tore through the entire house ransacking it as they went, the agent noticed the Paolo Soprani on a chair next to the table. He was about to throw it onto the floor but suddenly changed his mind when he noticed the Romani flag hanging above the table.

"You don't love Romania anymore, Rosca? You don't love my country?"

His country.

Emil didn't want to answer. The Securitate agent smiled. He ripped the flag from the wall and threw it onto the floor before stepping on it and finally spitting right in the middle of the wheel.

Emil couldn't help himself anymore. "Ceaușescu will make you pay for that, you goddamn bastard!"

The brute took one long step toward him, face to face, staring him down. "What did you just say, you son of a bitch?"

"Ceaușescu will put you in jail for what you just did!"

The man looked at Emil for a moment, then burst out laughing. "Ceaușescu? He's the one who sent us!"

They were handcuffed and dragged out of the house and into the yard. Emil walked first, his son following him. They saw flames bursting out of the windows of several homes on the street, the shouts of Romani men and women as they fled into the night, taking with them only what they could carry. Emil recognized some of his neighbours being arrested, stuffed into the back of prisoner trucks, packed like sardines without a care. A mass arrest taking place all across the neighbourhood at once. What was happening? Why? Why now?

Emil and his son received a modicum of privilege. They were seated in the back of a heavy ZIL-114, the acne-scarred agent in front. Soon they were driving away down the muddy road. The car interior reminded him of the one in Vorkuta. A new model, just as luxurious. Nothing good could come out of this ride.

Emil held his son close.

The ZIL fell in line behind several other trucks, down Colentina Boulevard. Emil understood they were being driven to police headquarters. It had to be a mistake. His friend, Nicolae, couldn't be betraying him, not after all these years.

But instead of going down Moşilor Avenue, the Securitate agent ordered the driver to take a right. Emil, worried, didn't dare look at his son, afraid of revealing his own fear to him.

"What's going on? Where are we going?"

The agent turned to Emil. "Chitila. I almost forgot about your wife."

Emil closed his eyes. He knew it was useless to try to talk to this brute. He slid down the seat, still hugging his son against him. The world was once again falling apart.

It was dark in Chitila. Honest Romanians were sleeping soundly behind locked doors. The Securitate bastards knew the address already; they didn't even miss the alleyway on the left, the one you had to take to avoid a dead end. They had been here before — that much was clear. They'd monitored the place, knew what they were getting themselves into.

The ZIL came to a stop in front of a small, modest house. It, too, plunged in darkness. The agents forced Emil and his son out of the car. Emil saw he had an opportunity. One last chance.

He shouted as loud as he could in Romani, "Eugenia! Run! Run, Eugenia! Run away now!"

The butt of a weapon swung into his stomach, and he folded over, his breath short. His son started crying loudly. Another blow, this one to the back of his head. Emil collapsed. Agents ran into the house, turning on every light, waking everyone up. Emil was about to lose consciousness when he heard a tumult coming from the house. He looked up and saw Eugenia and Alina standing before him in their night clothes. Eugenia, her belly wide, fear in her eyes, a policeman holding her by the hair. Emil's eldest son held on to his father; he didn't want to let go of him for a moment, not even to go to his mother. Emil realized the neighbours were staring at them through their windows, not daring to come any closer for fear of being arrested themselves.

The Securitate agent turned toward the street and shouted, "Your neighbours are Gypsies! Do you know what we do to them?"

Emil heard his wife cry out.

Then a gunshot.

Eugenia fell to the ground, hands over her stomach. Blood leaking between her fingers. Eugenia dying on the sidewalk. Ignoring his son's cries, Emil took his own head in both hands. He wanted to die. He shouted, moaning into the night, the total indifference of the Securitate men the only reply. Stone-faced, they dragged him back to the car.

A few hours later Emil, dressed in overalls, sat on a short bench, the sort used to milk a cow. The room was completely dark, not a single opening for light to get through. He had no idea of its size, though the echo of his shuffling feet made him think it was cavernous. His ankles were tied to the bench, he realized, as he tried to move his legs farther apart. He couldn't remember when he'd been tied up. Probably when he reached this jail. Or was he at the headquarters of the Securitate? The second option made more sense. Meanwhile, Emil thought, on the other side of Bucharest, Ceauşescu, the Genius of the Carpathians, slept soundly, dreaming of his House of the People.

The Romani leader couldn't believe what the Securitate agent had told him. It simply couldn't be that Nicolae had deserted him.

Impossible.

It had to be a mistake. Nicolae would burst through the door any moment and apologize.

A light exploded in the dark, blinding him. He couldn't turn his head away from it. Emil blinked and blinked and finally made out a desk, a man sitting behind it. He wore a suit and tie. A face as serious as death behind small round glasses. He had the air of a professor as he read through a huge dossier in front of him. Emil's file probably.

There was a long period of silence, then the man said, "Emil Rosca, I'm Vasil Lionu, the prosecutor named by the Ministry of Internal Affairs to shed light on accusations of sedition and incitement to armed revolt."

Sedition? Armed revolt?

"You know the law. It's forbidden for any Romanian to have contact with a foreigner unless special permission has been granted by the Securitate."

"Nicolae Ceaușescu authorized my trip!"

"We aren't speaking of London."

Emil didn't understand.

Lionu pulled a sheet out of the dossier. "Rossen Markov and Paul Vaneker. You met both of them willingly on June 14, 1968."

That was three years ago, and the bastards had decided to go after him now.

"Funds of unknown origin are circulating in Romania …"

"They're being used for the education of Roma."

"Ah, so you're admitting —"

"I demand to speak to Nicolae Ceaușescu!"

The prosecutor took his glasses off.

Emil added, "He's my friend. Godfather to my children. I'm sure he has no idea what you're doing to me."

"Where does the money come from, Rosca?"

"I want to see Ceaușescu."

Lionu ignored him. At length, in a tired, emotionless voice, the prosecutor proceeded to enumerate all of Emil's "crimes," followed by the number of whatever article of the law he'd broken. A long litany, as useless as it was absurd, a mantra almost, during which Emil thought only of Eugenia, poor Eugenia, and Christina, as well, and every Roma in his neighbourhood, in his *kumpaníya*. All his fellow Roma who had tried to forget, to annihilate memory, to pretend they were safe. Emil realized that forgetting was death, especially for a people whose future was constantly refused them. He thought of his father, Anton; they'd been separated when he was still so young. Thought of his mother, and his brothers, and the sisters he'd barely known.

The world walked on its head, he thought. No, it was more like the world walked on the heads of all Roma.

"Of course, there's no point in denying it," Lionu concluded.

"Leave me alone!"

The prosecutor put his glasses back on. "The punishment has already been determined. Why burden the court with these crimes committed by a Gypsy?" His eyes narrowed. "The same crimes as always for your people. Treachery, spying, collaboration with the enemies of the people."

Emil heard footsteps on his left.

And out of the darkness, a ghost appeared: Dr. Hans Leibrecht in a white lab coat. He was older, more bent than in Auschwitz, but his eyes were filled with the same evil light.

Emil couldn't believe his eyes. He felt cast back to Dr. Mengele's clinic twenty-eight years ago in Block 10 of the Stammlager.

"Do you still play the accordion, Emil Rosca?" Leibrecht asked in German.

Emil was speechless.

Leibrecht smiled, then slipped his hand in his pocket and took out a straight razor, its blade glinting.

Emil shivered.

"Do you know that I have no idea what they did with our samples in Berlin? At the institute, I mean. Mengele was convinced he could demonstrate the inferiority of the Gypsy race by the shape of your ears."

Leibrecht barked what in another man might have been laughter. "Those were the good old days, right, Emil? We had fun in Auschwitz, didn't we?"

Emil closed his eyes. He knew what was coming next.

"Such a shame we were interrupted that day …"

Emil, his eyes still closed, waited for the knife to reach his face. A few breaths, and still nothing. Emil opened his eyes and shouted out in horror.

His eldest son, unconscious, lay on a gurney.

Just as Emil had in Block 10.

Leibrecht walked to the child and slowly rolled the gurney closer to Emil. He could hear his boy breathing softly.

An angel.

"Gypsies have the most beautiful ears, don't they?" Leibrecht smiled wider. "I'll show you what you missed, Emil Rosca. Look, look and see what you avoided that day. Look closely …"

35

As soon as he was released by Peter Kalanyos, Max rushed to Málaga to grab a flight. On the way to the airport, he called Toma Boerescu in Bucharest. The old man didn't answer. His second call was to Marilyn Burgess. He told her the anti-Roma movement had nothing to do with this whole affair: it was an inside job. Kalanyos was responsible for the Zăbrăuți Street fire and the deaths of Cosmin Micula and Laura Costinar. What was more, he was holding Kevin hostage and threatening to kill him if Sacha wasn't brought back to him.

Silence on the other end of the line, as if Burgess couldn't believe him. "Does it have anything to do with drugs?"

"I don't think so. I doubt Sacha plays a role in the rest of Kalanyos's dealings. What's more, Kevin is still in Romania."

"I'll take care of it. I'll be in Bucharest tonight."

Max gave her Toma Boerescu's address, mentioning the threats Kalanyos had made. Burgess promised to send someone to check up on the old man. It was too late probably. After the call, Max tried to reach Boerescu again, but his fixer still didn't answer the phone.

From Amsterdam's Schiphol Airport, Max grabbed a cab to the Renaissance Hotel near Centraal Station. The hotel seemed the perfect place to lie low: it was filled with American tourists on holiday. Spacious rooms, thick duvets, efficient, anonymous employees, a bar busy with airline crews and travellers in transit, victims of jet lag — it would have been the perfect place to rest and recuperate if Max had had the time. Instead, he'd chosen the place for the discretion it provided him.

Aspekt-Ziegler's headquarters were spread across a series of eighteenth-century homes between Vijzelstraat and Leidsegracht in a posh neighbourhood in which the city's favoured sons had once lived. Original facades had been preserved along a canal lined with centenary elm trees. The manufacturing plant was near Zaanstad in the northern suburbs of the city — a factory that now ran at half capacity. Since its expansion in Asia, Aspekt-Ziegler had subcontracted production of most of its orders to the Philippines.

Over the phone, Max had introduced himself as a representative of JPMorgan Chase vacationing in the Netherlands. Someone had told him about the house Aspekt-Ziegler owned in Granada. His boss had asked him to check whether they might rent the house for a retreat the following summer. Frank Woensdag wasn't in, so the operator transferred his call to Eva Kerkhoven, Woensdag's assistant.

Kerkhoven invited Max to her office on the top floor under the attic. From the waiting room, Max could see the crescent moon canals, roads filled with cyclists despite the cold weather. He imagined Raymond Dandurand coming to this magnificent city to plead for his company's survival in 1998 after the contract with Nordopak had fallen apart.

"Mr. Payne?"

Tall, elegant, maybe sixty years old, Eva Kerkhoven wore a suit and had reading glasses around her neck. It was immediately clear that her greatest responsibility was to save her boss the inconvenience of people trying to meet him; this Payne character was just another man waiting to annoy Woensdag. She offered Max her hand, which he took as warmly as possible, offering his widest smile despite the woman's rather stony glare. Kerkhoven explained that Frank Woensdag was vacationing in Indonesia and wouldn't be back before February. His colleague, Bernard Rutgers, might be able to help. Unfortunately, Rutgers was at the Zaanstad factory for a meeting.

"He won't be back in today, I'm afraid."

Afraid, most of all, that Max would want to stay the whole day.

Frank Woensdag and Bernard Rutgers were charged with managing Aspekt-Ziegler's real estate. The company was looking to get rid of some of its properties over the medium term, which explained why the Granada house had been put on the market.

"Are you looking to rent? We have an agency over there, which takes care of —"

"I know. My boss asked me to get in touch with Frank directly."

Eva Kerkhoven repressed a tic of impatience. She might pretend to manage the company, but Max had no intention of giving her the satisfaction of pretending to believe her.

"I can arrange a meeting with Mr. Rutgers if you would like."

Kerkhoven went into her boss's office to look through his schedule. So very busy, unfortunately. Max glanced through the open door into the office and noticed curling trophies in a small display case. He smiled.

"He won't be able to see you before next week. Would Monday afternoon work for you?"

At the tourism office in Centraal Station, Max's question was answered without a raised eyebrow. Why wouldn't a fanatic of curling want to have a game while waiting for his train to Paris? The Spaarnwoude Professional Curling Club had just expanded, demonstrating the affection the Dutch had for the Anglo-Saxon sport. Over the phone, Max pretended to be an American colleague of Bernard Rutgers and learned that the

Aspekt-Ziegler employee was currently sweeping in room 8.

"No need to bother him," Max told the club's receptionist. "I'm on my way."

Max reached the curling club just as Rutgers was coming out of the changing room. An employee pointed him out to Max. Tanned and thin, and a lot younger than Eva Kerkhoven. An ambitious young man on a path to the highest spheres of the company. Max walked toward Rutgers and told him the same story he'd given his assistant. "Your guard dog did her job, but the decor in your office betrayed you."

Rutgers smiled and guided Max to the bar. The place was decorated with wood panelling and smelled of old cigar smoke. It felt like the sort of private club you'd find in London when Great Britain ruled the world. Rutgers was a regular — that much was clear. A young woman brought him a box of Montecristos without being asked. Rutgers offered one to Max, who refused. But he did accept the beer the executive ordered. After the server left, Rutgers got straight to the point. "The house isn't for rent. It's for sale. Someone gave you the wrong information."

What was more, as soon as Frank Woensdag took his retirement, all of Aspekt-Ziegler's real estate would be liquidated. A few months away, not much more than that, he claimed.

"Originally, the property in Granada belonged to Aspekt-Ziegler's founder," Rutgers added.

"A bit off the beaten path, isn't it?"

"A gift from his friend, Francisco Franco."

"General Franco?"

"The one and only. During the civil war, Landermann fought alongside the Caudillo. In the 1960s, as a show of friendship, Franco gifted him the house. From a grateful nation and all that."

Old Landermann went there several times a year, organizing receptions where everyone who was anyone in the government came to pay their respects. At the time, of course, Aspekt-Ziegler tried not to put too much emphasis on its founder's particular friendships, even though the presence of General Franco in Spain was tolerated, much in the same way as António de Oliveira Salazar in Portugal or Georgios Papadopoulos in Greece. European companies went on with their trade and their partnerships, never feeling too bad about it. Still, at the time, Landermann caused headaches for the Dutch company's public-relations department.

"When Landermann died in 1994, it was a relief, really."

He was a vestige of another era, last witness to the dark years when three-quarters of Europe lived under the domination of totalitarianism.

"Which didn't stop Landermann from setting himself up in a mausoleum as big as a cathedral. It's worth the trip — and it isn't very far from here. At Nieuwe Ooster Begraafplaats …"

Which explained why Aspekt-Ziegler wanted to get rid of the Granada house.

Max went for it. "I was told you rented the house recently for a reception of some kind. A *Kris romani*? Strange, no? Landermann was a bit nostalgic for his fascist past, right? How does that square with a Romani meeting?"

Rutgers looked at Max, trying to evaluate the man before him. Max's questions had obviously raised doubts in his mind.

Seeing the man's hesitation, Max decided to double down. He pulled out Sacha's picture from his coat pocket and showed it to Rutgers. "Who is this?"

"Taken in the garden of the Granada house during the reception." He looked up at Max. "What are you looking for, exactly?"

"I need to find this child. The man behind him is called Peter Kalanyos. He's a criminal. He's linked to the murder of Ioan Costinar, a Romani leader. He's holding the child's father hostage."

"Who are you exactly? You're no banker."

"Let's just say I'm a friend of the family."

Rutgers's face closed up. He pulled his cellphone out. "What are you doing?"

"I don't know what you're after. I'm going to call New York to find out."

Max got up and left before Rutgers finished tapping out JPMorgan Chase's number.

Before returning to his hotel, after another unsuccessful attempt at reaching Toma Boerescu in Bucharest, Max followed Bernard Rutgers's suggestion. He made a quick stop at the cemetery the man had mentioned. The cab driver dropped him off at the southern gate, asking whether he should wait for Max, who told him no. As the cab drove off, Max passed through the gate into the deserted cemetery. The only sign of life was the lit-up windows of a small house on his left. Soon night would fall; Max had thirty minutes or so of daylight left. He found a map of the cemetery and located the section with Werner Landermann's mausoleum. He began walking north among the tombstones.

Max wondered whether Landermann had negotiated the service contract with Raymond Dandurand. The deal that had made Raymond's company in the early days. Probably not. In the early 1970s, Landermann was already an old man who'd let go the reins of his company, according to Rutgers's insinuations. Max wondered with whom Raymond had negotiated at the time.

The mausoleum was impossible to miss. Bernard Rutgers had been right. An enormous, garish monument halfway between a bank and a jail. Celestial angels playing trumpets, wearing bay leaf crowns, riding Roman chariots. All of it in grey stone with Landermann's name in golden letters. Pretentious in life, pretentious in death. But only Javier, the barman in Granada, to miss him. No mention of his wife on the mausoleum; however, she was probably buried not too far away.

Max soon found her tombstone. It was more modest than her husband's, naturally. And outside the mausoleum, as if he'd been afraid that she would steal his thunder.

Christina Landermann had died in 1997 at the age of seventy-eight.

Max walked near it. On and near the tombstone, large buttons, like you'd have on a dress shirt or a coat. Strange. Max realized there were quite a few of them around the mausoleum. Twenty or so at least that the wind had scattered all over the place.

"The Roma. They come sometimes and pay their respects here."

Max turned around. The cemetery guard was there, leaning against a rake, observing the mausoleum. The small house at the entrance was probably his.

"A way to show their grief, I guess. They tear the buttons off their clothes and throw them on the tomb. To calm the *mulo*, you understand?"

"The *mulo*?"

"The spirit of the dead. A ghost." The caretaker smiled. "If you stay, you'll see him. The *mulo* only comes out at night and at noon. Only when there's no shadow."

Max was intrigued. "And why do the Roma care about this woman?"

The guard shrugged. He had no idea. "I asked Paola whether it bothered her. She told me it was fine."

"Paola?"

"Landermann's daughter."

36

The connection between Aspekt-Ziegler and the Roma had been Christina Landermann. Mourners had come to pay their respects: Roma tearing the buttons off their coats before her grave. Had she been behind the agreement that made Raymond Dandurand's fortune? That question stemmed from the realization that Max had just had. And what had been Christina Landermann's role within Aspekt-Ziegler itself? He wouldn't be getting any more answers from Bernard Rutgers; the man would be too suspicious of Max now. Paola, however might know a thing or two.

Paola Landermann — Christina's daughter — finished work at six. She had a gig in accounting at the Academisch Medisch Centrum, one of Amsterdam's most important hospitals. Max left her a message, pretending to be a representative for an American insurance company wanting to hand her a reclamation cheque. Paola called him back almost immediately, and they agreed to meet.

Max met her in the hospital lobby at six.

"I hope it's one of those novelty cheques!" Paola was perhaps fifty or so and smiled as she walked toward Max, briefcase in hand.

He led her to a café off the lobby, immediately disappointing her. "There's no cheque. I only needed to get in touch with you."

"But ..."

Paola was confused. And slightly worried. Max quickly told her of his visit to the Amsterdam cemetery, giving her the details of the relationship between Raymond Dandurand and Aspekt-Ziegler. He revealed what he knew of Kevin's presence at the garden party in Granada, where he'd finally gotten proof that Kevin's son had survived the rivière Saqawigan accident.

As he spoke, Paola became increasingly intrigued. Max described where his investigation was taking him, closing in on a Romani connection, something intimately linked to the Roma.

And the most recent link was Christina Landermann.

Paola only had answers when it came to her own mother. For years — even when her father was still alive — Paola's mother had made generous donations to the Romani community, funding literacy programs in the Netherlands and abroad, clinics, pharmacies, all of it with money out of Aspekt-Ziegler's philanthropy accounts. In addition to this front-line work, she'd also funded political initiatives like the World Romani Congress in the early 1970s.

"After my father died, our house in Granada was often lent to Roma from across the world, who used it as a meeting place."

"Do you know why?" Max asked.

"My mother was the daughter of an early Nazi supporter. She grew up in the inner circle, completely obsessed by the strength and persuasion of Hitler, Himmler, Goebbels, and the rest of them. She spent a few years in Auschwitz. On the right side of the barbed wire — at least that's the way she saw it at the time."

Paola lowered her eyes, uncomfortable. "My mother sought redemption, forgiveness, I guess you could say, for everything the Nazis had done. Especially toward the Roma."

"Forgiveness for your father's deeds?"

She hesitated, then said, "Him and the others. Werner was her second husband. He changed his name in 1946. During the war, he was called Matthias Kluge. Her first husband was also posted at Auschwitz — Oskar Müller."

"Did Matthias Kluge, did your father approve of your mother's philanthropy?"

"He never knew anything about it, or perhaps he pretended he didn't." Paola smiled. "My mother didn't reveal my father's past to the media and let him pal around with his old fascist friends in Granada, and in exchange, he let her give money to her lepers, as my father would say." Paola hesitated, then added, "A marriage of convenience."

Max showed her a picture of Sacha with Peter Kalanyos. Paola shook her head. She'd never seen the child, or the Hungarian Rom. She didn't know Kevin from Adam, either. Paola had never set foot in the Granada house and had never heard of Raymond Dandurand. She also doubted her father would have let Christina negotiate an agreement with a North American contractor.

According to Paola, neither Landermann nor the top brass at the company would ever let Christina make any important business decisions.

"My father didn't take her very seriously. To his eyes, Christina only became interested in the Romani cause because she was bored. She was a housewife. For some it's museums, for others the philharmonic, but her own interest fell squarely on the Roma."

"Clearly, you didn't agree with him."

"No. But I'm still not sure I understand what truly animated her. Christina was secretive, didn't confide much. It took years for me to know … and still …" She paused. "My mother lived in her own secret world. She let no one in. Not even her only daughter."

Paola sighed, visibly troubled. "I regret it today. Not having known her. Not having made more of an effort to get to know her."

At least that explained the relationship between Christina Landermann and the Roma. Still, there remained a missing link: the one that tied Raymond Dandurand — and by extension Kevin and Sacha — to the Roma. If Raymond had had a relationship with Ioan Costinar, he would have likely been familiar with

Christina, as well. But how had these meetings taken place? And in what context?

According to Paola, her mother had had no influence on Aspekt-Ziegler's activities, but she must have had an ally, an accomplice within the company. Someone high up who would have been able to make business decisions, someone Landermann trusted. A friend of her husband, perhaps, who she'd manipulated into helping her carry out her plan. She would have had to take money out of the company and redirect it to the Roma. Had Raymond taken advantage of the same largesse, unbeknownst to Landermann?

Max tried to think back to the context that had led to Aspekt-Ziegler's decision to partner up with Nordopak in order to penetrate the American market. The work Raymond and Gérard Lefebvre had done to make sure Nordopak stayed afloat. Max had to find a way to put the pieces of the puzzle together.

He called Caroline in Montreal and asked her to go through Kevin's papers in his Old Montreal apartment. Max remembered having seen a file on Nordopak.

Two hours later Caroline called back with details on the file: mostly business plans, memoranda, press releases, all dated from after Kevin's return from New York. She added that for anything older Max should get in touch with a man called Guido Bergamini at Cambiano's headquarters in Turin. All of Nordopak's archives had been transferred there after it had been bought out.

It took a day for Max to finally reach Bergamini, the man in charge of putting order to Nordopak's archives.

Some of the material had been organized already, some not. It would be a lifetime of work.

"I've got a favour to ask," Max said to Bergamini.

"Prego."

"In 1973 Nordopak signed a contract with Aspekt-Ziegler. I was wondering what information you might have about the agreement, the names of its signatories, the names of the employees who worked on its ratification."

To justify his interest, Max claimed he was one of Nordopak's retirees preparing an article for the company newsletter. Bergamini believed him but warned Max not to get his hopes up, since he might not find anything at all.

After leaving Bergamini his cellphone number, Max called the NIOD Institute for War, Holocaust, and Genocide Studies in Amsterdam. He scheduled a meeting with Simon Stern, a professor at the institute, for that very afternoon.

The institute was in Amsterdam's City Centre on Herengracht. It taught courses on the Holocaust and genocide in general and collected documents and information on the crimes of the Third Reich, among other activities. Over the phone, Stern told Max that his organization often collaborated with the International Tracing Service in Bad Arolsen, north of Frankfurt, and distributed the results of its research to similar centres all over the world. By gathering as much information on the events of the Holocaust as possible, academics and curators of centres across the globe, like Stern's institute, had made the Shoah the most well-documented genocide in the history of the world. Ironically enough, they were helped by the Nazi obsession with paperwork, as well as the Jewish community's insistence on remembering.

Simon Stern was waiting for Max in a conference room on the first floor of the institute. "Good afternoon, Professor Harris. Welcome to Amsterdam."

Max was playing the part of a teacher travelling through Holland on vacation, though taking a bit of time to find new ways to get his students back in Chicago interested in history. He sought suggestions on how to really imprint on his students the extent of Nazi horror. To shake them out of their torpor and reveal the truth.

Stern was entirely sympathetic to the teacher's predicament. He wasn't the only one seeing forgetfulness creeping in. Parents would sometimes come to the institute to speak with him, confused and distraught by their children's indifference. Some of these parents were Jews themselves. For them, forgetting, a fading of memory, was the worst possible sin. They saw their children shrug, uncaring, at the Holocaust. Ancient history from another age. There were more recent genocides to care about.

Max thought it might just be about marketing. Old crimes in black and white lost to newer ones in colour and stereo sound. One of the NIOD Institute's chief purposes was precisely, humbly, to preserve the memories of genocide.

Tall, his back bent, Stern had eyes that burned with energy despite his venerable age. When he offered Max his hand, the latter looked for the number tattooed on the former's forearm. Max knew Stern was a camp survivor. The old man caught Max's glance.

"The tattoos were only in Auschwitz. I was in Buchenwald. Yellow triangle on striped pajamas. But the result was the same."

Stern was captured in the last few months of the war after being hidden by a German family for four years.

"Can you imagine? A typical Bavarian family. Blond hair, red cheeks, a young mother with a bright smile. They were like ad copy for the Third Reich. And yet …"

One day their neighbours turned them in for a few ration tickets. Stern managed to flee before the Gestapo came, but he was caught a few days later, famished, as he trudged toward the Allied lines.

"Did the family survive?"

"Miraculously, yes."

Stern guided Max through the institute. They passed shelves full of documents where technicians busied themselves scanning and preserving them electronically for posterity.

"In Poland the Germans were caught off guard. The Soviet advance was faster than they anticipated. Especially near Kraków."

When the Wehrmacht soldiers began their retreat, camp leaders at Auschwitz blew up the crematory ovens and gas chambers and took with them every prisoner who could still walk.

"Too little too late, in a sense," Stern told Max.

When they reached Auschwitz, the Russians discovered the sheer extent of the horror, of course, but also important caches of documents, which were sent back to Moscow. Since 1991 the Frankfurt International Tracing Service and the NIOD Institute had gotten most of the documents back, which gave Stern and his team a better idea about the situation of detainees in Auschwitz and nearby camps.

"I'm looking for a German," Max told him. "Werner Landermann. He was an officer at Auschwitz to the end."

"Aspekt-Ziegler's founder?"

"He was called Matthias Kluge then. I'm also looking for one of his colleagues — Oskar Müller."

Stern put his glasses on and gestured at a young woman to come over. She smiled at Max as she neared. Clara, the computer specialist. The old man spoke a few words in Dutch, and Clara quickly found the list of Auschwitz officers.

"There he is. Matthias Kluge, an accountant at the time. Low-ranking, however. He was only a corporal."

A young man typing away on his calculator as smoke rose over the ovens at Auschwitz.

"He probably worked on IBM equipment," Stern murmured. He turned to Max. "IBM received through its German subsidiary, Dehomag, a contract for the registration and classification of detainees."

"Even though the Americans were at war against Germany?"

"Not before 1941. And by then the camps had already been in operation for seven, eight years."

Kluge working away on IBM equipment in the shadows of killers. He'd gotten off scot-free at the end of the war, hidden behind greater evil. Just like IBM, he'd never answered for his complicity in the genocide.

"The same goes for Bayer, the pharmaceutical company," Stern said. "It used prisoners as guinea pigs."

The institute professor told Max that Siemens, BMW, Thyssen, Daimler-Benz, Krupp, and IG Farben were all companies that had used prisoners for test subjects or forced labour without any consequences after the war. Most of those firms were still in existence today.

"The Allies didn't want to repeat the mistakes of 1918," Stern continued, "when they humiliated Germany with the Versailles Treaty's conditions. As early as June 1944, when it became clear the Nazi defeat was inevitable, the Allies began working to ensure that Europe would recover as quickly as possible, Germany first in line."

And so Kluge and other lower-ranking Nazis had been able to walk away from the destruction unscathed. And some, like Kluge-become-Landermann, made a fortune in postwar Europe.

"Why did he open his company in the Netherlands?"

"Europe was in ashes, but in some places the ashes hid fertile soil, while in others there was only salted earth. Warsaw, Dresden, Frankfurt, Rotterdam were all in ruins. But Kraków, Prague, and Amsterdam remained relatively unscathed. Kluge found willing and qualified labour in the Netherlands and discovered infrastructure that was relatively intact."

"Did he build his company on riches pillaged from the camps' prisoners?"

Stern shook his head. "It's possible, but I doubt it."

By the time they reached the camps, detainees had nothing on them except for the clothes on their backs and, rarely, jewellery they'd managed to hide. Theft occurred earlier in the process, when the poor men and women had been arrested. Once they reached the camps, the *kapos* were first in line, especially those who unloaded trains, as at the Judenrampe. A man like Kluge, confined to the offices of the Kommandantur, didn't have access to the prisoners.

Stern led Max to a shelf and asked him to pull out a book — a photo album with a leather spine. It had been seized by a Russian soldier from an SS officer and contained portraits of the garrison, much like every other army in the world would have. Soldiers standing at attention, looking serious. Others relaxing, playing cards, drinking schnapps. Women, as well, among them Christina Landermann, at the time married to Oskar Müller.

Max looked through the pictures. What had they thought would happen? That they would meet for pretzels and beer two decades later to laugh and joke about the good old days? Such delusion, such cruelty. It revolted Max.

"A number of officers lived outside the camp in homes confiscated from Poles when Birkenau was constructed. That's probably where these pictures were taken."

"Is Matthias Kluge in any of these photos?"

"In this album, no. Probably elsewhere."

"And Oskar Müller?"

"The conductor …"

Max glanced at Stern, confused.

"There were orchestras in Auschwitz, several of them, really. Led by detainees, except for one. Müller's orchestra." Stern leafed through the last few pages. A group picture, musicians in black coats. "There he is. Oskar Müller and his orchestra."

Max scanned the picture.

Stern continued. "They were unlucky, these poor musicians. The day before the camps were liberated, Müller gathered the orchestra in one of the Stammlager's blocks. He pulled out his service weapon and killed them one after the other. Then he shot himself in the head."

The old man pointed out the accordion player. A frail young man behind a huge instrument, all patched up. "The only one who survived was Emil Rosca. Have you heard of him?"

The name meant nothing to Max.

"A Romanian Rom, a descendant of the famous Rosca family."

Another Rom. Once again Max's search returned to them.

"What happened to him?"

"He was arrested by the Soviets and sent to a gulag in Vorkuta. He was freed by Nicolae Ceauşescu." Stern sighed. "Later the dictator got him, anyway, and Rosca disappeared in his jails."

Hitler, Stalin, then Ceauşescu. That man had suffered through an unenviable life.

"Perhaps you've heard about his son? Ioan Costinar? A leader of the Romanian Romani community. He, too, was killed. It was a few years ago now."

Max looked up.

Emil Rosca interned at Auschwitz, father of Laura's husband. Member of Oskar Müller's orchestra, Christina Landermann's first husband …

‡

Back at the Renaissance Hotel, two messages were waiting for Max. The first was from Marilyn Burgess. Max called her back immediately.

"Bad news. Your fixer's apartment was ransacked."

"And Boerescu?"

"We've got no idea."

Max sighed. Peter Kalanyos wasn't the sort to make an empty threat — that much was clear.

The second call was from Italy. Guido Bergamini, the archivist. He'd left his home phone number for Max, who returned his call right away.

"The agreement was signed in Granada," Bergamini explained. "In Werner Landermann's house."

It had been signed in the summer. Landermann had been spending his holidays there. Raymond had gone to that house, just as Kevin would years later to find his own son. Three generations tied to the same home in the shadow of the Alhambra.

"Among the signatories on the Canadian side there's a Gérard Lefebvre. And on the Dutch side we've got Landermann, Frank Woensdag, and Lars Windemuth."

Woensdag again.

Mr. Wednesday.

The other two were Landermann's colleagues, Bergamini explained, at least according to the company's own papers.

And where might Max find Mr. Windemuth?

"He's retired near Zutphen. There's something else, as well. The document makes it clear that the agreement will only take effect on November 12, three months after its signing, which is a strange detail that doesn't really make sense to me."

It made no sense to Bergamini, but to Max the date was familiar: Kevin Dandurand's birthday.

37

Kevin was born on November 12, 1970. His birthday had been used as a symbolic date for an agreement that would make his father rich. Had it been a moment of vanity for Raymond? A wink by an enthusiastic new father? Or did the date have deeper significance? Kevin at the heart of a deal between Nordopak and Aspekt-Ziegler. And Sacha, too, through his father. What role did the two of them play?

Max drove to Zutphen along a forest-bordered highway that eventually led to Germany. His mind returned to Kevin's role in Raymond's sudden prosperity. As if Kevin had been part of his father's deal with Aspekt-Ziegler somehow. But in what context? And why?

Roxanne was from Romania.

Kevin told Max one day how Raymond had met his mother while travelling through Europe on one of his many business trips abroad.

Don't be mad at him, don't resent him for anything. Ever.

Roxanne's words to her son when he revealed to her Raymond's infidelities, Sharon and Josée's existence.

Roxanne vowed eternal gratitude to Raymond. Why?

Zutphen, capital of Achterhoek, a roadside sign informed Max as he crossed the Ijssel River. He found a room at the Berkhotel in Kloostertuin before going out for breakfast at Gastenhuys de Klok, following a suggestion by a gas station attendant just outside Amsterdam. Max was to meet Lars Windemuth in front of Sint Walburgiskerk, the old city's most impressive monument. He'd told Werner Landermann's former colleague the same story he'd given Guido Bergamini.

It was much colder here than it had been the day before in Amsterdam. As he danced from one foot to the other in front of the church among a sprinkling of tourists, Max regretted not having worn warmer clothes.

"You're a journalist?" Lars Windemuth asked.

"Sort of."

White hair that used to be blond, thinning. A healthy old man, though his ruddy nose betrayed his affection for spirits — brandy, he'd later admit. Max gave him his spiel.

"You visited headquarters? Met anyone there?"

Max gave an evasive answer, turning the conversation back to what he was after. "I'm interested in a very specific period — Aspekt-Ziegler's deal with Nordopak in the early 1970s."

Windemuth smiled. "It was a wonderful time. I was young, the whole world was ours. Everything seemed possible."

"So why Nordopak? Why did Aspekt-Ziegler choose such a small company in Montreal?"

"A business decision like any other. Why so curious?"

He looked sideways, hesitant; he was hiding something.

"I'm not as confident as you are," Max said.

"I'm sorry?"

"I'm not so confident it was a business decision like any other. Other factors were taken into consideration, weren't they?"

Windemuth looked around them. "Why don't we go have a drink?"

A noisy bar near the church filled with patrons finding refuge from the cold. The place was warm and comfortable. After ordering a beer for Max and a brandy for himself, Windemuth described the work he used to do for Aspekt-Ziegler: he sought market opportunities, attempted to diversify product lines. At the time the future was in America, not Asia, as it was today.

"We dreamed of opening offices on Madison Avenue! Branches in California. To make Americans believe in our products, our ideas, our methods."

"The alliance with Nordopak was your idea?"

"Frank Woensdag's idea. He convinced Landermann to give the contract to the Canadians."

"Why?"

Windemuth shrugged. "Dandurand's company seemed exactly the sort of business we'd want to partner with."

"Come on now! The company was treading water."

"Exactly. Dandurand was easier to negotiate with."

"And what about Landermann? He didn't object? It was an important decision."

"By then Woensdag was the one at the helm, really, and the old captain was mostly left with a symbolic role. That would be the best way to describe it. Landermann hung around, signed on the line at the bottom of the page, but held himself far from the spotlight."

"Because he was a former Nazi?"

"Among other things. And he drank a lot. And spoke loudly. And shared his opinions. Which were …"

"Controversial."

"That would be one way to put it."

Woensdag had convinced him to stay in the shadows, Windemuth continued. Especially since at the time the hunt for former Nazis was on. Everyone dreamed of putting their hands on the collar of Josef Mengele, for example. Though no one could find him.

Windemuth furrowed his brow. "One day, in a meeting with Israelis, Landermann began boasting how he'd supervised the doctor's spending allowance in Auschwitz. Can you imagine?" He sighed. "No, you couldn't bring Landermann anywhere."

"And Christina in all of this?"

"His wife? She was discreet, but a hard worker. And she held something over her husband. She never set foot in the factory or at headquarters, but you could tell she cared how the company fared."

"Did she know anything about Aspekt-Ziegler's expansion plans?"

"Thanks to Woensdag she did. She's the one who got him into the company in the first place. In 1963, I think."

"And so he felt like he owed her something."

"What are you trying to say?"

"Christina put the pieces in motion for the Nordopak deal, didn't she?"

Windemuth took a long swallow of brandy, giving himself a little courage. Clearly, the question embarrassed him.

Max waited for him to put his glass back down. "Did Landermann know about the child?"

The old man's eyes widened.

Max had hit the nail on the head.

"What child? What are you talking about?" Windemuth acted surprised, obviously trying to hide the truth.

"The keystone of this whole deal, right? The child Raymond agreed to raise in exchange for a long-term deal with Aspekt-Ziegler."

Silence fell.

"Little Kevin, right? Only three years old."

Suddenly, a voice behind Max said, "Landermann died without ever knowing a goddamn thing."

Max swung around. Another old man behind him. Bald, dark eyes, tanned, leathery skin.

A Rom.

The man scanned the room before sitting next to Max and offering his hand. "Frank Woensdag."

"I thought you were in Indonesia."

"You thought wrong. I can't tolerate the heat." He smiled. "And I'm probably the only Rom you'll ever meet who hates to travel."

The Mercedes was headed north. Lars Windemuth drove while Woensdag sat with Max in the back. Landermann's former underling was answering Max's questions honestly without trying to hide anything, which surprised Max.

Yes, Christina had gotten him the job with Aspekt-Ziegler in the middle of the 1960s to make sure she could divert a portion of the company's profits toward Romani causes. She was particularly sensitive to their condition in Eastern Europe.

With a few colleagues, Woensdag had created a fake research-and-development department. It was used as a way to send money to Eastern Europe without raising Landermann's suspicions, or those of the political authorities of the recipient countries.

A little before her death in 1997, seeing her end in sight, Christina had placed a large sum of money in a Swiss bank account created to continue her philanthropic work with Roma across the globe.

"And how was Raymond Dandurand involved in all of this?"

"Aspekt-Ziegler could have chosen any number of companies far more suited to help it make a move into the American market. Christina was the one who wanted the contract to go to Raymond's business."

Max waited for the rest.

"Christina and Raymond got to know each other during his various business trips to Europe. At the time Dandurand was desperately seeking new contracts. He'd harass Landermann with his never-ending calls. They would eat together, Christina, Dandurand, and Landermann, and Dandurand talked non-stop about his company. That's how she became interested in him."

The Mercedes left the highway, and Woensdag continued. "I didn't understand, didn't know why she was so insistent. So I asked her. She told me Dandurand was willing to agree to quite the favour."

"Adopting Kevin?"

"Yes."

"Where was the child from? Romania?"

"Christina was discreet about that. She called me three months after the signing to tell me the children had arrived."

"There were several children?"

"Kevin and two others. I went over to Christina's apartment. Landermann was in Spain, I think. I mean, that's where he spent his summers. She told me that Dandurand would be adopting a young woman and a boy."

A young woman? Roxanne?

She wasn't Kevin's mother, but actually his big sister.

Max imagined the scene: Raymond coming out of Dorval Airport with a baby carriage, Gérard Lefebvre looking on dumbfounded. Raymond telling him he'd just saved Nordopak, thanks to a wedding and an adoption …

413

"And the other child?"

"A family in Great Britain. But it was harder for that one. The boy didn't have any ears …"

Ioan Costinar.

Kevin's brother.

A businessman in trouble agreeing to an impossible offer. Raymond becoming rich from his deal until the Dutch company severed all ties with his company in 1998, once Christina had passed away. By the time Raymond had been conned by his son and Max, Woensdag had already been pushed aside, replaced by a new generation of executives. Gone was Dandurand's secret ally in the company.

His solution? Find new collaborators sensitive to his problems.

And so Raymond went to Woodlands, Manitoba, to meet with Ioan Costinar because he was familiar with the Landermann widow's affection for the Romani cause. As a representative of the World Romani Congress, Costinar managed the funds Christina had left in an account just before her death. But Costinar hadn't made a deal with Raymond, and Raymond had returned to Montreal with nothing at all.

Or perhaps not quite nothing.

Raymond had been noticed by Peter Kalanyos, who had no relationship to Ioan Costinar. Kalanyos decided to take advantage of the situation. He travelled to Grande-Vallée a few days later, after killing Costinar, to murder Dandurand and take the child.

But again and always — why Sacha?

The Mercedes came to a halt in front of an opulent stone home hidden from the road by a row of spruce. Max got out of the car and looked around, taking a deep breath of brisk country air. As Windemuth drove around the house to park the car behind it, Max noticed a tricycle and toys. A child stood a few metres away, watching him, fear painted on his face. From where he stood, Max couldn't see the red mark on his neck, but there was no doubt, anyway: it was Sacha, little Sacha, Sacha from the pictures, Sacha-the-Red, Kevin's son.

"Sacha …"

Just as Max began walking toward him, a silhouette appeared from behind the trees. A woman walking straight to the boy to take him by the hand.

Josée Dandurand.

38

Emil Rosca's cellmate at Rahova Prison still remembered the hell of Pitești, where he'd been locked up in
the early 1950s. It had been Gheorghe Gheorghiu-Dej's
model prison, his masterpiece, his creation. Enough
to make Stalin jealous. In the evenings, after darkness
fell, Emil's cellmate told him his stories, a way perhaps
of making him appreciate their current conditions of
imprisonment. Pitești had been a "re-education centre,"
sadism its foundational philosophy.

"At first, Emil, we had to confess our sins and
denounce our former accomplices on the outside."

"Then we had self-criticism sessions where we
denounced our allies and accomplices within the prison.
After that we were forced to confess publicly, turning

our backs on our families, religion, wives, and friends. And, finally, the last step was re-education. We were sentenced to re-educate our best friend and torture him with our own hands."

The victim become the perpetrator.

During de-Stalinization, Pitești's leaders, including a number of "re-educated" citizens, were accused of purposely wreaking havoc and terror to discredit the Communist regime. Most were sentenced to death.

And the perpetrator become victim again, the circle complete.

Under Nicolae Ceaușescu, cruelty hadn't suddenly disappeared, quite the contrary. It had changed, though, into a more insidious, psychological terror. In the first few weeks of his imprisonment, Emil attempted in vain to get in touch with the Conducător. Ceaușescu was always away somewhere, he was told, travelling across the world, invited by foreign dignitaries, even in the West, where he'd become a golden child of sorts.

And then, little by little, Emil became used to his new life. After Auschwitz and Vorkuta, he came to believe that prison was his lot in life, his fate, his punishment.

His very own Gypsy curse.

One morning during roll call, a few months before being released, Emil learned that his children had died. He was standing with his fellow cellmates at attention in a row, like every morning, a guard walking behind them, counting out loud enough for another guard with a notebook in hand at the other end of the room to hear.

The roll call guard shouted Emil's name and number, moved to the next man, then suddenly turned and walked back to Emil, tapping his shoulder. "By the way, Rosca, your three pathetic children are dead. Rotting now. It's been more than a week. Fever took them, and we can thank fate for that."

Emil attempted to hide his hurt; he knew weakness would only be exploited. But the pain in him was like an ulcer bursting, like a cancer making itself known. He saw double but didn't falter, didn't give the bastards the satisfaction.

That night some of the other prisoners shared their rations with Emil, which he hadn't been able to swallow. He could only think of his children. Ceauşescu had succeeded where Hitler's concentration camps and Stalin's gulags had failed: the great line of Luca le Stevosko finally extinguished. Thanks to Emil, Ceauşescu had taken and kept power over his countrymen; he had used his naïveté and trust. All that Emil had left was regret at not spitting in Ceauşescu's face that day in Vorkuta, as his father might have. Unlike his father, Emil wouldn't have the opportunity to die with honour. He would rot away in prison for believing the lies of a *gadjo*.

Another Romani prisoner informed him that his children's possessions had been burned according to Romani tradition, just as Eugenia's belongings after she was killed. The ceremony had followed a *pomána*, a funeral feast, in which three living children played the role of the three who'd passed. The soul of the children having not yet reached the kingdom of the dead, the *pomána* helped give them courage for the long road ahead.

In the following days, Emil thought of ending his life. But he couldn't. Suicide would be conceding victory. A show of weakness.

By the time he was let go in the middle of the winter two years after his arrest, an emaciated and weakened Emil realized with terrible sadness that the living conditions of his people had greatly deteriorated. His house had been razed and a multi-storey building had been slapped together over his old mansion: it already looked as if it were crumbling. Electrical wires dangled from the windows, no one having even bothered to connect them to the electrical posts down the street. A balcony had collapsed into the parking lot, raising neither alarm nor complaint. Complain to whom, anyway?

The houses that had used to be owned by other members of the *kumpanía* had disappeared, as well, replaced by fallow ground, now home only to a few mangy dogs.

In the streets, Roma rummaged through piles of trash for something to eat. Others wandered to and fro, hoping activity would warm them, dressed in threadbare clothes stuffed with newspapers or cardboard.

So this was how Ceaușescu and his bastard henchmen thanked the Roma for putting them in power!

In a café in the suburbs north of Bucharest, Emil couldn't recognize a single face, despite the fact it had been a rather well-known hangout for Roma. The barman told him that he still saw Roma in the neighbourhood from time to time. Thanks to his help, Emil found a few Lovari and a group of Kalderash, and the latter led him to Sergiu, Eugenia's brother. They told him that Sergiu regularly visited Buftea Market. He would come into town in his truck, his pride and joy. According to another barman, Sergiu ferried Roma between farms during harvest season.

Emil walked more than twenty kilometres to see this brother-in-law. Sure, the man talked too loud and was rather rough around the edges, but he was the last of Emil's clan. He decided he'd ignore the poor opinion he'd always had of Sergiu. They'd never really had any affinity, but Emil couldn't care about that anymore. Seeing Sergiu would be like seeing Eugenia and his three children. It would be an attempt to regain a window into his life destroyed by Ceaușescu and the bastards who followed him. Sergiu was all the family he had left.

For a whole day Emil stood around Buftea Market before finally spotting his brother-in-law. The man's laugh hadn't changed, nor had his manners. You could hear him from a kilometre away.

When he finally noticed Emil, Sergiu looked like a man who'd seen a ghost. Without hesitation he took him in his arms. "I thought you were dead! They set you free! I can't believe it!"

"Not completely free."

Emil was assigned to a residence and couldn't leave Bucharest, much less Romania. Even his presence in Buftea was prohibited. Once a week, Emil had to meet with a Securitate agent. If he was caught breaking a single rule, he'd be sent back to prison. Though, in truth, the whole country would be his prison now until the day he died.

Sergiu kept staring at him, still disbelieving. "Come, I've got something to show you."

Emil climbed into the back of the truck, where he sat on jute bags among wooden crates. The truck left the city through busy streets. Emil glimpsed a roadside billboard: Nicolae and Elena surrounded by beatific schoolchildren. Disgusted, he looked away.

Sergiu lived in a home built with stolen materials, he proudly informed Emil. Other Roma had joined him in this improvised neighbourhood on the road to Găeşti. They all knew they'd be chased out of their new homes sooner or later.

For now it was their fiefdom.

A woman welcomed Emil as he jumped out of the truck. He didn't recognize her; surely, Sergiu had married again after his wife died during the destruction of the *kumpaníya*'s homes.

Suddenly, Emil jumped back, startled. Behind the woman, his two sons appeared, and their older sister, Alina, now a beautiful young woman.

He ran toward them and took them in his arms. He'd never been so happy. His three children were alive! He'd been lied to in prison — more torture to break his spirit. His eldest son wore a hat year-round to hide the scars left when his ears had been sliced off, Sergiu explained. Each side of his face bore large scars, long healed now. The pain must have been excruciating, but the wounds were superficial, and the boy hadn't become deaf.

Alina had been tortured, as well, and by the same Dr. Hans Leibrecht. She would never be able to bear

children. The doctor had practised on her the sterilization methods he'd developed in Auschwitz.

Emil held his daughter to him. They stood together
for a long time without moving.

He felt a presence at his feet. His youngest had
been a baby when Emil was arrested. Thankfully, the
Securitate hadn't put its hands on him. Neighbours had
hidden him under a pile of old clothes.

His three children with him.

His broken children.

His family he'd thought lost forever, now with him
again.

The happiest day of his life.

"Wait, that's not all." In the kitchen, Sergiu climbed
onto a chair and pulled out an enormous box from the top
shelf of a cupboard. Inside, Emil's old Paolo Soprani. The
gormónya had a few more battle scars from the Securitate
raid, but it had survived. "A keepsake to remind me of you."

Suddenly, incapable of holding back anymore, Emil
burst out in sobs. He cried for a long time, surrounded
by his children and Sergiu, of whom he'd been so con-
temptuous once upon a time but who today was giving
him a reason to live.

"I'll prepare a hedgehog," Sergiu's wife announced
with a celebratory smile.

Other Roma, told of Emil's return, joined them.
Kalderash, and Lovari especially, a few Tshurari: Emil's
reconstituted family.

"What will you do now?" Sergiu asked.

Emil had been thinking about this very question
since the beginning of the meal. When he had believed

his children dead, the future had been meaningless. But now only his children mattered. Sooner or later Ceaușescu would hear about his children's existence, or be overtaken by paranoia once again. Emil couldn't take the risk of being with his children when that happened.

The next day he sent a message out of the country.

Three weeks later it was time to act.

As planned, Emil rented a room at the Atlas Hotel beside the Timișoara terminal so that his children could rest for a few hours before continuing their journey. They lay in a pile on a too-soft mattress and were soon fast asleep. Emil dozed in a chair that dated from the 1950s. The night before they'd all climbed into Sergiu's truck and driven on back roads to avoid police roadblocks. Today, in Timișoara, was the last day of their travels in Romania.

As the children slept, Emil tried to understand why Ceaușescu had been so cruel to him and his family. His old friend had decided to isolate himself, as had Stalin, indeed as most dictators did, sooner or later. Up until recently the Roma had been an unstructured group without a political agenda. After the London congress, they'd begun to organize. Ceaușescu had chosen to act decisively while they were still weak, instead of waiting to face a stronger force later, one with credible leaders like Emil.

One thing was certain: Emil would never forgive Ceaușescu for what he'd done to his wife, Eugenia, and his family. And he'd certainly not keep the children where the Conducător might get his hands on them.

He heard the whistle of the train from Belgrade. The station was probably full of Yugoslavian tourists. They dressed well, walked with their noses high, just like Westerners, treating Romanians with condescension.

The next morning, as the train left for Belgrade, it would stop near Moravița on the edge of the Yugoslavian border, where Romanian passengers would get off, leaving only Yugoslavian passengers and the very few Romanians with exit visas — party cadres mostly. Their papers would be examined by Romanian border guards. Then they would go on to Vršac on the other side of the border, where Yugoslavian border guards would repeat the process.

And on that train, counterfeit papers in hand, Emil's three children would be on the road to freedom.

Emil's youngest pulled on his sleeve. It was still early, but Emil hadn't been able to fall asleep beyond a light, fitful doze. Had they been followed? Sergiu had been careful as always. And the hotel often housed Roma. The boss himself was a Lovari. A guy you could trust, Sergiu had insisted.

In the morning, the owner led them to a park near the train station, through little-used side streets, before heading back to his hotel. At that early hour in winter the place was deserted. While the two boys played a little farther away, Emil sat with Alina on a bench. He thought of his life that had brought him here, to this city, at this moment. The end of the road, he told himself. He thought of all the broken promises made to his father and himself. Commitments forgotten as easily as they'd been made. Once again, he cursed his naïveté, which had led Eugenia to her death, mutilated his eldest son, and made his daughter sterile.

He'd made his decisions for the good of the Roma and to further grow the legend of the Rosca family, but all he'd managed to do was lose his wife and put his children in harm's way. He could never forgive himself for that.

A woman walked toward the two boys, a German woman in a heavy winter coat. Christina. She squatted at their level and spoke to them as if she'd always known them. His eldest son glanced back at his father questioningly. Emil smiled. The younger one had already fallen under the charm of the German woman, who had offered him a chocolate.

Emil turned to Alina. "You're responsible for your younger brother now. You'll never be able to have children, but you'll raise your brother like your own son. Swear to me you'll never tell him anything. Never tell him about Romania, about his father, about his family."

His daughter wanted to know why.

"To protect him, Alina. To protect us all. Those who hurt you, they're dangerous, powerful people who can find you anywhere."

"And Ioan?"

"You'll be separated. You'll never see him again. To protect all three of you. There's no other way." He kissed Alina, trying to hide his tears. "Go now."

Alina stood before Emil one last time. Her whole body shook. She turned and ran toward Christina, who asked her to hold her little brother's hand. The German woman took Ioan by the hand and led all three children toward the edge of the park. Emil and Christina looked at each other. For a moment, he felt like running to her, taking her in her arms, kissing her, feeling her heat one last time, but he didn't dare put his children's lives in danger. His children were used to separation by now; they'd be fine. They had already spent two years without him. For them, Christina would be another substitute mother. They would soon forget their father.

When the group of four reached the end of the street, Emil got up and followed at a distance. Full of obvious affection, Christina bent over to say a few words to the children. Emil watched them go with her toward the country she'd chosen for them. He hadn't asked where they were going in case someone tried to torture the truth out of him. Emil told himself that at least he'd have done one good thing in his unfortunate life: he'd given his children the possibility of better lives outside Romania, far in distance and time from the horrors Emil himself had suffered through.

Emil stopped following them. It would be too dangerous to continue. Christina and the children were already crossing a large boulevard, heading toward the train station. His children were moving quickly; Christina had probably promised them ice cream. Leaning against a fence in the park, he saw them disappear among the crowd of travellers.

"Hey, you fucking Gypsy! Where are your papers?"

Emil whipped around. Two policemen stood beside him, with a third cop behind them. The three of them shivering. They were probably waiting to return to the station to warm up. Emil was their last identity check before their break. He was trapped by the fence — nowhere to run. Emil took his papers out and handed them to the officer, who backed up a step before taking them, as if afraid of being contaminated.

The officer understood from the papers that Emil had broken his parole conditions.

Emil offered no resistance as they dragged him toward a car. They roughed him up a little. It wasn't mean-spirited; they were merely trying to warm up a little. They drove back to the station, their prey in the back of the car.

They had to stop a few blocks later as the Belgrade train passed in front of them. Between the two officers, in the back seat, Emil craned his neck to watch it go by. He saw passengers moving from one car to the other. Tourists straightening their jackets or checking on their luggage. Perhaps making their way to the dining car. They were probably all happy to be returning to Belgrade and the relative freedom offered by Marshal Tito. Romanians certainly hadn't been lucky in the dictatorship lottery. Among the passengers were Christina and his three children, but he didn't see them.

The train disappeared, the gate lifted, and the police car started off on the road again. Surprisingly, Emil felt reassured, content. His children would have a fresh start — that was all that mattered. His existence no longer held any importance at all. From here on out, all he needed to do was wait to die, and then he'd finally be free.

39

A fire burned in the large hearth. A country holiday, Max thought to himself. All that was missing
was some eggnog and a few Christmas songs. And
yet the atmosphere was tense. From the kitchen, Max
heard glass clinking: Lars Windemuth preparing a
few cups of coffee. On the floor, Sacha played with an
elaborate set of plastic cubes, seemingly ignoring the
presence of adults. He was closed in on himself, seemed
lost, confused.

Max wondered what Sacha understood of the situation. He'd been torn out of his home for a second time,
torn from a usurper father, but the only father he'd ever
known. Back in Montreal, Kevin and Caroline would

surely seem like strangers to his eyes. He would forever remember his life in Romania, would miss it, probably. Max understood Kevin's desire to rebuild his family as it was before the tragedy, but did he really understand what he was getting himself into? Nothing would be given freely, nothing would be easy for the parents. And for Sacha it would be harder still.

And then there were the legal aspects to consider. Officially, Kevin's son had died in rivière Saqawigan. If he suddenly came back to life, a crime had been committed, kidnapping, fraud, something! The authorities would be forced to crack open the case of Raymond's death: who knew what would be revealed then?

Josée sat next to Max. "Kevin stopped in Paris on his way back from Spain, from Granada. He showed me Sacha's pictures."

Kevin had told her his plan: he'd take Sacha away from his kidnapper by himself without recourse to the judicial system.

"I tried to convince him he shouldn't," Josée added. "There'd been a kidnapping. Romania would need to respect the relevant international agreements."

But Kevin didn't believe he'd find recourse in the law.

How could he possibly win his case? His past legal problems would undermine his credibility. And then Peter Kalanyos could easily just disappear somewhere, taking the child with him, this time for good.

He had to act now.

Kevin had asked Josée to help him protect the child. The kidnapping would occur in Romania, but then he would need to take Sacha out of the country quickly and stash him safely somewhere, far from Kalanyos and his men.

"That wouldn't solve the legal problems of undoing Sacha's death," Max said.

"The practice where I work has a section dealing with international adoptions. The little boy Kevin would bring back to Montreal wouldn't be Sacha — officially — but another child, just another Romanian orphan."

Why had she agreed to help her half-brother? She'd never been that close to him in the first place. Kevin had revealed to her a face of her father she hadn't known. She wanted to play a role, a tiny one, to correct the pain he'd caused his son.

"And so Kevin put me in touch with Frank Woensdag."

Things had gone according to plan at first. Kevin succeeded in isolating Kalanyos in a Bucharest café while Laura Costinar took the child out of his house and brought him to Josée. Thanks to the adoption documents prepared by her practice, with their official authorizations forged by Cosmin Micula, the photographer, Josée reached Amsterdam without a hitch, Sacha in tow. She went to Woensdag's place, as planned, and waited for Kevin and Laura to arrive.

But they hadn't been able to leave Romania in time and had fallen into the hands of Kalanyos and his men.

"Kalanyos still has Kevin," Max said. "He wants to trade the child for Kevin. I spoke to him in Granada. He's going to kill Kevin if he doesn't get Sacha back."

Josée sighed. Both she and Woensdag glanced at the child. Max could sense how worried they were, completely at a loss.

Discreetly, Lars Windemuth placed a tray on the coffee table — hot bowls of café au lait, which everyone ignored.

One question still hadn't been answered, one Max had been thinking about since the beginning of this whole affair: why was Sacha so important to Peter Kalanyos? Why had the criminal gone so far, taken so many risks, to get the child back? He'd killed Laura, Micula, and many Roma. Gotten in the crosshairs of Adrian Pavlenco. Hunted Max down.

Woensdag sighed deeply. He seemed exhausted, as if he hadn't slept in days. "To understand that answer you've got to go back quite a few years and follow the difficult path of a naive Rom, ambitious but generous, as he went from a concentration camp in Poland to a Bucharest suburb terrorized by Ceaușescu, with a stop in Vorkuta, one of the most sinister gulags of Stalin's reign."

The man's father was Anton Rosca, a descendant of Luca le Stevosko. Anton's ancestor had fought alongside Mihail Kogălniceanu to abolish slavery in the nineteenth century. This fight gave his family a reputation respected by all Roma.

After the First World War, Anton Rosca had tied his fate with that of Carol II, reinforcing his authority on the country's Romani clans. Romanians and their political leaders in particular didn't know the Roma well. They couldn't understand these former slaves, didn't understand why they travelled constantly. Their culture, their lifestyle, was completely foreign to Romanians despite the fact they'd inhabited the same country for centuries.

In October 1933, Anton was one of the principal promoters of the first international meeting of

Roma thirty-eight years before the London congress.
Delegations from across Europe came to Bucharest to
try to create a unified Romani front.

What did Anton want for Romania? Romanestan,
where he could be king? No, and Carol II would have
never dismembered his own country, something the
Russians and Germans would soon do for him, anyway.
Anton simply wanted his people to have a role to play in
existing political structures.

Carol II refused. In any case, he had very little
authority over his rebellious parliament, his inchoate
democracy. Adding the Roma to the mix would have
been political suicide. Anyway, Carol's reign was coming
to an end. Unbeknownst to the Romanians, in August
1939, the Russians and Germans had agreed to divide
Poland, Romania, and other territories with the signing
of the Molotov-Ribbentrop Pact.

And so, after the invasion of Bessarabia and northern Bukovina by the Soviet Union the following year,
Carol II was forced to abdicate and hand over rule to
his young son, Michael. The latter sat on a powerless
throne. Romania's strongman at the time was General
Ion Antonescu, who sided with the Germans and
imposed right-wing policies across the country.

Antonescu hunted Jews and Roma, and Anton tried
to flee with his family. He was caught in a mass arrest,
though he wasn't identified. Deported to Auschwitz,
Anton made sure no one knew his true identity, a Roma
specialty. From inside the camp, unknown to all, Anton
led the resistance against Antonescu in collaboration
with Paul Vaneker, the Dutch *gadjo*.

But the Germans soon identified Anton and executed him after he refused to work for them. With Anton dead and his children exterminated, the Nazis felt they had nothing to fear from the Rosca anymore. They could be placed in the same category as the Krieks of Poland, Joseph XIII's Sinto clan, and all the other great Romani families mowed down by history.

Woensdag rubbed his eyes nervously, discovered the bowl of coffee in front of him, and took a long sip of it. Max did the same.

Sacha continued to play, ignoring the adults' conversation.

"Anton Rosca had a son who miraculously survived Auschwitz," Woensdag continued. "The Germans didn't realize it."

"Emil the accordionist."

Ioan Costinar and Kevin Dandurand's biological father. Sacha's grandfather.

In 1945, the Russians tossed Emil Rosca into a coal mine, like so many other former detainees. Stalin feared the prisoners who'd spent so much time with the enemy. Many of them went straight from the Nazi camps to the gulags. Emil was one of them.

At the end of the war the Allies divided Europe among them. The Russians received Eastern Europe after promising the Americans and British they would allow a right to self-determination for these countries. A promise Stalin made causally but never intended to respect.

In Romania the reversals of alliances and the strength of the resistance led to the creation of a coalition of political parties. Among them was a minority Communist

Party trying to rise to power. Moscow interfered in the 1946 elections and manipulated the creation of the new government, ensuring its control over the country. This led to the abdication of Michael, Carol II's successor.

"An inevitable abdication," Woensdag said. "Stalin threatened to execute five thousand students if Michael kept the throne. The king had no choice, so he fled to Great Britain."

The rest was a predictable mess: confiscation of private property, nationalization of companies, collectivization of agriculture.

The peasants fought rabidly against these changes. Armed resistance groups were formed. With the possibility of open civil war burning up the countryside, the Communists sought support wherever they could find it. That was when the little accordion player from Auschwitz came to mind. In 1949 Nicolae Ceauşescu, Gheorghe Gheorghiu-Dej's protégé and a rising figure in the regime, found Emil in Vorkuta and brought him back to Bucharest, luring him with the promise of Romanestan, a promise he, too, had no intention of respecting.

Rosca and Ceauşescu became good friends, a friendship that fell apart in the 1970s. Increasingly paranoid, exercising power over the country as a disease ravages the body, Ceauşescu threw Rosca to the Securitate, his secret police.

However, Emil had time to send his daughter and two sons to safety. In 1989, after the revolution, the eldest son returned from Great Britain under the last name of Costinar, accompanied by Victor Marineci. In London, where he'd studied, Emil's son had collaborated with the World Romani Congress as the titular head of the Romanian Romani community in exile — supported by Marineci.

Members of the new democratic government discovered the political power represented by the Roma. A power that had to be seduced, cajoled, wheedled, just like that of any other stakeholder. With Marineci's help, Ioan Costinar picked up where his famous father had left off. Within a few years, he became the spokesman that his father and grandfather had been before him. An educated, credible, convincing representative oriented toward the future.

Ioan's only problem: he and Laura hadn't managed to have a child, though they'd tried for years. Discreetly, they'd consulted with doctors in Great Britain, but to no avail.

Among the Roma, a child was the foundation of the family. Without children a Rom couldn't expect to lead other Roma.

"That's when things turned sour," Woensdag said. "For years I thought Ioan was a good man, beyond reproach …"

Max couldn't believe what he was hearing. "You're saying he's the one behind all this?"

Woensdag shrugged. "That's what Kevin believes."

According to Kevin, Raymond, looking anywhere to save his company, reached Woodlands, Manitoba, with the intention of asking Ioan Costinar for help. The businessman knew Ioan had access to the considerable funds Christina Landermann had taken from her husband's company. Christina had helped Dandurand once already when Raymond had agreed to adopt Kevin and wed Alina, who became Roxanne. Dandurand was going for broke.

Costinar learned that his brother, Kevin, had a son …

"Couldn't Laura and he adopt any child?" Max asked. "Why Sacha instead of another?"

"Before dying, in order to ensure that the money taken from Aspekt-Ziegler would always remain in the hands of the Rosca family and be managed by them, Christina arranged with her account's administrators in Zurich for a very particular deal. To have access to the money, in addition to the regular conditions, whoever wielded the account would have to undergo a DNA test to prove he or she was a member of the Rosca clan.

By secretly "adopting" Sacha, Ioan Costinar would gain the respect of all Roma. Sacha would become the king-in-waiting who would one day take over his adopt-ive father's business. After Ioan's death, Sacha would continue to have access to Christina Landermann's money, and so would be able to continue his father's good work.

In exchange for the child, Costinar promised Dandurand enough money to save his business.

Not long after, however, through circumstances Woensdag didn't know, Peter Kalanyos inserted himself into the deal.

"He and Costinar knew each other?" Max asked Woensdag.

"No, not at all. But, according to Kevin, Kalanyos got wind of the deal and understood Sacha was a gold mine. There was money in the boy."

Shortly after Ioan Costinar's murder on his way to Winnipeg's airport, Raymond Dandurand fell into the waters of rivière Saqawigan, and Sacha was off to Romania. Thanks to Sacha, Peter Kalanyos inherited the Rosca fortune.

No one knew the importance of the child, and so no one worried about another son in the Kalanyos family — his children didn't go to school in the first place. Among the Roma, the composition of families was always rather complicated, at least in the eyes of *gadjo* authorities.

The only thing that mattered was that the Zurich bank considered Kalanyos Sacha's legitimate guardian. The Hungarian Rom had the fake papers to back it up.

A perfect plan. Almost.

Kalanyos soon learned that the child wasn't the only inheritor to the Rosca name.

Max looked up at Woensdag. "But wasn't that the case? Ioan killed. Kevin and Gabrielle didn't know their origins. Alina died a long time before. Only Sacha was left."

"You're forgetting the father, Emil Rosca. After the revolution, Emil came out of prison. He was finally able to travel freely. He went to Amsterdam a number of times to see Christina while Landermann was vacationing in Spain." Woensdag smiled sadly. "He survived such horror, that little accordion player. He's even with us here today."

A door opened behind Max.

He whipped around, surprised.

An old man, his walker before him, struggled slowly into the room.

Toma Boerescu.

40

The Airbus began its descent beneath heavy clouds. Max O'Brien's mood darkened. Soon snow would fall on Bucharest, maybe just as the plane landed. The city was invisible, hidden behind a veil, revealing itself only at the last minute as the plane's wheels touched tarmac. Max had never been nervous in planes before, but this time his shirt stuck to his back and his hands were moist. The flight had gone smoothly. When the plane had taken off in Amsterdam, Sacha had watched the snowbound landscape of the Netherlands through the window in silence. After the Airbus finally reached the clouds, Sacha had gazed with fascination at the grey stuff around him, though he could barely see the tip of the wing.

Max thought back to Toma Boerescu, a.k.a. Emil Rosca. His incredible story, Sacha its end point. This grandson Boerescu would never have known about had become, in the course of things — by the acts of men, really — his only family, besides Kevin and Gabrielle. Christina hadn't listened to her lover's advice when she'd sent Ioan to his adoptive parents in Great Britain. She wouldn't accept the loss of his culture, so she'd chosen a Romani family, though one well integrated in *gadjo* culture. They had known about the importance of the little boy from Romania ...

"I was sent back to prison after Timişoara," Boerescu had told Max when the latter learned his true identity. "I was sure I'd never get out."

Unbeknownst to him, Christina had overseen Ioan's education from afar. She'd refused Emil's defeatism, thinking of the future, even though she'd lost faith in the possibility of true political reform in Romania or elsewhere in Eastern Europe. Boerescu agreed. The early 1980s had seemed to confirm their pessimism. And then, within the span of a few short weeks, the world had changed.

Freed, Boerescu could have taken up arms once again and supported Ioan, now an adult. Yet his life had taught him only harsh lessons, and he decided to live anonymously. Too many of Ceauşescu's cronies still held sway in the new Romania. For example, wasn't this new MP, Vasil Lionu, the prosecutor who had presided over his mock trial in 1971, constantly denying his links to Ceauşescu? The one who'd allowed Hans Leibrecht to savagely mutilate his son and daughter? The colour of the table napkins had changed, but it was the same bastards chowing down on the feast.

It was best if everyone thought Emil Rosca had died in the dungeons of the old regime, his existence forgotten once and for all.

"But I did follow what Ioan and Victor Marineci were doing," Boerescu told Max.

After Ioan's tragic death — victim of Romania's extreme right wing, or so Boerescu believed at the time — the old man had come out of the woodwork. Four times a year Boerescu discreetly travelled to Zurich in place of his son to cash a part of Christina's funds, which he then handed over to the World Romani Congress. He was almost caught a few times but always managed to hide his true identity on his return to Romania. Boerescu wasn't aware of the role Peter Kalanyos had played in Ioan's murder, nor did he know of Sacha's existence. He still thought the death of his son had been directed by neo-Nazis.

"Until Kevin appeared in Romania," Boerescu said.

Kevin didn't know about his adoption. Neither Raymond nor Roxanne had ever whispered a word to him about it. With them dead, his true origins could have remained a secret forever.

Josée had taken up the story. "But the letter Kevin received after Lefebvre's death sent him on a mission."

In the man's safe-deposit box was an envelope to be given to Raymond Dandurand or his heir. Michaud sent Kevin a package that contained, among other things, papers revealing details of the agreement between Nordopak and Aspekt-Ziegler in 1973. An agreement of which he was the central piece. It was a copy; the original had probably been destroyed by Raymond.

"Lefebvre had added a handwritten note, describing the details of Raymond's search and revealing the names of the people who'd been responsible for the unconventional business deal," Josée said.

Lefebvre had kept all of the information under lock and key since Raymond had come back from Amsterdam with a wife and a child in tow. That was how Kevin had discovered Christina Landermann's role in the whole affair, and the help offered by Frank Woensdag.

Over the course of a few days, Kevin had communicated with Woensdag and learned some of the details of the transaction. Among those facts was that his mother had been, in truth, his sister. What was more, he'd had a brother, a Romani leader named Ioan Costinar murdered six years earlier.

Kevin was intrigued — as Max would later be — with the coincidence between the dates of Raymond's and Costinar's deaths.

When Kevin sought out Laura Costinar to dig deeper, he'd learned from Frank Woensdag that she'd be attending a *Kris romani* in Spain in a house owned by Aspekt-Ziegler. A meeting of various clans, mostly from Hungary, to speak about the new Europe's growth eastward.

Max could guess what happened next. Once in Granada, Kevin had managed to gain access to the garden party. It had been open to *gadje* — journalists and supporters — and Kevin had seen, in the middle of a crowd of Romani children, his own son, Sacha-the-Red.

The next day Kevin told his story to Laura, sharing his suspicions and his intent.

"Was she aware of the agreement between Raymond and her husband about Sacha?" Max asked.

Boerescu had straightened up. "Ioan had nothing to do with this whole mess. I know it! He would never have kidnapped his own nephew, never!" There was a long silence, then the old man added, "Peter Kalanyos is responsible and no one else."

Woensdag nodded. Clearly, this wasn't the first time Boerescu had taken up Ioan's defence.

"Laura would have never tolerated it," Boerescu continued. "She knew nothing of any agreement. She also had no idea that Kalanyos was behind her husband's death."

When Kevin had told Woensdag of his son's presence at the Hungarian's party, it became clear that Kalanyos was the keystone of the whole tragedy. The man's criminal past only reinforced suspicions.

"When Frank told me about Kevin's journey," Boerescu said, "and when Laura explained what he'd discovered, it became clear that Kalanyos was responsible for my being tailed in Zurich as well as Sacha's kidnapping."

Kevin became obsessed with bringing his son back to Canada, while Laura wanted to get Kalanyos in front of a judge. They joined forces, and Max asked for Josée's help.

"And Cosmin Micula," Max asked.

Sergiu's son, whose family had taken in Boerescu's children during his detention in Ceauşescu's prisons.

Kevin's "almost cousin."

To Boerescu, Kevin's plan was a completely insane enterprise that didn't have a chance of succeeding. He'd refused to lend a hand. When Kevin and Laura were kidnapped by Kalanyos, Boerescu had finally decided to intervene and help Max, who'd just arrived in Bucharest.

For Kalanyos, Max was, at first, only another shit-kicker trying to get his hands on his adoptive son. And so he tried to pin Laura Costinar's death on Max, hoping the Roma would catch him and lynch him. But Boerescu made sure that wouldn't happen.

The old man smiled. "Sorry to have lied to you, Max ..."

"Kevin knows about you? About everything you've done?"

"He doesn't know me. I've never even met him." A veil fell over Boerescu's face. "Ioan is innocent. I'm sure of it. He can't have done what Kevin says he did. If I've come out of the shadows now, it's in part to redeem his memory."

As the plane came in for its final approach, Max put his hand on Sacha's shoulder. The little boy whipped around, his eyes wide, filled with fear, as if Max were about to hurt him. Max couldn't communicate with the child — they didn't share a language. It wasn't easy, but after a moment Sacha turned back to look out the window. Just then the wheels hit the tarmac.

From here on out, Max thought, things could go either way. He felt as if he were in some formidable poker game, the stakes life or death. He wasn't sure he was holding the nuts. All he was betting on was that the cards dealt to Kalanyos weren't as good as his.

The night before, Max had communicated with the Hungarian, telling him that Sacha had been found and Max was ready for the trade. Kalanyos would get Sacha back in exchange for Kevin. The Hungarian had demanded that the exchange take place in Bucharest itself, in Ferentari, where everything had begun. On Zăbrăuți Street, to boot.

Max would have preferred neutral ground.

"You'll come only with Sacha, not another soul. No weapons, of course. And without a police escort."

"And Kevin? What guarantees are you giving me?"

"None at all."

"If something happens, Kalanyos, I'll kill you with my own hands."

The Hungarian had barked a laugh. "I guess that means I'll see you in Bucharest soon?"

Max had called Marilyn Burgess to give her the details of his conversation with Kalanyos. There was no way Sacha could actually be given back to Kalanyos. Burgess and her team would set up in Ferentari. Snipers in the surrounding buildings. Kalanyos wouldn't stand a chance, she had assured him.

Max would have liked to share her optimism. He was mostly worried for Kevin and Sacha. Whether Kalanyos got away or not didn't bother him overmuch. Burgess and her team could get their hands on him some other time. That was, if he let Kevin and Max go; he might see it as his obligation to kill both of them.

Max would have to play hardball. There was no room for error.

The pilot asked all passengers to keep their seat belts buckled until the plane came to a complete stop, which would take only a few minutes. There were planes at every gate: rush hour at Otopeni. Romanians coming back from Western Europe, gifts in tow. Reuniting with their families and walking out onto home soil. The storm had begun, and snow was falling heavily.

A taxi — driven by one of Burgess's men in disguise — would be waiting for Max and Sacha outside the airport terminal. Other vehicles would both lead and tail them, switching up their roles occasionally to confuse any surveillance Kalanyos might have put in place. As soon as the Hungarian appeared with Kevin in Ferentari, Marilyn Burgess would snap into action.

The confrontation augured nothing well. There might be a shootout. Peter Kalanyos didn't seem the sort of man to go for half measures. He wanted Sacha back and clearly wouldn't hesitate to get rid of Max and Kevin.

A nervous Max leaned toward Sacha to get him to take the small backpack he always had with him. When Max handed it to him, Sacha's eyes opened wide.

"Uncle Victor!" he shouted.

Max whipped around. Before he could react, Victor Marineci was hugging the child. With dozens of passengers around him, there was nothing Max could do. Marineci spoke a few soft words to him in Romani, the word *Féro* — Sacha's new name — spoken several times. The boy returned to his seat all smiles.

Marineci glanced at Max. "A thief who keeps his word. Now that's a new one!"

Max didn't know what to say, shocked by the sudden appearance of the Romani MP.

"We've never had an opportunity to meet, Max O'Brien."

Max suddenly understood how Peter Kalanyos had discovered Christina's secret accounts in Switzerland. "You're quite the traitor, aren't you, Marineci?"

Max was about to jump him when Marineci raised his hand. Softly, he said, "Peter and his men can hear us. I've got a wire on. If they hear sounds of a struggle or I stop responding, they'll disappear. Who knows what might happen to your friend then?"

Max turned to Sacha, who smiled up at Marineci as if he were part of the family. The MP ruffled his hair and spoke a few more words in Romani.

"I can't help but spoil the boy," he said to Max. "I saw him almost every week. He's such a smart child …"

Max was disgusted.

"We're going to leave the plane, the three of us together," Marineci told him calmly. "In the hall, instead of turning left toward Immigration, we'll go right. The door is usually locked, but it'll be open for us tonight." He smiled. "Being an elected official comes with a few perks …"

Max couldn't believe he hadn't seen this coming.

The Airbus slowly rolled toward a gate that an Air France plane had just vacated.

"Peter will be waiting for us in his car at the far end of the airport parking lot. With your friend. That's where we'll make the trade, you understand?"

In Ferentari, Burgess and her team would be twiddling their thumbs while God only knew what would be happening to Max and Kevin. He had no chance of warning her, either.

The plane shook slightly, locking with the gate. Passengers jumped to their feet and grabbed luggage from the overhead compartments. Marineci helped a teenager pull down her bag.

"Thank you," she said.

The young woman followed the line of passengers toward the door, and Marineci turned to Max. "Do you also need a hand?"

Max had no idea what to do, what to think, how to get out of this predicament. He was trapped in a line of passengers, while Marineci spoke soothing words to the child in a language Max couldn't understand. A child telling his uncle all about his trip. They got along well, the two of them. Max was the stranger here; he was the bad guy, the kidnapper.

"Can't you see how happy he is? How cruel must your friend Kevin be to want to take him away from his family."

"Sacha is his son!"

"He never knew him, or barely. They don't even speak the same language." Marineci tidied the boy's hair with his hand, and Sacha leaned against him. "They've got nothing in common. At all."

Outside the plane, as predicted by Marineci, no one said a thing when the MP and his travel companions moved in the opposite direction of the other passengers.

"What got into you?" Max asked. "Why did you have Costinar killed?"

Marineci sighed. "Poor Ioan would never have had such success in the first place if it hadn't been for me."

It had been a harmonious relationship at first. Costinar was the face of the operation, making speeches, mobilizing the troops. Behind the scenes, Marineci pulled the strings. Soon the éminence grise understood that his protégé was a gold mine, a man who might make a difference, not only in Romania but across Europe. Since the European Union had come into existence in 1993, Romania had been petitioning to join it, and Brussels now seemed to favour the idea. Ioan Costinar was destined for greatness.

"But Ioan refused to play the game," Marineci said.

"Or maybe he could sense that your ambitions weren't in line with the hopes of the Roma!"

Marineci laughed. "Perhaps."

At the end of the corridor, in a deserted waiting room, a uniformed driver stood. He smiled obsequiously when he saw the trio approach.

"This is Laszlo," Marineci said.

Without another word, the driver took the MP's bag and led the three passengers down another corridor with tall glass windows that gave onto the landing strip. Snow was falling in earnest now, wind blowing the heavy drifts almost horizontally.

Marineci gestured toward the driver. "Laszlo works for Peter, so don't try to make a scene."

Kalanyos now knew, thanks to the wire Marineci wore, that Max had respected his end of the bargain — Sacha was back on Romanian soil. Soon Kevin would be worth nothing to Marineci and his accomplice. If Max could manage to take Sacha with him and run, Kalanyos would need to keep Kevin alive, at least a while longer.

"Raymond didn't go to Woodlands to see Ioan, did he? He came to see you."

Marineci smiled. "Better late than never, right?"

He and Raymond had known each other for years. When Sacha was born, Marineci had gotten in touch with the businessman to tell him the child was worth a fortune, though he hadn't given him all the details. Marineci had offered a large sum of money to get his hands on the boy.

Toma Boerescu had been right. His son, Ioan, had nothing at all to do with the kidnapping.

The businessman's financial problems had happened at the right time for Marineci. A perfect opportunity to get rid of Costinar, while still keeping control over the money the Romani leader had access to. Of course, Marineci couldn't take the risk of keeping Dandurand alive. Raymond would come back to him sooner or later the next time he got into a bind and ask for more money. The emperor had become a witness to be eliminated.

"I didn't know Emil was still around," Marineci said. "Though he's so sick, he won't be alive much longer. In a few months, no one will be able to stop me from going to Zurich and emptying the accounts."

The wind blew across the strip, forcing the door shut. Max had to put all of his weight on it to open it. The four stood in the parking lot, where snow was already piling up in drifts. Max raised his coat collar, while Marineci hugged the child close to him. Sacha seemed worried again, as if he could sense the importance of the moment. Soon he would be given back to his kidnappers — to him, his true family. Meanwhile, his father, his true father, would be murdered. Like Raymond, Laura, Micula, and the others had been.

So many killings, so much violence, and Sacha unaware of it all.

Headlights flashed straight ahead. The driver guided the group toward Peter's car.

Max had to act, and now. Once they reached the car, it would be too late. As soon as they had Sacha, he and Kevin were dead. What could he do? Max could easily neutralize Laszlo, whatever Marineci might think. And the MP wouldn't be too hard to handle, either. But if he acted now, then Kevin would be as good as dead. Marineci had made it clear: if Kalanyos realized there was a fight going on, he'd beat it. And then who knew what would happen?

Max had never felt so powerless.

When they finally reached the car, the front door opened. The driver stepped out; he was one of the men who'd pummelled Max in Granada. Inside the car he could make out two passengers in the back seat: Peter Kalanyos, still in his leather coat, and Kevin, head bent over his chest. He was practically unconscious, in pretty rough shape. Perhaps he'd been drugged.

Another car appeared on their left and stopped near them. Laszlo guided Sacha and Marineci toward it, and they climbed in the back. The car's driver moved to the passenger side, and Laszlo got in behind the wheel.

The child didn't even glance at Max; for Sacha, Max was already in the past tense.

Kalanyos lowered his window. "I was right to trust you, Max O'Brien."

"I wasn't."

"You didn't really think I'd make the mistake of meeting you in Ferentari?" The Hungarian laughed. "I know you more than you think, O'Brien, and I know when you're trying to con someone."

Behind Max the car with Sacha and Marineci was disappearing into the night. As he'd feared from the beginning, Max and Kevin were at the mercy of a killer.

Kevin raised his head in the back seat but didn't seem to recognize his friend.

"You have the child. Now let him go."

Kalanyos showed his teeth. "And give you a chance to call Amnesty International, or the police, or who knows what?"

"I've got no credibility, you know that. If I speak to the authorities, I'll be arrested. Now come on, give me Kevin!"

Max felt the barrel of a gun pressed against the back of his neck. Kalanyos got out of the car. The driver gestured for Max to climb in and take Kalanyos's still-warm seat. Max whipped around, knocking his assailant's gun out of his hand and twisting his arm. Kalanyos tried to get back into the car, but Max kicked the door closed. The Hungarian was trapped between the door and the frame, with Max leaning against the handle.

Neither of them could move now. Max looked up and saw the driver rush back toward him. Punching the man in the face, Max followed that with another in the stomach, while Kalanyos caught his breath. Max then threw the driver against the car and struck his head against the frame several times. The driver collapsed.

When Max turned around again, Kalanyos had a weapon drawn on him. "End of the road, O'Brien."

Kalanyos's finger squeezed, and a shot ripped through the night and the falling snow. A man's body flew backward while Max dropped to the ground. They hit the pavement at almost the same time, one bloodied, one not.

Max heard tires screeching and doors slamming shut. He got to his knees and saw Marilyn Burgess offering her hand. "Clearly, you can't be left without supervision for even five minutes."

Burgess's men flooded the scene, neutralizing the driver.

"Sacha's with them," Max told her as he leaned into the car to check on Kevin, who was regaining consciousness, the sound of gunshots shaking him out of his torpor.

"Actually, Sacha's with us," Burgess said. "We have him safe and sound." She helped Max pull Kevin out of the car. "We got in touch with Laszlo last week and offered him a choice — he could work for us or spend the rest of his life behind bars. What would you have done?"

Max smiled. "So you knew about Marineci?"

"We had our doubts. As soon as Kalanyos's name came up, we spoke with our Hungarian counterparts. Marineci had been seen with him a number of times over the past few weeks. It became clear he'd played a role in this whole affair. We didn't know the extent of it just yet. Laszlo told us the plan. About the trap here in the parking lot."

Max glanced at Kalanyos's body on the ground, Burgess's men already at work cleaning up the scene.

"Adrian Pavlenco has been informed of what's gone on," Burgess continued. "In a few minutes, his agents will find the body of Kalanyos in an abandoned building in Ferentari."

"And Marineci?"

"Officially, he'll resign for health reasons. In fact, he'll stand trial before a *Kris romani*. I think you can guess the verdict." Burgess watched her men load Kalanyos's body into the trunk of the car. "Everything Marineci owns will be confiscated and he'll be exiled for life from the Romani community. There's no more heinous punishment for a Rom. Worse than death."

41

Spring, at last. The weather warmer, passersby smiling at one another after a long winter of heavy coats and grey skies. In the taxi driving him into the city, Max felt as if he were waking up from a long night filled with dark dreams. He had the strange impression of walking along a precipice in the dark on an uncertain road and coming out, mostly by good fortune, unscathed. In a way, he, too, had been saved. Every new day was an opportunity to tidy yesterday's mess. Each new life could erase the horrors of past lives. A feeling that wouldn't last — probably not, anyway — but still, today, optimism filled him.

Three months earlier in Amsterdam Max had taken Kevin and Sacha to the airport, where Josée waited for them with the adoption papers and other legal documents necessary to bring the child back to Canada.

Max would take his own flight back to New York, though he'd pursue a meandering way home, with a few stops here and there so as not to raise suspicions. The media weren't talking about him anymore, or Kevin. The Romanian police had concluded that Peter Kalanyos had tried to pin Laura Costinar's death and the Zăbrăuţi Street fire on Max and Kevin. The two men had been exonerated, but Max didn't want to run any unnecessary risks: he was still the subject of an arrest warrant from both the Canadian and American authorities for his previous activities.

As Josée Dandurand had adjusted Sacha's small backpack, Kevin took Max by the arm. "I thought he'd be here with us."

"He's a shy old man who doesn't want to impose himself," Max said.

Kevin seemed disappointed.

Max led him to a newspaper stand so he could grab something to read for his trip. As they riffled through the French-language newspapers, a man dressed all in grey had appeared, leaning on a walker.

Toma Boerescu.

Kevin recognized him immediately. Shocked into silence, he could only gaze at the old man — a small, stunted, fragile figure who, through sheer misfortune, had been caught in nearly every storm of the twentieth century.

"Nice to meet you, Kevin," Boerescu finally managed to say, his voice breaking.

Kevin glanced at Max, as if asking what he should do, how he should react. "You're returning to Romania?"

"Soon."

Another moment of silence.

"It's a pleasure to meet you," Kevin said. "I wish I could have known you earlier."

The two men looked at each other, uncomfortable. Max felt like a third wheel. He was searching for an excuse to get out of there and leave them alone. But a glance from Kevin told him he should stay and offer his friend support.

"Alina took good care of you?" Boerescu asked Kevin.

"She was the perfect mother."

Boerescu nodded. "Poor Alina …"

A flight was called over the public-address system. It was time for Kevin, Josée, and Sacha to board.

"You know what makes me happy?" Boerescu asked, smiling. "Having had wonderful children, the greatest gift Eugenia, your mother, could ever have given me."

Kevin stood silent, unable to say anything.

"I think of her often, you know. And I think of Alina, as well."

Kevin nodded.

"I saw you just now with Sacha. I didn't want to interrupt. I … I'm proud of what you've done for him, Kevin." Boerescu, too, fell silent, moved to tears. "I'm proud to have you as my son."

Words Kevin had never heard before.

Max looked away.

"I'm proud of you, too," Kevin finally said. "Proud that you're my father."

‡

Kevin, Sacha, and Josée had landed in Montreal late in the afternoon of December 24. They picked up Gabrielle and drove directly to Refuge Sainte-Catherine, where a Christmas table was being set. Volunteers were out in strength to serve a meal provided by sponsors. Earlier that week a high-ranking elected official had even come to put on his chef's hat and an apron to cook for the less fortunate — in front of television cameras, of course. A public-relations ploy the refuge's board was only too happy to accept, especially around Christmas, when the most help was needed.

But the cameras were gone today. Back to the routine, the usual procession of broken and unfortunate souls looking for a warm meal and a bit of conversation.

While Josée and Gabrielle stood a bit behind discreetly, Kevin walked into the cafeteria holding Sacha by the shoulder, his hand on the nape of the neck, right over the red mark. Caroline was serving a young man with a Mohawk when she noticed them.

She walked toward them indecisively. Kevin lifted his hand, revealing the mark on the child's neck. Caroline burst into tears. She hugged Sacha against her tightly, too tightly. The child seemed confused, unsettled by this stranger's emotions. As if these past four years had made him not only a stranger, but a little strange. This was their son, yes, but different.

In time, Max was sure things would settle down.

For the last few weeks, according to Gabrielle, Sacha had gotten increasingly comfortable in his new environment. What the teenager told him about her mother had filled him with hope. Kevin and Caroline were living together again — in Grande-Vallée, in the renovated country home. The house had become their own refuge, their shelter, their den. They had felt the need, the four of them, to remove themselves from the world to try, amongst themselves, to catch up on lost time, to find new ways to live together. Max had respected their wish and made himself scarce, calling rarely, or sending an email, but never insisting.

Sacha was learning French with Marie-France Couturier, progressing rapidly according to Gabrielle, whom Max spoke with more often than her parents. She and her little brother were inseparable. Sacha would be going to school in September, in Montreal most likely, since Kevin wanted to teach again.

Every day Kevin ran along rivière Saqawigan. He crossed the fateful bridge — which now had a lane reserved for cyclists and runners — made a loop at the end of the bridge, and jogged back to his family. Kevin took a moment every now and then to think of his adoptive father, trying not to judge him, though never excusing his behaviour. Raymond had been a victim of both circumstance and pride, a dysfunctional father for whom Kevin had never really been a son, but the keystone of a business contract. His real family, besides Sharon and

Josée, had been his employees, those who worked for him and who'd contributed to his fame and fortune. Kevin had never been part of that, and he swore to himself he would never act toward his son as his father had toward him.

And then, one day, an important piece of news: Caroline was writing for a local newspaper, the *Matane Weekly*, which mostly ran pieces on hyper-local affairs, like threats to the local shrimp population or the reconversion of the old fishing port into a cruise ship terminal. Max was glad to learn that she had found her desire to live again, to write, to wake up in the morning with something other than dark thoughts on her mind.

Serenity at last.

Kevin and Caroline had come out of the shadows. Life was giving them a second chance.

Max walked into the lobby of Hotel Estheréa in the heart of Amsterdam. From his room he could see the crowds of tourists straggling along the Singel and other canals, taking advantage of an early spring. A barge honked its way up, slowly drifting toward the other end of the city.

Since his meeting was scheduled for the next day, Max took a quick nap, then went out to eat seafood at Lucius, a restaurant near his hotel. He wandered around the neighbourhood, just another tourist with a bit of free time.

The next day Max rented a car and drove out to Nieuwe Ooster Begraafplaats. He recognized the guard at the cemetery gates, the same man who'd sent him after Paola Landermann months before. The poor man had his hands full today: a group of children ran around the cemetery, weaving and bobbing among the tombstones. And there were families, as well, laden with flowers, looking for the resting place of an aunt or cousin. The guard was both disciplinarian and guide.

Max parked his car near the entrance and walked among the crowd of visitors all the way to Werner Landermann's mausoleum, still as gaudy as ever. A man stood right next to it, lost in thought before Christina Landermann's tomb. Toma Boerescu. Frank Woensdag had driven the old man to the cemetery, and around noon he would pick him up so the two of them could get a bite to eat at a pub near the flower market. For Toma and Woensdag, this was a ritual repeated every time the old man visited Amsterdam. Every year, on Christina's birthday.

Boerescu ignored the families and children around him. He wore his usual coat, though without the fake medals this time. He no longer needed to pretend for Max, no longer needed to make him believe in a long if not very illustrious career with the Bucharest police.

Very little else had changed since last winter, except for the walker. During his last trip, when leaving Amsterdam to return to New York, Max had passed an orthopedics store on his way to the airport. He had called the number posted on the window and ordered the most expensive walker they had, then had it delivered to Woensdag's house in Zutphen where Boerescu was staying at the time.

By the time Max had reached Schiphol Airport and headed to security, his cellphone had rung.

"Thank you, Max!" Boerescu had cried out.

Max had smiled, showing his passport to the desk agent.

"It's wonderful. It'll be the most beautiful walker in all of Bucharest, I'm sure of it." Then Boerescu had said, "Safe travels, Max."

Latcho drom.

Kevin and his father had met up in February, with Frank Woensdag. All three had gone to Zurich to make Kevin the sole beneficiary of Christina Landermann's succession, once Toma Boerescu passed away. On the same occasion, Kevin had ceded to the World Romani Congress control over the funds, as long as they were only used for health care, literacy, and the defence of Romani rights. Christina's objective all along.

Since then father and son had remained in touch. Boerescu had watched Sacha's progress from afar, glad to hear he was adjusting to life with his true family. For the first time since Christina's death, he seemed to have found a certain form of peace, of serenity.

Toma Boerescu turned slightly toward Max as he neared. The old man seemed more fragile than the last time Max had seen him, which had been at Christmas. Sickly. Victor Marineci had been right: Boerescu wouldn't live through the year.

He looked at Max. "I've had this cough for weeks. The doctor wants to give me more pills. I feel like I could open my own drugstore." He went for a smile, but it faltered before it reached his eyes. "Six months, a year maybe. The doctor isn't very optimistic. I let myself imagine the worst."

He sniffed, tapped his chest. "A little coal left in there from Vorkuta, apparently." Boerescu coughed again, as if to prove what he'd just said. "I spent my life running from death. I don't have the strength to run away this time."

Max gestured toward the old man's walker. "Magnificent, you were right," he said, trying to change the subject.

Boerescu's face lit up. "All the old folks in Bucharest speak about it behind my back. They look at me sideways when I go by!"

"They're just jealous."

Boerescu chuckled, then coughed again. He pointed at Christina's tomb, covered in buttons. "The Roma who travel through here come at night, jump over the fence."

"And the *mulo*?"

Boerescu darkened. "As if we needed a bogeyman to fear! The world is horrible enough as it is."

He looked at Christina's tomb again. "I was at her side when she died. I felt completely useless. An old man, incapable of stopping her cancer from destroying her. She saved my life three times, and I couldn't even save her once."

Boerescu wiped his eyes. "She told me, 'You're wrong Emil. Every day you saved my life. Every day over all these years.' She said that knowing I existed somewhere helped her go on each day to repair a little of what her family, her father, her husband, and the others had destroyed. That I had saved her life a million times over."

The old man fell silent, gathering his thoughts, leaning against his walker. "Christina held on to my hand until the very end. I closed her eyes after her last breath. That's all I managed to do. And then her hand fell out of mine."

He turned to face Max full on. "I was beaten. I was tortured. My whole life was pain with a few moments' respite in between. They killed my wife, mutilated my children. But that dead hand falling from mine, Christina's hand, that was the most painful moment of my life, the most horrible torment inflicted on me. That hand falling for the last time, that hand that had caressed my face in Auschwitz. Her declaration of love."

Boerescu straightened with difficulty. Painfully. As if every inch of his body was in pain. With sudden energy, he ripped a button off his coat and threw it onto Christina's tomb.

The two men talked for a little longer, and when it came time to part, Max hugged him close. He felt that ailing body against his, that body that had suffered so. Max couldn't find the right words. Boerescu said nothing, either. They parted in silence.

Max walked back to his car near the cemetery's gate, knowing he'd never see the old man again. Just as he was about to get into his car, Max heard an accordion's tune very faintly. He turned around. And there was Boerescu, still in the cemetery, playing his Paolo Soprani, leaning against his walker. Max wondered where Boerescu could have hidden the instrument. He hadn't noticed it before; it had probably been stashed behind a tombstone.

The music, hesitant at first, slowly became more melodious, stronger. People stopped, kids and adults alike, to watch this old man play a song both familiar and unknown.

A Romani tune.

Max closed his eyes. It was no longer a dying old man playing, no, but a young boy, far, very far away, in another world entirely. A young Romani boy lost amid cruelty and hate, alone, discouraged, looking for love and light in the grey ash of the human soul.

WHERE ARE THEY NOW?

Many people who lived and died in our own time are mixed in with the fictional characters of this novel. At the end of the war Heinrich Himmler was caught by the British but committed suicide before he could be brought to Nuremberg to face his accusers. Eduard Wirths also committed suicide after his arrest. His subaltern, Josef Mengele, found refuge in South America. He drowned off the Brazilian coast in 1979. Johann Schwarzhuber was arrested by the Allies in May 1945, then was tried and condemned to death. Rudolf Höss, captured by the British in 1946, was found guilty at Nuremberg and handed over to Polish authorities. He was executed by hanging in 1947 in Auschwitz at the entrance of the crematorium.

Ioan Antonescu was taken prisoner by the Soviets and brought back to Romania in 1946, where he was found guilty of collaboration with the Nazis and put to death.

Gheorghe Pintilie, the Securitate's first director, responsible for the arrest and deportation of more than four hundred thousand people, died in 1985. After holding the post of vice-premier of the Soviet Union, Andrey Vyshinsky became the country's minister of foreign affairs and its permanent representative to the United Nations. At the moment of his death in New York in 1954, Nikita Khrushchev denounced him as the principal herald of terror under Stalin.

The character of Paul Vaneker, the Dutch spy working with the Roma, was directly inspired by Jan Yoors, who told of his activities in the Resistance alongside the Roma in *Crossing: A Journal of Survival and Resistance in World War II*. He died in 1977 in New York where he'd had a career as a visual artist since the 1950s. Carol II of Romania fled to Portugal, where he died in 1953. His son, Michael, forced to abdicate in 1947, lived with his family in a number of European countries. At the age of ninety-five, he splits his time between Romania and Switzerland; he is the only monarch to reign in the interwar period who is still alive today.

During the war, Slobodan Berberski was a member of the Yugoslav Resistance. A pioneering figure in Romani literature, he died in 1989. In 1978 Jan Cibula was elected president of the International Romani Union at the Geneva congress. He died in 2013. Having served as the director of the Roma Community Centre in Toronto, Ronald Lee remains active in the defence of Romani rights in Canada and elsewhere in the world.

ACKNOWLEDGEMENTS

I wish to thank the following people for their help in writing this novel. Author and journalist Ronald Lee shared his deep knowledge of Romani culture and history and offered me telling information about the 1971 Romani congress, which he attended as a delegate. I also drew on his expertise for some of the Romani vocabulary used in the novel. Constantin Anghel, a Romanian Rom, offered rich details on the lives of the Roma in that country. Similarly, Anamaria Luta gave me information on Romanian society before and after 1989. Dr. Gilles Truffy answered my numerous questions on the medical aspects of the story. Francine Landry offered her generous comments and suggestions throughout the writing of this book.

I also want to thank the entire team at Libre Expression, especially Johanne Guay, Carole Boutin, and

Jean Baril. I'm privileged to have worked with the extraordinary editor, the late Monique H. Messier, who offered wonderful advice and constant encouragement.

Thanks also to Jacob Homel for this translation, and to editor Michael Carroll, and the team at Dundurn Press.

To get in touch with the author:
mbmysteries@gmail.com

IN THE SAME SERIES

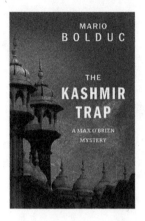

The Kashmir Trap
Mario Bolduc
Translated by Nigel Spencer

Max O'Brien's nightmare has begun again. Eleven years after the tragic disappearance of his brother, an ambassador in Central America, Max's nephew, also a diplomat, is assassinated in New Delhi. Max is on the run from police, and this time the professional con man decides to find those responsible for the crime. Determined to track down the truth, he arrives in India just as the country is preparing for war with Pakistan. His inquiry leads him to Kashmir — the heart of the conflict — and the depths of his own soul.

The first book of the thrilling Max O'Brien Mystery series, *The Kashmir Trap* explores the parallel lives of two brothers who have made very different choices. Violence and the growing tension between India and Pakistan set Max on a course of redemption, revenge, and death.

🌐 dundurn.com   ▦ dundurnpress
🐦 @dundurnpress   📷 dundurnpress
📘 dundurnpress   ✉ info@dundurn.com

FIND US ON NETGALLEY & GOODREADS TOO!

▦ DUNDURN